THE LOST FLEET

BEYOND THE FRONTIER

STEADFAST

THE LOST FLEET

BEYOND THE FRONTIER

STEADFAST

JACK CAMPBELL

ACE BOOKS, NEW YORK

THE BERKLEY PUBLISHING GROUP
Published by the Penguin Group
Penguin Group (USA) LLC
375 Hudson Street, New York, New York 10014

USA • Canada • UK • Ireland • Australia • New Zealand • India • South Africa • China

penguin.com

A Penguin Random House Company

This book is an original publication of The Berkley Publishing Group.

Library of Congress Cataloging-in-Publication Data

Campbell, Jack (Naval officer)
The Lost Fleet : Beyond the Frontier : Steadfast / Jack Campbell. — First edition.
pages cm. — (The Lost Fleet ; Book 10)
ISBN 978-0-425-26052-4 (hardback)
1. Science fiction.   2. Space warfare—Fiction.
3. Imaginary wars and battles—Fiction.   I. Title.   II. Title: Steadfast.
PS3553.A4637L667   2014
813'.54—dc23
2013047004

FIRST EDITION: May 2014

PRINTED IN THE UNITED STATES OF AMERICA

10   9   8   7   6   5   4   3   2   1

Cover art by Michael Komarck.
Cover design by Annette Fiore DeFex.

To my sister Dianne, for whom "steadfast" is an apt description. Thank you.

For S., as always.

ACKNOWLEDGMENTS

I remain indebted to my agent, Joshua Bilmes, for his ever-inspired suggestions and assistance, and to my editor, Anne Sowards, for her support and editing. Thanks also to Catherine Asaro, Robert Chase, J. G. (Huck) Huckenpohler, Simcha Kuritzky, Michael LaViolette, Aly Parsons, Bud Sparhawk, and Constance A. Warner for their suggestions, comments, and recommendations.

THE FIRST FLEET OF THE ALLIANCE

ADMIRAL JOHN GEARY, COMMANDING

SECOND BATTLESHIP DIVISION
Gallant
Indomitable
Glorious
Magnificent

THIRD BATTLESHIP DIVISION
Dreadnaught
Orion (lost at Sobek)
Dependable
Conqueror

FOURTH BATTLESHIP DIVISION
Warspite
Vengeance
Revenge
Guardian

FIFTH BATTLESHIP DIVISION
Fearless
Resolution
Redoubtable

SEVENTH BATTLESHIP DIVISION
Colossus
Encroach
Amazon
Spartan

EIGHTH BATTLESHIP DIVISION
Relentless
Reprisal
Superb
Splendid

FIRST BATTLE CRUISER DIVISION
Inspire
Formidable
Brilliant (lost at Honor)
Implacable

SECOND BATTLE CRUISER DIVISION
Leviathan
Dragon
Steadfast
Valiant

FOURTH BATTLE CRUISER DIVISION
Dauntless (flagship)
Daring
Victorious
Intemperate

FIFTH BATTLE CRUISER DIVISION
Adroit

SIXTH BATTLE CRUISER DIVISION
Illustrious
Incredible
Invincible (lost at Pandora)

FIFTH ASSAULT TRANSPORT DIVISION
Tsunami
Typhoon
Mistral
Haboob

FIRST AUXILIARIES DIVISION
Titan
Tanuki
Kupua
Domovoi

SECOND AUXILIARIES DIVISION
Witch
Jinn
Alchemist
Cyclops

THIRTY-ONE HEAVY CRUISERS IN SIX DIVISIONS
First Heavy Cruiser Division
Fourth Heavy Cruiser Division
Eighth Heavy Cruiser Division

Third Heavy Cruiser Division
Fifth Heavy Cruiser Division
Tenth Heavy Cruiser Division

Emerald and **Hoplon** lost at Honor

FIFTY-FIVE LIGHT CRUISERS IN TEN SQUADRONS
First Light Cruiser Squadron
Third Light Cruiser Squadron
Sixth Light Cruiser Squadron
Ninth Light Cruiser Squadron
Eleventh Light Cruiser Squadron

Second Light Cruiser Squadron
Fifth Light Cruiser Squadron
Eighth Light Cruiser Squadron
Tenth Light Cruiser Squadron
Fourteenth Light Cruiser Squadron

Balestra lost at Honor

ONE HUNDRED SIXTY DESTROYERS IN EIGHTEEN SQUADRONS
First Destroyer Squadron
Third Destroyer Squadron
Sixth Destroyer Squadron
Ninth Destroyer Squadron
Twelfth Destroyer Squadron
Sixteenth Destroyer Squadron
Twentieth Destroyer Squadron
Twenty-third Destroyer Squadron
Twenty-eighth Destroyer Squadron

Second Destroyer Squadron
Fourth Destroyer Squadron
Seventh Destroyer Squadron
Tenth Destroyer Squadron
Fourteenth Destroyer Squadron
Seventeenth Destroyer Squadron
Twenty-first Destroyer Squadron
Twenty-seventh Destroyer Squadron
Thirty-second Destroyer Squadron

Zaghnal lost at Pandora
Plumbatae, **Bolo**, **Bangalore**, and **Morningstar** lost at Honor
Musket lost at Midway

FIRST FLEET MARINE FORCE
Major General Carabali, commanding

3,000 Marines on assault transports and divided into detachments on battle cruisers and battleships

ONE

ADMIRAL John "Black Jack" Geary, accustomed to gazing down upon worlds from hundreds of kilometers high and looking into the vastness of space in which a man could fall forever, felt slightly dizzy as he leaned over the crumbling remains of a stone wall to peer down the other side, where the land dropped away for about ten meters in a steep slope littered with rocks. Beyond, a land green with vegetation rolled to the north into the low hills that marked this small portion of Old Earth. He remembered land like this, in parts of his home world of Glenlyon, a planet he had not seen for a century.

Geary squinted against a wind that brought scents of growing things and animals and the enterprises of people. Not like that inside a spacecraft, which despite the best air scrubbers known to science, always held a faint taint of crowded humanity, caffeinated beverages, and heated circuitry.

"Not much left, is there?" Captain Tanya Desjani commented, looking at what had once been the wall's foundation.

"It's thousands of years old," Historic Properties Steward Gary

Main replied. He seemed as much a part of the landscape as the wall itself, perhaps because members of his family had served as Stewards of the wall for generations. "The wonder is that there's anything left at all, especially after the ice century of the last millennium. The Gulf Stream helps keep this island of ours warm, so it got very cold up here when the stream lost a lot of push. The rest of the world got warm, and we got cold, but then England has always been a bit contrary when it comes to the rest of the planet. Since then, everywhere else on Earth has been cooling down, and we've been warming up."

Geary smiled crookedly. "I have to admit it feels strange to be on a planet that has known humanity for so long that people can speak of the last millennium."

"That's all quite recent, compared to this wall, Admiral," Main replied.

"Hadrian's Wall," Desjani mused. "I guess if you want to be remembered for thousands of years, it helps to build a big wall and name it after yourself. I remember the Admiral and I talking about that Empire of Rome, and I thought it must have been pretty small. Just part of one planet and all. But, standing here, I realize it must have felt awfully big to people who had to walk it."

Main nodded, running one hand above the fitted stones remaining in the wall. "When this was intact, it was about six meters high. Forts every Roman mile, and numerous turrets between them. It was an impressive fortification."

"Our Marines could have jumped over it in their combat armor," Tanya said, "but if all you had was human muscle, it would be tough, especially if someone was shooting at you while you tried to climb it. How did it fall?"

"It didn't. Rome fell. As the empire contracted, the legions were called home and the wall abandoned."

Geary looked down the length of the wall, white stone against green vegetation, thinking of the massive demobilizations that had taken place inside the Alliance since the war with the Syndicate Worlds had ended. *The legions were called home, and the wall abandoned.* It sounded so painless, but it meant that defenses once regarded as vital were suddenly surplus, men and women who had once carried out duties considered critical were no longer needed, and things once thought essential were now judged too expensive. "The borders and their horizons shrank," he murmured, thinking of not just the ancient empire that had built this wall but of the current state of the many star systems in the Alliance.

Tanya gave him the look that meant she knew exactly what he was thinking. "They say this wall was garrisoned for centuries. Think of all the soldiers who stood sentry on it. Some of them might have been among our ancestors."

"Many people think Arthur might have been a king during those times," Steward Main said. "That maybe his knights held the wall for a while after the Romans left."

"Arthur?" Geary asked.

"A legendary king who ruled and died long ago. Supposedly," Main confided, "Arthur didn't die but remains sleeping, awaiting a time when his people need him. Of course, he's never shown up."

"Maybe your need hasn't been great enough," Desjani said. "Sometimes, sleeping heroes from the past do appear just when they're needed."

Geary barely managed not to glare at her. But his sudden shift in mood was apparent enough to cause silence to fall for a few moments.

Main cleared his throat. "If I may ask a question of you, what do you think our other guests think of all this?"

"The Dancers?" Geary asked. An alien landing shuttle hovered nearby, mere centimeters above the ground. "They're amazing engineers. They examined the remains pretty carefully. They're probably impressed."

"It's hard to tell, Admiral, since they're in their space armor."

"You probably couldn't tell even if you could see their faces," Desjani told him. "They don't display emotions the way we do."

"Oh, right," Main replied with remarkable understatement. "Because they, uh . . ."

"Look to us like what would happen if a giant spider mated with a wolf," Tanya finished for him. "We've speculated that we look as hideous to them as they do to us."

"Don't judge them on their looks," Geary added.

"I wouldn't, sir! Everyone's heard how they brought that fellow's remains back. How did he get out as far as their territory in space?"

"A failed early experiment with using jump space for interstellar travel," Geary said. "We don't know how, but he finally popped out at one of the stars occupied by the Dancers."

"His ship and his body popped out," Desjani corrected, a rough edge in her voice. "He must have died long before then. Died in jump space."

"That's bad?" Main asked.

"About as bad as it gets." She took a deep breath, then forced a smile. "But the Dancers treated his remains with honor and brought them home when they finally could."

"That's what I heard," Main said. "Those Dancers did better by him than many a human I've encountered would have, I'll tell you." He glanced at the sun, then checked the time. "We should move on when you're ready, Admiral, Captain."

"Give us a few minutes, will you?" Desjani asked. "I need to talk to the Admiral about something."

"Of course. I'll be right over there."

Tanya turned her back on the curious crowds hovering a few hundred meters away, citizens of Old Earth who were fascinated not only by the newly discovered alien Dancers but also by the humans from distant stars colonized by those who had left this world long ago. She turned her wrist to show Geary that she had activated her personal security field so their words could not be heard by others or their lip movements or expressions seen clearly. "We need to talk about something," she repeated to him.

Geary suppressed a sigh. When Tanya Desjani said that, it meant the something she wanted to talk about was something he wouldn't want to discuss. But he stood close to the wall, right next to her, though he didn't lean on the ancient structure. That just felt wrong, like using a book from the far past as a footrest. "Something about walls?"

"Something about here." She turned her gaze from the landscape and caught his eyes. "Tomorrow, we leave Old Earth, return to *Dauntless*, and head for home. You need to know what people will be thinking."

"I can guess," Geary said.

"No, you can't. You spent a hundred years frozen in survival sleep. You've been among us for a while, but you still don't understand us as well as you should. But I know the people of the Alliance right now because I'm one of them." Tanya's eyes had darkened, taken on a hardness and a fierceness he remembered from their first meeting. "I was born during a war that had started long before I arrived, and I grew up expecting that war to continue long after I was gone. I was named for an aunt who died in the war, saw my brother die in it, and fully expected that any child of mine might die in it. We could not win, we would not lose, and the deaths would go on and on. Everyone in the Alliance, everyone but you, grew up the same. And while we were growing up, we were taught that Captain Black Jack Geary had saved the Alliance when he died blunting one of the first surprise attacks by the Syndicate Worlds that started that war."

"Tanya," he said resignedly, "I know—"

"Let me finish. We were also taught that Black Jack epitomized everything good about the Alliance. He was everything a citizen of the Alliance should be and everything a defender of the Alliance should aspire to. Quiet! I know you don't like hearing that, but to many billions of people in the Alliance, that's who Black Jack was. And we all heard the rest of the legend, too, that Black Jack was among our ancestors under the light of the living stars, but he would return from the dead someday when he was most needed, and he would save the Alliance. And you did that."

"I wasn't really dead," Geary pointed out gruffly.

"Irrelevant. We found you only weeks before power on that damaged escape pod would have been exhausted. We thawed you out, then you saved the fleet, you beat the Syndics, and you finally brought an end to the endless war." She ran one hand slowly across the rough stone of the wall, her touch gentle despite the force of her words. "Now, despite a victory that is causing the Syndicate Worlds to fall to pieces, the Alliance is also threatening to come apart at the seams because of the costs and strains of a century of war. In that time, you've come to Old Earth."

"Tanya." She knew he would be unhappy with this conversation, with being reminded yet again of the beliefs that he was some sort of mythical hero. For a moment, he wondered if an ancestor of his had stood here, very long ago, peering into that same wind for approaching enemies, burdened with the responsibility of protecting everyone else. "We came to Old Earth to escort the Dancers. If the aliens hadn't insisted, we wouldn't have come here."

"You and I know that, and some members of the Alliance Grand Council know that," Desjani said. "But I guarantee you that everyone else in the Alliance believes that you chose to come here, to Old Earth, the Home of us all, the place our oldest ancestors once lived, to consult with those ancestors. To learn what you should do to save an Alliance that more and more citizens of the Alliance fear may be beyond saving."

He stared at her, hoping that Tanya's security measures really were keeping the nearby observers from seeing his expression. "They can't believe that."

"They do." Her eyes on him were unyielding. "You need to know that."

"Great." He faced the remnants of the wall, staring north to where the wall's enemies had long ago been. "Why me?"

"Ask our ancestors. Though if you asked me," she added, standing right next to him as she also gazed outward, "I'd say it was because you can do the job."

"I'm just a man. Just one man."

"I didn't say you would do it alone," Tanya pointed out.

"And our ancestors haven't been talking to me."

"You know," she added in the very reasonable voice of someone repeating common knowledge, "that our ancestors rarely come out and tell us anything. They offer hints, suggestions, inspirations, and hunches for those who are willing to pay attention. And if they care about us at all, they will offer those things to you if you are listening."

"The ancestors here on Old Earth," Geary said as patiently as he could, "didn't get raised in an Alliance at war and indoctrinated about how awesome I am. Why should they be impressed by Black Jack?"

"Because they are our ancestors, too! And they know what Black Jack is! Remember that other wall they took us to? The, uh, Grand Wall?"

"The Great Wall?"

"Yeah, that one." She gestured to the north. "Now, this wall, the one that Hadrian built, was a real fortification. It kept out enemies. But that Great Wall over in Asia never could do that. The people there told us it was so damned big, so long, that it was impossible for the guys who built it to support a large enough army to actually garrison it. They sank a huge amount of money, time, and human labor into building that Great Wall, and whenever an enemy wanted to get through it, all they had to do was find a spot where there weren't any soldiers and put up a ladder, so one of their own could climb up and over, then open the nearest gate."

"Yeah." Geary nodded. "It doesn't make a lot of sense, does it?"

"Not as a fortification, no." She waved again, this time vaguely to the east. "Those pyramids. Remember those? Think of the time and money and labor that went into those. And then those big faces on the mountain a ways north of where we first stopped in Kansas. The four ancestors whose images were carved into a mountain. How much sense did that make?"

He turned a questioning look on her. "This has something to do with me?"

"Yes, sir, Admiral." Desjani smiled, but the eyes that held his were intent. "That Great Wall said something about the people who built it. It told the world, we can do this. It told the world, we're on this side of the Great Wall, and all the rest of you are on the other. Those pyramids must have really impressed people a long time ago, too. And the four ancestors on the mountain? It didn't just honor them, it also honored their people, and their homes, and what they believed in. All of those things were symbols. Symbols that helped define the people who built them."

He nodded slowly. "All right. And?"

"What's the symbol of the Alliance?"

"There isn't one. Not like that. There are too many different societies, governments, beliefs—"

"Wrong." She pointed at him.

Geary felt that vast sinking sensation that sometimes threatened to overwhelm him. "Tanya, that's—"

"True. I told you. You still don't understand us." Her face saddened. "We stopped believing in our politicians a long time ago, and that meant we lost belief in our governments, and what is the Alliance but a collection of those governments? It can't be stronger than they are. We tried putting faith in honor, but you reminded us how that caused us to warp the meaning of 'honor.' We tried putting faith in our fleet and our ground forces, but they failed, you know they did. We were fighting like hell and dying and killing and not getting anywhere. Until you came along. The man who we had been told all of our lives was everything the Alliance was supposed to be."

Tanya tapped the wall next to them. "Black Jack isn't just this wall, the guy who physically protected the Alliance from external enemies, he's also that Great Wall and those pyramids and those four ancestors. He's the image of the Alliance, the thing citizens think of that *means* the Alliance. That's why he is the only one who can save it."

He had to look away once more, to gaze across that sere landscape again, seeing overlaid upon it images of the battles he had already fought, of the men and women already dead. "Senator Sakai said something like that to me, but he was a lot more pessimistic." During the war with the Syndicate Worlds, the Alliance government had created the myths around Black Jack to inspire and unify its people at a time when the example of that sort of hero was desperately needed. Now the man that myth had been built around somehow had to save the Alliance that had created it. "Ancestors help me."

"Well, duh, isn't that what we've just been talking about?"

Geary felt a crooked smile form and looked at her again. "I never would have guessed what people born during the war were thinking. What would I do without you?"

"You'd be lost," Desjani said. "Totally, hopelessly lost. And don't you ever forget it."

"If I do, I'm sure you'll remind me."

"Maybe. Or maybe I'll just go back to being me." Her gesture this time encompassed the crowd maintaining its respectful distance behind them. "To these people, I'm commanding officer of the most impressive warship they have ever seen. I'm the girl who wiped out the so-called warships of the so-called Shield of Sol that had been bullying their way around this star system while pretending to protect it from inferior forms of human life like you and me."

"Too bad for the Shield of Sol that we debased humans from the distant stars are a lot better at fighting battles than they were," Geary said.

Tanya grinned. "Pure bloodlines, lots of medals, and pretty ships are no substitute for smarts, lots of firepower, and experience. Anyway, the people here at Sol think what I am, what I've done, is all pretty remarkable. Once we get home to the Alliance, though, everybody there is once again going to be looking at me as just the consort of Black Jack."

He felt anger at that, anger that banished the despair of moments earlier. "You aren't anyone's consort. You're Captain Tanya Desjani, commanding officer of the Alliance battle cruiser *Dauntless*. That's the only way everyone should see you."

Tanya laughed. "You're so sweet when you're being delusional." Despite her warm gear, she shivered as a gust of wind hit. "The locals think this is warmer? I think we've done enough sentry duty on this wall. I've been spoiled by spending so much time inside climate-controlled spacecraft. What's that last place we're supposed to see today?"

"Stonehenge. A religious site."

"Oh." She smiled again. "Good. I need to pay my respects before we leave Old Earth."

"I don't think whoever built Stonehenge worshipped the same things we do," Geary pointed out.

"They didn't use the same names," Desjani objected. "That doesn't mean the same things didn't matter to them or that they weren't trying to grasp the infinite in the same ways we do."

"I guess so." He took a deep breath, looking down and grimacing. "This old world bears a lot of scars that were inflicted by human wars and other forms of destruction. Have we learned anything? Or are we going to keep repeating the same mistakes?"

"We're going to do our best, Admiral. But the wars aren't over. Not by a long shot."

————————

WHEN their shuttle lifted from a field near the wall, Geary watched with surprise as the Dancer craft shot upward and kept going. He hauled out his comm unit and called *Dauntless*. "General Charban? Can you find out what the Dancers are doing? They're supposed to be following us."

"And they're not," Charban had no trouble guessing. The actions of the aliens doubtless always made sense to the Dancers themselves, but humans had found them often hard to predict or understand. "I'll try to find out what they're doing."

A few minutes later, as the shuttle split the sky en route its next destination, Charban called back. "All the Dancers will say is *go our ship*. They're returning to one of their ships."

"You understand them as well as anyone," Geary said. "Are they unhappy or bored or what? Any guesses?"

"What's the next location they were scheduled to see?"

"We're going to a place called Stonehenge. An ancient religious site."

"Religious?" Charban asked. "That might be the reason. The Dancers have never responded when we tried to discuss spiritual beliefs. Maybe they think such things are private or secret. Let me check what we sent them . . . yes, we told them that Stonehenge is a place where humans talked to something bigger than themselves. That's the nearest we can come to saying religious site. They may not feel it is appropriate for them to be there. That's my best guess."

"Thank you, General. Let me know if the Dancers say anything else. We'll see you tomorrow."

The massive rocks at the place called Stonehenge didn't look that impressive to eyes accustomed to what modern equipment and modern engineering could do. Imagining humans constructing this place with bare hands, muscle, and the most primitive of tools made it feel much more remarkable. Moreover, as Geary left the shuttle where it had set down close to the ancient circle of stones, he felt an even greater sense of age here than at the wall.

"This is *old*," Tanya said. "Look, there's a flame." She walked toward a fire pit to one side of the stones and knelt.

Geary stayed back, giving her privacy and looking around. The locals who had been waiting for them were approaching with the strange combination of wariness and welcome that many people on Old Earth seemed to feel toward the distant children of this world.

Beyond them . . . "What is that?" he asked the first woman who approached him, her coat adorned with the crest those on this island wore to identify themselves as custodians of the past.

She looked over her shoulder, then made an apologetic gesture. "A different kind of monument, Admiral. Perhaps, in a way, a monument to the things people worshipped in a time in the past for us but in the far future to those who built Stonehenge."

Geary squinted at the objects. "They look like ground fighting vehicles."

"They are. Or, they were." The female steward sighed. "At one time, many weapons of war were built with totally robotic controls. They could and did operate without any human intervention."

"Autonomous robotics? What were those people thinking?"

"That they could cede control and yet maintain it," she replied, her voice growing caustic, then taking on the cadence of someone reciting words often repeated. "Those broken machines were Caliburn Main Battle Tanks, part of the Queen's Royal Hussars. Someone managed to override and alter their programming, causing the most massive and destructive armored vehicles ever constructed to break out of their garrison and head for this site, with instructions to destroy the ancient stones here. Much of the automated equipment that could have stopped them was disabled by computer viruses and worms planted by the same people. Fortunately, humans carrying antitank weaponry were able to destroy the vehicles though at considerable cost in life. The last of the Caliburns, the spearhead of the attack, were knocked out just before they reached the stones."

She waved toward the crumbling metal-and-ceramic monsters. "They were left here, as a monument to the heroism of those who stopped them and as a reminder of the folly of entrusting our safety to something incapable of loyalty, morality, or wisdom." Her voice changed, losing the tone of rote recitation. "You don't use such weapons, then? In your wars among the stars?"

"No," Geary replied. "Every once in a while someone proposes it, and a few times it has been tried with experimental units, but the results tend to be similar to what happened here. As erratic as humans can be, they are still immensely more reliable and trustworthy than anything that can be reprogrammed in a few seconds or mistake a glitch in its programming for reality."

He knew he should be focused on the ancient monument, but for some reason he couldn't explain, the wrecks of the armored vehicles held his attention even as he and Tanya were given a quick tour while the setting sun drew long shadows off the standing stones. It seemed only a few minutes had passed before they were ceremoniously escorted back into their shuttle. "Can we fly low over that?" Geary asked as the shuttle lifted.

The pilot gave him a startled look, but nodded. "It might get me in trouble, but I'll say you insisted," she added with a grin.

"Why were you surprised by my request?"

"Because not many who come here want to see that. Most would rather that ugly pile of rust and high-tech pottery was gone, but it's an historic site just like the big stones, so they're stuck with it. Me, I'm glad it's here."

"Why?" Tanya asked.

"Something my dad said when he brought me here the first time," the pilot said, twisting her controls to bring the shuttle in a slow pivot over the ruins of the archaic armored vehicles. "I looked at them old, dead monsters, and I said, *It's a good thing they stopped them*. And my dad looked at me and said, *No, it's a good thing they* had *to stop them because if they hadn't, we might have made ones a lot bigger before we learned our lesson.*"

"You've got a smart dad," Tanya remarked.

"A-yeah." The pilot grinned at her. "He wanted me to work at the law, like he does. But he accepted my being a pilot when I said it was that or I'd ship out for the stars. *They're all crazy out there*, he said. You lot don't look too crazy to me, though."

"You don't know us very well," Geary said.

ANOTHER reception committee awaited them at the castle. "Here's where you'll spend your last night on Earth," the pilot said as they left her, laughing at what Geary guessed must have been a joke. He went through the process of introductions and greetings, the faces and names and titles of the various officials blending into the blur of others he had met during what had turned into a whirlwind tour of Old Earth. Back in the Alliance, most star systems had a single government spanning all of the planets and orbiting facilities, but here there seemed to be a new government, a new batch of officials, and a new set of titles every hundred kilometers.

"It's a real castle," Desjani said in disbelief.

"Yes, Lady Desjani," one of the officials responded.

"I'm not a lady, I'm a captain."

"Uh . . . yes . . . Captain. The oldest portion dates to the eighth century, Common Era. Have you ever seen a castle?"

"I've seen fake castles," Tanya said. "You know, buildings that aren't very old but were made to look like castles for amusement parks and resorts or for people with a whole lot of money to spend. There are a few on Kosatka, where I grew up. Like the one at—" Her voice cut off abruptly.

"Tanya?" Geary asked in a low voice.

"Memories," she murmured back to him. "My brother and I, when we were kids. Don't worry. I'll be all right."

Her younger brother, dead in the war. Desperate to change the subject and distract the locals who were watching Tanya with discreet curiosity, Geary locked on one of the last things said. "The eighth century? Is that Roman?"

"After the Romans left," a man replied. "The Dark Ages, we called them."

"Dark Ages?" Desjani said with forced cheerfulness. "No wonder they needed a castle."

"Yes. After the Roman Empire fell apart, there were many wars, barbarian invasions, a general lawlessness and suffering. Terrible loss of life and destruction. It was an ugly time," the man said, sounding as if he had lived through it.

"It's hard to imagine such a breakdown of government and society," a woman added.

"Not if you've seen it," Desjani replied.

Another awkward silence fell, giving Geary time to wonder why Tanya seemed to be particularly undiplomatic tonight. "The Syndicate Worlds," he explained. "They're coming apart. We've seen revolutions there, collapse of local authority, and internal fighting."

A second long pause was broken by the man who had spoken first. "Are you helping them?"

"We . . . can't," Geary said. "In most cases, we can't. It's too big. Even if the Alliance hadn't been bled white by the war—"

"The war the Syndics started," Desjani interjected harshly.

"—we wouldn't have the resources. We're doing what we can, but it's very little compared to the scale of the problem." They didn't like hearing that. Geary had run into this before on Old Earth, a difficulty in comprehending the sheer vastness of humanity's reach even though human-occupied space made up only a small portion of a single arm of the galaxy. Nor did he want to explain that the immense costs of the war had left the star systems in the Alliance bickering over even reduced commitments to common goals and unwilling in a time of cutbacks to invest in helping former enemies.

But there was another point that usually swayed his audiences, or at least cut short their arguments. "Besides, the Syndicate Worlds is an authoritarian state. They maintained rule by force. Now some of their star systems are seeking freedom, autonomy. We won't help the Syndic government terrorize their own people in the name of maintaining order. We've helped defend some star systems which have declared themselves free." Technically, only the Midway Star System qualified as having been defended by the Alliance against Syndic reconquest, but one star system fit the definition of the word "some."

"And we've defended them against the enigmas," Desjani added, still sounding defiant. "We stopped the enigmas from taking over star systems occupied by humanity."

A woman smiled broadly. "You must tell us about these different aliens! Please come in. We have a dinner ready for you."

Grateful that at least one person present was trying to steer the talk away from difficult topics, Geary smiled in return.

The smiling woman led Geary and Desjani to their seats in a dining room with walls hung with shields and banners whose decorations were bright enough to advertise them as recent reproductions rather than ancient artifacts. "I'm Lady Vitali."

"Vitali?" Tanya asked. "We have a Captain Vitali in our fleet. He commands the battle cruiser *Daring*."

"He could be a relation," Lady Vitali said. "Our family has a long naval tradition. Does he cause much bother? Raise a bit of hell at times?"

"No," Geary replied.

"Perhaps he's not a relation, then. Tell me about the enigmas!"

As everyone ate, the locals listened intently as Geary, for perhaps the tenth time during this brief visit to Earth, described what little had been learned about the enigmas. That led to a discussion about the Dancers, then the third alien race so far discovered, the single-mindedly expansionist and homicidal Kicks.

"You've seen a great deal among the stars. Have you enjoyed your stay on Earth?" Lady Vitali asked Desjani.

Tanya paused, as if trying to ensure that her next words weren't combative or inappropriate, then nodded. "It's like visiting a place of legend. I never thought to see any of it in person."

"What impressed you the most?"

"The statue we saw of that woman. Joan. When I looked at it, I felt like she might have been an ancestor of mine."

"Joan of Arc? You could do much worse. I like to imagine Nelson was one of my ancestors. Fortunately for us, and for them I suppose, they were too far separated in time to have fought each other." Lady Vitali grew serious. "We prefer to think we have outgrown war here, but we haven't. We've simply strangled it in bureaucracy and red tape."

"Perhaps that's the best humanity can hope for," Geary remarked.

"No. I don't believe so. We frustrate the belligerent, who head for the stars to fulfill their agendas. We make it hard to start a war and easy to leave. All we're doing is exporting aggression to the stars."

"Is that why some of you look at us like we're the latest barbarians to come here?" Desjani asked.

"Of course it is. We admire what you and your ship did to those boors who called themselves the Shield of Sol, but we also . . . worry about it. We don't want war as you are accustomed to it to come here again."

"We're leaving tomorrow," Geary said. Back to the not-technically-a-war-anymore aggression by the remnants of the Syndicate Worlds, back to the many hidden threats in the Alliance, and back to the menaces posed by the enigmas and the Kicks.

"You're our children," an old man said in a gruff voice. "We sent you to the stars, then we left you on your own while we blew the hell out of Earth and the other planets here in some more wars. We hoped that *you* would learn some wisdom that we have lacked, that *you* would someday come home with the secret of peace. But how could you be better than your mothers and your fathers? You're our children," he repeated, taking a long drink of wine.

"We look to our ancestors for wisdom," Tanya said.

"Don't bother looking here," the man said, putting down his empty glass. "We're not wise. We're tired. Maybe somewhere out there, you'll find an answer. Maybe those Dancers know the secret."

Recalling the terrible defenses with which the Dancers defended their region of space, Geary did not think so, but he nodded politely. "It's possible. We'll keep looking, and maybe we will find the answer."

"And we'll keep blowing the hell out of anything that gets in the way of humanity's quest for peace," Tanya grumbled in a voice too low for anyone but Geary to hear.

He wasn't certain how many hours elapsed before he and Tanya could politely say their good-nights and make their way to their rooms. Certainly it was late enough for the fabled constellations of stars seen from Old Earth to shine brilliantly above.

They had intended to take full advantage of this final night, now that all official duties were over and, for a few brief hours, they could simply be man and wife rather than admiral and captain. Once back aboard *Dauntless*, any romantic familiarity would be off-limits. Two suites had been set aside for them, but they both went into his. The door had no sooner closed behind them than Tanya smiled at Geary. "Come here, Admiral."

But, like many plans, this one did not survive contact with reality. Their lips had barely touched when a soft but insistent knock sounded on the door.

"It had better be *very* important," Tanya growled.

Thinking the exact same thing, Geary yanked open the door.

Lady Vitali stood there. When they had left her a few minutes before, she had seemed fairly tipsy. Now she looked at them with no signs of intoxication apparent. "I must apologize for an unexpectedly abrupt end to our hospitality. Among the other inventions which Earth may have given the universe was the idea of assassins. Some who fit that name are en route this place as we speak."

After so many surprises in combat situations, Geary's mind took only a second to reorient this time. "Assassins? Are we their target?"

"I believe so. Or, rather, my sources of information believe so, and I believe them. Unfortunately, their message only just now reached me. I have called some friends who have a shuttle, which will take you to your ship in orbit. It will be here within fifteen minutes."

Geary's instinct to act warred with sudden suspicion. "No offense, but why should we trust you in this?"

"Because I was told that if you needed to be convinced of my trust-worthiness, I should mention the name Anna Cresida."

Tanya caught his eye and nodded. Anna Cresida, the last name of a close friend dead in the war paired with a false first name, was the code agreed upon by the senior personnel aboard *Dauntless* to inconspicu-ously authenticate critical information they might have to pass to each other while on Old Earth or to indicate a dangerous situation if one arose.

"Who told you that name?" Geary asked.

"It's a long story, and time is short, Admiral. Nor is any answer I give likely to convince you if you do not accept the name itself."

"She's got a point," Desjani said. "I just called *Dauntless*. From where they are in orbit, a shuttle from her will take forty-five minutes to launch and get here. If time is that critical, Admiral, I recommend that we accept the ride offered by our host. You and I are pretty good at fighting in space, but I for one don't want to face assassins on the ground."

"All right," Geary relented. He knew that Tanya had good instincts in such matters, so if she was willing to trust Lady Vitali, that counted for a great deal.

Lady Vitali's somber expression was softened by a smile as she looked as Desjani. "I envy you the command of such a craft as that battle cruiser of yours, Captain."

"From what I see at the moment," Tanya replied as she threw their spare clothes and other possessions back into their travel bags, "you might have qualified to command one."

"That's the first diplomatic thing you've said tonight. I knew you could do it."

Geary broke in sharply. "Whose assassins are these?"

"I have little idea," Lady Vitali said. "My sources, which I assure you are very capable, haven't been able to discover the origin of the money behind this. But I can tell you this much, Admiral. The money does not come from any place on which the light of Sol shines."

"Those Shield of Sol people from the outer stars?" Desjani asked.

"Possibly. The ones who escaped being killed by you didn't know why their late and unlamented senior officer was so keen on attacking your ship, and we can't ask that senior officer because, unfortunately, the technology available to us is not capable of reconstituting bodies and brains that have been blasted into their component atoms. You might be a little less thorough in your destruction of your opponents next time, Captain."

"I'll keep that in mind." Desjani hefted her bag and held Geary's out to him.

He took the bag, then studied Lady Vitali. "How did you manage to get things done so quickly tonight despite the bureaucracy and red tape you spoke of earlier?"

Lady Vitali's broad smile was back. "You would be amazed what can be done with the right combination of ingenuity, threats, and promises, Admiral. Or maybe you wouldn't be surprised if half of what we've heard of you is true. If I discover anything about the source of this threat to you, I will send it on, though it may take a long while to reach you given the distance involved and lack of routine traffic between our home and yours."

"Understood. Thank you. We're in your debt."

"Oh, nonsense. If you believe that you owe me anything, then if I ever reach your neighborhood, point me in the direction of the best beer."

As they reached a side door of the castle, moving in silence through narrow stone corridors with just a dim light held by Lady Vitali, Geary wondered how many times others had fled this castle in centuries past, their flight perhaps illuminated by torches rather than modern lights, horses rather than a shuttle their method of escape. For a moment he felt displaced in time, so that he would not have been surprised if there had indeed been saddled horses awaiting them beyond the walls of the castle.

Once out near the landing area, one wall of the castle rising behind them and everything else shadowed by the night, the glamour of their late-night getaway faded abruptly, and worries set in once more. Could Lady Vitali really be trusted? Could this be a plot to get him and Tanya out in the open, where they would be better targets for assassins already awaiting them?

On the heels of that thought, Geary saw a darker shape detach itself from the rest of the night sky and come in to land with a degree of quietness that spoke of military-grade stealth technology. "Will you be all right?" he asked as Lady Vitali urged them to the shuttle.

"Oh, quite. Don't worry about me. I have some other friends who will be on hand to greet our uninvited guests. But we wouldn't want you to be caught in the cross fire! Off you go. Have a nice trip home." Lady Vitali waved cheerfully as the closing boarding ramp cut off their view of her and of Old Earth.

"Lady Vitali has some interesting friends," Geary remarked to Tanya, as they strapped into their seats, the shuttle already accelerating upward.

"And at least one of them is aboard *Dauntless*, it seems," she replied, checking her comm unit. "That's the only way she could have known the made-up name Anna Cresida. My ship is tracking us, by the way.

Old Earth's stealth tech is at least a couple of generations behind ours. The tracking confirms that we are on a vector to reach *Dauntless.*"

"Good. We were warned that some of the various governments and authorities on Old Earth might try to involve us in their own affairs. Do you think this might be some ploy to make us suspicious of other governments in Sol Star System?"

"No," Tanya replied with a shake of her head. "If it were that, she wouldn't have told us the money appeared to be coming from outside the star system. And, obviously, someone else from *Dauntless* thought she was trustworthy enough to share our code phrase. I think you and I narrowly avoided meeting our ancestors here in the wrong way." She paused, then laughed. "I finally get it. What that one man said about us being their children. Everyone in the Alliance thinks of Old Earth, and Sol Star System, as someplace unimaginably special, a place of tranquillity and wisdom far surpassing our own. But that man had it right. We're not different from them. The violence and politics and sheer stupidity we deal with are here, too. They've always been here.

"When humanity left Old Earth for the stars, we didn't leave any of it behind. We took it all with us."

She paused, eyeing her comm unit. "*Dauntless* says we're veering off a direct vector to her."

"What are we headed for?" Geary demanded. "Where does the new vector aim?"

"No telling." Her eyes met his. "*Dauntless* was cut off in mid-message. Our comms are being jammed."

TWO

GEARY, his expression grim, tapped the comm panel near his seat. "No response from the pilot."

"None here, either," Tanya said, rapping a fist against the surface of her seat's comm panel. "What do you suppose they're planning?"

"Didn't you say *Dauntless* was tracking us?"

"Yes, indeed." She smiled unpleasantly. "If I know my crew, and I do know them better than anyone, my battle cruiser is currently accelerating to a fast intercept with this shuttle."

The shuttle lurched as it twisted up and to their right. "Evasive maneuver," Geary commented, checking his comm unit again. "The automated antijamming routines on my unit have found something."

Desjani studied hers. "Mine, too. It found a path through the jamming to something, but it's not *Dauntless*. Oh, hell, it's internal."

"The control deck on this shuttle," Geary suggested.

"Probably. We might be able to screw with their controls if we established contact, but our units can't shake hands with the Earth systems. This won't get us anywhere."

The shuttle rolled to their left.

Tanya frowned, then looked at Geary. "If they are trying to evade *Dauntless*, why aren't they diving into atmosphere?"

"You think there's—?"

The panel next to Geary suddenly flared to life, revealing a woman in the flight-engineer seat on the control deck. "Whatever you're trying to do, please be so good as to stop. The signals coming out of there are confusing our systems."

"Stop jamming our comms," Desjani demanded before Geary could say anything.

"Your comms?" The woman appeared to be genuinely puzzled as she checked some of her readouts. "Oh. Our stealth systems cut in jamming automatically when they identified your signals."

"Then manually override them," Geary said.

"If you emit signals, you'll compromise our stealth!" the woman pleaded. She looked to one side as if listening, then back at Geary. "Your ship keeps adjusting its track to maintain an intercept. You must still be sending it some locating data despite our jamming."

"My ship doesn't need any help from us to track this shuttle," Desjani said. "You can't evade her. I strongly suggest you give up trying."

Puzzlement appeared on the woman's face again. "Evade your ship? We're not trying to evade *them*."

Tanya glared at the woman's image. "Who are you trying to evade?"

"We don't know, exactly, but our flight controllers on the ground say there are at least two other stealth craft up here that are trying to close on us. We're trying to remain clear of them until we reach your ship, which is very difficult when we have only vague ideas of where the other stealth craft are and is being complicated even more by your systems interfering with ours."

"If that's true," Desjani said in a voice that contained considerable skepticism, "then stop jamming our comms so my ship can send you position and vector data on those other craft."

"*Precise* positions and vectors," Geary added.

"You can—?" The engineer turned again, speaking rapidly to the pilot, her words and lip movements obscured by the security functions in the panel.

But Geary could make out her expression, which quickly went from questioning to insisting to demanding. "She's reading the pilot the riot act."

"Good," Desjani retorted. "Pilots need that done to them every once in a while. It's the only thing that keeps them even a little humble."

The woman looked back at Geary. "I'm overriding the jamming of your comms and releasing the lock on the control-deck hatch. Please come forward so we can see the positioning data your ship provides."

Tanya unstrapped from her seat and triggered the hatch, watching as it opened and gesturing Geary to stay back. "All right. It looks safe. Come on, Admiral. This shuttle crew may be playing straight with us, but I've still got a bad feeling about this."

The flight deck was roughly similar in layout to an Alliance shuttle. The basic design must have been settled on long before humans went to the stars, Geary speculated. He grabbed a handhold to steady himself while Tanya took a free seat next to the male pilot. "I've got comms again," she announced. "*Dauntless*, give me a remote look at the vicinity of this shuttle."

She tapped her unit to bring up the 3-D display, which popped into existence above her hand.

"There are three of the Gorms!" the flight engineer cursed. "And closer than we thought."

"You don't know who they are?" Geary asked.

"No. Whoever they are, they must have been waiting for us up here. We got snookered, Matt," she said to the pilot.

"They were watching for anyone lifting out of there en route that warship," the pilot agreed. "Good thing they've had as much trouble seeing us as we did seeing them."

"But your ship can see us and them that easily?" the engineer asked Desjani. "How?"

"Do you really expect me to answer that?" Tanya asked.

"No. But it was worth the asking, wasn't it?"

The pilot had been studying the display and now turned and climbed slightly to avoid the nearest other stealth craft, which was just below them and angling in their direction. The second craft was in higher orbit, tracking slightly away as it searched for them, and the third lower, but rising and converging on their track. All around, following their own orbits or trajectories, scores of other spacecraft, satellites, shuttles, and ships operating without any stealth equipment wove through space oblivious to the four hidden craft playing hide-and-seek among them.

"Martian," the flight engineer declared, pointing to the nearest pursuer.

"Are you certain?" the pilot said.

"Absolutely. The signature on that bird is Martian. I can't tell if the other two are also Reds."

"Why are people from Mars after us?" Geary asked.

"Hired guns," the pilot answered. "If you've got money, and you want a job done, no questions asked, Mars is the place to put up your offer. The only difference between the three primary Red governments is how much they charge for looking the other way and how much control they actually have over their countries. Speaking of looking the other way, you haven't been up here or seen me or the flapping ear or talked to either of us. All right?"

"You get us to *Dauntless*, and officially we won't breathe a word otherwise," Geary promised. "Flapping ear?"

"Flight engineer."

"Oh." He studied the movements of the three other stealth craft. "If your ground controllers can spot indications of those three, why aren't they trying to target them?"

"Target?" Both the pilot and the flight engineer shook their heads before the pilot continued speaking. "You mean engage with weapons? There aren't any antiorbital weapons allowed on Earth or in Earth orbit. Even if there were, our rules of engagement are straight out of Gandhi."

"What?" Desjani asked.

"We don't shoot," the flight engineer clarified. "Not if you're Earth-based or -controlled. Those three hunting us might shoot if they get a good chance at us, but that's because they're Reds, and because even if they're one hundred percent official property of some Martian government, there won't be anything on them to prove that."

"You can't shoot?" Tanya demanded as if unable to comprehend the words.

"Not while we're in Earth orbit," the pilot explained as he twisted the shuttle between the tracks of two other passing craft. "Beyond that, if we're past Luna, we can fire back, but only if we get hit at least twice. One hit might be an accident, you see. So we have to wait for two hits. Two hits means it's definitely deliberate. Then, if there's anything left of us, we can try shooting back."

"That is insane."

"I suppose it might look that way," the flight engineer agreed. "But, officially, it means we're at peace and staying that way. And we've got ships out beyond Luna. If something happens to us, and then some unfortunate accidents happen to any of those three craft before they make it home, well, that's just too bad."

"Hey," the pilot cautioned. "Watch the loose lips."

"I'm just letting them know how things work here," the engineer protested. "They should know."

"Why didn't any accidents happen to the Shield of Sol ships before we got here?" Geary asked.

The engineer and the pilot both shrugged. "If someone was planning that," the engineer said, "and I'm not saying anyone was, it would have been very hard because the Shield of Sol gang knew how we did things, being neighbors and all. They were on guard for it, and they were big, and they stayed together."

"You guys didn't play by the rules," the pilot added. "But we always have to. If anyone shoots at us, all we can do is dodge."

Desjani smiled. "My ship will intercept us in seven minutes, and we *still* don't have to follow your rules. If those Martian craft give us any trouble, they'll be sorry."

Both the pilot and the flight engineer gave her horrified looks. "No," the engineer protested. "You can't. Not in Earth orbit."

"I know it's crowded up here, but my ship's fire-control systems can make the shots at the right angles—"

"*No.* You *can't* shoot in Earth orbit. It's not about rules or regulations. It's . . . wrong."

Desjani stared at the two, perplexed.

Recalling some of the things they had seen on the surface, Geary nodded slowly. "It's because of your history, isn't it? The damage that was done to Old Earth from orbit."

"Yes, sir," the pilot confirmed in a low voice. "Not just things being dropped on us but what happened when fighting up here disrupted space-based systems that had become critical. There were some ugly things on the ground after that. All hell, and everything that could deal with it knocked out, too. For a while, no one knew if Earth would pull through or if we'd end up like the dinos through what amounted to racial suicide. Nobody from down there is going to start a fight up here. And if you do, well, it will mark you, and in the worst way. I don't doubt you could take out anything you wanted up here. But it would be a mistake. A very big mistake."

Tanya shook her head and looked down at her comm unit. "All right. I understand. Dropping rocks on civilian targets is an ugly thing."

Something in her words or her tone of voice might have given away some of the recent history that haunted the Alliance fleet, because the two from Earth eyed Desjani with startled dismay. Geary spoke quickly to distract them. "Can you stay clear of the craft pursuing you until *Dauntless* reaches us?"

The pilot jerked his attention back to Geary and nodded. "With the data your ship is sending us, yes. It's not certain, because they might accidentally box us in, and I have to stay clear of all the other traffic up here, which can't see us and might run into us if I don't avoid them."

"But you said they might shoot?"

"They might," the flight engineer confirmed. "They're not from here, they're hiding their origins to keep their bosses in the clear, and the reputations of the Reds couldn't sink any lower without going below absolute zero. Uh-oh. That low one is coming up more, and the high one is dropping and swinging in. They must be picking up something from those transmissions of yours."

Tanya raised her eyes to study the pilot and the flight engineer. "Do you prefer having the precise data on those guys, or do you think I should shut down the data feed?"

Both hesitated, then the pilot grimaced. "I'd rather have the good picture, ma'am."

"Captain."

"Right. Captain. From their movements, our hunters still only have a vague idea of where we are. But they know where we're going, to meet up with your ship, which they can see coming. That narrows down our possible vectors a lot for them."

"I'll see if I can tweak our gear to mask what they're picking up," the flight engineer added, concentrating on her controls.

A few minutes passed, the shuttle making gentle adjustments up, down, right, left, to weave along vectors toward the most open path between their hunters and all the other objects moving through this portion of space, all while still heading toward an intercept with *Dauntless*.

Geary had almost relaxed when he heard Tanya draw in breath in a hiss between her teeth. "Something's happened. Those guys are zeroing in on us."

The pilot nodded, stress visible on his face. "They shouldn't be. But they've started reacting to our movements as if they've got a much better idea of where we are than they should."

"Whatever gear they've just activated, it's not as good as what *Dauntless* is using to track them." Desjani switched her gaze to Geary. "About a generation behind our best gear, I'd guess."

"Which means a generation ahead of what's in this star system?" he asked. "It looks like whoever wants us provided money and some equipment."

"Can I do anything against it?" the flight engineer asked.

Desjani made an angry gesture. "I don't know. I'm not a tech. If we had Senior Chief Tarrini here, she'd probably know exactly what to do with your gear to confuse the guys hunting us."

"We could have Tarrini pass instructions to the flight engineer over my comm unit," Geary suggested.

Tanya shook her head. "It would take too long for her to study the equipment remotely, figure out how it's configured and what to tweak. By the time that was done, *Dauntless* would already be here, or we'd already be screwed. It is older stuff, though. Do you know anything about it, Admiral?"

It was his turn to make a negating motion. "The gear I trained on was at least three generations behind what the Alliance uses now. Maybe four generations. And I wasn't a tech, either. I just have a general knowledge of how it works."

"This is what happens when you only have officers and no chiefs or other enlisted," Desjani grumbled. "Plenty of people to give orders but no one who knows how to carry them out. How good are you?" she asked the pilot.

The pilot smiled crookedly. "Pretty damned good."

"Every pilot thinks that." Desjani looked to the flight engineer, who nodded confirmation.

"He's not bad," the engineer said. "Got a decent feel for the bird. Only crashed once since I've known him."

"That wasn't a crash," the pilot replied, his voice sharp. "It was an abrupt landing aggravated by adverse conditions."

"Glad to hear it," Desjani said. "Because it's up to you to get us through those guys. What do I tell *Dauntless*, Admiral?"

He knew what she meant. *Do I give the Alliance battle cruiser permission to fire on the three pursuers if necessary?* It shouldn't have been that hard a question to answer; except from the way these people of Earth had reacted to the idea it was clear that doing so would cause a huge outcry, far greater than any upset over the annihilation of the Shield of Sol ships in the outer reaches of the star system.

"Just tell *Dauntless* to get here as quickly as she can," Geary said.

"She's coming around the curve of the planet now and braking to match velocity with us. Estimate three more minutes until we're alongside."

The shuttle lurched up, swinging to the left as it did so. "Weren't expecting that, were you?" the pilot muttered fiercely, his eyes fixed on the display over Desjani's comm unit.

The closest hunter slid past just beneath them, not realizing it had missed by a few hundred meters getting close enough to establish a firm lock on the shuttle's position.

But the evasive maneuver had brought them up toward the higher hunter, and now the pilot brought the shuttle back down with a swift change in vector. "They'll see that!" the flight engineer warned the pilot. "You're maneuvering too hard."

"I know! They're getting too close! We can't hide any longer. Our only chance is to keep dodging away from them until that battle cruiser gets here!"

"But they might—"

"I don't have any other options!"

The shuttle ducked and darted through space, evading each time one of the hunters threatened to get too close, maneuvers complicated by the need to avoid hitting anything else around them. Geary's breath caught as they zipped over a stodgy tug plodding obliviously through space, then narrowly avoided hitting a satellite racing along on its fixed orbit. Despite the pilot's evasive moves, the net kept tightening around them, the distances to the pursuers shrinking as they gradually converged on the desperate flight of the shuttle.

"One minute until *Dauntless* gets here," Desjani reported.

A high-pitched keening sounded just as she finished speaking. The flight engineer silenced the alarm and called to the pilot. "They're targeting us! Trying for a lock-on!"

"Try active jamming!"

"If I do, they'll fire on the jamming source! We wouldn't last five seconds! I'm doing all I can with passive countermeasures."

"*Dauntless*," Desjani said in a voice whose calm tone contrasted with the frantic words of the pilot and the flight engineer. "We are being targeted. I see you forty seconds from intercept, stern on. Override the collision-avoidance systems and maximize after shields. Your relative speed at contact should be enough to brush aside the two closest of our pursuers without hazarding the ship."

"Captain?" the reply came. "We can nail them with hell lances easy."

"Firing is not authorized," Desjani said.

"Captain, just to be clear, you are directing us to make shield contact with the closest pursuers of your shuttle."

"That's correct. Do it."

"Follow your captain's orders," Geary said, leaning in toward her comm unit. *I just concurred in ordering my flagship to deliberately collide with other spacecraft.* "Are you sure?" he muttered to Desjani.

"I know my ship," she insisted. "And I know maneuvering in space.

Right now, those guys after us are moving just a little faster than we are and in the same direction, so they can stay close. *Dauntless* is slowing to match our speed, so when her shields make contact with any of them, the impact should be at a relative velocity of only about ten meters per second and dropping."

"About ten meters per second? There's a significant amount of mass in whatever is hunting us. That will still be a dangerous impact."

"*Dauntless*'s shields can handle it."

It was one of those moments in which he either accepted her judgment or undercut her, and he knew that Tanya had a lot more combat experience than he did, as well as a lot more experience with current warships. "All right."

"Steady out," Desjani ordered the pilot. "Get on a vector and hold it. I don't want my ship hitting you, too, because you're bouncing around."

With a stunned look at her, the pilot did as he was told, settling the shuttle onto a single course and speed. Almost instantly, the three pursuers, unaware of how accurately they were being tracked by *Dauntless*, turned onto intercept vectors that would get them close enough to lock onto the stealthed shuttle and open fire.

A bright star coming toward them grew rapidly in size as the remaining distance dwindled, *Dauntless*'s main propulsion units straining at full capacity to reduce her speed to match that of the shuttle. Her dark, shark-shaped hull was invisible behind the hellish glare from the propulsion units.

One of the pursuers, with less nerve or more brains than its companions, broke off and accelerated away moments before *Dauntless* slid with enormous grace and enormous mass into position next to the shuttle. One of the pursuers took a glancing blow from the battle cruiser's shields, knocking it off in a wild tumble as the craft's stealth systems failed under the impact and made clear to all there was a small vessel careening uncontrolled among them. Other ships and craft frantically dodged the wreckage, filling emergency communications with warnings and complaints about the sudden appearance of a navigational hazard.

The third pursuer wasn't nearly so lucky. *Dauntless* hit it almost dead center on her stern, bracketed by the energies being hurled out by the battle cruiser's main propulsion units. The craft blew backwards under the impact, disintegrating as it went, the pieces, most of them too small for anyone to worry about evading, showing up easily now to all observers.

The pilot and flight engineer were staring at the menacing bulk of *Dauntless* next to them as if fearing they would be next.

"My ship is opening up her shuttle dock," Desjani told them with a smile. "Drop your stealth systems, and they'll guide you in."

AS Geary and Desjani walked down the ramp off the shuttle, the sound of six distinct bells resounded through the dock, followed by the announcement "Admiral, Alliance fleet, arriving," then four more bells and "*Dauntless*, arriving."

"No damage from the, uh, accidental collisions," the battle cruiser's second in command reported, saluting, his expression unaccountably grim despite that good news.

"Well done," Desjani said, with a brief I-told-you-my-ship-could-do-it glance at Geary. "A lot of people saw those collisions. We'll file a standard collision report with the Sol Star System authorities about encountering stealthed craft we could not see in time to avoid. With their reverence for rules here, the local authorities are certain to still abide by the one that says stealth craft are obligated to stay clear of all others, and any collision is automatically their fault. Is everyone else back?"

"No, Captain. We're short two officers. Lieutenant Castries and Lieutenant Yuon. They didn't report back on time to the shuttle that returned their group, and local authorities have so far failed to locate them."

"Why wasn't I informed earlier?" Desjani said in a low, angry voice.

"I was waiting on a report from the local authorities, Captain," her second in command replied, both his posture and his voice stiffening. "When I tried notifying you, you were already aboard this shuttle."

"Why did you wait on a report from the locals?" Desjani asked.

"Because we thought that they might have decided to elope, and the locals were certain they could locate them quickly."

"Castries and Yuon? When did they become a couple?"

"They haven't, officially, Captain. They're usually arguing, though."

"Oh, for the love of my ancestors! That is *not* a surefire sign of pending romance! I want to find those two lieutenants now. If they were civilians, they might be eloping," Desjani said. "Since they're officers in the Alliance fleet, they would instead be deserting. But I don't like this. It doesn't match what I know of Castries or Yuon. I take it the locals didn't find them yet?"

"No, Captain. But they remain confident that they will find them within an hour. Old Earth is laced with so many surveillance networks that just about everything anyone does gets spotted."

"It sounds like a Syndic planet," Desjani grumbled.

"All of the senators are back?" Geary asked.

"Yes, Admiral. And both envoys as well. We didn't have time to tell the Dancer ships what we were doing, but they stuck with us when we came for you, holding position exactly one hundred kilometers from us through every maneuver we did, so they are also accounted for."

Among those awaiting them was Master Chief Gioninni, carrying a bottle. Desjani beckoned to Gioninni and examined the bottle. "Whiskey from Vernon? Is this from the ship's supply?"

"Yes, Captain, properly signed for and everything," Gioninni assured her with a slight wariness as he judged her mood. "You know the tradition. When sailors get rescued, the ship pays a ransom to whoever picked them up. From what I hear, the folks on this bird deserve the ransom."

"They do," Desjani agreed. "But we'll hold them here while you also get some beer sent to the dock. We owe Lady Vitali a ransom, too."

"Beer, Captain?"

"Yes, Master Chief. The good stuff. Not from the officers' supply. Get it from the chiefs' supply."

"If you say so, Captain. I will, uh, have to charge—"

"I'm sure I can count on you to take care of the paperwork, Master Chief," Desjani said. As Gioninni hastened off to do her bidding, she looked at Geary again. "He'll write off twice as much beer as he actually provides to the shuttle."

"I was wondering why you were trusting Gioninni to play it straight in the face of that kind of temptation and how large his profit margin would be. Are you going to nail him for it?"

"Not for that, but I'll use it to make him cough up the extra bottle of whiskey he surely pulled out of our stocks when he got that one. He won't have left any tracks, so it's the only way I'll get the extra bottle back. Do you think my missing lieutenants fell afoul of the same sort of people who came after us?"

"Let's hope not. But if Castries and Yuon did, the locals may be our best hope for locating them."

"That was my thought," Desjani said. "Which is why I approved of Gioninni's ransom payment and sweetened it a little."

Several minutes later, they watched the shuttle depart and begin its dive back into the atmosphere of Old Earth, lighter by two passengers and heavier by bottles of some of the best whiskey and the best beer the Alliance had to offer.

"So much for our vacation," Desjani commented. "For some reason, I don't feel very rested. I hope you're not too eager to leave, Admiral."

"No, Captain," Geary said. "Even if we weren't waiting to hear more from the locals, I don't want anyone thinking we're bolting out of here as if we were guilty or scared. We'll hold here for at least the next few hours. That will also give us time for the envoys to get across to the Dancers that we're leaving Home and heading back to our homes."

She saluted, all formality again now that they were back aboard her ship. "Yes, sir. I'll pass that on to General Charban as soon as I get to the bridge."

"Thank you, Captain. I'm going to drop off my gear in my stateroom, then I'll join you on the bridge." He returned the salute, then left the shuttle dock, walking through the now-familiar and comforting passageways of *Dauntless*, passing officers and sailors and Marines whom he knew by sight and in most cases by name now. Technically, Old Earth was Home to all humanity, and, technically, Geary's personal home was on the planet Glenlyon in the star system of the same name. But the reality was that *Dauntless* was as close to a real home as he had in this time a century removed from his own.

And he had become increasingly grateful for that.

HE found Alliance Envoy Victoria Rione waiting at the hatch to his stateroom. "Did you get the message about talking to the Dancers?" he asked. She had been visiting locations on Earth for the past week as well, supposedly just as a tourist/touring representative of the Alliance, but he suspected Rione had been up to more than that.

"Yes," she replied. "Charban is handling it. There is something else we need to talk about."

"The missing lieutenants?"

"Among other things."

"Good. There's something else I need to ask you as well," he said, waving her inside the stateroom and following her. He didn't feel an urgent need to reach the bridge despite his concerns for Castries and Yuon. If any word came about them, it would reach him just as quickly here as on the bridge, and Rione might have some important information. "Have a seat."

She had already made herself at home, lounging into one of the seats around the low table in the stateroom. "I understand that you had an interesting trip back to the ship."

"It wasn't boring. And I understand you had a working vacation on Old Earth," Geary observed, sitting down across from her.

Rione gave him a blandly uncomprehending look. "Why do you say that?"

"We encountered Lady Vitali."

"Lady Vitali of Essex? I hear she throws a good party."

"She does. But I want to know how Lady Vitali knew to tell me the name Anna Cresida when I needed to know whether or not to trust her."

Rione studied him, her eyes hooded with calculation, then shrugged and made a casting-away gesture with one hand. "I told her. One of my clandestine assignments on this mission, one I'm not supposed to let you know about, was to establish ties with some of the governments in Sol Star System. Our experience with the surprise attack by the Shield of Sol ships only emphasized the importance of that task. Lady Vitali is one of those contacts who struck me as potentially very useful to us."

"Did she?" Geary sat back, glaring at Rione. "She appears to have rendered very valuable aid to Tanya and me, but Lady Vitali didn't strike me as the sort to just be used by people."

"You're absolutely right about that," Rione agreed, examining her fingernails as she spoke. "She, or rather her government, doubtless intends using us as well. They help us, we help them."

"So you trusted her, and who knows how many other people on Old Earth, with a code name that was only supposed to be shared among us."

Rione raised an eyebrow at him. "Trust has nothing to do with it. Self-interest is the factor here. You can rarely go wrong depending on that. You had a demonstration of that on your trip back to this ship, didn't you? Lady Vitali's government saw just how useful we can be to them when your captain annihilated those Shield of Sol ships. So, if Lady Vitali's friends learn anything more about those craft that tried to interrupt your shuttle trip, or learn anything from the surviving assassins who were after you on the ground, they will let us know so that, in the munificence of our gratitude, we might offer more favors in return."

Surviving assassins? He wondered if Lady Vitali was personally deadly enough to have helped take down the attackers, or if she just controlled events and directed others from behind that friendly smile. "The favor we need the most at the moment is information about Lieutenant Castries and Lieutenant Yuon."

"I know. I've already asked all of my contacts for anything they can find out. Even if it is something that officially their governments won't admit to, they'll tell me."

For reasons he didn't quite understand, Geary believed that Rione's confident statement was right. "All of your contacts? Just how many contacts did you establish with how many governments?"

Another wave of her hand, this one careless. "Oh . . . ten . . . twenty . . . something like that. I haven't had much time to work."

Geary shook his head in open amazement. "Every time I think I've figured you out and know exactly what you're capable of, you surprise me with something else."

"I'm a woman, Admiral."

"I don't think that entirely explains it." Geary tapped the controls on the table between them, bringing up an image of Sol Star System, the planets and minor planets and multitudes of smaller objects tagged with names out of the distant past. Venus. Mars. Jupiter. Luna. Callisto. Europa, whose doom still haunted the rest of human space. And Old Earth herself. "I hope they can help find our lieutenants, but beyond that, what good does the Alliance think agents working for one small part of one planet can do for us? In the Alliance, none of those governments still ruling over portions of Old Earth would count for anything. They're far too small and far too weak."

Rione looked annoyed. "Our enemies are already at work here. Hopefully, they aren't involved with the matter of your missing officers, but regardless, I want to know who told those Shield of Sol ships to attack us, and who paid for assassins and stealth spacecraft, and who spied on our movements and attempted a few other tricks that our various hosts managed to block or frustrate. Aside from that, you're military. You know the importance of certain places, an importance that is based on factors that may have nothing to do with equations of physical strength and power. *Any* place on Old Earth carries a lot of leverage inside the Alliance. I don't know all the ways we can use that. But I know I can use it in ways others may not expect. Any individual who can claim backing from Old Earth, leaving aside little matters like how small a portion of Old Earth that backing actually comes from, will gain additional prestige in the Alliance from that alone, perhaps enough so to give him a crucial edge."

Geary leaped to his feet, his angry gaze fixed down on her. "Him? You mean me. Backing from Old Earth? For what purpose? What the hell makes you think you can use *me*?"

She looked up at him steadily, cool and unruffled. "I have no intention of trying to use you. The last thing you need is for someone to be trying to guide you in the right political moves. Your greatest strengths are your lack of political ambition and your refusal to even think about political tactics."

"I'm doing what any good officer would do!"

Her smile was mocking. "I can name a dozen senior fleet officers off the top of my head who reached their exalted ranks by using political tactics and would be pursuing more political tactics right now if they were in your shoes. Tactics such as cultivating relationships with the likes of Senator Costa, Senator Suva, and Senator Sakai."

"But not you?" Geary demanded.

"Me? I'd be a liability. All you would want me for is a scapegoat."
She waved him back. "Relax. I never wanted you to charge in and take
over the Alliance, remember? The Alliance doesn't need someone who
thinks he or she is the savior of us all." Rione stood up as well, her eyes
on the display, one finger rising to point toward Old Earth. "You've
been there now. We've been there. We've seen the history of our ancestors firsthand. How much tragedy grew out of individuals certain that
they had a special destiny or that they deserved to rule?"

He considered the question, his jaw tightening with frustration,
then spun away from her and looked at the familiar starscape displayed
on one bulkhead. "What the hell am I supposed to do? I don't think
I'm someone like that, but a tremendous number of other people
believe it. Senator Sakai thinks who I am could easily destroy the Alliance."

"He's right." She made a helpless gesture, both hands partially
raised as if anticipating defeat. "I don't know what to do to save the
Alliance. There are many forces working to tear it apart, and many
people contributing to those forces either through greed or malice or
hope or despair or good intentions. I don't know how to counter the
stresses built up by a century of war, and the debts from a century of
war, and the simple and understandable but also naïve desires of many
people to live as they wish without bowing to some distant authority,
which they forget was created because its absence led to much worse
things than its existence does. Senator Costa thinks she knows an
answer built around an iron fist. Senator Suva still believes the answer
lies in good intentions and everyone's singing in harmony around a
common campfire. Senator Sakai no longer believes there is an answer.
But you . . ."

She shook her head, looking at him. "You aren't wise enough to
think you know the answer or wise enough to think you know there
isn't an answer. Which means you're probably far wiser than the
others. And you're the most powerful piece on the board."

"A piece you would, however, be willing to sacrifice," Geary said.

"Only if necessary. And I would feel bad about it afterwards."

He couldn't help smiling at her sardonic reply. "You wouldn't feel bad for long. Tanya would kill you."

"Very likely, yes. Though I'm sure that your captain would prefer to have grounds for murdering me that didn't involve your death." Rione went back and sat down, rubbing her forehead with one hand. "I haven't been able to figure out something that's very important, and you're the only person on this ship I can talk to about it. I was able to confirm from their reactions that all three of the senators on this ship know about the new warships being built despite public declarations that new construction was halted when the war ended. That means that Suva and Costa, who are ideological opposites, agreed to the project. What rationale convinced both of them that a new, secretly constructed armada was a smart idea?"

"They don't see eye to eye on much," Geary agreed, looking back at the depiction of Sol Star System. "But they appeared to find some common ground when the Dancers returned that man's remains to Old Earth."

"That won't last," Rione said. "More importantly, they both must have signed off on that secret armada some time ago, well before the Dancers gave them reason to rethink their attitudes toward others."

"Senator Sakai voted for it, too, I think. Did they tell you who would command that secret force?"

Rione gave him a demanding look. "No. Do you know?"

"Sakai told me it would be Admiral Bloch."

She didn't answer for almost a minute, then shook her head, looking pained. "Why? Why did the Grand Council agree to such a thing? It doesn't make sense. Bloch manufactured for himself a reputation as a great fleet commander, a reputation I believe was unsupported by actual ability, but even if they still believe Bloch could be a match for you, they know that Bloch had been planning a coup before the Syndics captured him. If that attack on the Syndic home star system hadn't been a disaster that led to your assuming command and his being captured, if Bloch had won that battle, had defeated the Syndics, he would have turned his victorious fleet against his own government. The Grand Council was desperate enough for victory that they were willing to risk that."

"And you would have done your best to kill him even though it would have meant your own death as well."

"I thought my husband was dead in the war. I didn't have anything else to live for except preserving the Alliance. And, yes, you've never asked, but some of my fellow senators knew what my intent was. I was their fail-safe to stop Bloch." Another long pause as Rione thought. "They must believe that this time they have some other means of ensuring he doesn't betray them. But what?"

Geary sat down again across from her, catching her eyes with his own. "While we were at Midway, we heard firsthand about some of the tricks the Syndics employed to keep their high-ranking individuals in line."

"No," Rione said, shaking her head again. "Costa would have signed off on tactics like holding Bloch's family hostage, but Suva never would have agreed to that. Neither would Sakai. It would have to be something the entire Grand Council would support, and I have no idea what that might be."

"We'll have to find out."

"I'll do my best." For a moment, before the feelings were masked, anguish could be seen in her eyes. "For the Grand Council to openly move against you, when you've done nothing but support the Alliance, would be irrational. But I no longer have confidence in my own ability to understand the motivations of the Grand Council. You created a condition they had never experienced and never imagined facing. Peace. They are flailing for answers and, I suspect, acting out of fear rather than reason. I have no doubt that you could beat Bloch in a fight even if you were badly outnumbered, but that would mean civil war. If it comes to that, it could create damage to the Alliance too great for anyone or anything to repair."

"There's always duct tape," Geary suggested in what he knew was a weak attempt to lighten their shared worries.

That brought only a thin smile from her. "As much as it impressed the Dancers as humanity's finest achievement, I doubt that even duct tape could repair the Alliance if it broke that badly. Who do you think is behind the attacks on us here?"

"Lady Vitali said the money was coming from outside Sol Star System."

"I believe she is right," Rione said. "But from where?"

"The Shield of Sol ships were after not just this ship but also the Alliance senators aboard her," Geary pointed out. "Since those senators represent a wide range of different views, targeting all of them would imply a source somewhere in Syndicate Worlds space."

"Possible, but unlikely. Syndic space is much farther from here than Alliance space is, and Alliance space is far from close." All trace of humor had fled again as she looked steadily at him. "I admit I was surprised by the boldness of the attempted strikes at you today. I shouldn't have been. There are powerful people in the Alliance who would willingly sacrifice their purported friends and allies in the name of some supposedly higher purpose. That's an old trick in crime and politics, to include some of your own people among the casualties in order to make yourself seem among the victims. We joked about my doing that to you, but I wouldn't because I think you're the only hope the Alliance has. Others, though, think you are either in the way of their preferred solution or the source of the danger. While Black Jack was dead he made a marvelous martyr for the government, serving exactly as needed. Don't delude yourself. There are those who would prefer to return to the days when they could use Black Jack to their own ends because he was, they thought, safely dead and unable to act on his own. You truly do not know which of those people can be trusted in anything."

Geary sighed, looking down for a moment, then back up to catch her eyes again. "If I can't trust anyone, why should I trust you, Victoria?"

"I didn't say you couldn't trust anyone. You've got your captain. As for me, I'm not asking you to trust me because I'm some paragon of virtue upon whom the light of the living stars shines with special warmth. You know I'm not." The thin smile was back. "No. You can trust me for the same reason I decided to trust Lady Vitali. Self-interest. I want to save the Alliance, and I believe that only a living Black Jack can make that happen."

It was uncomfortably close to what Tanya had told him at the ancient wall, and he had learned that on the rare occasions when those two women agreed on something, he had better listen. "Just how do I make that happen?"

"By staying alive. Without that, nothing else is possible."

THREE

HOURS crawled by as *Dauntless* held orbit near Old Earth and Tanya Desjani grew steadily more ill-tempered.

Her outlook had not been improved by the responses of two of the Alliance senators aboard the ship. Senator Costa had scowled when first told of the missing officers. "Is this going to delay our return to Alliance space?" The silence that had followed her question brought a slight flush to Costa's face before she made an inadequate attempt at a dignified retreat.

Senator Suva had not done much better, her first reaction being "You're not going to charge those two officers with a crime, are you?"

Fortunately for the reputation of the Alliance Senate, which could not have sunk much further in the eyes of the fleet in any event, Senator Sakai had also responded to the news with a question, but one which raised his status considerably in the eyes of the crew. "What can I do to help?"

For her part, Victoria Rione remained dead serious in her words and gestures, a disquieting sign of how concerned she was. "I'm hearing nothing," she confided to Geary. "I don't think my sources are lying. They truly can't find them, and if your missing officers had run off together for a romantic honeymoon amidst the ruins of Earth, they would have been found long before this."

Nearly ten hours after the disappearance of the lieutenants, Geary was pretending to get administrative work done in his stateroom when his comm panel buzzed urgently. Desjani looked fierce and angry as she spoke to him. "We've received news about my lieutenants from the locals."

"Did they find them?"

"No. What they found was proof that Lieutenant Castries and Lieutenant Yuon have been kidnapped and taken off Old Earth." She tapped a control and the screen split to show an elderly man waiting patiently. He was sitting behind an impressive wooden desk which must have been several centuries old, a painting of a single, solitary volcanic peak crowned with snow hanging on the wall behind his left shoulder. Everything about the office, including the man behind the desk, spoke of age and history. "Please summarize for the Admiral what you just told me," Desjani said to him.

The old man inclined his head slightly toward Desjani, then looked at Geary. "After much sifting of data, we discovered DNA samplings taken at a cargo facility in our area of responsibility, samplings which match those of your officers."

"DNA samplings?" Geary asked.

"From minute particles, flakes of skin, the sort of thing humans shed constantly." The man made an apologetic gesture. "The amount of DNA was very tiny, requiring much extra effort to find and analyze, but we have no doubt of our finding. Based on the other records at that cargo facility, we are confident that your officers were smuggled off the planet using modified cargo containers, which are sometimes employed by criminals for such purposes."

Geary rubbed his head with both hands as he absorbed the news. "They're not on Earth anymore? Do you know which ship those cargo containers went to?"

"We do." The man held up a restraining hand before Geary could say anything else. "But they are no longer on that ship." He touched some controls of his own and the screen split again, now also showing the boxy shape of a cargo vessel orbiting Old Earth. "You see here that another craft docked with the ship. You see? A small, stealthy craft, which only became clear to our sensors when it was locked to the ship. After a brief time, it broke free, and we lost track of it." The elderly man bowed his head again. "I regret to say that we have been unable to establish the position and vector of that craft though we have picked up a few traces that may well correlate to it."

"A stealth craft?" Geary studied what could be seen on the third screen. "Tanya, that looks like one of the stealth craft that tried to intercept our shuttle."

She nodded. "That's what I thought. The characteristics match. Which means it's from Mars and probably on its way back there now. Request permission to—"

"Your pardon," the old man interrupted, his voice gentle but somehow carrying enough authority to check Desjani's words. "If this craft is from Mars, and such an origin would not surprise me in the least, they will not be going back there, not while carrying your officers. They will seek another location, one where they may hide, and where if they are located, it will not compromise the identities and allegiances of their superiors."

"Any guesses where they would hide?" Geary asked.

The man pondered the question for a moment before replying. "The belt, or beyond. There are many places among the asteroid belt or the outer planets where a craft of that size could lie unnoticed given its ability to conceal itself."

Desjani had been studying something to one side and now looked back at the elderly man from Earth again. "These traces you picked up. How confident are you of them?"

"That they belong to the craft we seek? Fairly confident. That they show precise locations? I have little confidence of that. You see how large the probability cones are around those trace detections."

"I do," Desjani conceded. "But I've been driving ships for a long time. I can look at something like that and feel where it's leading. That craft is heading for Jupiter," she concluded.

The old man reacted with only a slight rise of his eyebrows, which was replaced by a long moment of deep thought. "That is a likely destination for someone seeking to hide. Jupiter has sixty-seven natural moons, a planetary ring of much smaller objects, and twenty major human facilities orbiting the planet in addition to numerous smaller artificial objects. There are many small settlements among the moons of Jupiter, and the craft we seek is capable of landing on bodies with atmospheres as weak as that of the Jovian moons. In particular, Io's turbulent surface activity would help conceal the craft, while Ganymede, like Mars, is notorious for its many ties to organized criminal activity."

"They left Earth orbit nearly twenty hours ago," Desjani grumbled. "They could be halfway to that asteroid belt by now. Admiral, I'm working up an intercept based on their probable vector and those trace detections. If we get close enough, we'll spot them. Request permission to leave orbit and proceed to intercept."

Geary glanced at the elderly man, who made no sign of approval or disapproval. *You want to leave this to us, do you? Let the barbarians do their own dirty work.* "What velocity are you using?" he asked Desjani.

"It ramps up to point three light before we start braking again for the intercept."

That would create quite a spectacle in Sol Star System, an Alliance battle cruiser roaring toward the orbit of Jupiter at a pace that would make nearly every other spacecraft here look snail-like by comparison. And, for the occupants of that Martian stealth craft, it would mean watching a massive warship heading at great velocity for something very close to an intercept with them.

"Yes, Captain," Geary said. "You may proceed toward an intercept with the criminal stealth craft. Let's put on a show that will impress whoever took our lieutenants. Thank you, sir," he added to the old man, "for your assistance in this matter."

"I have done nothing," the man replied, his expression totally serious. "Tell that to anyone who inquires. This contact and my transfer of information to you have not been fully approved and vetted by my government. Such an approval process will take some months to complete, so I have conducted a dry run. A simulation of passing such information to you, so that I would be ready when approval comes. Officially, I have done nothing."

"I understand," Geary said. "Your simulation was highly effective. Thank you for letting me evaluate it."

"The pleasure was mine. The needs of friends must not be neglected. Perhaps, at some future date, we shall have needs that you will be pleased to consider addressing." Another small bow toward Geary, then the old man's image vanished.

Tanya Desjani had not wasted another minute. As Geary finished speaking, *Dauntless*'s thrusters were already slewing the battle cruiser about, followed by the surge of the main propulsion units kicking in and hurling the warship out of the mass of space traffic near Old Earth.

Geary watched the globe that was the Home of all humanity diminish in size as *Dauntless* accelerated away from it toward an intercept with the craft that was itself heading toward the orbit of Jupiter. He had never expected to visit Jupiter, or this star system. He wondered if, once the lieutenants were rescued, he would ever return.

AT their closest, Earth and Jupiter were only about thirty-five light-minutes apart. A mere six hundred thirty million kilometers or so. But that could only happen when both planets were on the same side of the sun and lined up perfectly in their orbits. Even if the two planets had been that close when *Dauntless* began her hunt, neither of them was going to stay still. Planets had to be intercepted, chased or cut off, as they raced along their orbits. In the case of Jupiter, the gas giant had been moving around the star Sol at better than thirteen kilometers per second since long before the first human raised a wondering gaze to the night sky, and might still be doing so when the last human had gone to whatever fate awaited the species.

In this case, *Dauntless* faced a long, curving route through space adding up to one and a half light-hours before she would reach Jupiter. She would have to accelerate part of the way, then brake at the end so as not to overshoot her target, reducing her average velocity to about point one six light speed.

"It will take us just under ten hours to get there," Desjani told Geary. "Which would be fine, except that the guy we're chasing has a ten-hour head start on us."

"He can't have gone as fast as we will," Geary said.

"No. Even if he could accelerate at the same rate we could, which I seriously doubt, he would have to limit acceleration to keep from compromising his stealth so badly that even the sensors in this star system could spot it. But once we get within a light-hour of that guy, *we* will be able to see him no matter what."

Geary settled into his seat on the bridge of *Dauntless*, gazing at the curving tracks on his display. Two showed brightly, that which *Dauntless* would follow, and that which was estimated to be the track of the craft they were hunting. Around those two long curves, a crazy quilt of dim arcs marked the projected movements of numerous other spacecraft and natural objects. Some of those arcs were changing as he watched, moving away from the bright line of *Dauntless*'s vector, marking course changes by spacecraft that had projected *Dauntless*'s path and wanted to stay well clear of the mad people from the stars and their powerful warship. "What are we going to do when we catch them?" he asked Desjani.

She gave him a puzzled look. "Tell them to turn over our two offi-cers or die."

"What if they refuse? They've got Castries and Yuon as hostages."

Tanya waved one hand in a nonchalant manner. "And I've got a pla-toon of Marines."

"You don't think this might require more . . . subtlety . . . than Marines usually employ?"

"Fleet Marines are trained in hostage-rescue ops," Desjani insisted. "And, personally, I think heavily armed Marines in full battle armor is just the kind of subtle approach this calls for."

"Tanya," Geary said carefully, "the people who kidnapped Castries and Yuon will see us coming. We can't surprise them. We don't have a stealth-configured shuttle or Marine scout stealth armor."

She glared at her display. "What approach does the Admiral prefer?"

"There are a lot of local law-enforcement craft near Jupiter. Police, Space Guard, and some specialized investigation and enforcement outfits. A kidnapping falls into the category of routine procedure for them."

Desjani kept her eyes looking front, but her frown deepened. "We're supposed to depend on them? It will take them six years just to get bureaucratic clearance to talk to us."

"If that happens," Geary said, "we will act."

She finally looked at him again. "Promise?"

"Yes. But I need to ask them for assistance before we act unilat-erally."

"Fine. We'll ask, they'll stall, and we'll handle things."

He had a strong suspicion that she was right.

THEY were six light-minutes from Jupiter, less than an hour's travel time away, when a symbol popped into existence on the bridge dis-plays. "Got him!" Desjani exulted, adjusting the battle cruiser's course to achieve a perfect intercept.

"He's awfully close to Jupiter," Geary said.

"Yes, but we've got him now. We can track him wherever he goes."

Geary judged the positions of the various law-enforcement space-craft at or near Jupiter, then decided on a simple broadcast. "This is Admiral Geary on the Alliance battle cruiser *Dauntless*. We have a solid track on a stealth craft operated by criminals, which is carrying two of our officers who were kidnapped on the surface of Earth. I am attaching our tracking data for your use. I request all possible assistance in intercepting the craft and rescuing our two officers. To the honor of our ancestors," he added in the formal ending that seemed both necessary and appropriate. "Geary, out."

He waited impatiently as the minutes crawled by. It would take six minutes for his transmission to be received by the ships near Jupiter, and even though *Dauntless* was currently closing the distance at a velocity just under point two light speed, it would still take at least five minutes for any answers to cover the distance back to *Dauntless*. How long would the police and Space Guard ships debate what to do before they replied to him?

As it turned out, he saw the movements of a number of those ships before the replies began coming in. Some were positive, as from Lieutenant Cole of the Sol Space Guard cutter *Shadow* near Callisto. "We are moving to intercept the criminal vessel. Kidnapping is a crime under Sol System law, no matter the origin of the victim, so this falls under our jurisdiction. We are informing our superiors but require no special approval from our chain of command to take action."

Others were more cautious, as from Senior Officer Bular on Police Pursuit Craft Twelve of Jovian Orbiting Habitat Sparhawk. "We are moving toward the craft you have identified but have requested clarification from our headquarters. We will require approval from them prior to taking any action against the craft you say is involved in criminal activity."

And some were along the lines of the reply from Inspector Toyis of the Special Ganymede Bureau of Investigation. "We regret that we are unable to respond to your request at this time. Your request for action has been forwarded to our head office, where it will receive full consideration. You will be notified when our head office has reached a decision. If you are no longer in Sol Star System at that time, our head office will not attempt to forward its decision but will maintain it on file for ten standard solar years. When inquiring about the status of your request, reference Standard Application For Assistance, Forwarding And Consideration Form 15667 Revision Twenty Five, Serial 3476980-554-3651."

Desjani stared at her display after that message ended, looking as if she didn't know whether to laugh or be angry. "Admiral, after we finish with the kidnappers, is it all right if we destroy the head office of the Special Ganymede Bureau of Investigation?"

"I'm tempted, but no," Geary said. "Permission to destroy their head office will probably require some sort of special form, and we can't hang around waiting for their reply to our application to annihilate them."

"They probably do have a form for that," Desjani agreed, then indicated three ships weaving orbits about another moon of Jupiter. "Did you see the reply from these guys?" She tapped a control.

Geary saw a lean, hawk-faced man's image appear before him. "This is Commander Nkosi of the Special Quarantine Enforcement Division. We are in receipt of your request but are unable to assist. Our orders require us to maintain positions enforcing the quarantine of Europa. No exceptions are authorized. If the criminal craft comes close to one of my ships, we will act if we can do so without leaving our assigned region."

"Europa quarantine duty?" Geary asked. "I can see why they aren't allowed to leave their posts."

"No," Desjani agreed. "I'll give those guys a pass for not being able to help. Can you imagine having to spend weeks and months orbiting Europa? Looking down at those old cities and installations filled with nothing but the dead?"

"I wouldn't enjoy it." He gazed at the depiction of Europa on the display. "It's so bright. Covered with ice sheets. I remember when in school they showed us the vids from Europa, I was struck by how bright the moon looked. It seemed impossible that it was contaminated by a bio-engineered plague that had wiped out every human on that moon."

"He altered course," Desjani said, pointing to her display, where the stealth craft's projected track had swung slightly. "Just a small adjustment. He doesn't realize yet that we're tracking him."

Over the next half hour, it became apparent that enough vessels near Jupiter were moving on intercepts from enough different angles that the stealth craft was boxed in. Its only path for escape would have been back toward Sol, but *Dauntless* was coming on relentlessly from that direction. And, by now, whoever was on that stealth craft must have seen all those ship movements and realized what they meant.

Rione had come onto the bridge, taking the observer's seat at the back and peering at the display there. "Am I right that it is merely a question now of which ship that stealth craft surrenders to?"

"You're correct," Geary said.

"I came up here to tell you that the ransom demands had been received, but those demands appear to have been overtaken by events."

"What did they want in exchange for our officers?" Geary asked.

"Technical specs and equipment," Rione said, intent on her display as if watching a movie play out. "All stealth-related. They want our state-of-the-art. Which they would then sell to everyone with enough to offer in exchange."

He didn't answer, feeling a tight sensation inside at the realization that he could not have agreed to that. If they hadn't been able to intercept that craft, he would have been faced with a very ugly decision.

Tanya must have realized the same thing. She didn't look toward him as she spoke in a low voice. "They would have understood that you couldn't agree to that. We all would have understood."

"Do you think that would allow me to ever forgive myself?" he asked.

"No. But it's the only comfort I would have had to offer. Thank the living stars—" Her voice broke off and she sat straighter, eyes intent. "What's he doing?"

Geary focused more closely on his own display as he saw the stealth craft, within minutes of being intercepted by some of its pursuers, suddenly veer onto a different vector and accelerate. "He's heading for the only opening that's left." He wondered if his voice reflected the horror he was feeling.

"That's not an opening!" Desjani protested. "He's heading into Europa's atmosphere!"

"Why was that opening left for him?" Rione demanded in shocked tones.

"Because no one in their right mind would go that way!" Geary answered. "Get the word out to all of the other ships," he ordered the bridge crew. "Tell them what that craft's new vector is."

They were close enough now that it took only a few minutes for the updated information to reach all of the pursuing ships, but those critical few minutes made all the difference. The quarantine-enforcement ships had been caught flat-footed as well by the sudden maneuver and were now twisting about frantically to reach the stealth craft.

But only *Dauntless* had a solid track on the stealth craft, and *Dauntless* was still too far away. As the nearest ships fumbled for attempted intercepts, the stealth craft penetrated Europa's atmosphere.

"He's braking," Desjani said. "He's braking hard. Ancestors save us. He's going to land."

As they watched helplessly, the stealth craft came in to a gentle landing on the riven ice sheets that covered forbidden, dead Europa.

For one of the few times that Geary had known her, Victoria Rione had shed all pretense and feigned indifference. She was staring aghast at her own display as she called across the silence filling the bridge. "What can you do? Admiral, what can you do?"

"I don't know," he said. "If there is anything we can do, I'll find it."

DAUNTLESS had settled into orbit about Jupiter, close to and matching the motion of Europa. About a dozen other ships were matching her orbit, waiting to see what the Alliance battle cruiser would do. The stealth craft sat silently on the surface of Europa, not broadcasting any demands but able to be spotted by every ship now that it was resting on the ice.

Geary sat in his stateroom with three other people: Tanya and Victoria Rione, who had managed to take up positions as far as possible from each other, and Dr. Nasr. "Doctor, do you know anything about the bug that wiped out life on Europa?"

Dr. Nasr nodded, his mouth twitching with distaste. "I know enough. It is a bacterium, genetically modified from an original form which caused no ill effects and is indeed beneficial to the human body."

"Is?" Rione asked. "You're certain that it's still there? Still viable?"

"Yes."

"Why didn't they use something lethal?" Geary asked. "As long as they were making a bioweapon, why not start with something that was already bad?"

"Because," Nasr explained in a quiet voice, "they wanted to ensure that the bacteria did not trigger bioalert sensors. By using something originally innocuous, they hoped they would slip unnoticed past any defenses." He closed his eyes as if trying to block the sight of visions of the past. "In this, they were extremely successful. Their own bio-defenses did not spot or give an alert on the bacteria when they escaped their control."

Desjani made an angry noise deep in her throat. "They were clever enough to make something that deadly but too stupid to program their own defenses to spot it?"

"I am guessing," Dr. Nasr replied, "from my own experience, that the creation of the deadly bacteria was held within a highly classified program. It was kept secret from those who could have reprogrammed the defenses because such reprogramming might have compromised the existence and characteristics of the virus. I do not know this for certain, but I feel confident that was the reasoning employed." The bitter tone of his voice left no doubt as to the doctor's opinion of that reasoning.

"You're probably right," Geary said. "Stupider things have been done in the name of secrecy. Why are you sure the bacteria are still there? They killed every human on Europa centuries ago."

"So you think the quarantine is a matter of habit or tradition rather than need?" Nasr asked. "No, Admiral. The bacteria are still there. Certain bacteria can survive much longer than centuries even when exposed to the radiation, vacuum, and other conditions of space. From what I know, from how the bacteria spread across Europa and the countermeasures taken to enforce the quarantine, the genetically engineered bioweapon was made to go dormant under harsh conditions, then activate when in a suitable environment to infect human hosts. You would have to assume the bacteria are present anywhere you landed on Europa, even if only a few of them."

"And one bacterium would be enough," Geary said.

"One would be enough."

"Why did those idiots land there?" Desjani demanded.

"Because they are idiots," Rione said, upset enough to actually answer Desjani directly. "They were hired for a job, chased, trapped, and saw a way out. They took it. Even though it was stupid."

"Actually," Geary said, "they may have thought it was incredibly clever."

"What could possibly be clever about it?" Rione demanded.

Geary pointed to the image of Europa floating above the table like a very large Ping-Pong ball with tan patches and striations all over its surface. "They knew no one could chase them down there, and for some reason the locals aren't firing on them. They must have known they can sit on the surface without being attacked. They're probably planning to sit there for months. We can't wait here for months. When we leave, they can lift, go stealthy again, and escape past the blockade."

Dr. Nasr shook his head. "No. It would not work. No one, no friends of theirs, would accept them for fear of the plague."

"Exactly. That's the stupid part of their clever plan. But if they can get off the surface and away from Europa, they can spread the plague."

Rione gazed at the image of Europa. "The quarantine ships couldn't stop them? That gives us leverage if we can come up with a plan."

Once again, Nasr shook his head. "We cannot go down, and we cannot allow them to come up. The craft did not land near any of the dead cities, but we do not know how much the plague may have spread across the surface of Europa. It only takes one bacterium," he repeated.

Geary looked toward Desjani. "Any ideas?"

She shook her head angrily. "No. We can't use the Marines. Their battle armor would keep out the plague. It's designed to do that sort of thing. But we don't have battlefield decontamination gear with us, and can't be sure that would be good enough against this bug. If something was on the outside of their armor when they came back aboard *Dauntless...*" Her words trailed off because they all knew what could happen, and none of them wanted to spell it out.

Several seconds passed without anyone's saying anything, then Dr. Nasr held up his forefinger, his eyes clouded with thought. "The battle armor will keep out the plague. Do you have the details on this armor?"

"Of course," Desjani said. "Full specs. What do you need?"

"I am wondering about sterilization," Nasr said slowly, the words spaced out as his thoughts produced them. "Not simply decontamination. If we sterilize the battle armor before it comes aboard, if we can apply sufficient energy to the outside of the armor without harming those inside..."

"Outside the ship?" Geary asked. "What do we have that could do that?"

"Hell lances!" Desjani said. "Scale down the energy. We can calculate exactly how much we need and blast every square millimeter of the battle armor!"

"I need to do some research," the doctor cautioned.

Desjani had already walked quickly to the nearest comm panel. "Gunnery Sergeant Orvis! I need you on the double in the Admiral's stateroom. Bring every spec you've got on your battle armor." She tapped another address. "Senior Chief Tarrani. Admiral's stateroom, on the double. We need to talk hell lances from a surgical perspective."

She paused after that and looked at Geary. "Should I call Master Chief Gioninni? Are we going to try to make a deal with these guys or just go in shooting?"

Rione frowned and also addressed Geary. "Any diplomatic matters should be handled in proper channels."

"This isn't a diplomatic matter," he replied in as diplomatic a way as he could manage. "This would be making a deal with criminals."

"Making deals with criminals is a major part of most diplomacy. Didn't you know that? Do you believe that this Master Chief Gioninni is somehow expert at dealing with criminals?"

Geary paused, then spoke with great care, aware that Desjani was desperately trying to avoid laughing. He felt the same way, in part because of the giddiness brought on by the realization that they might, just might, be able to develop a viable rescue from what had appeared to be a hopeless situation. "Master Chief Gioninni is . . . very familiar with . . . extralegal means of . . . conducting business."

"I see," Rione said in a frosty voice. "Whatever he does, whatever he says, could produce extremely serious consequences for the Alliance and for your missing lieutenants. You had best keep that in mind."

"Perhaps," Desjani said in a slightly strangled voice brought on by her attempts not to laugh, "Master Chief Gioninni could work with our . . . diplomatic representatives."

"That's a good idea," Geary hastily agreed. "Tell him to contact

Envoy Rione and coordinate communications with the occupants of that stealth craft. We want to know how die-hard they are, or whether they can be convinced to give up Lieutenants Castries and Yuon without a fight."

"I'll see what can be done," Rione said. "You do realize, Admiral, that the occupants of that craft have signed their own death sentences. They have nothing to lose. Any deal is going to involve lying to them about being able to save their lives."

Nobody answered that immediately. Eventually, Geary shook his head. "We didn't put them in that position. They did it to themselves. If I have to lie to save Lieutenants Castries and Yuon from the stupidity and criminal acts of those people, then I am willing to do so."

"Don't bother yourself, Admiral." Rione smiled sardonically. "I can lie for both of us. That's also a big part of diplomacy. It's what I do for a living, remember?"

THE next hour involved considerable references to specifications of armor and weapons, debates about tolerances and backups, calling up medical references on the ability of bacteria to survive the most extreme conditions, and what little had ever been revealed about the bioengineered plague that had escaped a lab complex on Europa and wiped out every human on that moon with a speed and efficiency that had terrified the rest of humanity.

In one corner of the stateroom, Victoria Rione and Master Chief Gioninni stood listening to the others and talking quietly to each other. After initial coldness on Rione's part, they seemed to be getting along famously.

Finally, Dr. Nasr looked at Geary and nodded. "Yes, Admiral. We can subject the outside of a suit of battle armor to sufficient heat and other forces to ensure that *nothing* survives."

"Excuse me, Doc," Gunnery Sergeant Orvis said, "but we should clarify that when you say *nothing survives*, you aren't including the Marine inside the suit."

Looking startled, Nasr waved his hands. "No. No. Of course not. The armor will protect the occupant. It will be ruined, though. External sensors burned out, joints fused, external coatings badly damaged. The occupants will be fine, but they will have to be cut out of the armor once we are done."

Orvis scratched his head, grimacing. "By *fine* we mean uninjured. Mostly uninjured. Nobody's going to be comfortable, though. It's going to get pretty damned warm inside that armor until it's pried open. But the closed-circuit backup life support inside the suits will keep oxygen going for the amount of time we need to worry about."

"Your Marines can definitely handle the discomfort though?" Rione asked.

It was Gunnery Sergeant Orvis's turn to look surprised. "Oh, sure. We're Marines. Too much heat and discomfort and getting shot at and beat up is just run-of-the-mill for us. It's when we're really comfortable that we get thrown off by how unusual it all is."

Rione paused, looking around with a bleak expression. "None of you have mentioned this yet, but what about the two officers? They will not be inside armor. They will have been exposed. A single bacterium would be enough, I heard. How do we deal with that?"

Dr. Nasr grimaced. "What we can do is bring extra armor and seal the officers inside. With any luck, if the fools on that ship have not gone outside or otherwise exposed themselves too much, there will be no contamination inside except anything our Marines might bring despite their own efforts to minimize the risk. But we must face such a possibility of contamination, so even after their armor is sterilized, the two officers will have to be placed in total medical isolation long enough to be certain that they have not been infected. It is the best we can do, and it will ensure that even if the officers are . . . as good as dead . . . the infection will not spread."

"I understand the need for solutions that are only the least awful compared to the possible alternatives," Rione said. "Thank you. That option offers our best chance and does not compromise our safety measures."

"My people will be careful to get those officers into the spare armor as fast and clean as they can," Gunnery Sergeant Orvis assured Rione.

"After that, you have to get everyone back up here," Geary said to Orvis. "Are you certain that you won't need one of the shuttles to land you on the surface and pick you up again?"

"We'll need one on the drop, Admiral, from high up, but not on the pickup. If we used a shuttle then, we'd be using it up. There's no way to fry the inside and outside of a bird the way the doc is talking about and have anything worth keeping." Orvis tapped his pad, and images appeared above it. "Europa's not a big moon at all. Not much gravity to worry about. A little over a tenth of a standard gravity. We'll need the shuttle on the drop to bring us down as low as the quarantine allows, then we'll jump and brake our landing with strap-on thrusters."

Tiny animated Marines in battle armor jumped from a tiny shuttle, falling down toward an image of Europa's surface.

"After we do the job," Orvis continued, "we get off by jumping and using what's left in the strap-on thrusters to kick us into orbit. The power assist in the armor combined with the thrusters should do the job."

"You can literally jump into orbit around Europa?" Rione asked skeptically.

"With the help of the extra thrusters, yes, ma'am. My Marines and I will have to jump as hard as the armor allows," Orvis conceded. "But we'll be highly motivated. About all you could do to motivate us more would be to dangle some beer out of an air lock. That'll give us something to aim for."

"Leaving out the motivational effects of the beer," Geary said, "what's your margin of error on reaching orbit?"

"Ten percent safety margin, Admiral," Orvis admitted.

"Not great, but big enough. Can the ice support being used as a jump-off platform?"

This time it was Desjani who nodded. "That's not a problem. *Dauntless*'s sensors have studied the surface. The stealth craft landed in an area where the ice is very thick and very hard. It might as well be solid rock as far as we're concerned."

Dr. Nasr tapped his own data pad. "The weapons on this warship can be recalibrated to an output that is sufficient to sterilize the outer armor but not deadly to the men and women inside it. We will be destroying the outer layer of the armor to ensure that nothing can get inside the ship."

Senior Chief Tarrini smiled. "The crew will get a kick out of shooting at Marines floating in space."

"I'd rather you hadn't brought that up," Gunnery Sergeant Orvis observed. "We've got exactly three spare suits of battle armor, but one of those is down hard because we had to pull some parts to keep another suit going. All we need is two, though. Once we get into the craft, the lieutenants can get into the armor, then we all leave."

Dr. Nasr sighed. "Can you send fewer Marines and try to rescue some of the others on the craft?" he asked.

Geary looked at the others, but they all looked back at him. *One more unpleasant benefit of being in charge. I have to answer that.* "Doctor, we have no idea how many people are on that craft. From the size of the craft, it could be as few as six or as many as thirty. If it's thirty, even if I send all forty Marines aboard *Dauntless*, the odds will not be very good for an assault."

"But if it is six?" Nasr asked.

"You understand, Doctor, that what Envoy Rione said earlier is all too accurate. Even if we get some of those people off Europa, the locals will very likely insist on executing them."

Nasr nodded, his eyes on the deck.

"But I will see what can be done," Geary promised. "Envoy Rione,

Master Chief Gioninni, when you talk to the people on that craft, see if you can find out how many of them there are as well as what kind of deal might be possible." If it served no other purpose, knowing how many criminals were on the craft would be very useful information for the Marines to have.

"Speaking of the locals," Desjani continued, "how do we deal with them? From the looks of Commander Nkosi and Lieutenant Cole, those two, at least, won't let our Marines just drop onto Europa, jump off, then sail away on *Dauntless*."

"Can we keep them off?" Rione asked Geary. "Prevent the locals from interfering with our operation?"

He could see the answer in Desjani's eyes. "No," Geary said. "Not unless we shoot them full of holes."

"Which I would prefer *not* to do in this case," Desjani added.

Senior Chief Tarrini mumbled something that sounded like "that's a first," then looked around as if trying to see who had spoken.

"I don't know how to handle the locals," Geary said. "Fortunately, we have four politicians aboard."

"*Fortunately, we have four politicians aboard?*" Desjani repeated. "That's one sentence I never expected to hear."

"I'm going to have a meeting with them. You, too, Doctor. I need to brief them on our plan, get their approval—"

Desjani made an inarticulate sound of protest.

"Get their approval," Geary repeated, "and work out how to do this without causing an incident that will be heard all the way to Kick territory."

"You're asking a lot," Rione cautioned. "But I can't disagree. We need governmental approval to do this."

Orvis looked to both Desjani and Geary. "Should I prep my people or wait for more word?"

Geary nodded. "Begin your preparations. You know what the mission will entail. We'll notify you when we get a start time."

Orvis stood and saluted. Many fleet salutes were still fairly sloppy since the practice had fallen out of use during the last decades of the war before being reintroduced by Geary. But the Marines had stubbornly clung to the practice all along, so Orvis's salute was a model of crispness. "I will require specific guidance on the hostage-takers, Admiral. Though from what I understand, maybe it would be a mercy to kill them all during the hostage-rescue operation."

"Maybe," Geary said in a low voice, not looking toward Dr. Nasr. "But for now your orders are to do what you need to do to rescue our people. If any hostage-takers get in your way, take any necessary actions to deal with them but do not kill anyone you don't have to. If those orders change, I will let you know."

"Understood, Admiral."

"Do you anticipate any problems getting all of your Marines to volunteer for the mission, Sergeant?" Dr. Nasr asked.

Orvis smiled. "When I brief my Marines on the task, I'll let them all know that they volunteered. Saves a lot of time that way."

After Orvis, Senior Chief Tarrini, and Master Chief Gioninni left, Dr. Nasr turned a troubled look on Geary. "There is still a risk to those two officers, you know, even if we get them off Europa safely. It will only take one plague bacterium clinging to the outside of someone's armor, then being transferred to them as they are put into the empty armor."

"What can we do if they get infected before they get inside the armor?" Desjani asked.

"Nothing. I cannot even risk treating them except by remote means. If they have been infected, they may die before we finish decontaminating the outside of their armor for them and the Marines. We will have to treat them as possibly contaminated. Once we bring them aboard, they will have to be locked into extreme medical isolation. We have a single compartment that allows that. It will be crowded with two in there, but there is no choice."

"There's no cure?" Desjani asked. "No treatment?"

"To develop a cure, someone would need a sample of the disease," Nasr explained. "Every existing sample has been confined to Europa. I will see if treatment simulations were run based on remote data, but I will be surprised if any are available."

"The locals might have them," Geary said. "They've been living with Europa for centuries. Surely they've thought about what to do if that horror ever escaped."

"Perhaps." The doctor shrugged. "But sometimes a taboo is too great to even bear looking at. Then, too, I remember a colleague of mine once arguing that research into cures was counterproductive, since it merely encouraged the behaviors that led to the ills. I did not agree, but such an attitude might rule here. Any suggestion that a cure might be found might produce pressure to relax the quarantine of Europa, and I understand why that could not be encouraged."

After the doctor and Rione had left, Desjani looked angrily at Geary. "Admiral—"

He held out a warning hand. "You know that I can't approve this on my own."

She glared stubbornly back at him. "No, I don't."

"This is too big an issue, and we have representatives of the government aboard."

"No."

"I have to ask them, Tanya."

"No!"

"Do you want to be present at the meeting as well?"

"*No.*" Her glare intensified as Desjani clenched a fist and pounded it lightly on the table. "But I will attend, anyway, Admiral, in an attempt to ensure that two of my officers are not doomed to die on Europa by the dithering and politicking of our esteemed Alliance senators."

FOUR

THREE senators of the Alliance, one envoy of the Alliance, an admiral and a captain of the Alliance fleet, and a doctor of the Alliance military medical corps sat around a small table inside the secure conference room aboard the battle cruiser *Dauntless*. Above the table floated an image of Europa and all the ships and other craft currently orbiting Jupiter near that moon.

Geary had finished describing the planned operation and was waiting for the reaction from the senators.

Senator Suva looked like she had a migraine headache. "Europa. Why did it have to be that place out of everywhere in this star system?"

"But it is Europa," Senator Sakai said. "Two of our people are there. The Admiral says we can do something. Do we take that action?"

"If we don't," Senator Costa said, "those two officers of the Alliance fleet die."

"How many officers have died in the last century? In the last year?" Sakai asked, his tone mild.

"That's not the point, and you know it! It's one thing to send members of our military on missions where they might die or even likely will die. It's another thing entirely to sit back and let two of our people die when we could do something to prevent it." Costa looked around the table, her gaze challenging. "That would make the Alliance look weak. Right now, the locals respect us. They've seen what this battle cruiser can do. We don't want them deciding that we lack the resolve to protect our own people and interests."

"But the two officers might already be dead," Suva protested. "Or . . . infected."

Everyone looked at Dr. Nasr, who shook his head. "If they were infected, they are dead, but the craft they are in must be making every effort to remain sealed against the risk."

"And the only thing stopping us is fear of stepping on the toes of the locals?" Costa demanded. "Then let's do it. We land the Marines, we get our people back, and by the time the locals know what's happened, we're at the hypernet gate and on our way home."

"Keeping it secret may be impossible," Sakai warned.

"But we *must*," Suva insisted. "The consequences would be immense if it is learned that we put people on Europa and recovered them."

"We only have to hide it until we're clear of here, then no one can prove anything," Costa declared. "They'll all know what we did, but they won't be able to prove it."

"The locals will see us conducting the operation. We don't have stealth equipment—" Geary began.

"Then how can we do this?" Sakai asked.

Dr. Nasr spoke with a sudden burst of pent-up emotion. "Why is this a question? The answer is simple. We cannot hide this. We should not try to hide it. Tell everyone. Tell them what we plan to do, how we plan to do it, what precautions we are taking, and let them watch as we do it all. Let them examine our equipment. Nothing else will convince them to trust us or to believe that our actions will not harm them. Why do we seek to hide it, to keep our plans secret? We are not the Syndics.

We are not the enigmas. Why do we try to keep so much hidden from those who have every right to know it?"

Senator Costa's expression had hardened as Nasr spoke. Senator Suva looked away. Senator Sakai seemed to be studying the far bulkhead, his face as impassive as usual. Rione, oddly, looked tired. But no one spoke for several seconds after the doctor finished.

Victoria Rione finally broke the silence. "You ask some very good questions, Doctor."

"No, he doesn't," Costa retorted. "Security demands secrecy. We keep things like this under wraps so we can protect the Alliance."

Costa's criticism instantly decided Suva, who gave Costa a scornful gaze. "We keep too many secrets! Who or what are we really protecting?"

Senator Sakai made a sharp gesture with one hand, forestalling Costa's counterattack. "There are secrets that are necessary, and there are those that serve no purpose. I would agree that secrecy has become too much a habit for us. My proof for this? None of us except this doctor thought of simply telling the truth to the people of Sol Star System. All we thought of was how to hide our actions. Do we still judge the need for secrecy in things? Or do we assume the need?"

"Do you agree with the doctor?" Geary asked Sakai.

"I do. His words have a wisdom we have forgotten. Truth does not fear the light."

"The First Truth," Rione said softly. "Yes. We have forgotten that."

"I've forgotten nothing," Costa insisted. "The only way to protect truth is to—"

"Lie?" Suva asked bitingly. "That is why we have so little credibility with the citizens of the Alliance! We don't tell anyone the truth anymore. We classify everything, in order, we say, to protect those citizens."

Costa looked fiercely back at her. "There are some secrets I am certain you would not want disclosed. Shall we spill them all?"

"That is a false argument," Rione said. "It is not a matter of all or nothing. No one here would argue with the need to keep some secrets. But it has become too easy to think only in terms of hiding information and not consider the rationale for whether it should be secret at all."

"So says the woman voted out of office by the Callas Republic," Costa said with a sneer, "and who now depends on the charity of the Alliance for home and employment."

Rione smiled sweetly back at her. "I freely admit to having told the truth to my people and to having been punished for that. Since we both agree that I have some experience with telling the truth, as well as plenty of experience with the lies that politicians routinely tell, that would give me grounds for having an expert opinion on the matter."

"Excuse me," Geary said, before the argument could become even more heated. "Everyone seems to agree that we need to act and that the plan can work. I have the impression that both Senator Suva and Senator Sakai support Dr. Nasr's suggestion that we approach the locals openly about what we intend doing and how we intend doing it, and allow them as much access as possible to verify that we are doing what we say. Is that correct?"

Sakai nodded. "It is."

Suva hesitated, stole a glance at Costa's furious expression, then nodded as well. "I agree."

"Then," Rione said smoothly, "we have a majority of the governmental representatives present in favor of proceeding and in favor of openness. I need not exercise Senator Navarro's proxy though I would have voted in favor as well."

"Whoever handles this," Costa warned, "is going to find that it bites them when we return to Alliance space."

Rione spread her hands. "I was feeling bored, anyway. Besides, it wouldn't feel like a proper return to the Alliance without my being accused of some serious misdeed."

With the critical decisions made, the three senators left, followed by Desjani and Dr. Nasr. Tanya gave Geary a warning look as she left, skating her eyes toward Rione to make it clear who the warning was about.

Once they were alone, Rione slumped down, rubbing her eyes with one hand. "We need to start with the commander of the quarantine force."

"Commander Nkosi," Geary said. "He is the key. Have you and Master Chief Gioninni had any luck talking to the people on the stealth craft?"

"No. They won't answer. It appears they intend sitting silently down there until we give up and leave." Rione lowered her hand and raised an eyebrow at Geary. "I have to confess that I did not think your captain would be smart enough to tolerate having someone of Mr. Gioninni's talents among her crew."

"She knows how valuable those talents can be," Geary said. "But she does watch him closely."

"Also a smart thing to do." Rione sat up straighter, took a deep breath, exhaled slowly, then reached for the comm controls. "Let's see whether or not we can make this happen."

Commander Nkosi did not waste time with preliminaries. "Admiral, I deeply regret the situation in which we find ourselves. Permit me to express official condolences on the fate of your officers."

Dauntless was so close to the ships enforcing the quarantine that there was no noticeable time delay in the conversation. "Those condolences may be premature," Geary said.

"Sadly, they are not."

"Allow me to tell you what we're contemplating doing. When I'm done, we can discuss whether or not those officers are effectively already dead." Geary went through the plan step by step, emphasizing the sterilization procedures to be used.

Nkosi listened patiently, his expression betraying no emotion. But when Geary had finished, the quarantine commander shook his head. "I can't agree to this."

"Commander—"

"My orders do not leave me any discretion in the matter, Admiral. If anyone or anything attempts to leave the surface of Europa, it must be destroyed. Nothing can be allowed to leave that moon. If your Marines attempt this operation, I will be duty-bound to make every possible effort to destroy them before they reach orbit."

Rione gestured toward where Europa lay. "Commander, can you see that stealth craft?"

"The one we are discussing? Yes. We have a good position on it. It has not moved since landing."

"Why aren't you destroying it now? Why wait until it tries to lift?"

Geary barely avoided giving her a sharp look. From the way Rione had asked the question, he had a very strong suspicion that she already knew the answer.

Nkosi made a face, then spoke with obvious reluctance. "Our orders are explicit. We cannot fire upon anything on the surface of Europa. The moon has not much more than ten percent of Earth's gravity. Any explosion of sufficient strength could cause . . . things . . . to be blown into space."

"Contaminated things," Rione said. "I understand. Now, you have a good fix on that ship when it is on the surface. How well can you track it once it lifts?"

Commander Nkosi glared at her. "Well enough."

"Commander," she said in a soft voice, "I have dealt with politicians for a long time. I've been a politician. I know when someone isn't being entirely candid. We already know the full capabilities of the tracking equipment in this star system. Once that craft lifts from the surface of Europa, your odds of being able to track and engage it are very small."

Nkosi looked away for a long moment, then back at her, his gaze now defiant. "I am not ashamed of my inability to lie well. You are correct."

"Then you cannot successfully engage the craft once it has lifted from the surface of Europa," Rione said, as if stating something already agreed upon, "and you are not allowed to engage it while it is on the surface. How do you prevent that ship from leaving Europa and going wherever it wants?"

"*You* can track it," Nkosi insisted. "You have shown us that."

"We can't stay here forever, waiting for that craft to lift," Rione replied, her tone hardening. "All they have to do is sit on the surface until we leave. A week. A month. We aren't even authorized to stay that much longer. And once we are gone, they go wherever they want, and you will not be able to stop them. The quarantine *will* be broken."

Nkosi paused. "If they try that, no one will grant them docking. Their own friends will destroy them."

"Leaving the debris to drift somewhere in space? Or perhaps they will land in a hidden location, perhaps a location on Earth, or Mars. What may happen then, Commander?"

Nkosi looked down, then back at her, his gaze appraising. "But you propose to prevent anything from leaving Europa by sending many Marines down to Europa and bringing them back?"

"You heard our proposal. We will send down Marines in battle armor, which is completely sealed against any intrusion. We will recover our two officers inside the ship, put them in spare battle armor, then our Marines and the two officers will jump off Europa, using assist propulsion units. Once they're off the surface, we will fire upon each set of battle armor in turn, covering every square millimeter with sufficient energy to blast anything on the outside of the armor, as well the outer layer of the armor, into component atoms. You and any other personnel you desire, including your medical personnel, can personally observe it all from our own ship. You can personally examine the equipment we will use before the operation begins."

"And what of the stealth craft?"

"Our Marines will ensure its systems are damaged so badly it will never lift from the surface."

Nkosi grimaced. "The moment the criminals on that ship got within fifty kilometers of the surface of Europa, they had no chance. But I am not a cruel man. I take no pleasure in that. You will not try to rescue anyone but your own officers?"

"We can't," Geary said. "We only have two spare suits of battle armor."

"You could send fewer Marines."

"No. Unless you can tell me how many criminals are on that stealth craft, I can't run the risk of making the odds against my people worse. If someone is going to die down there," Geary finished, "it's not going to be any of my Marines."

Nkosi looked down at his hands where they rested on the desk before him. "I can respect your logic. But there is no if. Those on the stealth craft will die. Your officers should die as well, not because I wish it, but because my orders allow no exceptions. I will ask permission to allow you to do this."

"How long do you think that would take?" Geary demanded, trying to keep the irritation out of his voice.

"Years," Nkosi admitted. "To get an answer, that is. Every government in Sol Star System would have a vote, and it would have to be unanimous."

"Then the answer would be no," Rione said.

"Only if we are lucky enough to still be alive," the commander replied. "I cannot deny the truth of what you say. The only way to keep that craft from escaping is to allow you to do this. Otherwise, everyone in this star system may die while the debate on what to do goes on, and the vote never takes place because everything orbiting Sol will be like Europa. I must allow this, but you must know the risk that I personally run by agreeing to allow it."

"Court-martial?" Geary asked.

"A very short one," Nkosi said. "The penalty would surely be that proscribed for anyone who fails in their duty to maintain the quarantine." He pointed downward. "A one-way trip to the surface of Europa."

Geary felt his next words catch in his throat. "I cannot ask—" he finally began.

"Wait, Admiral." Nkosi gestured again, this time outward. "Do you know what the duty of the quarantine force would be if the plague escaped Europa and spread among other locations in this star system?"

"I know that the original quarantine ships had to destroy refugee ships trying to flee Europa," Geary said.

"Yes. We would do that again, everywhere the plague spread. And our quarantine ships would take up positions at the jump points from Sol and at the hypernet gate your Alliance constructed, and we would destroy every craft that came toward those places trying to flee for safety. When the last refugee was dead, the last fleeing ship destroyed, all of this star system lifeless, our final duty would be to hurl our ships into the star Sol." Nkosi shook his head again, his eyes haunted by visions of that possible future. "Do you not think I would go to my own death to prevent that?"

"Is there any way to prevent them from punishing you?" Rione asked.

"Officially? No."

"You could come with us," Geary said. "Back to the Alliance."

Nkosi smiled. "I believe in facing the consequences of my actions, Admiral. I am old-fashioned in that way."

"I'm pretty old-fashioned myself. But you don't deserve to die."

"You don't have to," Rione announced, looking up from her data pad. "What is the single overriding imperative in your orders, Commander?"

He frowned at her. "We have discussed that. *Prevent any contamination from leaving Europa.*"

"*By any means necessary,*" Rione finished.

"How did you know what my orders say?"

"That's not important. The important thing is that our proposed operation is the only means available to you to . . ."

Nkosi's frown changed to a look of surprise. "To prevent contamination from leaving Europa. By the letter of my orders, I must allow you to proceed."

"That will make a good defense for you?" Geary asked.

"Good? No. Perfect. This is Sol Star System. Our people worship written procedures, rules, and regulations like others worship the divine. I cannot be prosecuted for following the letter of my orders. And so I shall not die."

Geary felt himself smiling for the first time in at least the last several hours. "Are the other ships around here under similar orders? What will they do?"

"They will ask for guidance from their supervisors," Nkosi said with a shrug. "It is not normally their responsibility to enforce the quarantine though they are obligated to assist if the quarantine force calls for aid. If I do not do that . . . the only one who might act is Cole on the *Shadow*. He does not shirk from what duty requires."

"Will we have to stop him?" Geary asked.

"I will speak to him. Cole is a hard-ass, but he is not a fool. He will see as well as I that we have no choice but to hope your plan succeeds." Nkosi caught Geary's eyes with his own. "I will be one of those aboard your ship to personally observe the operation."

"Certainly. We need you and any other personnel you want along over here as soon as possible, so we can make this happen."

"I will prepare a shuttle. First, let me call Lieutenant Cole and ensure that he acts with uncharacteristic caution and hesitation in this matter."

COMMANDER Nkosi was accompanied by two of his senior enlisted, whom he identified as experts in targeting and weapons systems, as well as by his senior medical officer, Dr. Palden. Nkosi stayed with Geary while Senior Chief Tarrini took the two senior enlisted in hand. Dr. Palden, a middle-aged woman with keen eyes, was already hurling questions at Dr. Nasr as they began walking toward sick bay.

"She is a good doctor," Commander Nkosi said. "Very dedicated. She is very keen on seeing your medical equipment."

"I want you to see our Marines before they depart," Geary said. He led Nkosi to the shuttle dock, where all forty Marines waited in ranks. In their battle armor, they looked more like ogres than humans, an immensely intimidating sight even to those used to it.

If Nkosi felt unsettled, he didn't betray it in any way as he closely looked over the battle armor and studied the specifications that Geary offered. "Extremely impressive," he finally said. "Our armor would be no match for these, but then we have been at peace for many years."

Next to the Marines, two extra suits of battle armor lay on the deck. Nkosi looked them over, then bowed his head, closed his eyes, and muttered something too low for Geary to hear. "This is the critical element," he said to Geary after raising his head. "Do your Marines understand that they must do everything they can to avoid contaminating your officers before they are sealed into this armor?"

"Yes, sir," Gunnery Sergeant Orvis replied before Geary could. "Admiral, have our orders regarding the hostage-takers changed?"

"No," Geary replied. "Take them out if you have to but only if you have to. If you can get in and out of there without killing any, that will be fine. Just make sure that craft's propulsion and maneuvering systems are too badly damaged for it to lift again."

Orvis saluted, his armored hand rising to the brow of the heavy helmet concealing his entire head. "Understand, sir. Break the ship, but not the crew, unless they make us do it the hard way."

"Satisfied?" Geary asked Nkosi.

"For my part, yes. I must speak with Dr. Palden, though."

Geary called sick bay. Dr. Nasr normally maintained an outward appearance of calm, but from the looks of him now, Dr. Palden had seriously rubbed him the wrong way. In response to Commander Nkosi's questions, Palden grudgingly conceded that the available equipment and planned procedures should be "adequate."

Nkosi checked with his senior specialists, who displayed much more enthusiasm. "This is really hot gear," one told the commander. "They can do what they say."

"I am satisfied," Commander Nkosi said.

"Board the shuttles and prepare to launch," Geary told Orvis.

HE led Commander Nkosi to the bridge, where Tanya Desjani was seated. "Begin the operation whenever you are ready, Captain," Geary told her.

"Thank you, Admiral." Desjani tapped her comm controls. "Commence hostage-recovery operation. Launch both shuttles. All personnel remain at full alert."

As he sat down in his own seat next to Desjani's, Geary called Envoy Charban, who had been holed up in his stateroom for the last two days maintaining constant contact with the Dancer ships. "How are you doing, General?"

Charban twitched his mouth before answering. "I feel like hell, Admiral. How do I look?"

"Like you feel," Geary admitted. From his appearance, Charban had already used more than one stim med patch to keep himself alert and awake. "Will the Dancers stay clear of Europa while we do this?"

"Let's do it, see what they do, then we'll both know." Charban ran one hand through his hair. "I think I've gotten across that they can't go to Europa, and they are staying well away. I'm pretty certain that they also understand why they can't go to Europa."

"You told them?" Geary wasn't certain of his feelings about that. *If it is necessary to keep them from going to Europa, then they had to be told. But I feel . . . ashamed to have to tell an alien species what my species did to that moon. Is that a reason to avoid being truthful, though?* "I guess this is one of those secrets that shouldn't really be secret."

"Excuse me?"

"I'll fill you in later. We're launching the shuttles now and should start the drop in about twenty minutes. If everything goes according to the timeline, we'll have the Marines back up here and getting their armor sterilized an hour and a half after that. Please stay on with the Dancers the whole time and do everything you can to keep them from diving into the middle of things."

"Yes, sir." Charban leaned back and made a deliberately casual salute. "Do you know what I want to know most right now? I want to know what they think of it. What they think of us. The Dancers, that is. They already knew we warred and we bombarded planets and inflicted awful atrocities on other humans, but did they know we were fools enough to create the thing that still haunts Europa? Now that they do know, will it change how they see us, will it alter their perception of us as part of some pattern they haven't been able or willing to get across to us?"

"Make sure the Dancers know that we're going down to Europa to save two of our people," Geary said.

"Certainly." Charban stared into the distance, his eyes unfocused. "We'll casually kill thousands, or tens of thousands, or millions, with our actions or inactions, but we'll then turn around and risk our own lives to save a few others. How can the Dancers ever understand us? *I* don't understand us. How can we ever hope to understand them?"

As the virtual window containing Charban's image vanished, Geary realized once again that there were no clear answers to Charban's questions.

"Both shuttles have launched, Captain," the operations watch reported. "They are descending toward the drop point."

"Very well." Desjani studied her display, then shook her head. "I never imagined that shuttles under my command would be deliberately getting as close to Europa as the quarantine allows."

"Did you ever imagine that two of your officers would be on Europa?" Geary asked.

"Now that you mention it, no."

Senator Sakai and Victoria Rione came onto the bridge, both standing in the back, out of the way, but watching the display at the observer's seat.

Geary gestured for Rione, waiting until she was inside his seat's privacy field before speaking. "Where are the other two?"

"Senators Suva and Costa?" Rione asked in an arch tone of voice. "They are in their own staterooms, disassociating themselves from this event."

"Disassociating?"

"Yes, Admiral. If this goes wrong in any of many possible bad ways, they will be able to claim that they were not actually involved, not fully informed, not properly briefed, and not truly responsible." Rione smiled. "Of course, if it all goes well, they will still claim credit for it."

Geary glared at his display for a moment before replying. "So Senator Sakai's decision to come to the bridge means he is associating himself with this operation?"

She nodded judiciously. "Better say he is owning it. His presence here, and near you, ties him to the outcome, no matter what it is."

"I'll have to thank him," Geary said. "Does this mean that Sakai is backing me?"

"Only in this," Rione cautioned. "He will judge every situation and decide each situation on its own."

"I can't fault him for that. I wish every senator were like him and, what was her name, Senator Unruh."

"Unruh impressed you, did she? You're right. But don't forget that Unruh, and Sakai, and every other senator on the Grand Council, were convinced to create that secret fleet and give command of it to Admiral Bloch. All of their individual hopes and fears came together to do something that you and I consider insanity."

"Didn't that happen before?" Geary asked. "I've been thinking about it, and when the Grand Council approved Bloch's plan for the strike at the Syndic home star system, didn't the same thing take place?"

Rione considered that, then nodded. "Yes. Patterns born of desperation. And every time you avoid disaster or win a victory, many of them become more desperate. I'm talking too much. Are you as worried about this operation as I am?"

"Probably more," Geary said.

"I'll leave you to focus on it." She went back to where Senator Sakai stood, but he felt her eyes still upon him.

Geary called up the virtual windows that allowed him to see the views from the armor of each Marine. After overseeing operations involving thousands of Marines, it felt odd to be able to view what was happening from the point of view of each individual Marine in this operation all at once. It reminded him of the days before the war, a century ago, when a typical training exercise might involve only a company of Marines at the most, and only a few ships. For a moment, the memories came to him vividly, of men and women he had known who had fought and died while he slept, and it took a tremendous effort of will to push away those images—and the emotions they brought with them—and bring his full attention back to the present.

Right now, all that the virtual windows revealed was the interior of the shuttles and the other Marines, but soon that would change. "Commander Nkosi, feel free to stand close enough to me to view my display. I want you to be confident that we hid nothing from you."

"Thank you, Admiral." Nkosi looked around the bridge of the battle cruiser, one hand reaching to touch the rough edges of Geary's fleet command seat. Geary remembered being startled himself at such rough edges on *Dauntless*, the marks of a ship built as quickly as possible with the expectation that it would soon be destroyed in battle. "I have never seen a purely military ship before. A true warship. It looks like what it is. An instrument of war."

Geary was pondering a reply when an alert flashed on his display. "Here they go."

The Marines were standing up and forming lines facing the hatches leading to each shuttle's exit ramp. Inside the confines of the shuttles, the Marines in their battle armor moved with slow, careful grace, like elephants around stacks of eggs still in their shells. "How much damage could they do to a shuttle interior if they bumped into it or hit it by mistake?" Nkosi asked.

Desjani shrugged. "How hard do they hit and where do they hit? It's not usually any problem. Our Marines actually take dance classes to learn how to move like that, to avoid hitting things by accident, you know."

"I did not know."

On the window for each Marine, Geary could see all of the data that Marine was being shown on his or her helmet display. External pressure readings were dropping rapidly as the shuttles pumped out the air in their passenger decks. As the readings hit zero, the hatches swung open, revealing the shuttle ramps leading downward a short distance before ending against the black nothingness of space. Europa was below them, unable to be seen from this angle. The great bannered spectacle of Jupiter itself was almost directly above and also couldn't be seen.

"Go," Gunnery Sergeant Orvis commanded.

The Marines shuffled forward, heading down the ramp, until the first in line reached the end and stepped off with a small leap to get clear. The next followed two seconds later, then the next, then the next, until every Marine was dropping through the very thin wisps of Europa's atmosphere. Dropping toward the most fearsome place in human-inhabited space.

Some of the Marines looked down as they fell kilometer after kilometer, tipping themselves forward until snarls from Orvis or one of the other Marine sergeants or corporals brought them straight again. On their displays, a small fragment of a sphere marked the surface they were plummeting toward, along with a number helpfully counting down the rapidly diminishing distance to that surface.

The images jerked as the assist jets began kicking in on the Marines, the thrust still gentle, just enough to control the descent. Even though the Marines were all looking straight ahead as they dropped feetfirst, more and more of the edge of Europa's horizon was appearing within their vision. "How can something so pretty feel so ugly?" one Marine whispered across the comm circuit linking them together.

"Yeah," another answered. "Like that lance corporal you used to date. What was her name again?"

A chorus of low laughter was cut short by Gunnery Sergeant Orvis. "Stow it! Eyes and heads on the mission!"

"They are nervous," Commander Nkosi commented. "I recognize that sort of talk. It is comforting to realize you people from the stars are not all that different from us."

"That's comforting?" Geary asked.

"Perhaps it should not be," Nkosi admitted.

Geary had focused his display on the drop zone, so by looking to one side away from the views from the Marine armor, he could see a segment of Europa's surface, the stealth craft resting on it, and the gently curving lines marking the projected paths of the falling Marines.

"Should we deploy chaff?" Corporal Maya asked Orvis, using the generic term for materials and devices that confused detection and aiming.

"Negative. If they haven't spotted us, we don't want to attract their attention, and if they have seen us, we don't want to advertise that we're coming in on a combat footing."

"How could they not see us, Gunny?" a private asked.

"If they're not looking," Orvis explained. "Did you apes listen to the predrop brief? The last thing those guys on the surface expect is for us to drop in, so even though we don't have stealth gear, we might still achieve surprise."

"What if we don't?"

"Then I'll tell the Admiral you were upset about getting shot at and sing you a lullaby to help you sleep when we get back to the ship! Everybody shut up and prep for landing! Weapons tight!"

Geary had kept one eye on the grounded stealth craft, watching for signs that those inside it had spotted the Marines and were preparing to fire. But as the Marines dropped the final kilometer to the surface, their assist jets braking them hard at the last possible moment, no reaction could be seen on the craft.

Watching the stress readings that jumped into red on the helmet display of every Marine, Geary winced in sympathy at the forces they were enduring as the jets labored at full thrust to slow their fall.

"If something goes wrong, will they break through the ice?" Senator Sakai asked.

"No, sir," Geary said. "The ice sheets are too thick and too hard. If the jets on any of the Marines fail, they will crater on the surface. It will crack the surrounding ice, but not enough to shatter or hole it." It all sounded so clinical when describing it, as if such a crater would not be the grave marker of a Marine who could not possibly survive such an impact. But he thought they were already past that point, the Marines' falls slowed enough that they could survive the impact if their jets failed now.

Orvis hit the ice hard enough to create some fine cracks under his armored boots. The gunnery sergeant tottered on his feet, facing the stealth craft, his weapon aimed and ready. He slid out his right foot to maintain his balance instead of following the normal practice of bending into a roll that would have ended up with him lying prone on the ice in a less exposed position. "Everybody remember to stay on your feet and minimize contact with the surface!"

All around him, the rest of the platoon landed in a staggered series of similar wobbly stances. None fell even though two had to take a few rushed steps to keep from losing their balance. Europa's extremely thin atmosphere could not generate any winds or resistance capable of pushing the Marines off their trajectories, so they had landed in almost perfect alignment, forming two bent lines around the sides of the craft.

Geary could see dozens of different views of the scene, each from one of the Marines. On the side with the ridge, the Marines were slightly higher and had a marginally different view of the stealth craft, but, otherwise, the views were similar. The surface ice of Europa here was darkened by minerals to a light khaki color and scored by low ridges and lines. The stealth craft had been brought to rest near a low, curving ridge that offered as much cover as could be found anywhere on the surface. It was small in relation to *Dauntless*, only perhaps three times the size of one of the battle cruiser's shuttles. From this close, however, the craft was impossible to miss, a smooth, curving shape rising above the skyline. The sky itself was as black as space, the atmosphere being too thin to catch sunlight, but the landscape was eerily lit by the faint light of Sol and the light reflected from the huge many-banded globe of Jupiter that dominated the view above this side of Europa.

"Move out!" The last Marine had barely come to a stop when Orvis called out the command and began running toward the spacecraft, along with half of the other Marines on each side. He and the others covered about a third of the distance to the craft, then stopped, weapons aimed and ready. Behind them, the other half of the platoon dodged forward, running through the area where their comrades now stood, covering the charge.

The sensors on the Marines' combat armor worked automatically and efficiently, scanning the spacecraft and identifying even subtle surface features. On the Marines' helmet displays, markers sprang to life over the image of the ship, designating various kinds of sensors, a few weapons designed for space combat, and maneuvering thrusters.

"Admiral, either we've achieved surprise, or they're waiting for us in there," Orvis reported.

Geary nodded from habit even though the gesture couldn't be seen by the Marine sergeant. "Make sure they can't lift. We can't afford to have them run."

"Yes, sir. Second Squad, Fourth Squad," Orvis called out as he dashed forward again. "Attack plan Alpha. Take out all assigned targets."

Ten Marines on one side of the ship halted, their weapons steadying before opening fire, as did ten Marines on the other side. The spacecraft's maneuvering thrusters were knocked out in a rapid series of shots that crippled the spacecraft's ability to control its movement if it tried to lift. Shoulder-fired weapons sent projectiles into the craft's single main propulsion unit at the aft end, doing enough damage to the external components to render the drive useless but not enough harm to threaten catastrophic failure of the drive components inside the hull.

Only seconds had gone by as the stealth craft was permanently grounded. The Marines who had continued running forward with Orvis were once again coming to a halt and raising their own weapons. "First Squad, Third Squad, engage assigned targets."

Energy pulses and projectiles from the Marine rifles slammed into the few weapons visible on the hull, destroying the external portions or sealing firing ports. Sensors on the spacecraft's outer hull were also knocked out by carefully aimed shots. "They're grounded, helpless, and blind, Admiral," Gunnery Sergeant Orvis reported.

"Good." Geary looked toward Desjani, who shook her head to indicate that no communications had been received from the stealth craft. Very likely the external transmitters on the craft had just been destroyed by the Marines, so if nothing had been heard before now, the kidnappers had lost their chance to try to negotiate. Nonetheless, he felt a strange reluctance to issue the next command, a hesitation that vanished in a flare of anger at the fools on the stealth craft who had made this necessary. "Get inside and finish the job." He could feel the weight of those words, as if they had real mass that settled on him and came to rest in his chest.

"Yes, sir. First Squad, Third Squad—"

"Gunny! There's something under the air lock on this side!"

Orvis opened a virtual window on his helmet display that gave him a view of what Corporal Maya had spotted. That gave Geary a window showing Orvis's view, with Maya's view in it in miniature. He actually wasted a precious second wondering how to enlarge it before mentally slapping himself and just looking directly at his own view from Maya's armor.

The image tightened and grew within the window as Maya magnified her view. "Got a body, Gunny," she reported.

A body? Geary heard a sharp intake of breath from someone on the bridge, but otherwise a tense silence had fallen.

"I don't see a suit," Orvis noted.

"Ain't one," Maya said tersely. "IR shows body temp matching surface temp. Must be frozen solid. Body is flat, but arms are locked into position slightly elevated."

"Been out here a little while, then," Orvis commented. "Sounds like whoever it was died while trying to climb back to the hatch and fell already half-frozen. Get in close while we cover you."

Maya flitted forward, her armor's sensors scanning the body for any signs of booby traps. Geary almost flinched again as he saw the object closer up. A woman, wearing only lightweight coveralls, lay splayed on her back on the ice of Europa, her body already frozen as hard as the ice beneath it. Her face, distorted by death and the physical damage caused by Europa's surface environment, was only partly visible beneath a coating of frost and icy strands of hair.

Geary stared at the image, trying to make out if the face was that of Lieutenant Castries. Had the hostage-takers decided that at least one of the Alliance officers had outlived her usefulness? Had they decided there was no sense in keeping alive another mouth to feed, and used a cruel and vicious means of disposing of her? Was Yuon's body also lying somewhere nearby, camouflaged by death and frost?

Had the Marines arrived too late?

FIVE

CORPORAL Maya crouched next to the body, not touching it and being careful not to let any part of her armor except the soles of her armored boots touch the surface of Europa. "I don't think she's one of ours," she reported, her voice professionally unemotional. Maya moved her rifle's muzzle with surprising gentleness to sweep some of the masking hair away, the frozen strands snapping like tiny icicles.

"That's not her," Desjani said, her voice rough. "That's not Lieutenant Castries."

"Did you copy that, Gunny?" Geary asked.

"Roger, Admiral. We're looking, and this is the only body out here."

"Air lock is right above me," Maya continued as she stood straight again. "She's got an empty holster. This wasn't a suicide. Somebody took her gun and tossed her out. You're right, Gunny. She was trying to climb back in when Europa got her."

Geary looked to another virtual window open next to that of the Marines, this one showing Dr. Nasr as he and the quarantine doctor watched the same events. "Doctor, is there any way to tell whether or not that woman was infected before she died?"

"No," Dr. Palden answered shortly.

"Do you mean was she ejected from the craft because she was ill?" Nasr asked. "It is very hard to tell with such little data, but if the reports we have of the plague are accurate, if she had been infected and showing the illness, she would have been too sick to try climbing back up. Once the plague manifested, disorientation and weakness came quickly. The others may have suspected she was infected, or the cause of her ejection may be unrelated to that."

Dr. Palden frowned but did not dispute Nasr's words.

"They pushed her out alive," Desjani said. "They wanted her to suffer. This was about thieves falling out, not the plague."

"I agree with your captain," Commander Nkosi said. "I have seen people shoved out of air locks by criminals like these before. They even call it *walking the plank*, as if they were romantic pirates rather than vicious murderers."

Orvis must have reached the same conclusion. "One less for us to worry about. All right, they know we're here because we had to knock on the outside of this bird to ground it. First Squad, Third Squad, commence forced entry. Weapons free. Take out any threats, but make sure you don't shoot until you're sure the target isn't one of our officers. No grenades or other area weapons. This is a hostage rescue, not an assault. Second Squad, Fourth Squad, provide cover, and make sure no one drops out of any secondary hatches."

Corporal Maya beckoned to her squad, bent her legs, then jumped nearly straight up, aided by the weak gravity of Europa and the power of her battle armor. She grabbed the outer hatch and brought her boots down on a narrow ledge running along the hull just below it, waiting while three of the Marines from her squad joined her. The rest of her squad gathered beneath them. On the other side of the ship, Sergeant Hsien and his squad did the same at the air lock on that side. The squads commanded by Corporal Bergeron and Sergeant Koury held their positions, their weapons aimed toward the stealth craft, ready to fire.

"Outer hatch is locked," Sergeant Hsien reported.

"Same here," Corporal Maya said.

"Crack them," Gunnery Sergeant Orvis ordered.

A private whose window data indicated a subspecialty in Demolition and Entry edged next to the air lock and placed a small box next to the external controls. "What is that?" Senator Sakai asked from the back of the bridge, jarring Geary out of his absorption in the events on the surface.

"It's called a skeleton key," Geary replied. "I've seen the Marines use them several times. They're designed to open doors by any means they can access."

But after several seconds, the private shook his head, producing a dizzying effect on those watching the view from his armor. "No go. Our gear can't get a grip on the software these guys have. It's nothing weird like the Kick junk, but it's too different from the stuff we or the Syndics use."

"Can you do a mechanical-override entry?" Hsien asked.

"Trying." Another couple of seconds passed. "It's hard to read stuff even just under the hull's outer surface with these stealth coatings in the way."

"Got a lock mechanism," the Demo and Entry Marine working on Maya's side reported. "Look about here."

"Where? There? Got it. Thanks. That looks close to our own designs. A mag field right here . . . got it."

Two Marines hauled the outer air lock hatch open while their companions held weapons at the ready. "Looks clear," Sergeant Hsien said, peering into the small compartment beyond.

"Open and clear," Maya reported.

"Fry 'em," Orvis directed.

One of the Marines on each side tossed a round object inside the nearest air lock, then joined their companions in huddling away from the outer hatch. Geary saw alerts flash on the display of each Marine as electromagnetic pulses flared inside the air locks, frying all but the most heavily shielded electronics, hopefully including any booby traps, weapons, or sensors.

"Ready," Maya said.

"Ready," Hsien echoed.

"All right. Inside." Orvis waited while some of the Marines crowded into the two air locks, and others jumped upward as space on the ledges cleared.

"Got some lightweight composite armor inside the hull," Maya reported. "Nothing on the inner door, though."

"Same on your side, Hsien?" Orvis asked. "Good. Prep Banshees. Prep to blow the doors. I'll count down. On one, fire the Banshees. Wait three seconds, then crack the inner doors and get inside."

"Fire Banshee when count reaches one, wait three, go in," Hsien repeated back.

"Fire on one, wait three, go in," Maya added to indicate she had also understood the orders.

One Marine at each air lock knelt and placed a short tube against the inner hatch. The two with the Demo and Entry skills stood by the doors and rapidly traced the edges of them with what looked like narrow tape, then laced a crisscross pattern across the surfaces of the doors as well before sticking small remote detonator tabs into the tape and stepping back. "Stand by," Orvis said. "Begin count. Three . . . two . . . one."

Geary saw the views from the Marines with the Banshee tubes jolt as the devices fired. The Marines scrambled to their feet, weapons ready, leaving neat holes where the Banshee rounds had punched through the inner air lock doors as if they were paper.

"Three . . . go!" Hsien and Maya yelled simultaneously.

The demo tape on the doors abruptly flared into brilliant light as it instantly ate through the material behind it. The inner doors blew out in fragments, the pieces flying past the Marines under the pressure of atmosphere venting from the interior of the stealth craft. The Marines surged into motion the moment the fragments were past, racing into the craft against the wind of the inner atmosphere pouring out into the barely present atmosphere of Europa.

Even through the Marine sensors, the scenes they confronted inside were of confusion and chaos. Each Banshee had burst after it tore through the hatch, setting off more EMP charges as well as dazzlingly bright bursts of light and thunderclaps of sound. Men and women carrying a variety of small arms had been covering the hatches from inside the ship, but now were reeling in disorder, some pounding on weapons whose fried circuitry had rendered them useless, others frantically grabbing at the inoperative breathing gear on their survival suits as they began to grasp that those circuits had been fried along with those in weapons.

The Marines, barely fitting inside the craft's passageways in their battle armor, fired with deadly efficiency. Within seconds, every criminal still holding a weapon had been hit, while a few others had fled.

A Marine private from First Squad paused, looking down at a figure writhing on the deck at her feet, then fired.

"Hotch!" Sergeant Hsien snapped.

"He was choking to death, Sarge!"

Hsien paused. "All right. No sense making 'em die slow like they did that woman they tossed out the air lock. We got six locals down on this side."

"Got five bad guys down here," Maya reported.

"Get moving," Orvis ordered. "Secure the rest of the ship."

The Marines from Hsien's and Maya's squads raced through the ship as fast as they could, literally hammering down hatches and doors with the strength of their combat armor. With only two decks in the fairly small craft, it didn't take them long. Behind them, at the air lock doors, other Marines hastily fastened emergency seals across the broken doors, keeping in what atmosphere remained in the grounded spacecraft.

"Heads up!" Private Francis called.

Geary yanked his eyes away from the screens of the Marines in First and Third Squads. Francis was in Fourth Squad, watching the outside of the stealth craft, and because of his angle of view had been the first to spot a small hatch near the underside of the spacecraft as it began opening.

Two figures in space suits dropped out, both carrying weapons, both firing wildly as they fell toward the ice.

Francis and a half dozen other Marines fired back, slamming shots into both figures before their feet even hit the surface. The two criminals landed in loose sprawls, to lie motionless.

"Got some here, too!" a Marine in Second Squad called. "Forward, just under the bow!"

This time, hand weapons were stuck outside the new hatch and fired without aiming, spraying shots as the ones holding the weapons stayed completely under cover.

"Do they think this is some stupid video?" Sergeant Koury grumbled, as she and the rest of her squad fired. Aided by the precise targeting abilities of their battle armor, the energy pulses slammed into the weapons sticking out of the hatch, knocking two out of the hands of those holding them while a third exploded in a flurry of propellant all going off at once. Three figures fell out of the hatch, one dropping to the ice and scrabbling feebly, while the other two pawed at survival suits with rents in them from which atmosphere was pouring out.

"Ancestors forgive us," Orvis mumbled. "Put them out of their misery, Koury."

"But, Gunny, we stopped doing that to the Syndics! What about prisoners?"

"We can't take them back. They're going to die fast now or slow later. You want to watch?"

"No," Sergeant Koury answered after a second. "But I'm not going to ask anyone else to do it." She raised her weapon and fired several times.

"They are being merciful," Commander Nkosi murmured next to Geary, as if trying to remind himself of that.

"Got four in here," a private in Third Squad called out from inside the craft. The view from his armor showed four terrified criminals huddled together between the beds in a sleeping compartment barely large enough for several bunks stacked along the walls.

"No weapons?" Sergeant Hsien asked.

"Don't see any, Sarge."

"Ask them if they know where the fleet officers are."

The private relayed the question over his external speaker, the sound coming out weakly in the thinned atmosphere left inside the spacecraft. "They say they don't know, Sarge."

"Then back out and leave one Marine to guard the compartment while the rest of you continue the search."

"Hey, Gunny," Corporal Maya called a minute later. "This looks like the hatch into the bridge."

Commander Nkosi nodded to Geary. "It should be the right location for a bridge on a spacecraft like that. The hatch is probably armored, in case of mutiny."

"We've seen that sort of thing before," Geary commented before calling Orvis. "Gunnery Sergeant, the local commander agrees that Corporal Maya has probably found the bridge. The hatch is likely armored, so it can serve as a citadel like the Syndics use."

"Thank you, Admiral. Sir, we've covered the whole spacecraft except whatever's behind that hatch. Our people must be in there, along with however many of the enemy are still active. We've accounted for twenty hostiles so far."

"It will not be a large compartment," Nkosi warned. "It will not hold more than a half dozen at the most. Blasting your way in could be hazardous to your officers if they are inside."

"We might not have much choice," Geary said. He glanced at Desjani. Her rigid face showed no feeling even though he could see anguish in her eyes. But she nodded in response to his unspoken question.

"You're right, Admiral," Desjani said. "Let's see what Gunny Orvis can do first, though."

"I'm on my way to that bridge hatch," Orvis reported, jumping up and pulling himself into the temporary air lock rigged from sheets of thin, transparent material that ballooned outward under even the gentle pressure still inside the ship. "Maya, I want your breaking and entering guy there along with half your squad. Don't do anything until I get there. From the sound of things, we can't afford to use a Banshee without risking serious harm to the fleet officers."

"Figures," Corporal Maya grumbled. "Jaworski, get your butt down here with me. The rest of you apes hold positions."

Orvis scrambled through the craft until he reached the hatch where Maya and her Marines waited. "Have you tried knocking? Did you push any buttons?"

"No, Gunny," Maya replied. "You said not to do anything."

"And you listened? You may make sergeant someday." Orvis walked to the bulkhead holding the hatch, examining it carefully. "I never saw one just like this. It does look armored, though. Let's see who's home before we blow the door down."

Orvis reached out a hand, one armored finger gently touching a comm panel next to the hatch. "That ought to be the call button, right?"

His question was answered a moment later when the comm panel lit up, showing a man brandishing a hand weapon, his face twisted by fear. "I've got them in here! You break in and I'll kill them both!"

"Martian," Commander Nkosi said, disgust clear in his voice. "That tattoo under his left ear. It's a gang mark. Red mobs use them."

"Hey," Gunnery Sergeant Orvis said to the criminal in soothing tones very unlike his usual way of speaking. "Relax. Can you hear me?"

"Yeah. Yeah. You break in and I'll kill them!"

"Understood. We don't want you. We just want those two officers."

"It's not my fault we're down here!" the hostage-taker cried, his words falling over each other as they came out too quickly and too loudly. "It was Grassie! She took us down before the rest of us knew she was aiming to land on Europa! It wasn't my fault!"

"Pal, I don't care whose fault it was, I just want our people back safe," Orvis assured him. "We'll let the locals worry about what to do to this Grassie."

The man laughed, high-pitched and rapid, the sound unnerving. "We already took care of her! Shoved her out the air lock while she tried to claim she had some plan to get us out of here! It's all her fault; she wanted to be on Europa, so we gave her to Europa!"

That explained the body outside the ship. "Idiots," Desjani said in disgusted tones. "They panicked and killed their pilot."

"They would have had a backup pilot aboard," Commander Nkosi said. "Or, at least, an autopilot routine so the ship could fly itself. But it was still a very stupid as well as brutal thing to do."

Gunnery Sergeant Orvis was speaking to the hostage-taker again, still using the same calm, measured tones. "All right. You took care of your pilot. So we got no problems."

"No . . . no problems?" The criminal sounded bewildered as well as frightened.

"That's right. You the only one in there with our people? What do you need?"

"What?" The criminal stared at Orvis.

"What do you need? You and me, we're just doing our jobs, right? Now, me, my job is to get those officers safe and sound. That's what I want. What do you want? You want a deal?"

"A deal?" The hostage-taker grasped at that like a man in a vacuum grabbing for a survival suit. "Yeah. A deal. I'll trade you those two."

"That's fair," Orvis said. "Trade them for what? What's the deal?"

"Uh . . . get me off this rock! That's the deal! You promise to get me off here along with you, then you let me go, safe, or I kill both of your friends!"

Orvis handed his rifle to a nearby Marine, then held his empty hands up in a nonthreatening way. "That's it? That's all you want?"

"Yeah! Promise you'll get me safe off Europa! In one piece!"

"Sure," Orvis replied. "We don't care what happens to you. You got a deal."

"I've got . . . ? That's it? You don't have to check with anybody?"

"Hell, no. I got full authority for this," Orvis assured him. "You let us in there, we get those two officers safe and sound, and we'll do what you ask."

Commander Nkosi turned an angry gaze on Geary. "Admiral, you can't—"

Geary shook his head, his grim expression stopping Nkosi's words in their tracks. He felt a sickness inside as he realized what Gunny Orvis intended, but no orders reached his lips to stop what would soon happen. *I need to own this, too. I knew it might come to this. It's my responsibility.* "I don't think you have anything to worry about," he told Nkosi.

"He doesn't," Desjani said. She didn't sound upset, just implacable. Geary wondered how many times she had faced similar situations and made similar decisions.

The traitor who had provided a Syndic hypernet key to the Alliance, and who had led the Alliance fleet into an ambush that might have been the death of that entire fleet, had died on this bridge. No one had ever told Geary who had pulled the trigger. But whether or not Tanya herself had executed the man, he realized that she could have.

A child of an endless war, she did what was necessary.

"But your man is promising—" Nkosi began again.

"We were at war for a century with opponents who would lie at the drop of a hat and commit any atrocity," Desjani interrupted. "We learned to do what we have to do."

Nkosi stared at her. "But . . . your own honor—"

"Don't," Desjani said in her most dangerous voice. "Don't go there. You have no right to judge us."

Nkosi looked away, clearly distressed, but he said nothing more.

"You promise? That's binding?" the hostage-taker was demanding once more.

"Yeah, I promise," Orvis said in a casual voice. "Yeah, it's binding." Unseen by the hostage-taker, but visible to Geary and the other watchers who could see activity on Orvis's helmet display, Orvis tagged the image of the criminal, then highlighted Corporal Maya's name. Almost instantly, Maya's acknowledgment glowed green on Orvis's display.

"Look," Orvis pressed, "you've only got so much life support left, and the longer any of us hang around this ice ball, the more risk we're all running. Let's get this done, all right?"

The hostage-taker hesitated, then nodded. "All right. Remember. You promised. I got a record of it."

"That's fine. I got a record of it, too."

A low thunk sounded as the bolts holding the hatch retracted, then the hatch swung open. Atmosphere puffed out as pressure inside the bridge equalized with what was left inside the rest of the spacecraft. Orvis entered slowly, still unarmed, his hands once again held out as far as they could be and get through the hatch. A few other Marines followed behind him, their weapons pointed toward the deck or the overhead, everyone moving in a relaxed way. Last of all came Corporal Maya, her weapon pointed slightly away from the hostage-taker.

The criminal obviously still didn't trust the Marines. He had the pistol barrel pressed against Lieutenant Castries's forehead. Castries was dressed in a shapeless coverall and propped into a seat. Her eyes were closed and her body slack.

"Drugged," Dr. Nasr told Geary. "If she were merely unconscious, her respiration would be more rapid."

Lieutenant Yuon lay on the deck next to the chair holding Castries, unmoving except for the slow rise and fall of his own breathing.

His attention focused on Orvis and the other Marines in the front rank, the hostage-taker did not notice Maya's weapon shifting slightly as she took aim. "How are we going to—?" he started to say.

At such close range, the shot and impact seemed to occur simultaneously. The hostage-taker jerked as the energy pulse from Corporal Maya's weapon blasted all the way through his head and impacted on one of the screens behind him.

Orvis stepped forward quickly, grasping the pistol and pulling it away from the limp hand of the dead criminal as the body dropped to the deck under Europa's gentle gravity.

"Stupid git," Maya commented conversationally. "Even the Syndics aren't dumb enough to fall for that anymore."

"That's because the Syndics taught us that trick," Orvis said with brutal directness.

"Gunny, we couldn't take him back! The only way to keep him from killing these two squids was to tell him what he wanted to hear."

"It was still a false promise. Remind me when we get back to the ship to apologize to my ancestors and beg forgiveness for the lie."

"Sure, Gunny," Maya said, her voice now subdued. "Won't be the first time, will it?"

"Hell, no. Wish it could be the last." All traces of gentle persuasion dropped from Gunnery Sergeant Orvis's voice. "All right, you apes! Get them into the spare armor, on the double! Minimize physical contact with them until they're sealed in!"

"Minimize . . . what, Gunny?" a private asked.

"Don't touch them!"

"How are we going to get them into the armor without touching them, Gunny?"

"Make sure you don't touch them when you touch them, that's how. Now get it done!"

As those aboard *Dauntless* watched the Marines gingerly sealing the unconscious bodies of Castries and Yuon into the spare battle armor, Commander Nkosi shook his head. "If I had done that, I would be going to jail."

"Lucky you had us here to do it, then, isn't it?" Desjani replied bitingly.

"This isn't over," Geary said to break up the painful debate. "We still have to recover them."

Nkosi licked his lips before speaking again. "Sir, you must understand that if my physician does not certify that your Marines' armor has been decontaminated, my ships will fire upon those men and women before your ship can recover them. My presence here will not stop my ships from acting as I ordered."

"I would expect no less," Geary said. "So far, your physician seems satisfied, though." He did not bother saying what everyone knew, that *Dauntless* would not sit passively while the quarantine ships attacked Alliance Marines. "We've dealt with that stealth craft for you," he reminded Nkosi.

Orvis was checking the seals on the armor now holding Lieutenants Castries and Yuon. "Looks good. Let's go. Pull out, everybody."

As the other Marines began moving, Maya and three of her squad carrying the two suits of armor with the lieutenants in them, one Marine called out a plaintive question. "Sarge? What about these guys? The four in this berthing compartment?"

"Leave them," Hsien snapped.

"But—"

"Just leave them!"

The Marine moved away fast, as if trying to flee the compartment where the last four criminals were still alive. The other Marines went quickly, too, clearing passageways rapidly, past the dead criminals who had fought at the air locks and going out through the temporary air lock as swiftly as they could.

Orvis waited on the ice, counting as he watched Marines come out and jump from the air lock to land nearby. "That's everybody."

"Gunny?" the private who had been guarding the four prisoners asked.

"I know what you're going to ask," Orvis said. "We can't help them. They did this to themselves."

"Gunny," another private said, "that ship is a mess now. It's gonna be unlivable in—"

Orvis pointed toward the wrecked ship. "We left the weapons dropped by the guys we killed inside. Some of them still work. And we left the med supplies and drugs undisturbed. There's more than enough drugs for them to knock themselves out and not feel a thing when the end comes. That's the best we can do for those four who are still alive. You understand? That's the best we can do. Unless you want to climb back in and finish them yourself."

"No. No, Gunny. I got too many nightmares as it is."

"You and me both. Now line up. We jump in sequence. Check your jets. Put everything you got into the jumps, and your jets will kick in automatically as you clear the surface."

The Marines formed a loose column on the surface of Europa, most of them looking upward to where Jupiter loomed. No one looked down at the hard, dirty ice under their feet. "Follow the drill," Orvis cautioned. "Three-minute intervals. You screw up, and even I can't save you. Maya, those two officers still out?"

"Yeah, Gunny. Must be nice to sleep late, huh?"

"Funny. You and the others with the officers slave their armor to yours, so they'll automatically jump along with you."

"Got it. All right, Gunny, their armor is in zombie mode."

Geary looked toward Desjani, who was studying her display. "Are we in position?"

"We're ready. Shuttles, stand by."

"Gunnery Sergeant Orvis, we're ready for you."

"That's it," Orvis announced to his Marines. "Ready? Begin count. One."

The first Marine in the column, his knees already flexed, straightened in a convulsive leap, the power of the armor and the weak gravity combining to hurl him high upward even before the jet assists cut in and yanked him away from Europa with startling speed.

Three minutes later, a second Marine jumped. Then a third, a fourth . . .

Geary watched their progress on his display, a string of shapes rising from Europa. It struck him suddenly that these were the first humans to leave that cursed moon since before the human-created plague struck long centuries ago. From this high up, he could see one of the domed cities that had held nothing but the dead during those centuries, many of the solar-powered lights still functioning even after so long to create a false image of life and warmth in a place that held neither.

As the first Marine rose into orbit, one of *Dauntless*'s shuttles snagged him with a tether that shot out and latched onto one leg. The shuttle brought the Marine into position near *Dauntless* and waited.

Desjani touched a comm control. "Senior Chief Tarrini, target is one Marine. Make sure you get everything."

One of *Dauntless*'s hell lances fired. The particle beam, which at full strength would have easily punched completely through the Marine's battle armor, had been carefully adjusted to put out just enough energy to flay the armor of its outer layer. As the armor jerked under the impact of the stream of charged particles, Geary heard the Marine inside grunt under the force of the blows transmitted through the armor. Stress data appeared on his helmet view, along with warnings as damage rapidly accumulated to everything on the surface of the armor. Then the image and sound cut off as the last external comm relays on the armor evaporated under the lash of the hell lance.

The shuttle used the tether to rotate the Marine carefully, ensuring that the weapon played over the entire surface of the armor.

"How does it look?" Geary asked Dr. Nasr.

Dr. Palden answered before Nasr could. "That spot needs another hit. And there. What about under the tether clasp?"

"That will be hit when the shuttle releases the tether," Nasr said, his tone of voice uncharacteristically short.

"Proceed," Dr. Palden said grudgingly.

Several seconds later, the two doctors gave their approval. The shuttle ejected the used tether so that it fell toward Europa, then shot out another to grab the next Marine, while the second shuttle swung over to pick up the first Marine. Geary blew out a gasp of air as he looked at the heat readings on the outside of the first Marine's battle armor. "I sure hope Dr. Nasr and Gunnery Sergeant Orvis were right about the Marines inside the armor being able to endure that."

Desjani, who was beginning to relax, smiled thinly at him. "Doctors make mistakes sometimes, but gunnery sergeants? Doesn't happen."

As the next Marine was pummeled by the hell lance, the first was hauled into the second shuttle, where everyone paused while the doctors carefully examined their data. "He is fully decontaminated," Nasr said.

Dr. Palden scowled as she checked the same data, saying nothing.

"There is a person inside that armor," Dr. Nasr finally prodded her.

"I need to be sure!" But five seconds later Palden shrugged. "It's good."

"Get him out," Desjani ordered.

Geary watched sailors kneeling by the rigid figure of the Marine. Master Chief Gioninni was personally supervising the work, and Geary had earlier observed *Dauntless*'s hull technicians practicing on the broken set of battle armor, slicing it into pieces to get the precise settings needed for their equipment. But he still felt worry as incredibly sharp blades with edges only a single molecule wide sliced into the

Marine's armor. Such a blade could cut completely through a human arm or leg without even noticing the resistance.

But there were no signs of trouble as the cutters came off the armor. "Put the 'shroons on," Gioninni ordered after inspecting the cuts.

Geary had no idea what the official name for 'shroons was. Like everyone else, he had only heard the nickname universally used for more than a century for the means to crack or pry open objects using only the tiniest of openings as a start. Rumor had it that the nickname derived from the ability of mushrooms to crack concrete slabs as they grew.

Following Gioninni's command, the techs slapped 'shroon pads onto the cuts in the Marine's armor. Unseen, tiny filaments slid down from the pads into the cuts, then began expanding and growing, inexorably pushing the openings wider and wider despite the immense strength of the inner layers of material on the battle armor. Reaching the extent of their reach and life span, the 'shroons shriveled and dropped away.

"Get him out," Gioninni said.

The techs knelt again and slid the Marine out of the split armor. The private looked back at them with a dazed expression, still bemused by the blows from the hell lance and the subsequent heat inside his armor. Helping him to a seat, one of the sailors offered a drink which the Marine sucked down avidly.

Lowering the drink bulb, the Marine locked an accusing look on the sailors. "Gunny said there'd be beer."

"You'll get beer when we get back to the ship," Gioninni assured him. "Right now, that stuff the docs cooked up is best for you."

"Look at them bruises on him," one of the techs commented in awed tones. "You look like you just came back from some really great liberty," he told the Marine.

"Don't feel like it," the Marine grumbled, taking another drink and grimacing.

"That's all right," the sailor assured him. "You guys did good down there."

"Hell," the Marine said. "We did our job. Those goons never had a chance." He stared gloomily at nothing as the sailors prepared for the next Marine.

It seemed to take an eternity to decontaminate every Marine and pry them out of their ruined armor. But, finally, Gunnery Sergeant Orvis, the last, climbed out of his armor unassisted, his face mottled with bruises already forming, disdaining any help from the weary sailors. Orvis looked at the piles of destroyed armor, shaking his head. "Operation complete, Admiral. The bean counters are going to raise hell about all this trashed armor, though."

"I'll let Captain Smythe worry about that," Geary said, knowing that his senior engineering officer would find some account to charge the expense to that would, if not justify the expense to the bean counters, at least confuse the bean counters as to whether they should object to the charge. "But the op isn't complete yet." The two sets of battle armor holding Lieutenants Yuon and Castries still lay intact inside the shuttle, their exteriors darkened and radiating heat. "Dr. Nasr will meet you at the shuttle dock. Help get those two sets of armor to the total-isolation compartment in medical."

"Yes, sir. Admiral, I have to tell you, it was pretty tough inside that armor. We need to get those officers out of that as soon as possible."

The shuttle had almost reached *Dauntless* as they spoke. Within a minute, it had landed, and the ramp was lowering. The worn-out Marines, groaning just loud enough to make their unhappiness apparent but not loud enough to draw a rebuke from Gunnery Sergeant Orvis, put on insulated gloves and hoisted the armor-encased officers onto medical stretchers that raced off with Drs. Nasr and Palden running behind.

Geary felt an irrational urge to trot down to sick bay himself, but he was still watching the overall situation and so waited on the bridge, viewing remotely as the stretchers deposited the two officers inside the total-isolation compartment. The two barely fit in the small room, which was intended for only the most extreme emergencies and could normally hold just one person.

Dr. Nasr moved with assured speed as he activated autonomous devices within the total-isolation compartment. After ensuring that the seals on the compartment were in place and solidly locked, he set the devices to work cutting the officers out of the armor. It was a longer and more complex process than when sailors could do some of the work and oversee the rest, but eventually the limp bodies of both officers were free of their protective shells.

Remote diagnostic sleeves attached themselves to the two officers, taking samples and readings which were relayed to Nasr. "No sign of infection," he declared in a relieved voice.

"No sign of *active* infection," Dr. Palden corrected.

Instead of replying, Dr. Nasr ordered the equipment inside the isolation compartment to begin supplying both lieutenants with solutions for liquid and nourishment, as well as some drugs to counteract those keeping them unconscious.

After several minutes, Lieutenant Castries blinked and looked around groggily. She tried to stand up, wavering on her feet, and staring down in confusion at the medical sleeves and other devices attached to her. Geary winced in sympathy at the bruises vividly marking her visible skin, hoping that whatever the docs were giving Castries and Yuon including some powerful painkillers.

Dr. Palden peered intently at the readouts, her expression suspicious. "Disorientation and weakness," she said like someone condemning a prisoner.

"Completely explainable by her ordeal and condition," Dr. Nasr shot back. "Body temperature is stabilizing at normal. Brain functions show no deterioration or abnormality."

"That is so," Palden admitted reluctantly.

Lieutenant Castries had lifted her gaze to stare at the monitor in the compartment. "What happened? Where . . . Is this *Dauntless*?"

Geary broke in to answer. "Yes, Lieutenant. You're safe aboard *Dauntless*. Do you know you were kidnapped?"

"What? No. I was on some street and . . . now I'm here." She looked around, spotting Yuon, who was beginning to stir. "Him, too? Why are we both in here? And what the—?" Castries was staring at the broken battle armor in absolute bafflement.

"You are in complete medical isolation," Dr. Nasr explained. "You show no signs of current infection, but will have to stay totally isolated in that compartment for the next three weeks."

"Infection?" Castries was staring at her hand, which seemed to be covered with colorful hues of black, purple, and green as bruises developed.

"You have been on Europa."

"I've— That's— What—? I'm actually awake? This is real? I have to spend three weeks in here?" Castries suddenly realized something and her stare shifted to Yuon, who was blinking himself to awareness. "Three weeks in this little hole with *him*? What have I done to deserve this?" she wailed.

"A sedative may be required," Dr. Palden noted dispassionately.

Relieved at seeing Castries all right, and at having the risky rescue operation successfully completed, Geary could not keep himself from laughing briefly as he looked toward Desjani. "I think that lays to rest any possibility that Castries and Yuon could be an item."

Tanya grinned. "You never know. They're going to be stuck in there together for three weeks, so there's always the possibility of hostage syndrome."

Geary escorted Commander Nkosi back to the shuttle dock, where they were met by the two doctors, as well as by Senior Chief Tarrini and the two weapons specialists that Nkosi had brought with him. Behind Geary came Senator Sakai and Victoria Rione. As Geary entered, he saw that a jovial Master Chief Gioninni had backed the two weapons specialists into a corner, where he was apparently thanking them profusely.

Nkosi paused before entering his own shuttle, gazing at his comm unit. "My ship has relayed a message to me. Sol System government orders me not to permit your operation until further consideration."

Geary smiled. "Sometimes light-speed limitations and communications lag can be your friends."

"Certainly, especially when those to whom you send reports and who send orders back are close to a light-hour distant." Nkosi hesitated again. "I will tell them all that I saw."

"That was the idea," Geary said, no longer smiling. "We didn't try to hide anything. And we only did what you would have done if your orders permitted it, and what you would have done as soon as you could."

"Yes," Rione emphasized, "we did as *your* rules required. Ensure that you tell everyone that, Commander. We carried out the actions that Sol Star System rules *made* us carry out."

Nkosi gazed steadily back at her. "I will ensure that is widely known. Enforcing the quarantine of Europa is a lonely, boring, and on rare occasions horrible experience. I will not hesitate to remind the people of Sol Star System what their rules require of others and require of my own crews. And I will tell them that your actions were not only necessary but have eliminated an awful threat to us all."

"Thank you, Commander," Senator Sakai said. "The Alliance is grateful for your cooperation in this."

"Hopefully, you won't be the only ones who are grateful for that!" Nkosi saluted, then turned and walked into his shuttle. Behind him came Dr. Palden and the two weapons specialists. As the hatch to the shuttle closed, Geary saw those two hauling out large comm devices and shaking them with puzzled expressions.

The moment the shuttle left the hanger, Senior Chief Tarrini and Master Chief Gioninni broke into laughter.

"What did you do?" Geary asked.

"Nothing bad, Admiral," Tarrini assured him. "You saw those big units those two specialists had? Comm units, hell. Even Sol Star System isn't that far behind on their tech to require something that large. Those were collection devices. They were scanning and recording everything they could while they were close to our weapons."

"So we set up a strong mag coil in that corner," Gioninni said with a chuckle. "I backed them into the corner while telling them how grateful we were for them helping out, then Senior Chief triggered the coil. The field was strong enough to send all of their files down the backassward black hole of degenerate data."

"An unfortunate accident," said Senator Sakai with a rare smile showing. "I believe my own files have encountered that black hole on occasion."

"Senator," Geary said, "with the permission of the Alliance government, I would like to head for the hypernet gate now and get on our way home."

"Permission granted," Sakai said, solemn again. "Is that how you say it properly?" He looked around at the others. "Thank you for finding a solution that saved those two young officers and for the excellent work in carrying it out. I would like to thank the Marines personally when the opportunity arises."

Tarrini was eyeing Sakai as if uncertain of the politician's motive in saying "thank you," but Gioninni grinned. "You are welcome, Senator. It may be a few days before the Marines are up to meeting you, though. They're all pretty beat-up."

"And they will, I think," Dr. Nasr added, "need additional meds and therapy to cope with the events on the surface." Despite his dour words, since Dr. Palden left, Nasr had been acting as if a dark cloud had lifted.

"It was a dirty job," Geary agreed. "I'm sorry we had to ask that of them." He tapped the nearest comm panel. "Captain Desjani, head for the hypernet gate. We're going home."

Only a few seconds passed before he heard cheers echoing through the passageways of *Dauntless*. The word had spread fast.

He didn't feel like joining in the jubilation, though. The events on Europa had cast too dark a pall over his feelings. All he could feel was a tired sort of relief that, once again, an unavoidable job was complete.

SENATOR Costa would sometimes take a seat in one of the dining compartments, engaging crew members in conversation. Geary had long ago figured out that Costa's goal in this was not simply to ingratiate herself with the crew but to find out what they knew and gauge their feelings on different issues.

He usually made only a polite greeting when he saw her doing that, but this time as he walked by Geary saw the two sailors sharing Costa's table getting up to go, their meals finished. Before the senator could stand as well, Geary came to the table where Costa sat. "How are you doing, Senator?"

Costa's smile was as insincere as that of a Syndic CEO. "Not badly, Admiral."

"May I join you?"

"Of course. I'm surprised that you're seeking out a conversation with me."

Around the two of them, the nearest tables were being unobtrusively vacated as the sailors at them moved away. Other crew members who were walking past changed their paths so that they also did not come close. In a matter of seconds, without any obvious message or conversation, a large unoccupied region had appeared around the table where Costa and Geary were, granting them some measure of privacy even in this public area.

Senator Costa didn't seem to have noticed, instead waiting expectantly for Geary's reply, but he noticed one finger tapping the small bracelet on her left wrist twice. Because of his time around Rione, Geary recognized what had happened. Costa had activated a personal security field which would garble the sound of their voices for anyone trying to listen in.

The senator could be blunt when she wanted to be, and on this occasion Geary decided to do the same, keeping his voice at a normal volume to see how Costa would react. "I was just wondering what information you've gathered about how the crew feels," he asked as he took a seat opposite her.

The senator's artificial smile widened. "Is there anything that you are worried about me learning?" Her own voice wasn't pitched low, so his guess had been right. She wasn't worried about being overheard.

"No." Geary met her eyes with his own. "I want you to know how the crew feels about the Alliance government."

"And how they feel about you?" Costa said.

"There is no disloyalty to the Alliance here."

Costa didn't reply immediately, her false smile being replaced by an appraising look. "I know you toured as many ruins and wrecks on the surface of Old Earth as we did, Admiral. We didn't have time to see a fraction of what was there, let alone the remnants of the devastation sometimes inflicted elsewhere in this star system."

"I saw them," Geary said. "It's . . . sobering."

"How much was built by the old, great empires, and how much destroyed when those empires fell? No one can calculate the answer to either question." Costa leaned forward, her expression now challenging. "What will be the cost if the Alliance falls? We've seen examples of that in territory that once belonged to the Syndics. What would you do to prevent it, Admiral?"

"I don't want it to happen," Geary said.

"Everyone says that," Costa said with a dismissive wave of one hand.

"The Dancers showed us that we have much in common as humans, that we need to see what we share rather than only the things that we differ on. You said so yourself."

"Of course I did," Costa admitted, with none of the emotion she had betrayed during that event on the surface of Old Earth. "But that doesn't mean that I have to accept so-called solutions based on soft sentiment rather than hard reality. What will you do, Admiral? What is your solution?"

"I'm doing it," Geary said. "I am supporting the government, I am following orders, and I am defending the Alliance against every threat I know of."

"Every threat?" Costa's gaze grew colder. "Are you issuing a warning to me?"

"That was not my intent," Geary said. "I'm not threatening anyone. I am following orders and taking what measures I can to preserve the Alliance."

"Passive measures! All of them! Would you block others from taking the actions needed to save the Alliance? Would you take the necessary actions yourself?" Senator Costa pressed.

Geary said his next words with great care. "Opinions differ on what will save the Alliance and what actions are necessary."

"But you feel qualified to decide? You who slept through the long trauma of the war with the Syndics?"

"I experienced the beginning of that war," Geary said, hearing a trace of anger enter his voice and trying to eliminate it. "I was there at the end of it, as well." *I brought about the end of it, but I won't say that. I won't boast about something like that which I survived and so many others did not.* "When I awoke, I was told about a lot of things that had been done because they were judged necessary to win the war. None of them had worked, and some had, in my judgment, actually kept the war going. As a result, I am skeptical of things that are claimed to be necessary to save the Alliance."

Costa smiled again, a movement of her lips only. Nothing else about her expression reflected emotions appropriate to a smile. "Modest words. But if you block others, you are yourself deciding what is necessary and what is not. Some of us do not want to see the Alliance go the way of those ancient empires, do not want to see the chaos and destruction that would follow. We will not permit that to happen. You know the need for a firm hand, the need to employ force without hesitation, just as we did on Europa."

Just as we *did?* Senator Costa had apparently decided to claim ownership of that action now that it was successfully concluded. "Force should never be used except with wisdom and restraint," Geary said. "What if the actions you deem necessary to save the Alliance actually bring about the chaos and destruction you want to prevent?" he asked, remembering when Senator Sakai had asked him pretty much that same question.

Another fake smile, as Costa leaned back with feigned informality. "Who said anything about me?"

Geary managed his own false smile. "No one. I'm sure you wouldn't propose actions without concern for those who would pay the price for those actions."

"We all have to be willing to sacrifice, Admiral."

"It seems to me that some people are expected to sacrifice a great deal more than others."

Costa's look of benign superiority slipped. "That sounds like a very subversive sentiment from someone who claims to support the Alliance government."

"Not at all," Geary said. "The only sentiment I expressed was that I respect the people subject to my orders too much to be careless with their lives."

The senator dropped all pretense of camaraderie, her gaze on Geary hardening. "You're so very sure of yourself. Maybe you should be wondering, Admiral, why the actions I think are necessary have the backing of your fleet headquarters as well as ground forces headquarters. We could use your support as well. But we don't need it."

She stood up, waved a farewell, and walked off through the groups of sailors who opened a path through them for the senator.

Geary tried to keep his feelings from showing as he stood up. *So, whatever actions Senator Costa is pushing aren't being done behind the backs of fleet headquarters and ground forces headquarters. My own superiors are backing the construction of a secret fleet and support placing Admiral Bloch in command of that fleet even though Bloch planned to stage a military coup before he nearly destroyed the Alliance fleet and was captured by the Syndics.*

Ancestors help us all.

SIX

"**IS** there a reason you've been routing these lawsuit notifications to me?" Rione asked, both looking and sounding annoyed.

Geary rubbed his eyes before looking back at his stateroom comm panel and answering her. "What lawsuit notifications?"

"At last count, one thousand, three hundred and twelve."

"Lawsuits? From who? About what?"

"Let's see." Rione pretended to study a screen in her own stateroom. "Third and fourth cousins of some of the criminals who died on Europa alleging wrongful death, property-damage claims, violation of ecological regulations—"

"Ecological regulations?"

"We left litter on Europa," she explained. "Um . . . violation of medical quarantine, those brought on behalf of the entire population of Sol Star System, unlawful confiscation of personal weapons, violation of castle doctrine—"

"What?"

"It's some law about being able to defend your home. Assorted law-

yers are claiming that the stealth craft was the home in question and
la-di-da." Rione gave him a flat look. "It appears that a substantial fraction of the population of Sol Star System are lawyers, and it appears
that many of them see the Alliance as a cash cow for lawsuits over our
actions to recover our two officers and a few other events. You haven't
been forwarding these to me?"

"No," Geary said. "I hadn't seen them." Which told him exactly
who had been forwarding those messages to Rione. Tanya must have
gotten quite a kick out of doing that. "But I guess you or the senators
are the most appropriate recipients."

"Given the lack of an Alliance embassy or interests section in this
star system, I suppose we are."

"What are you going to do with them?"

She pondered the question. "I'll need to get agreement from our
three senators on this—"

"Hell."

Rione smiled. "It shouldn't be that hard in this case. I think all
three will agree that sovereign immunity doctrine applies, and therefore I should simply forward all of these notifications back to Sol Star
System authorities to deal with. In a few centuries or so, the bureaucracy here will have finished deciding how to handle them, then everyone's descendants can worry about it."

"That sounds like a good solution," Geary said. "What with the
attempts against us, the kidnapping of our lieutenants, and now these
lawsuits, I'm beginning to understand why the Alliance doesn't send
official representatives to Sol very often."

She nodded. "Sol Star System is heavily infested with lawyers. If
that's not grounds for a quarantine, what is?"

"Have you heard anything more from any of your friends in this
star system?"

"All that I have heard so far is that whatever outcomes occur as a
result of our visit and our actions will take a long time to shake out. We

don't fall into the routine or established narrative here, so most of the population has no knee-jerk reaction to fall back on. They will debate and discuss for a long time rather than rush to judgment."

"Except for the lawyers," Geary pointed out.

"Well, naturally. That's about money. I understand that you received a message from Sol as well."

Of course, Rione would have known that. "Nothing for you to worry about. I asked a question before we left the first spot we visited on Old Earth, and the answer was sent to me."

"The abandoned town?" Rione asked. "In Kansas? What did you ask about it?"

"One of our escorts said the area was finally recovering from all the blows it had received at the hands of man and nature, and the town might live again. I asked her later if that was true, if there were any plans to rebuild there."

"Why did you care? We've seen entire star systems that have been abandoned by humans, perhaps forever."

"I don't know why it mattered to me," Geary admitted. "But I suddenly felt the need to know the answer, and, as I eventually learned, it was yes. Some people have already begun plans to move back there and reconstruct the old town. They're descendants of those who once lived there, and they want to honor their ancestors by making that town live again now that crops will once again grow there."

"It was in pretty bad shape," Rione observed.

"They'll rebuild. They're planning on reconstructing the old courthouse by hand, just like their ancestors did."

"Interesting symbology," Rione murmured. "Literally rebuilding the past. Refusing to accept a negative outcome and forging a new one. It's a pity we couldn't rebuild Europa."

"Why did you bring up Europa?" It was only after speaking that he realized how harsh his voice had sounded, how tension had filled his brain with an angry red haze that refused to focus on any particular image.

She looked at him, her expression displaying a hint of sadness. "While that operation was taking place on the surface of Europa, most of the people on the bridge of this ship were watching what the Marines were doing. I was watching you."

"And?" He still sounded angry, still felt that hot tension inside, but he wasn't sure why.

"A year ago, I don't think you could have done it. Everything we did on Europa was necessary. And most of it was also distasteful at best and terrible at the worst."

He looked down, avoiding her eyes, focusing on his hands, which had clenched into fists. "We didn't have any choice." As he said the words, Geary knew they were defensive, as if he was trying to convince her rather than stating a truth.

"I know that. But I believe that a year ago, you still couldn't have forced yourself to give those orders, to allow those actions. You have learned to deal with things you would have once found too horrible to contemplate."

Geary took a deep breath, his eyes still locked on his impotent fists. Was that what made him angry? Or afraid? "Just like you. And Tanya. And everyone else alive today."

"Not just like us." He had expected some return anger from her, but just heard the same sadness. He looked up again, watching Rione closely as she kept speaking. "You haven't learned to live with it. Oh, we take our meds and other treatments to keep going, but we accept that as part of life. The actions and the treatments are *necessary*. To you, the actions are still *wrong* even while you recognize the necessity at times. That's why I watched you, Admiral, instead of watching the Marines. I wanted to see if what the Marines had to do still hit you hard. And it did."

"That was important to you?" Geary asked.

"Yes. I needed to know that, if you had been in the place of that Marine, you could not have pulled the trigger to kill that hostage-taker.

The Marine could do it, I could have done it, anyone else on this ship probably could have done it. But not you. And that is very important, Admiral. You are still closer to our ancestors than you are to us. Don't let that torture you. Embrace it. I didn't understand it at all when I first met you, but now I think it is very important, though I'm not certain what its eventual impact will be. When is the last time you talked to Senator Suva?" she asked in an abrupt change of topic.

"Probably at the meeting where they voted to approve the rescue operation on Europa," Geary said. He didn't call her on the sudden shift in the conversation, glad to be leaving Europa behind in any way that he could.

"She knows you talked to Costa and that you talked to Sakai. You should seek her out."

"Am I supposed to talk to her about anything in particular?" Geary asked.

Rione shrugged. "How much you look forward to continuing to serve the Alliance, how much fun we had at Sol, whatever. Just speaking to Suva will reassure her that you aren't plotting with Costa and Sakai behind her back, and maybe she will spill a little more information like Costa did to you."

SENATOR Suva was in her stateroom. She invited Geary inside politely enough but stayed seated and didn't offer him a seat. "Yes, Admiral?"

"I wanted to ask if you were all right," Geary said. "You haven't been out among the crew since we left Europa."

"You keep track of my movements, Admiral?" Suva's voice stayed low, but an edge of steel crept into it.

"Rarely," Geary said. "But it's my job to be aware of your general activities as well as your health. You've made a habit of walking through the ship once a day to talk to members of the crew. But you haven't done that since Europa."

"How nice of you to be concerned." Suva looked away, her eyes hooded. "With all that we ask of the men and women in the Alliance military, it's a small thing for me to meet some of them and ask how they are, how their families are doing, whether they need anything."

"You may think it's a small thing," Geary said, "but it has impressed some of them. They believe that Alliance politicians are all alike, and that those politicians don't care about the fates of men and women like them. It doesn't hurt at all for them to learn that politicians, like other people, can't be categorized so simply. But the crew has noticed that you stopped doing your meet and greets since Europa."

As the silence lengthened, he wondered if Senator Suva was going to reply. She looked down, twisting a small loop of wooden beads between her fingers. Geary recognized it as similar to the souvenirs many of *Dauntless*'s crew members had picked up on Old Earth.

Finally, she grimaced, her gaze still fixed away from him. "I have never . . . had the . . . opportunity . . . to watch our military carry out such an . . . operation."

He wasn't surprised at her reason. "What happened on Europa was ugly. No one was comfortable with what we had to do. And I gave the orders to carry out that operation."

Her gaze shifted to him, appraising, worried. "The point is, Admiral, they obeyed those orders. They were willing to obey those orders."

"If there had been any alternative—"

"I have been trying to understand them," Suva finally said. "Perhaps I'm afraid I will understand them and not like it. Because of what they are willing do."

"You think they like war?" Geary asked. "You think they like what happened on Europa?"

"I mean exactly that. I can't imagine . . . how? I couldn't do it. I could not."

"That's why we're lucky we have people who can do those jobs," Geary said. "I don't know if I could shoot someone. I've never actually done that." Suva looked sharply at him, skeptical now. "If I had been in more of the war, involved in a boarding action, it could have happened. But it never did, so I've never pointed a weapon at one specific other human being and pulled the trigger. But if you think it's somehow easy on those who have done it, you're wrong. The Marines we sent down to Europa were badly rattled by it. They are combatants, not executioners. If the Alliance made a ribbon for that operation, I don't think any of the Marines would wear it."

"I could not have done it at all," Suva said. "I will get out and once more talk with the crew, but there are some things I find it very hard to empathize with."

"You voted to conduct that operation," Geary pointed out.

"I was not fully informed of what that involved," Suva replied.

Were those the exact words that Rione had used to describe one of the excuses that Costa or Suva would adopt? He tried not to let anger appear on his face or in his voice. "If you were aware of any alternatives," he said once more, "I wish you had mentioned them."

"It's your job to produce alternatives for military actions, Admiral. You gave us one choice."

"I gave you two choices. Do what we did, or leave our officers on Europa along with a threat that might cause the infection to be spread elsewhere in Sol Star System. If there had been a third or a fourth choice, I would have offered them." He paused to ensure his next words were the right ones. "I made a recommendation in favor of an action I believed to be in the best interests of our two kidnapped officers, in the best interests of the Alliance, and in the best interests of everyone in Sol Star System."

She did not answer for several seconds, then spoke defiantly. "Narrow definitions of what is best can lead us into actions that are not really in anyone's best interest. I believe in acting in the best interests of humanity. All humanity. I'm not ashamed to say that I love humanity. As a species, we have enormous potential, unlimited horizons, and an immense ability to care for others. I like that, and I intend working for that even if I am the only one willing to do so."

Geary ran one hand through his hair as he looked at her, feeling frustration replace his earlier anger. "Why do you think I don't feel the same way?"

"I think that you're too powerful and too willing to use the force at your disposal. In that, you are no different from S—" She bit off her next words.

He could guess what they would have been, though. *Senator Costa.* Or maybe even *Syndics.* The thought of being compared to a Syndic CEO made it harder to control his voice. "This may be difficult for you to believe, but I have exercised a great deal of restraint in the use of force. I am very careful as to how and when I employ what power I have, and only use it when I must."

"Is that a threat?"

"What?" Just as with Costa, an innocuous statement had been read as a personal threat. *I know that I want senators like Suva and Costa to understand my crew better, but I'm having a hard time understanding the senators. They look for hidden meanings in the most straightforward statements.*

Well, damn, of course they do. That's the sort of battlefield they fight on, the sort of tactics they use. They're engaging me as if I were one of them. Is that a compliment or an insult? The last thought cooled his temper and any desire to escalate the verbal sparring. Instead, Geary spoke as openly and bluntly as he could. "It was the exact opposite of a threat. I will not threaten the government of the Alliance."

"I cannot afford to trust you on that, Admiral," Suva said.

"Then why not trust Senator Sakai?"

"Because Sakai is burned out. He no longer cares."

"What about Senator Navarro?"

"A hypocrite."

"Senator Unruh?"

"Arrogant."

Geary could not help smiling ironically. "For someone who loves humanity, you don't seem to like very many people."

Senator Suva's eyes narrowed as she gazed at him. "Perhaps I have been too candid with you."

"Not at all. I agree with Dr. Nasr. There are too many secrets, too many things declared secret, or kept secret not because of real need but out of habit." Geary paused, wondering if he should say what had just jumped into his mind. But it felt like the right thing to say now, and perhaps Suva was the right person to say it to. "And then there are the things kept secret because no one wants to admit to them."

Suva's gaze was challenging now. "Such as?"

"The kind of biological warfare program that once wiped out human life on Europa."

Whatever she had been expecting, it wasn't that. And unless Suva was a brilliant actress, his words had shocked her. "The Syndics did that?"

"I don't know whether the Syndics had such a program or not."

"Then who—?" Suva took in a long breath. "Are you implying that the Alliance had such a program?"

"I'm saying that it did. I know that it did. The program was supposedly shut down sometime before I was recovered, but I don't know that for certain. I'm not supposed to know what I do know of it."

Suva's voice quavered with tension. "I . . . I find this very hard to believe. Why should I believe you?"

"Why should I lie about something like that?" Geary asked. "You must have heard something about what Victoria Rione's husband was suffering from."

"I heard some information," Senator Suva confirmed, her voice steadying. "Some of it very prejudicial to Rione."

Why am I not surprised? "I can tell you with absolute certainty that she had nothing to do with what happened to her husband. That was entirely the work of the Alliance government, or portions of it, under the veils of secrecy."

"If it was the sort of project you claim, they would certainly have kept it very secret! They've kept it secret from me!" Suva was angry now. "Are you saying the military had nothing to do with it?"

"The military did have some involvement. I don't know how much. I don't know if they were running the show or just providing support."

His frank admission that there had been some military aspect to the program appeared to once again surprise Suva. "Assume it is true. Why has no one else spoken up?"

"I can't speak for everyone else, but I know why Rione's husband didn't. He was mind-blocked."

"That's why—?" Suva was seething now. "I don't like being lied to, Admiral."

"I have never—"

"You're not among those I am thinking of. Why are you telling me about this?"

"Because it scares the hell out of me," Geary said. "I'd like to be more certain it was completely shut down. You're keeping secrets from me. What secrets are being kept from you? And how dangerous to the Alliance are those secrets?"

Suva sat back, covering her eyes with one hand, what could be seen of her face suddenly haggard with worry. "I'm not proud of every decision I have made, Admiral, and if I had my wish, no man or woman would ever again have to die in defense of their homes and families. I have to make imperfect decisions based on imperfect information."

"I understand that. I often have to do the same, knowing that a bad decision on my part could have catastrophic consequences."

She lowered her hand, gazing intently at him. "Perhaps we understand each other better than I thought. I will look into this matter, Admiral. But do not assume that means I have become one of your followers. The welfare of the many has to outweigh individual concerns about what has to be done to save the Alliance."

Once again, it reminded him of a recent conversation. "Senator Costa said something very similar to me not long ago," Geary said.

"I am nothing like her," Suva said, her face flushing. "I will look into this information of yours. But I have difficulty fully trusting the source. I have to worry about many things, Admiral. I have to worry about people who will follow your orders to do things I could not do. I have to worry about your deciding there is no alternative to issuing certain orders."

"No one could seize control of the Alliance by force and hold it," Geary said.

She stared at him, her face rigid. "Some people, *one* person, is so revered by the populace that he would not need to use force. All he would have to do is give orders . . . and they would be obeyed."

"*I* will not give such orders," Geary said with more force than he had intended.

"Can I afford to believe that? Is that all, Admiral?"

"Yes, Senator." Geary left the stateroom, wondering what questions Suva would pose to her colleagues after *Dauntless* got home, and whether Suva would reconsider the wisdom of the secrets she was keeping. But at least Suva had laid out some of the reasoning by which she might have justified voting for actions that seemed otherwise inexplicable.

ABOUT half an hour until *Dauntless* reached the hypernet gate. Geary was almost to the bridge when the battle cruiser shuddered like a living creature that had felt a tremor run through its body.

He sped up, reaching the bridge a few seconds quicker, and slid into his seat next to Tanya Desjani's. "What happened?"

Her answer wasn't to him, but to the commander visible in a virtual comm window next to the captain's seat. "See if you can identify the original source. Let me know if anything else comes in."

Sighing, she leaned back, then turned a glare on Geary. "Another system virus, courtesy of the good folk in Sol Star System."

"That seemed like an effective one," Geary said.

"It was. The vast majority of the worms, Trojan horses, viruses, vamps, 'bots, zaps, and assorted other malware that have been thrown at us while we're here has bounced off like an ion hitting a magnetic field. The local hackers don't know enough about our systems to make their stuff stick." Desjani waved one hand around. "But this last one was tough. My top code monkey says it's an import. He recognized portions of it as resembling offensive malware employed in Alliance space."

"Maybe another present from someone back home trying to mess with us." Geary looked around. "But we're all right now?"

"Oh, yeah. No problem. Since it was cobbled together from known malware, our system security spotted the thing and shut it down immediately. What you felt was some of our systems having to reset after being swept." She gave him a lopsided smile. "The source was a message, allegedly from a young lady on Old Earth to one of our sailors, with 'special pictures' attached."

"Ancestors help us," Geary said. "The sailor opened them?"

"He's a sailor. Of course he opened them." Desjani pointed toward the hypernet gate. "I cannot wait to get out of this star system. Sol Star System isn't some special place of wisdom and peace. It's the snake pit where humanity has had the longest to work on our worst impulses. We're lucky that Castries and Yuon were the only two members of the crew actually kidnapped. I don't mind too much that no one here thanked us for getting rid of those Shield of Sol clowns. And it doesn't matter to me that no one here seems to care that we risked our Marines to save our own people and prevent any contamination from leaving Europa. It doesn't even bother me much that Lieutenant Cole on the

Shadow keeps sending us frequent status reports to let us know that he's watching us for any signs that we're breaking any more of the endless rules in this star system."

The small Sol Space Guard cutter had doggedly followed *Dauntless* toward the gate, like a small terrier trailing the dire wolf of the battle cruiser. "What does bother you?" Geary asked.

"That they keep trying to mess with us!" She glared at her display. "Should we ask for formal permission to depart from traffic control or just head out when we reach the gate?"

"Technically, we're supposed to ask for permission. And we wouldn't want to upset the Sol Space Guard."

"Ancestors, no," Tanya agreed. "Not with the indefatigable Lieutenant Cole on our tails. I'm not sure I'm joking about that, by the way."

"My instincts tell me we'd be better off not crossing him, too. But I'm also tired of being here. We'll send a formal notification of our departure to Sol Star System authorities, then head out without waiting for a reply."

"You've got fifteen minutes until we reach the hypernet gate," Desjani advised cheerfully. "I hear you've been talking to politicians."

"I often talk to some politicians," Geary reminded her.

"I mean in addition to that woman and retired General Charban."

"Yes." He made sure the security fields were activated around his and Desjani's seats before saying more. "One is willing to make every required sacrifice to save the Alliance, as long as someone else actually makes those sacrifices. Another loves humanity but doesn't seem to trust or like many humans."

"I can guess which two those are," she replied dryly. "How about our new pal?"

"Who do you mean?"

"Senator Sakai." Desjani gave Geary a questioning look. "I'm wondering if he's sincere, but he's been a lot more . . . open, lately."

"Open?"

"You know. Talking to members of the crew. Showing more obvious interest in things instead of just watching with that poker face he used to have all the time."

"I've seen some of that," Geary said. "I wondered if Sakai was doing it around others."

"He is." She watched the hypernet gate, which was growing visibly larger now as they approached it. "I noticed he started changing after watching the Dancers on Earth."

"After they returned the body, you mean? The impact of that seems to have worn off for Suva and Costa, but if it has stuck with Sakai, it could gain us a strong supporter." He paused, thinking. "Though I wonder if the event has worn off for the other two, or whether they are trying to pretend it didn't affect them. Maybe in the long term, it will still make a difference."

"And in the short term?"

"In the short term," Geary announced, "I must inform various important people of our impending departure." He touched one control. "Senators, we will be entering the hypernet gate in about ten minutes." Another control. "General Charban, the Dancers are sticking close to us but please ensure they know we're going to enter the gate in about ten minutes so they don't suddenly take off before then." A third touch. "To Lieutenant Cole on the cutter *Shadow*, be advised that you are within the radius of the hypernet field we will employ for *Dauntless* and the six Dancer ships. We appreciate your escort to this point, but unless you intend accompanying us back to Alliance space, I recommend that you quickly open the distance between your ship and ours by at least five hundred kilometers." A final tap. "To Sol Star System authorities, this is Admiral Geary aboard the Alliance battle cruiser *Dauntless*. We will be departing Sol Star System via the hypernet gate in nine minutes. Thank you for your cooperation, assistance, and the warm welcome given us. Farewell. To the honor of our ancestors, Geary, out."

Desjani raised one eyebrow at him. "Warm welcome?"

"A lot of people on Old Earth were nice to us."

"And a number of other people in this star system shot at us. I guess that also qualifies as a 'warm welcome.'" She nodded toward her display. "It appears that Lieutenant Cole isn't coming along after all."

Geary took a look at his display, seeing that *Shadow* had pivoted and was rapidly moving away from *Dauntless*, heading back into the star system, back toward Sol and the battered Home of humanity.

Tanya paused, perplexed. "You know, I've gotten so used to Lieutenant Cole's status reports that I might actually miss them."

"You're joking."

"No. Seriously. For the next few days I'm going to be wondering off and on what Lieutenant Cole and his cutter are doing right now, what Lieutenant Cole is thinking right now, what Lieutenant Cole had for dinner . . ."

He grinned. "From what I understand, when one ship is in a hypernet and the other is in normal space in a distant star system, the concept of right now is ambiguous at best."

Desjani looked thoughtful. "One of my friends went into high-end theoretical physics. She told me a few years ago that one of the ongoing debates was whether humanity carried our own sense of time with us to other stars, that the presence of humans in the different star systems was what produced a unified sense of time among them despite the span of light-years between them. Don't look at me like that. It's actually a profound question that we don't know the answer to."

"We don't know what time is?" Geary asked.

"Not really. Some ancient scientist said that *time is what prevents everything from happening at once.* My friend told me that, too, and said the quote still pretty much summarized everything that we know about time. I never forgot that quote because it reminds me of how little we know even today about the most fundamental things."

He gazed at his display, looking past the depiction of Sol Star System to the galaxy and the universe looming beyond. "There's so much we want to learn. So much we need to learn. Why do we as a species spend so much time trying to destroy ourselves when we could be spending it trying to understand ourselves and the universe we live in?"

Tanya shook her head. "Maybe they're related. Maybe whatever drives us to want to learn also drives us to compete in ways that can destroy us."

"The Dancers may give us some insight into that," Geary suggested.

"Yeah. If we can ever figure them out. Understanding the Dancers may be harder than understanding time."

Her hand went to the hypernet controls. "Destination set as Varandal. The Dancers are within the radius set for our hypernet field. Request permission to head for home, Admiral."

"Permission granted."

The stars and everything else outside the ship vanished. Unlike jump space, with its gray monotony and strange flashes of light, when traveling by hypernet there was literally nothing outside the bubble containing *Dauntless* and the six Dancer ships. And, literally, *Dauntless* and the other six ships weren't moving. But in sixteen days, they would pop out of the hypernet gate at Varandal, hundreds of light-years away, thanks to the mysterious and still-dimly-understood quantum connections between the gates.

Geary could sense the tension on the bridge relaxing and feel the same sensation inside himself. "Do you ever find it odd," he asked Tanya, "that we're more comfortable right now?"

"Why wouldn't we be?" she asked, stretching like someone coming off a long and grueling task. "No one, and nothing, can touch a ship once inside the hypernet."

"Yeah, but, according to what Jaylen Cresida told me, that's because while we're in the hypernet we don't actually exist except as some sort of probability wave."

She made a face at him. "That's just how the rest of the universe sees it. From our frame of reference, we exist, and I'm not going to let you ruin a chance to unwind by overthinking things." Desjani turned to face the bridge watch team. "Keep an eye on things. Pass the word for half-watch shift holiday routine for the rest of the day."

"You are in a good mood," Geary muttered as they left the bridge.

"I can start ordering floggings again tomorrow. For now, I'm going to talk to my ancestors for a little while, *our* ancestors that is, to give them some thanks for the safe recovery of my two lieutenants, which it wouldn't hurt you to do, either, before I try to catch up on some paperwork."

"I'm going to look in on sick bay, first," Geary said. "I want to see how Castries and Yuon are doing."

"Not all that well," Desjani said with a grimace. "But you'll see."

It wasn't one of the blocks of time set aside for routine sick call by crew members concerned about nonemergency medical issues, and there weren't any medical emergencies at the moment, so when Geary reached sick bay, he found Dr. Nasr sitting at a desk deep in study. Nasr only gradually became aware of Geary's presence, blinking at him like a man coming up from deep sleep. "Is anything wrong, Admiral?"

"Nothing beyond the usual at the moment." Geary always felt uncomfortable in sick bay. He had been brought to *Dauntless*'s medical spaces after being recovered from the damaged escape pod in which he had drifted, frozen in survival sleep, for a century. From here, he couldn't see the bunk in which he had awakened, disoriented and dazed, to learn that everyone he had once known was long dead, and that while he was supposedly dead he had been turned into the myth of Black Jack. Even his first sight of Tanya, an officer inexplicably wearing the Alliance Fleet Cross which no one had earned for almost a generation in Geary's time, was bound up in the shock of those moments.

He suppressed his uneasiness, trying to look unruffled as he gestured toward the bulkhead behind which Lieutenants Castries and Yuon were confined in medical quarantine. "How are the patients?"

"You can view them remotely," Nasr advised Geary as he brought up a virtual window.

Geary peered into the window floating before him, seeing Yuon and Castries in the small compartment. They were sitting with their backs to each other, as far apart as the tiny space permitted (which was barely beyond touching distance), pieces of the Marine battle armor they had been cut out of piled between them like a wall. Far from betraying romantic involvement, Yuon and Castries were acting like a brother and a sister who could barely tolerate each other's existence. "How much longer do they have to stay in there together?"

"Two weeks, four days more," Nasr said. "I am certain that Lieutenant Castries could provide you with the exact hours and minutes remaining as well if you asked it of her."

"Lieutenant Yuon doesn't seem too happy, either."

"The feelings do appear to be mutual," Dr. Nasr agreed.

"No signs of infection yet?"

"None. You will be informed immediately if there are any signs."

Geary watched small medical devices crawl up the right arms of Yuon and Castries, both of whom studiously pretended not to notice. "How often are you drawing fluids?"

"Every four hours." Nasr eyed the images with concern. "They are . . . unhappy with their circumstances. They have, I believe, gone through denial, anger, and bargaining. They are now in depression. I am not sure they will ever reach acceptance."

It might have been funny except for the obvious misery of the two lieutenants, who had one moment been walking along a street on Old Earth, and the next found themselves awakening together in the tightest form of medical quarantine current technology could achieve. "Are they being medicated?"

"Yes. Minimum necessary doses." Nasr squinted at the two figures again. "I will have to increase it. I do not know what else I can do to ease their mutual distress."

"I know how they feel, I think," Geary said. "From what I've seen of Castries and Yuon, they get along all right normally, but these are not normal circumstances. On my first ship, there was another junior officer and I who did not get along at all. The only thing that made it tolerable was that we occupied different watch sections. When I was awake and working, he was usually asleep, and vice versa. We rarely had to actually interact. If we had, we probably would have been like those two are now."

The doctor frowned, then smiled. "We should speak more often, Admiral. That is an excellent solution."

"It is?" Geary asked, flattered by Nasr's praise but also uncertain what solution he had apparently just provided.

"Yes." The doctor was already at work, entering commands on the unit he held in one hand. "I will shift the sleep cycle of one of them and keep the other awake, using the proper dosages of medications. Within a few days, I will have their patterns firmly established, so that when one is awake, the other is asleep. While they will continue to physically share the compartment, they will not have to endure the conscious presence of the other but can even feel some degree of privacy with their forced company rendered insensible."

"Will that be safe?" Geary asked. "Doping them for the next few weeks like that?"

"Perfectly safe," Nasr said, waving his hands in a dismissive way. "And much, much safer than keeping them both awake and aware of each other for that period! I am grateful to you, Admiral. I made the elementary mistake of assuming I knew what the question must be, which made me see the wrong paths to the answer."

Geary looked at Dr. Nasr, running the physician's words through his mind. "We need to be sure we're asking the right question in order to get the right answer? Is that what you're saying?"

"Yes. If you only think you know the question, the answers you come up with will not be adequate or correct."

Geary left sick bay, deep in thought, barely aware of greeting the sailors he passed as he walked. What the doctor had told him was important. Very important. Something told him that.

Unfortunately, whatever that something was could not tell him *why* the words were important.

AMONG the many things he had once never considered worrying about was what he might find when arriving at an Alliance star system. It would have been like being concerned every time he got home for the night and opened the door, wondering what might be inside. Certainly there was the chance of a surprise, but not the sort of surprise that might threaten not only him but also all he cared about.

But that, and many other things, had changed in the last century.

He was on the bridge again, which felt fairly crowded with all of the official representatives present. The three senators were at the back, pretending not to fight over precedence for the observer's seat and its display. General Charban and Victoria Rione, the two envoys, stood to one side, pretending to be engaged in a casual conversation, having formed an unlikely alliance of their own against the covert pressures being brought against each of them.

Desjani was doing her best to ignore all of the representatives, pretending to be totally absorbed in preparing her ship for arrival at Varandal.

That left Geary to offer respectful greetings in a manner he hoped would not be interpreted as pretend, and to notice a certain level of tension among the three senators. They seemed to be just as worried about what they might find at Varandal as Geary was.

There wasn't any transition jolt confusing the mind such as occurred when coming out of jump. Instead, the stars appeared around them as *Dauntless* arrived at Varandal, the only immediate and obvious indication that they had left the bubble of nothing inside the hypernet and were surrounded by the real universe again. Geary dropped his study of the three senators and scanned his display, waiting as impatiently for it to update as he would when showing up at an enemy star system.

"*Dreadnaught* is gone," Tanya said just as he also caught that. "So are *Dependable* and *Conqueror.*"

"There are some heavy cruisers and destroyers missing, too," he said.

"Looks like two divisions of heavy cruisers and four squadrons of destroyers." Desjani shook her head. "A task force of some kind."

"Why would Jane leave Varandal when I left her in temporary command of the fleet?" Geary demanded, keeping his voice low.

"If you're thinking she just hared off on her own initiative, I don't think that happened," she cautioned. "This looks like an ordered movement to me."

"Those three battleships weren't in very good shape. They needed a lot of repair work. Why would anyone order them—"

Senator Costa's voice broke into their discussion. "Some ships are missing! Why? Where did they go?"

Geary took a moment to ensure that when he turned to answer, his irritation at both the question and the suspicious tone in which it had been voiced wasn't showing. "I will let you know as soon as I know, Senator."

"You're asking us to believe that major components of this fleet have gone somewhere without your orders?" Costa asked.

Rione answered before he could. "Why is that so remarkable? Fleet headquarters, or the government, could have sent the entire fleet on some task while we were gone. Were you expecting something different here?"

That question, though posed in a diffident and mild tone, made Costa flush slightly. "What are you implying?"

"Nothing! Is anyone implying anything?" Rione could sound amazingly innocent when she wanted to.

Costa's flush changed into a glower. "I will go collect some updates on the situation here. I am certain there will be messages waiting for me," she announced, pivoting to march off the bridge.

Suva had said nothing, scanning the situation with wary eyes.

Senator Sakai, though, walked up to Geary's seat. "Admiral, I would be grateful for your honest appraisal of what we are seeing here."

"It's still hard to tell much." Geary hedged, trying to decide how much to trust Sakai. After all, Sakai must have voted in favor of a number of actions that struck Geary as misguided at best. *But if he is trying to help, if what we saw on Old Earth has made Sakai rethink things, then I would be a fool to keep him at arm's length.*

"But I am concerned," Geary continued. "The battleship that is commanded by the acting fleet commander is gone, along with the rest of her division. She wouldn't have left unless ordered to go, but none of those battleships was in good enough condition to conduct a combat mission after they were badly damaged fighting the Kicks and the enigmas."

"I will see what I can learn," Sakai told Geary, then left.

Geary beckoned to Rione, who came close enough to be inside the privacy field he activated around his seat. "Do you think that Costa or the other two senators were expecting anything to be happening here?"

"I don't know," Rione said. "Costa sounded as if she was worried as well as suspicious, so if she was expecting something, it is not what we see. Suva has a deer-in-the-headlights look. I would guess that she has no idea what is going on and therefore is worried about what you, and Costa, and everyone else, is up to. But Sakai is sincere. I will stake my reputation on that."

"Your reputation?" The words slipped out before Geary could stop them. He waited, expecting Rione to flare with cold fury.

Instead, she laughed. "You're right. My reputation is something I would want to lose."

"Not with me," he insisted.

"I did lose it with you," Rione said with self-mockery, a rare open (if oblique) mention of their brief liaison before they had learned that her husband had not died fighting the Syndics but was still alive as a prisoner. "I'll see what I can find out," she added, parroting Sakai, then left the bridge.

Desjani was still studying her display. "Admiral," she said in low tones, "I don't entirely trust what we're seeing."

He focused intensely on his display, seeing the many warships, each accompanied by status markers. The fleet looked like it had accomplished a lot of repair work while they had been gone.

A whole lot of repair work. An impossible amount of repair work. "Everything looks really good," he commented back to her in a skeptical voice.

"That's what I was thinking. The status feeds, the *official* status feeds, look like they've been heavily gun-decked. But this can't be the work of a few officers falsifying the status of their ships to make them look good. Everybody must be doing it." She gave him a frustrated look. "Let's hope whoever has been in charge since Jane Geary left can explain what's going on."

"It's probably Duellos," Geary guessed, though he wondered if that was only because he hoped that was the case.

"Captain Duellos would be the wisest and best choice," Desjani agreed in a way that made it clear that the last thing she expected from fleet headquarters was choices that were either wise or good. "The comm traffic we're seeing is all routine, for what that is worth."

"If not Duellos, maybe Tulev," Geary suggested.

"If they went by seniority, it would be Badaya." Tanya eyed him. "I admit that I've been wondering how much of his conversion to the wisdom of letting the government stay in control is real. He used to be very enthusiastic about the prospect of a military coup."

"I've convinced him otherwise," Geary said with more certainty than he felt. "If Badaya had done something, we would be hearing all about it in the messages and news feeds we're receiving."

"Except that the status reports for the warships in the fleet look faked," she reminded him. "How do we know the rest of this stuff hasn't been scrubbed and sanitized to present an image of normalcy?"

"I don't think 'normalcy' is a word," he grumbled.

"Yes, it is."

Instead of continuing the debate, Geary called up one of the news feeds which *Dauntless* could now receive. Even after so much time in space, he still half expected the news to be immediately filled with excited reports of *Dauntless*'s return to Varandal. But it would be hours before the light from *Dauntless*'s arrival got to the inner star system, and hours more before the reactions to that in the news would be seen by the battle cruiser. Instead, the news seemed to be the same mix of political turmoil and dissent, economic worries, concerns about what was happening in those Syndic star systems nearest to Alliance territory, and speculations about the future of the Alliance. A "special report" on the two new alien species whose existence had been discovered by Geary's fleet in the regions beyond Syndicate Worlds space contained a great deal more speculation and some information he recognized as coming from his own reports to the government. Word that *Dauntless* had escorted the six Dancer ships to Sol Star System had clearly spread far and wide, with various "experts" who had never actually encountered the Dancers or any other alien species holding forth on the perceived wisdom and significance of that mission.

At best, it was entertaining. But the plethora of message traffic and video feeds they could receive was more than anything else exasperating because none of them addressed the fact that Captain Jane Geary and her battleships had left Varandal or revealed who had been in charge of the fleet since her departure. All Geary and the others aboard *Dauntless* could do was wait the more than three hours it took for a welcoming message to be sent and finally reach them.

Humanity might still be trying to figure out what time was, but there was no doubt in Geary's mind that time deliberately ran slower at times like this. The three hours felt like an entire day of waiting. He was nonetheless startled when a high-priority message was received within seconds of the earliest possible time they could have expected one.

"Badaya?" Desjani murmured as that officer's image appeared.

The message-origin identification on the transmission left no doubt that Captain Badaya, once the loosest cannon among those in the fleet who proposed a military coup to replace an Alliance government seen as corrupt and incompetent, was acting commander of the fleet.

As if anticipating the reaction to seeing him, Badaya grinned wolfishly.

SEVEN

BADAYA smiled wider. "Welcome back, Admiral. I am in command of the fleet."

He paused, while Geary glowered at his image and Desjani muttered some curses involving a quick trip to the afterlife and abundant torture therein for Badaya.

"Or, I *was* in command," Badaya continued. He seemed to be enjoying himself immensely. "I will now, of course, return command of the First Fleet to you. My report of significant activity while serving as acting commander of the fleet will be very brief because not much of significance happened. I am looking forward to seeing you in person, of course.

"Just to clarify things, I was *ordered* to act as fleet commander until your return. *Ordered* by fleet headquarters, in the same set of orders that tasked Captain Jane Geary to take her battleship division and some supporting forces to recover some Alliance prisoners of war from former Syndicate territory. Captain Geary followed her orders, as did I."

Badaya smiled again, and Geary finally understood the reason for his delight. "They expected him to run amuck," he said to Desjani. "He knew that, and he didn't do it. He's happy because he screwed up the plans of whoever decided to send Jane off and specified Badaya to be acting fleet commander."

"Why is it that people I don't like keep doing the right things?" Desjani complained.

"I am now once again subject to your orders, Admiral," Badaya finished with obvious satisfaction. "The fleet has followed all orders, just as you ordered. Our honor remains unstained. To the honor of our ancestors, Badaya, out."

Geary sat silently for a few moments after the message ended, then looked over at Tanya. "What do you think?"

"I think," she said, "that Captain Badaya knew exactly what we would be worried about, me especially, and took considerable pleasure in letting me and those senators, who you notice are listed as cc recipients on that message, know that he has done exactly as ordered and has done nothing treasonous, dishonorable, criminal, treacherous, seditious, corrupt, insubordinate, subversive, or stupid."

"No loose cannons here," Geary said. "He wasn't exactly subtle about the everyone following their orders thing."

"Badaya?" she asked. "Badaya's idea of subtle is a supernova."

Geary shook his head as he stared grimly at his display. "He was smart enough to see that someone wanted him to screw up."

"Why would anyone want to encourage someone to try to overthrow the government?" Desjani asked. "Or just act against the government? I don't get it. Who wins if that happens?"

"Nobody." But as soon as he had said it, he realized that was wrong. Some people might imagine they would win in the short haul. And the Syndics, who had everything to gain by sowing the same kind of chaos in Alliance space as now afflicted many areas of Syndicate Worlds space, might win in the long haul as well. He couldn't believe that any senior officer or politician in the Alliance would collude with known Syndic agents, but those working on behalf of the Syndics who had kept that relationship secret probably were whispering the wrong things into the right ears. If nothing else, those agents would be feeding any fears of what Black Jack might do, and urging actions that would only make sense inside bubbles of secrecy and paranoia.

The war had ended in victory, but the peace might still be lost.

"Admiral?"

Geary had forgotten that General Charban was still on the bridge. He turned to see Charban holding out a data pad. "What is it?"

"A message from the Dancers."

"For me?" The screen displayed a string of symbols along the top, and a line of words beneath them. *Happy. Home. You. Good. Complete.* "They're congratulating us on getting home?"

"Yes," Charban said. "Though we're still uncertain exactly what the Dancers mean by concepts like happy and good. Sometimes their happy seems to mean something more like appropriate or even finishing a task. Good appears to be tied up with their concept of patterns. If what happened fits the pattern they see, it's good. But other times good seems to be referring to some other concepts that we're still trying to work out."

"All right." Geary looked at the message again. "Complete. What does that mean?"

"Something is done," Charban replied. "Their task? Our task? A pattern? It's hard to say."

Tanya shook her head. "The Dancers can't spell it out any more clearly than that?"

"I think they could," Charban said. "I'm certain that they could. But they won't. As I've said, they are keeping communications with us at a very basic level for reasons of their own."

"Have you asked the Dancers why they're doing that?" Geary said.

Charban smiled. "Not being a diplomat by training, I have asked that question. Every time I have done so, the answer has been the same. *Good.*"

"Good?"

"Maybe they're praising you for asking the question," Desjani suggested wryly.

Charban grinned. "It's possible. I'm inclined to think they are telling us that they are acting the way they are for good reasons. All that we have to do is figure out what those reasons are."

It was Geary's turn to shake his head. "General, I can't figure out the reasons why some of our fellow humans are doing what they're doing."

"Yes. We keep looking for the mirrors that will show us important things about ourselves, but instead the images we see raise as many questions as they do answers. Sometimes I think the universe and the living stars are laughing at us, and we won't really understand anything until we get the joke. You know, like that old Catch 42 expression that stands for *the meaning of life is that in the end you always get screwed*."

"Let's hope that's not it," Geary said.

THE next day, a government courier ship reached them and came alongside *Dauntless*. Geary, resplendent in a full-dress uniform, which Tanya had inspected with a critical eye before grudgingly approving of his appearance, went to the shuttle dock for an official farewell to the three senators.

Costa looked as confident as always, Sakai was once more revealing little, but for the first time that Geary could recall, Suva had an uncharacteristic sense of uncertainty to her.

"When will the Dancers proceed to Unity?" Costa asked.

Envoys Charban and Rione were both present as well, and at the senator's question Charban turned a pleading eye on Rione.

"We have asked," Rione said. "The Dancers have not given any clear reply until half an hour ago, when they communicated that they will *not* be going to Unity."

"Why not?" Senator Suva demanded. "Unity is the capital star system of the Alliance. They need to see it. The rest of the Senate and the full Grand Council should meet with them."

"We have told them that," Rione replied. "Their answer today was *Varandal good now.*"

"It seems to me," Costa said, "that we need some new people communicating with the Dancers." Even though she could not hide her amusement at Suva's unhappiness, Costa clearly was not pleased with Rione's news.

Charban smiled apologetically. "The Dancers have to want to communicate with them. They prefer to speak with certain humans."

"We have only your word for that!"

"The academic experts who accompanied the fleet into Dancer territory said the same thing in their reports," Geary said.

"Not all of the experts agreed with what was in those reports."

"Senator," Rione said, "you are welcome to have anyone speak directly to the Dancers and ask any questions they desire. Envoy Charban and I will assist in any way that we can. But I can safely predict that the answers you get will be the same as we have received."

Sakai glanced from Rione, to Charban, to Geary. "Do you have any better guesses as to why the Dancers came to human space? Was it primarily to return the remains to Old Earth? Or was there more involved?"

"I believe," Charban said slowly, his eyes gazing into the distance as he formed the words with care, "that there was a great deal more involved. Things that matter a great deal to the Dancers. I am not confident that all of those things would be recognizable to humans, but I have no doubt the Dancers came here to accomplish something they thought important to us and to them."

Suva studied Charban closely. "You have words from them that talk about such things?"

"No, Senator. No direct statements. Just a growing feeling from my many attempts to communicate with them and understand them."

"I wish whatever you had was more definitive than that," she replied, her voice flat.

"Believe me, Senator," Charban replied with the same polite

deference, "I wish I had something more definitive as well. We know what we have seen them do. That is the only certainty."

Costa looked around with a warning gaze. "Speaking of what the Dancers have done, I am officially notifying everyone here that all activity within Sol Star System has been classified by order of the Grand Council. No one is to speak to the media about it, no videos or other records are to be released, and no one not present at Sol is to be informed of anything that happened there without the prior approval of the Grand Council. You are not even to discuss those matters among yourselves because of the possibility of being overheard by someone not cleared for the information."

"You can't do that!" Charban said with unaccustomed heat, his earlier respectful demeanor vanished.

"Yes, we can," Costa said, nailing him with a glare. "And we have. Do you understand, Admiral?"

"I understand," Geary said, trying not to let his voice tremble with anger. "But I would like to know what possible reason there would be for such an action."

"It is vital to the security of the Alliance," Senator Suva said, "that the activity in Sol Star System be fully analyzed and evaluated by those responsible for the safety and security of us all before raw data is set loose to be misinterpreted and misunderstood." It was hard to tell how much she actually believed what she was saying.

Costa smiled. "Someone who sent Marines down to the surface of Europa and recovered them should not question the wisdom of keeping certain matters under wraps."

"I supported conducting that operation openly and I do not believe it should be kept secret," Geary said, wondering why Rione had not warned him of this beforehand. He stole a glance her way and saw Rione displaying an unusually open amount of surprise.

"I have a voting proxy from Senator Navarro—" Rione began.

"Which ceased to be in effect once we arrived back at Varandal," Suva informed Rione.

Sakai looked straight ahead, his expression as hard and unrevealing as stone.

"Do you understand the Grand Council's orders?" Costa demanded of Rione.

"I understand every word," Rione assured her in a toneless voice.

"Then we are done here." Costa headed for the shuttle, followed by Suva and Sakai.

As the shuttle ramp began closing, Geary nodded toward the craft. "I take it you were as surprised as we were?" he asked Rione.

She nodded but held up a cautionary hand. "We're not supposed to talk about it."

"Costa and Suva clearly supported that decision, but Sakai didn't seem happy."

She smiled enigmatically. "Sakai didn't express any emotion at all. But I suspect that you are right. Without my proxy vote, it would have been two against one when Costa and Suva unexpectedly cooperated."

"What can we do to stop this nonsense?" Charban demanded.

"Legally?" Rione asked in reply. "Nothing. Admiral, please excuse me. I have some personal business to attend to."

"Personal business? I admit I was surprised that you didn't go with them," Geary said.

"There have been lots of surprises, haven't there? I should be able to learn all there is to know about the status of my husband without leaving this fine ship, and I want to stay in communication with the Dancers."

She was leaving something out. He knew she was. But Geary didn't call her on it.

"Admiral—" Charban began once more.

"I will see what I can do," Geary said.

Charban, still upset, left the shuttle dock in Rione's wake.

Desjani waited until the shuttle had departed, then gave Geary a sidelong look. "That woman wasn't angry."

"Rione? No. She pretended to be surprised, but if she had really been blindsided by the news she wouldn't have shown it. Rione knew the senators were going to drop that bomb just before they left. Sakai must have warned her."

"I can read her attitudes enough to know what she's going to do, Admiral. There will be records in the ship's comm system if she does . . . anything. Those records could cause major problems."

"I think I can guarantee there won't be any records," Geary said. "Not from this ship."

"Not from—?" Desjani glanced toward the outside of the hull. "The courier ship?"

"I'd bet on it. If Sakai tipped her off, she had time to set something up. Either an automated routine she slipped past the safety nets on the courier ship's comm system, or one of Rione's agents aboard the courier ship who'll do the same thing."

Tanya laughed. "So, *if* there's any leak, it will come from the ship the senators are on? Explaining that ought to keep them busy for a while. How in the hell do those idiots expect me to keep my crew from talking about anything that happened in Sol Star System?"

"Damned if I know," Geary said. "Dr. Nasr was right. Classification has nothing to do with reality anymore. Some things have to be kept secret, but this? Billions of people in Sol Star System know what we did there, and have records of what we did there. None of this is secret or can be kept secret. But I imagine the government will continue to officially deny everything even after—I mean, even *if*—that information leaks. Somehow leaks, that is. By means I don't know about."

THE next day, Geary was standing in sick bay, waiting for Dr. Nasr to release the quarantine on Lieutenants Yuon and Castries, when Desjani joined him. "You've got a call from Admiral Timbale, sir."

Geary walked to the comm panel on the nearest wall and called up the message. Admiral Timbale, the fleet officer in charge of all the facilities at Varandal, had a long-suffering expression. "Admiral, I have been instructed by representatives of the Grand Council to pass on to you orders that two civilian-leased courier ships en route the hypernet gate, and two more en route jump points for other star systems, be intercepted and stopped by any means necessary. The courier ships are believed to be carrying information classified by the Alliance government. I was told to emphasize to you that these orders must be carried out. Timbale, out."

Geary frowned at Desjani. "Why didn't you call me from the bridge as soon as this came in?"

"Because I was just about to come down here, and"—she gestured in the general direction of Varandal's hypernet gate—"it's impossible to stop those courier ships with any Alliance warship. All of them are too close to the gate or the jump points they are heading for, and none of our warships are close enough. The only jump point being patrolled is the one to Atalia. If we had been told to stop those courier ships four hours ago it would have been possible, but not now."

"All right." He didn't question Desjani's assessment. Government orders might not take into account reality, but physics had never shown any tendencies to change the rules of the universe just because someone in a position of human authority was demanding it. "Do we know why we were ordered to stop those courier ships? Why the government thinks they are carrying classified information?"

Desjani's look of feigned distress was almost laughable. "We're starting to get news feeds which are full of details about events in Sol Star System while we were there. Apparently, the local news sources waited until we couldn't stop the courier ships before they started broadcasting the reports."

"Is there any indication of the source of the reports?" Geary asked.

"Not that we were told."

He didn't need any special displays or information to analyze the situation or attach to the message, so Geary tapped in the commands to transmit his reply from here in sick bay. "Admiral Timbale, this is

Admiral Geary. Unfortunately, there is no possibility of intercepting any of the courier ships before they depart due to the positions and vectors of those couriers and all available warships. Please advise the representatives of the Grand Council that we regret the physical impossibility of carrying out their order and stand ready to assist in any other way they request. Geary, out."

Dr. Nasr, painstakingly reviewing every piece of available data on the two lieutenants, had not even noticed the nearby conversation and message transmissions. Now, finished, he stood up and nodded tiredly as he spoke for the record. "I can find no indications of infection. Based on the information provided by Sol Star System authorities, any infection must have manifested one week prior to this. I therefore recommend that the two lieutenants be allowed to leave quarantine."

Geary spoke with equal solemnity. "I concur in your recommendation and order that Lieutenants Castries and Yuon be removed from quarantine."

Nasr touched the controls to speak to the two lieutenants. "In two minutes, the seal on the hatch confining you will open. You are to remove all clothing before leaving the compartment. Do not attempt to take any objects with you when you leave. You will be met by two personnel in isolation suits who will ensure you undergo full physical decontamination, after which you will be allowed your freedom of the ship once more. Do you understand?"

"I understand," Lieutenant Yuon said.

"Remove all clothing?" Lieutenant Castries asked. "I have to be naked in here with him?"

"Only for a short time," Dr. Nasr assured her.

"Ancestors help me. I really am in hell."

"I hear suffering is good for the soul," Yuon snapped at her.

"If that were true, I'd be a saint by now!"

"Lieutenant Castries!" Dr. Nasr broke in. "Do you understand?"

She visibly calmed herself before answering. "Yes, sir. I understand."

"Commence stripping. The hatch will open in one minute, thirty seconds."

Geary looked at Desjani. "Is there any medal we can give Lieutenants Castries and Yuon for enduring all of this?"

"I seriously doubt it. I just hope they can still work together after being given a little time to recover from this. I'd hate to break up a good watch team."

A ship's captain had to be practical, Geary reflected. "Doctor, how long is it until I can meet with the two lieutenants?"

"The decontamination procedure will take about half an hour. You are welcome to observe—"

"No, thank you, Doctor. They've been through enough. Those two don't need higher authority watching as they undress and go through decontamination. Give me a call when they are ready," Geary directed. But as he turned to leave, he found General Charban waiting. "Yes?"

"Can we talk, Admiral?" Charban asked.

"Certainly. Captain Desjani, I'm going to my stateroom. Please notify Envoy Rione that I need to talk with her."

Charban did not say anything for the first minute of their walk toward Geary's stateroom. When he finally spoke, he sounded oddly wistful. "Someone beat me to it."

"What's that?"

"You know what I mean, Admiral. I long ago had my fill of official stupidity." Charban was looking straight ahead, but his eyes did not seem to see the passageway they were in, instead gazing upon some other images that lived in his memory. "I saw too many men and women die because of official stupidity. Too many die for no reason or bad reasons. I know you don't think much of my judgment in that respect."

"General," Geary said slowly, "I didn't grow up with the war. I didn't spend my entire life at war. I don't judge those who did."

"But you do, and I don't blame you for it." Charban sighed heavily, his eyes growing haunted. "There was a moon in Semele Star System, the only thing worth living on in that entire star system. A red giant sun orbited by a few small rocks and one gas giant, and the moon orbited the gas giant. The Syndics had heavily fortified it. They had it, so we had to have it. I led my soldiers down onto that moon and we fought. The warships with us bombarded that moon until it was no longer worth having, but the Syndics kept fighting. I never understood that, Admiral. I never understood why the Syndics fought so hard against us when their government was so vile. But the former Syndics at Midway explained it to me. They were fighting to protect their homes. That was all. Not their government. Their homes. Their families. That's what they believed."

Charban came to a halt, still staring ahead of him. "We lost half of my division killing every Syndic on that moon. Two weeks after that, we left. Repositioned, in official jargon. I don't know whether or not the Syndics once again garrisoned the moon. All I knew was that I had lost half of my division so that we could occupy a place that we then left. I couldn't do it anymore. I put in my papers. I had served long enough. They had to grant me retirement. Why I survived and others did not, I don't know. But I couldn't do it anymore, Admiral. And I couldn't believe in it anymore. I couldn't believe that the people deciding strategy and plans had any idea what they were doing. I couldn't believe that the men and women we were sending to their deaths were accomplishing anything by their sacrifices."

"I understand," Geary said. "Truly. I do understand."

Charban blew out a long breath, then finally looked at Geary again. "Yes. I think you do. Did you leak all of those reports to the press?"

"No."

"Would you have? Don't answer. I think I know. But you must know this about me. I have no right to be here, to be alive, when I led so many to their deaths. I will spend what life is left to me trying to make a difference. I thought I could do that by entering politics. I don't believe that anymore. But there's a chance I can make a difference with the Dancers. A chance I can establish the beginnings of real understanding between our species and theirs. Would that be enough, Admiral?" Charban's gaze held his, the eyes dark with some hidden emotion. "Would it justify my still being alive, when they are dead?"

"General," Geary said, his voice soft, "I'm not wise enough to know the answer to that. I agree that when we first met I was skeptical of your own aversion to using force when I thought it necessary, but I do understand your reasons. What if the Dancers depart and don't allow any humans to accompany them back to their own territory? Will you reconsider politics then?"

Charban took a moment to answer. "Do you think I should?"

"I think we need more leaders who think more about the consequences of their actions and their decisions. I don't know that I would always agree with your decisions, but I do know you would take into account the long-term impact of them. And . . ." Geary had to pause to be sure he said the next thing right. "Those men and women you led, like the men and women I lead, died to defend their homes and families as well. I think their sacrifices deserve leaders who remember that, and who remember them."

Charban stayed silent for a longer time, before finally nodding. "Perhaps you are right. I will think about it. But now I am keeping you from meeting with Envoy Rione, and with this ship rejoining the rest of the fleet soon, I'm sure you have a lot of other things to worry about as well." He walked away, head bent in thought.

Rione was waiting at the hatch when Geary got to his stateroom, but she waved off his invitation to enter. "I need to catch a lift, Admiral."

"You're leaving?"

"Yes. There's a ship coming out to pick me up." A shadow crossed her expression, there and gone but unmistakable in its brief hint of worry and resolve. "I have found no clear information about my husband. I will have to hunt for the answers."

"If anyone has failed to live up to their agreements—" Geary began.

She silenced him with another sharp gesture of one hand. "If that is the case, I will take any necessary actions, and the less you know of that perhaps the better. This you must know, though. The Alliance has reliable reports that the Syndicate Worlds government on Prime is consumed with internal fighting. There have been more coups, attempted coups, and countercoups. The attempt to stop your fleet from returning from Midway was apparently one of the few actions that the Syndic central government has recently been able to agree on and try to implement."

"Why haven't I seen those reports?" Geary demanded. "Lieutenant Iger told me we haven't received any new material about the Syndic government."

"*You* haven't. Because the reports are classified in compartments for which fleet units are not authorized access." She shook her head in response to his immediate anger. "Don't bother venting to me about it. You know I agree with you. Here's the meat of the reporting. With the central Syndic government preoccupied with sticking knives in each other's backs, large portions of what remains of technically Syndic-controlled territory are reverting to an almost feudal power structure. Strong CEOs with access to the necessary wealth and firepower are asserting control over star systems in their local regions. They're exercising considerable autonomy in the absence of a firm presence from the central government."

"What's left of the Syndicate Worlds is falling apart?"

This time, Rione's gesture was indecisive. "Perhaps. Or perhaps the feudal power arrangement will stabilize the collapse. It's too early to tell. That's all I know."

"Have you heard anything about Captain Jane Geary and her ships?"

"No. That was apparently a pure fleet issue. Whoever sent her off didn't get their marching orders from any Senate source I can identify so far."

"Thank you." Geary hesitated, searching for the right words. "Good luck." It struck him suddenly that Rione might not be back, that if she found her husband and all was as well as could be, she had other places to be and other things to do than accompany this fleet any longer.

As he tried to think of the right way to say good-bye this time, Rione nodded wordlessly to him, then spun about and walked briskly away down the passageway.

He went in, pulled off the dress uniform top, and sat down heavily in the one really comfortable chair his stateroom boasted. The display above the low table before the chair was set for Varandal, so for a few moments he slumped down, watching the many ships and human installations orbiting the star, bright spots on the display as they swung in what seemed slow, lazy circles among the planets and other natural objects in the star system.

Geary frowned as he realized that six of those bright spots were accelerating together at an extremely impressive rate, heading away from *Dauntless* and toward . . .

His comm panel buzzed urgently.

"The Dancers have taken off like bats out of hell," Desjani reported.

"What?"

"The Dancers have—"

"I heard you! Where are they going?"

"Their vector is a beeline for the jump point for Bhavan."

"Bhavan?" One of the star systems adjacent to Varandal, Bhavan led deeper into Alliance space. "Why are they going to Bhavan?"

"Do you honestly expect me to be able to answer that question?" Desjani asked.

"No. Hold on." Geary hit acknowledge again as his comm alert sounded once more. A second virtual window appeared, this one showing General Charban. "Do you know that the Dancers are heading for Bhavan?"

Charban raised both eyebrows. "They are? That explains the message they just sent us. *We future return. Durnan.*"

"What?" Geary said again. "What does that mean?"

"Since you tell me they are heading for a jump point out of this star system, it means they are leaving Varandal to go to Durnan Star System and will return. That is my best guess, anyway."

Geary slumped back again, massaging his forehead as another headache loomed. "Tell the Dancers we'll escort them—"

"Sir," Desjani interrupted, "we can't catch them before they reach that jump point. Not at the rate they are going."

"We have to send an escort," Geary began stubbornly.

"Not if they won't wait for one," she replied.

"I will ask," Charban added in tones that implied he did not expect any useful result from the asking.

"General," Geary said with what he thought was immense patience, "if the Dancers go zooming through Alliance space on their own, refusing an escort, I will be held responsible. Everyone will be asking me why the Dancers left, where they are going, and what they are doing."

Charban nodded, unimpressed. "And then you will ask me to answer those same questions. I will tell you *I don't know*, and you will pass on that answer, because it's the only one we've got."

"General, dammit—"

"If you have a way to make them tell us what they're doing, Admiral, please employ it! Because I don't."

Geary paused, breathing slowly and getting himself under control. "I'm sorry, General. I know that you're doing your best, and that you have a better grasp of the Dancers than anyone else. See if you can get anything else out of them before the Dancers jump for Bhavan. Does Bhavan take them toward Durnan?"

"Yes, sir," Desjani confirmed. "They'll have to make a couple more jumps from Bhavan, though."

What if someone panicked and opened fire on the Dancers as they transited through those other star systems? What if whoever was in charge of defenses at Durnan took action? "How can we get General Charban to Durnan in time to ensure he can talk to the people there before they overreact to the Dancers arriving? Is there any way to do that, or are the Dancers taking the most direct route?"

Charban, a ground forces soldier confronted with a fleet question, merely shook his head.

Tanya was gazing off to one side intently. "I'm running some options . . . there's a way, Admiral. We can send the general on a ship through the hypernet gate here to Tehack. From there they can jump to Durnan, and should be able to get there at about the same time the Dancers do as they make three jumps."

"ID a ship for me," Geary ordered. "Heavy cruiser, close by, in good fighting shape and with close to one hundred percent fuel. Pick a light cruiser if none of the heavies fit the criteria."

"I'll get my people on it," Desjani said.

"General, get ready for a fast transfer and several weeks on a cruiser."

"Yes, Admiral," Charban said. "There may be some trouble regarding security. I have been informed that our comm equipment and software is not to be moved—"

"I hereby direct you to take all of the comm gear and software you need to talk to the Dancers. It's not going to do us any good sitting on *Dauntless* while the Dancers are at Durnan."

Geary paused, imagining hysterical news accounts of an "alien invasion force" swooping through the Alliance. "I'll notify our Grand Council representatives of what is happening and what we're doing."

"They won't be happy," Charban predicted. "But you might offer them this comfort. If the records of our visit to Old Earth had been kept secret, had not been mysteriously leaked to the media, then panic and fear might have resulted when the Dancers appeared alone in those star systems. But by the time the Dancers reach those places, the news will have preceded them. Our people will have seen what the Dancers did. Perhaps they will watch the Dancers pass by and wish the Dancers the blessings of the living stars."

"Wouldn't that be nice," Desjani said. She tried to keep her voice dry and sarcastic, but some real emotion leaked through.

"I'll bring that up," Geary promised. "Tanya—"

"*Diamond*," Desjani interrupted. "Heavy cruiser *Diamond*. She fits the bill. I'll notify her to break orbit and join up with us while you let the senators know what's going on."

"Good."

"But put a full uniform on before you call them. Sir."

"Uh . . . right." He had forgotten that he had pulled off the top of his dress uniform. The senators were going to be unhappy enough without making them think he was deliberately disrespecting them.

"THE representatives from the Grand Council were pretty mad about the whole thing, but even they had to acknowledge that we had no way of forcing the Dancers to stop."

The day after the wild scramble to deal with the departure of the Dancers, Geary's stateroom was crowded with several officers who were all physically present. Given the things that might be discussed, Geary hadn't wanted to use any form of conferencing software, no matter how allegedly secure it was.

One of the advantages of being fleet commander, though, was that he still got the comfortable chair.

"*Diamond* will get the, um, envoy there on time," Captain Duellos observed, smiling at the play of light in the wine in his glass. "And keep an eye on the envoy as well."

"That's not really necessary," Desjani said. "General Charban can be trusted."

Duellos raised an eyebrow at her. "That's a different assessment from you than the ones I heard when he first joined this fleet. Doesn't he want to be a politician?"

"I think we'd be lucky if he did."

Geary broke into the surprised silence that followed Tanya's statement. "Is there anything else that anyone can tell me about Jane Geary and her ships?"

Captain Tulev shook his head, slowly and stolidly, like a bull standing firm. "She left only a week ago. *Dreadnaught*, *Dependable*, and *Conqueror* were not fully repaired by any means, but all had enough combat capability to handle a mission for which no threat was expected."

"She was sent into Syndic space!"

"Yes. But, according to her orders, the star system where the Alliance prisoners awaited pickup is comparable to Atalia."

Captain Badaya leaned back, drumming his fingers on the arm of the chair, his expression that of someone tasting something sour. "I still think she'll get there and find nothing. Headquarters just wanted an excuse to get her out of the star system so they could appoint me temporary commander of the fleet. It's clear enough what they expected. I would assume temporary command, and I would promptly threaten the government with whatever ships I could get to follow those orders. A year ago, I might well have done that and played right into their hands."

"The point is," Geary said, "that you didn't."

"What are they after, Admiral?" Badaya asked, sounding almost plaintive. "Why would fleet headquarters want part of the fleet to rebel against the government?"

Tanya rested one side of her chin on her fist as she gazed at him. "It's like when someone tried to court-martial all of those ship commanders for running too low on fuel cells. Something guaranteed to make the hotheads explode. That almost worked."

Badaya looked even unhappier. "I played a role in that."

"Maybe that's why they thought you would be a sure thing this time," Geary observed. "Whoever they are. What I think they are looking for is a reason to dramatically reduce the size of this fleet."

Duellos had been watching the others. Now he spoke in a voice tinged with bitterness. "Why do they need a reason beyond the end of the war? Cut the budget some more, cut loose the officers and sailors the Alliance no longer *needs*, and reduce this fleet to a shadow of itself."

"They can't," Desjani replied. "Because Black Jack is in command. The people of the Alliance trust him far more than they trust the government. If the government obviously undercuts him without a good justification, it will be viewed as an attack on the champion of the Alliance by a bunch of corrupt politicians."

"If you ask me," Badaya said, "that's exactly what it would be."

Tulev nodded toward Badaya. "He speaks the words many in the Alliance would feel. Yes, if you look at events since the end of the war, our orders have repeatedly exposed us to situations that would reduce our numbers and capabilities. I have heard that there is much infighting among the government, but the different factions appear to agree on the need to lower the threat they see as posed by us."

"The threat posed by *me*," Geary replied forcefully. "They're playing these games, sending this fleet into situations where men and women can die and have died, because they fear me."

Duellos shook his head, his mouth twisted into a grimace. "That's only partly true. Yes, Admiral, you are the focus of the government's attention right now, but if you had not existed, and we had somehow won the war anyway, they would be just as fearful of this fleet. And this fleet would be actively resisting any attempts to reduce its numbers."

Tulev rarely smiled, and even though his lips curled a bit now, his expression still did not really reflect any humor. "The fleet would see such attempts as treasonous actions by a disloyal government, and the government would see the fleet's behavior as treasonous actions by a disloyal military."

"And the Alliance would end up going through the same kind of collapse the Syndicate Worlds is now experiencing," Geary said.

"If they keep reducing this fleet," Badaya asked, sounding bewildered now, "what will they use to defend the Alliance? They've seen that the Syndics still can't be trusted, they've seen the sorts of local warlords and piracy popping up where Syndic control has crumbled, so they must know they can't depend on good intentions or treaties to defend us."

Captain Smythe shrugged. "In the Admiral's day, a century ago, the fleet was considerably smaller than even what we have left with us at the moment."

"His day is right now," Desjani insisted.

"You're both right," Geary said to stop any debate on a subject that made him uncomfortable. "But a century ago, the paradox was that we didn't trust each other, but we trusted each other to keep things quiet. We could keep the fleet smaller because the Alliance counted on the Syndics keeping things quiet in their territory, and the Syndic fleet was also much smaller because they knew the Alliance would maintain order in its territory."

"That makes no sense at all," Badaya complained. "With all due respect, Admiral."

"It apparently worked," Smythe pointed out. "Until it stopped working. I'd love to find out exactly why the Syndic leadership decided to start that war."

"We guessed that the enigmas tricked the Syndics into starting it," Duellos said. "But I think the enigmas' seeds of war fell onto fertile ground because of the way the Syndicate Worlds is governed. Their Supreme Council are pretty much absolute rulers, which means they didn't have to listen to anyone counseling caution. They could just indulge their fantasies without fear of contradiction."

Tulev nodded heavily. "And out of that, what horrors grew. It is something anyone in power must fear, being surrounded by the flatterers and fools who say only what they think the powerful want to hear."

"Admiral Geary won't have that problem," Tanya remarked dryly.

Badaya laughed. "Not as long as you're around!"

"Speaking of saying what people want to hear," Geary said, "what's the real reason why all of the warships are broadcasting false readiness data?"

"Officially?" Badaya asked. "We were told that agents of unspecified foreign powers might be monitoring the readiness of Alliance combat forces, so we were to present the strongest possible image regardless of the true status of our forces."

"Foreign powers?" Tanya scoffed. "There's only one foreign power. The Syndics."

To Geary's surprise, the other captains shook their heads at her.

"Lately," Captain Smythe explained, "the phrase 'foreign powers' has been used in the media to describe the Callas Republic, the Rift Federation, stars outside Alliance space in the direction of Sol, and the Midway Star System and other former Syndic territories. Not to mention the press, which has itself been described as 'foreign interests' by members of the Alliance government."

"Does someone think we need more enemies?" Geary asked.

"Enemies can be useful."

"I do not think it is that simple," Tulev interjected, a slight frown crossing his brow in an unusual display of open emotion. "When people are afraid, when they are uncertain, they see more enemies. In this, they are sincere. It would be a mistake to assume all of those involved are cynically manufacturing more enemies to advance their own agendas. Many of them do see those enemies."

Captain Tulev paused, then spoke with his usual careful, emotionless precision. "You all know that my home star system was destroyed during the war, and that the survivors occupied defenses there afterwards, awaiting the return of the Syndics. I know that there have been many, many detections of incoming Syndic attacks in that star system since then. The great majority of them were illusions. Men and women swore they saw the indications, saw the detections of the enemy arriving, but data recordings showed no such reports from sensors. The defenders, fortified amidst the ruins of all they once knew, often see the enemy coming once more. They honestly believe they see those enemies. It is not a tactic or an attempt to mislead."

After a long moment of silence, Badaya laughed again, this time briefly and harshly. "Maybe that's us. We need enemies, too, don't we? To justify the continued size of this fleet?"

"We didn't imagine the Syndic attacks on the way back from Midway!" Desjani shot back at him.

"Granted." Badaya furrowed his brow in an almost comical display of deep thought. "But let's imagine we're average citizens of an average Alliance star system. They hear all about what the Syndics did, and they wonder why they should worry. That was in Syndic territory! Are the Syndics coming here to do such things? What about the enigmas and the Kicks? Immensely far away! Why the need for such a large fleet? Because the officers of that fleet see danger?"

"That's—" Desjani waged an obvious struggle to control herself before continuing. "All right. You have a point. We need to convince those citizens that the enemies we're worried about are real."

"And that some dangers are real as well," Duellos agreed. "Especially when the force assigned the task of dealing with dangers outside the borders of the Alliance, this fleet, is at about sixty percent readiness instead of the one hundred percent the data feeds claim."

"Hopefully, fleet headquarters and the government realize that," Geary said. "No other orders have come in since Jane Geary was sent off?"

"Not yet," Duellos said. "But they could come soon. You may not have noticed in the rush of your arrival, but three ships departed via the hypernet gate within a few minutes after *Dauntless*'s return. One was an official courier ship, while the other two claimed to be civilian ships with no government ties even though both were high-speed craft and, along with the courier ship, had been loitering near the gate for weeks. A lot of people wanted to know when Black Jack got back. Now some wheels are going to start turning. But what wheels and to what purpose?"

No one had the answers to those questions.

As the others left the stateroom for *Dauntless*'s shuttle dock, Captain Smythe lingered, waiting until Geary had shut the hatch again before speaking.

"I need to update you on funding," Smythe said, scratching his beard with one hand. "We're running into some problems."

Geary nodded, trying not to look grim. "People are catching on?"

"Catching on?" Smythe asked, surprised. "No. It's not that. The only one with a big enough view of what we're physically doing is Admiral Timbale, and he has made it clear to me that as long as the payment vouchers for work on our ships continue to clear, he has no interest in knowing anything about how we're getting all of those payments authorized."

Smythe wandered over to Geary's table and tapped in a few commands, producing an image of serried ranks of organizational codes and program codes connected by a rat's-nest of tangled lines and dotted lines. "This is a simplified summary of the sort of sources we're tapping for funds."

"Simplified? You're joking," Geary said, staring at the mess.

"Now, Admiral, this isn't a *bad* thing. From our perspective, it's a good thing. It's so complex and confusing that it gives us a lot of room to work." Smythe adopted a virtuous expression. "Within the system, of course."

"Of course," Geary agreed. "So what is the problem?"

"We can only tap money that's there. If the wells start to run dry, it doesn't matter what tricks we use to turn the spigots. We get less and less out."

"All of these accounts and programs are running out of money?"

"They are. There's major underfunding going on all over." Smythe waved a finger up and down. "To the extent that we're seeing money being bounced from place to place to hide the shortfalls."

"Bounced? You mean they're robbing Peter to pay Paul?"

"Oh, no, nothing that innocent." Smythe grinned, looking piratical now instead of angelic. "They're bouncing the money from place to place in such ways that they can double-count it as being in two or more places at once. There are little tricks that keep the money that remains moving so fast that it appears to be in multiple locations, and it gets counted as being in all of them. It looks like they have enough money to pay Peter, Paul, *and* Mary, but they don't actually let the money sit still long enough for checks to clear."

Geary sat down heavily, his eyes fixed on the mess. "I don't believe it. How are we getting money, then?"

"Because it's bouncing! That means it has to sit somewhere for just a very tiny moment before it jumps somewhere else. And, if you have the right software and the right green-haired talent to spot the patterns they're using, you can time your withdrawals to hit during that very tiny moment." Smythe frowned meditatively, looking into the distance. "Sort of like shooting skeet, I suppose. No. Like that old Whack-a-mole thing. With the help of the invaluable Lieutenant Shamrock, we are ready to hit the moles the instant they pop up, and taking a bit off the top each time."

Something about that phrasing made Geary give Smythe a stern, inquisitive look. "Is anything else coming off the top?"

Smythe managed to express simultaneous shock, piety, and sincerity. "No, sir! Some people might be tempted in such circumstances, but those people wouldn't be looking ahead. This can only last so long, Admiral. No matter how fast they bounce the balls, the point is going to come where the government either pays all of its bills or it defaults. If the Alliance government defaults, it would make current circumstances look downright idyllic. I think they'll find the money somehow.

"But when the government finally pays up, it can only do so by cleaning up the mess in its accounting, which will expose what was done. That is the point, sir, at which all of those accountants doing their best to carry out their orders to bounce the money will find themselves hauled up on charges for bouncing the money, while their superiors, the men and women who gave the orders to them, express surprise and shock at the whole thing before collecting another medal and promotion."

Geary snorted a cynical laugh and nodded. "You're probably right."

"I know I am, Admiral." Smythe spread his hands. "I have no intention of being one of those made a scapegoat in this. Nor would I position anyone working for me to be snared. Everything we are doing is proper and legal. If anyone catches on, they'll tell us to stop, not because it's illegal but because they don't want to spend that much money on us. But as long as they don't say we have to stop, we can do it, and justify it all by letter of rules and regulations."

Geary grinned. "We're all right, then?"

"Not entirely, Admiral. As I said at the start, we can't grab as much as we would like to. It's not there to grab. As a result, repair work on your ships has slowed down. It can't be helped."

Ugly. A fleet constructed to last a couple of years at best, every ship now exceeding its planned life span, more and more equipment failing due to "age" and less and less money to rebuild, repair, or replace everything that was breaking. But, if not for Captain Smythe, things would be a lot worse. "Thanks for all you're doing to keep this fleet as ready as possible. Put together for me your best estimate of the impact of the funding shortfalls on the fleet's readiness, looking downstream about six months if current trends continue. Then keep me apprised of any changes or major problems," Geary told Smythe. "Give my thanks to Lieutenant Jamenson as well."

"Certainly, Admiral." For the first time, Smythe displayed some discomfort. "As you know, Lieutenant Jamenson, our green-haired

Shamrock, has expressed interest in a transfer to intelligence. You had indicated that you would look favorably upon that, and I agreed with your reasoning that we should not penalize her for doing so well in her current job by denying her other opportunities. However, given current circumstances, I would like to delay such a transfer."

Oddly, that sort of personnel issue felt harder to deal with than the abstract discussion of money and equipment. "I'll talk to her, Captain. I'll explain what we're facing, and that we need her where she is for now." Geary rubbed the sides of his jaw unhappily. "I wish I could promise her that transfer in a month or two months, but I can't."

Smythe shrugged. "You know, Admiral, it may seem strange given Lieutenant Jamenson's ability to confuse and cloud issues, but she does like being played straight with. I think your idea is a good one."

"Has she found any more information regarding the new construction?"

This time Smythe shook his head. "Nothing direct. Though I strongly suspect that some of the funds missing from the accounts we're trying to tap have been redirected to cover cost overruns for building that new fleet. There is one odd thing, though. Support facilities. There aren't any."

"What do you mean?" Geary waved toward the star display. "With the reductions in forces going on, there must be a lot of underused support facilities that they can tap for use by those new ships."

"Yes, Admiral." Smythe pointed to the display as well, looking perplexed. "But, firstly, we can't find money being diverted to keep any of those underused facilities operational, and, secondly, if this fleet is being kept so secret, how can it maintain secrecy if it is sent to existing facilities in some star system full of people who would see those new ships? They would need new facilities, somewhere no one would spot them."

"That's a very good point." More puzzles. "If we could find Admiral

Bloch, we could probably find those support facilities and any of those new ships that have been finished."

"Maybe they're at Unity Alternate," Smythe said with a grin.

"Unity what?" Geary asked.

"Unity Alternate." Smythe's grin faded. "You don't get it? Oh. Of course you wouldn't. It's an old joke for us, but you wouldn't have heard it. At least fifty years ago, rumors started going around that an emergency fallback place was being constructed in case the Syndics hit the Alliance capital at Unity. Some secret star system with all sorts of facilities being secretly constructed so the government could carry on the war even if the worst happened."

"Secret star system? How could that work?"

"That's the problem, isn't it? We had the hypernet going in at that time, so marginal star systems were starting to be abandoned, but, still, any star system that we could jump to was accessible. Sealing one off would have been like posting a huge sign saying 'Secret Facility Here.' People actually looked, but no one found such a thing, so in time it became a joke. Anything mysterious, anything missing, was at Unity Alternate. Why hasn't leave been approved? The forms are at Unity Alternate. Where are my new specialists? They got sent to Unity Alternate. It's such an old joke by now that only old fools like me are likely to make it."

Geary sighed. "At least I'll understand next time someone else makes that joke. Speaking of missing objects, I see that *Invincible* is gone. Where did they take her?" The captured Kick superbattleship was immensely valuable in every possible sense of the word. He had not doubted that the government would take it somewhere else to slowly and carefully explore and exploit the vessel and everything in it.

Smythe spread his hands. "Your guess is as good as mine. Not only did they not tell us where they were going when they left by hypernet, I haven't been able to find out any news of where they went. Every press agency in the Alliance is looking for *Invincible*, but no one has found a trace of the ship."

"She's at Unity Alternate?"

"Exactly. See? You've already got the joke down." Smythe paused, then spoke in a more formal tone of voice. "There is one more thing, Admiral. A major problem. Since *Dauntless* returned to Varandal, word has gone out along various black-market channels of items for sale."

"Items?"

"Yes." Smythe gestured vaguely in what might have been the direction of far, far distant Sol. "Most of them are items from Old Earth or elsewhere in Sol Star System, which as far as I can tell may not have cleared customs and had duty paid on them but otherwise are innocuous enough. But there is also talk of collectors' items that have been on the surface of Europa."

"The surface of Europa?" Geary repeated, disbelieving. All of the armor had been destroyed. He was certain of that. And the Marines had brought back nothing except— "The clothes on their backs."

Smythe nodded. "Now fantastically valuable because of where they have been. I understand the desire to . . . operate in creative ways. How often can a pair of dirty underwear earn the owner a huge sum of money? If nothing else, the irony of the whole concept is priceless. But offering items for sale that are tied to Europa will not only generate a tremendous amount of interest from collectors, but also far too much interest from various governmental, law-enforcement, customs, medical, and other authorities. And if they start poking into that . . ."

They might notice how much money Geary was finding to keep his fleet repaired and operating. Master Chief Gioninni must be behind this sales scheme. The amount of potential profit, and the no-doubt technically legal aspects of the sales, must have blindsided Gioninni's usual caution. A word to Tanya about Gioninni and to General Carabali about her Marines' sideline should be all that was needed to eliminate that part of the sale. "I'll make sure that's shut down, Captain Smythe. Thank you for alerting me to it."

If only every problem were so easily resolved.

SIX days later, another courier ship arrived at Varandal, flashing into existence at the hypernet gate. There had been other courier ships showing before then, but Geary had watched this one's arrival with particular concern. Given the time required for a round-trip to fleet headquarters, today was the earliest orders might arrive for him after headquarters was informed of his return. It took hours for the light of the courier ship's arrival to reach where *Dauntless* orbited, but once Geary knew the ship was here, he also knew he wouldn't have long to wait.

Five minutes after seeing the arrival of the ship at the hypernet gate, a high-pitched tone that signified receipt of a high-priority, eyes-only message for Geary burst to life.

Four times he let the alert repeat, before he touched the desk control to silence it and view the message identification—*Alliance Fleet Headquarters. Orders for Commander, Alliance First Fleet.*

It took a conscious effort to open the message and view its contents. Geary braced himself, counting down before his finger tapped the command.

Three. Two. One.

EIGHT

LIKE the average fleet officer, Geary had always thought of fleet head-quarters as a distant place occupied by people whose primary jobs were to satisfy the desires of supreme commanders to have bigger staff empires than their counterparts, and to make up arbitrary, arduous, and absurd things to order the men and women in fleet units to carry out. But, since being reawakened and thrust into roles in which he dealt much more frequently with fleet headquarters, he had learned a lot more about that staff, and as a result, his distrust had grown by leaps and bounds.

As the message played, Geary saw two images standing before him instead of a single person. "This is Admiral Tosic," the tall, lean fleet officer said, his tone of voice challenging, "supreme commander of Alliance fleet operations." The former fleet supreme commander, Admiral Celu, had been replaced already? He wondered if Celu had retired voluntarily or if she had been pushed out.

The woman next to Tosic sounded less belligerent, but still forceful. "General Javier, supreme commander of Alliance ground forces."

"Your orders, Admiral Geary," Tosic began without any polite preliminaries, "are to take the First Battle Cruiser Division along with a squadron of light cruisers and three squadrons of destroyers to Adriana Star System. No additional fleet forces are authorized under any circumstances. Operation analysis at fleet headquarters confirms that a task force of that size will be adequate for the assigned mission, and current limitations on funding do not permit the luxury of deploying more forces than needed. Once at Adriana, you are to coordinate with Alliance ground forces to carry out the return of Syndic refugees to Batara Star System, taking any actions necessary and proper to ensure that the refugee problem at Adriana is resolved. Upon completion of that mission, return your forces to Varandal and await further orders. Tosic, out."

The images vanished. Geary regarded the area before him where they had been, then called up a star display to refresh his memory of Adriana and Batara, wondering why he had a dim memory of the latter star system. As he had recalled, Adriana was inside Alliance space, but Batara . . . "Tanya, can you come down to my stateroom? I want to discuss my new orders with you."

She was there within minutes, frowning, as Geary played the message again and Admiral Tosic delivered the orders.

"You know," Tanya remarked acidly as the message ended, "Tosic thinks he sounds powerful when he talks like that, but he really just sounds pompous. Where's Batara?"

"Here." Geary indicated a star display he had just reactivated. "I remembered it because it used to be part of the Hansa Group."

"The Hansa Group?"

"It was an association of four star systems that rejected all invitations to join with the Alliance or the Syndicate Worlds," Geary explained. "They wanted to be completely independent."

Desjani glanced at the star display. "Since Batara has been in Syndic space for a really long time, I guess that didn't work out too well for the Hansa Group."

"No. One day, the Syndics swept in, claiming they had been invited, and took over. That was about three years before the Syndics attacked the Alliance. It was the biggest war scare we had before . . . well, before we had a war."

"We didn't do anything?" Desjani asked, biting off each word as it came out.

"No." He remembered that all too well, the mix of anticipation in the Alliance fleet that the Syndics might finally get their heads slapped hard, and fear of whether such a limited operation to restore Hansa Group independence would escalate into a wider war between the Alliance and the Syndics. But he said nothing about that, guessing that Tanya and other people from this time would find such concerns incomprehensible.

"Maybe if we'd done something . . ." she growled.

"Maybe," Geary said. "Maybe it would have given the Syndics enough pause that they never attacked the Alliance. Or, it might have led to the same war, starting three years earlier. It's a road not taken, Tanya. We don't know where it would have led. Maybe to this exact same destination."

"Not exactly. You wouldn't be here." She eyed him, then smiled. "Or maybe you would be, if that was intended to happen no matter what." The smile faded as quickly as it had come. "Refugees from Batara are getting to Adriana? They would have to go through Yokai to reach Adriana. Yokai never fell to the Syndics during the war even though there were some nasty fights there. Why aren't the Alliance defenses at Yokai stopping the refugees now?"

Geary reached out to tap the image of the Alliance-controlled star, gazing at the data that appeared next to it. "I passed through Yokai a couple of times, a hundred years ago. Not a lot there. Small towns and orbiting facilities scattered around the marginal and uninhabitable planets that orbit the star. They subsisted mainly on the interstellar traffic passing through on its way to somewhere else. It looks like those towns disappeared a long time before the hypernet was constructed and eliminated most of that traffic, though."

She pointed again. "Everything that wasn't destroyed by Syndic attacks was abandoned or converted into fortifications and defense facilities."

"What happened to the people who lived there?"

"The ones who didn't die? The usual, most likely, since Yokai doesn't have any planets that are habitable for humans, had a fairly small population, and no cities. See, Yokai is a Special Defensive Zone, off-limits to all but the military. When the star system was designated an SDZ, the civilians who lived and worked there would have been relocated. A lot of them probably got sent to Adriana." She paused for several long seconds, looking at the star display in a gloomy way. "Not a lot of people, I guess, compared to a star system with a habitable planet and a good-sized population, but they all lost their homes."

"Alliance refugees," Geary said.

"Yeah. And now Adriana has a new batch of refugees to worry about. But why aren't they being stopped before they get there?" She peered at the display, suddenly intent. "Hold on." Tanya touched an inconspicuous symbol next to Yokai, waited, then touched it again. "I'm getting a classified data refusal. What information is supposed to be classified above the level of a fleet captain? You're fleet commander. Try hitting that."

He reached out and touched the same symbol, producing a notice that popped into existence. "I guess I'm cleared for it. Ancestors!" He couldn't help saying that as he saw what the previously hidden notice reported.

The civilians had been kicked out of Yokai many decades before. Now the military had also left. Even though the outer layer of information on the display had shown strong defenses still in place at Yokai, the classified notice dated to the most recent update of *Dauntless*'s information reported that in fact those war-related bases were now deserted, hastily closed down and mothballed as part of the drastic scaling back in defense outlays by the Alliance government. "That explains why Yokai isn't stopping the refugees. There's no one there to stop them. Or even report that they're coming through."

"They shut down the border defenses facing the Syndics there?" Desjani asked incredulously. "Were they *surprised* when that created problems?"

"They might have been surprised if they were deeply enough in denial," Geary said. "Or if different offices didn't tell each other what they were doing. Adriana must be mad as hell about this."

"They probably don't know," Desjani said. "Yokai is still an SDZ. Nobody from the Alliance is allowed to go there without official approval."

"But the Syndics know! They're coming through there! Why keep it secret from our own— Oh, never mind. I'll find out when I get to Adriana."

She cocked her head slightly to one side as she looked at him. "There's something else, isn't there? Something besides the mission?"

"Yeah." He inhaled slowly, trying to find the right words. "Tanya, once upon a time there was a . . . a community that lived at Yokai. It was their home. I went through Yokai twice on ships. I saw it. And I'm the last one alive who saw it. How many people still remember what was there?"

Tanya sighed. "Admiral . . . Jack . . . if you start trying to add up all of the things lost in the last century, you'll go mad. The list will never end."

"I won't forget."

"Fine. Don't forget. But you also have to remember what's going on right now. They want you to take a division of battle cruisers?" Tanya demanded with renewed anger. "But only one division. Sending you there with battle cruisers looks like massive overkill for a refugee return operation, but if money is as short as they say, they wouldn't

give you more than whatever bare minimum their ops analysis identified. Which means one division isn't enough, and this mission is a
bigger job than it appears to be."

"The last time I went through that region of Alliance space," Geary
said, "there were only two divisions of battle cruisers in the entire Alliance fleet."

"Yes, sir. I will point out what we both already know, that you are
talking ancient history, and that returning those refugees to Batara
means going into Syndic space, and based on what the Syndics did on
our trip back from Midway, one division of battle cruisers is guaranteed not to be enough to take on this mission."

"I don't have any alternative," Geary said. "The orders are clear and
unambiguous. And the money isn't there. Captain Smythe has told me
the same thing."

"Admiral Tosic has found plenty of money to build that new fleet!"

"Somebody has, but *we* don't have that money. I can ask Captain
Smythe to divert funds from repair and refit work on the old and damaged ships of this fleet, but those funds aren't enough as it is."

She glowered at nothing, then nodded. "Fine. *Dauntless* is ready to
go. I'll need a couple of days to get *Daring* and *Victorious* out of refit
status—"

"Tanya, the orders specified the First Battle Cruiser Division."

"You can't— Admiral, there isn't— The First Division only has
three ships since we lost *Brilliant*!"

"I know." He also knew why she was really upset, but he avoided
mentioning it directly. "This will give you a chance to let *Dauntless* go
into stand-down for repairs, which will also allow her crew to go on
leave and see their homes."

"You intend going into Syndic space without me?" Desjani flexed
her hands helplessly. "I— Admiral— Dammit."

"I'll have Duellos with me on *Inspire*."

"That's not the same thing! *Inspire* is not *Dauntless*, and Duellos is not . . ." She looked at him, uncharacteristically vulnerable. "Ever since we found you again, ever since we recovered you from that failing escape pod, I've kept an eye on you so you could . . . complete your mission."

"You tried to leave me once," Geary pointed out. "When the war ended and—"

"I knew that you would come after me!" Desjani lowered her head and grimaced. "I'm being a fool. I know it. But headquarters must be setting you up for trouble. You know they are. This mission sounds simple. But they want you to fail."

"And I will miss having you there to help me spot trouble before it spots me," Geary said with total sincerity. "And I will miss being aboard *Dauntless*. But Roberto Duellos is sharp. He's no Tanya Desjani, but I think he can do the job."

"How about your stress levels?"

She knew better than anyone how much post-trauma had been impacting him at times. "Better. Much better. I'm not sure why, yet. I'll be all right."

"Yes, sir." She looked up, straightening and smoothing out her expression. "These are your orders, this is your job, and I am a professional. What can I do to help?"

"You're doing it now. But I'll also appoint you acting fleet commander in my absence. That way I won't have to worry about anything going wrong here while I'm gone."

"Yeah. Right. What if Jane Geary makes it back while you're gone?"

"You retain acting command." He tried not to let worry show in his voice, but Tanya spotted it anyway.

"Jane will make it back," she reassured him. "*Diamond* and the Dancers might show up, too. I'll try to keep everyone here until you get back. What about taking one of the assault transports and some extra Marines with you?"

"That's not authorized, Tanya. I'll just bring those Marines assigned to the battle cruisers in the First Division. Ground forces are supposed to do any heavy lifting of that nature that this mission requires."

She paused, then gave him a keen look. "You should know that Roberto Duellos is under a lot of extra pressure. His wife hasn't quite given him an ultimatum of *the fleet or your family*, but it's getting close to that, and it's a devil's choice for him either way. If he leaves the fleet, he'll be lost, unable to find anything else that he cares about doing. But if he loses his family, he'll be just as lost."

Geary winced as he ran that dilemma through his mind. "He's likely to be distracted."

"No. He's too good for that. He *might* be distracted. Keep it in mind. Speaking of distractions, don't worry about those items from Europa that were offered for sale. That sale has been permanently shut down."

"You talked to Gioninni?"

"That depends how you define 'talked to,'" Tanya replied. "The message was conveyed in unmistakable terms. I told you it would be a good idea for Gioninni to watch Smythe because that meant Smythe would start watching Gioninni. There may be no honor among thieves, but there is competition."

"Thanks, Tanya. For everything."

"If you want to thank me, get your head out of the past, focus on the present, and get your butt back here in one piece . . . sir."

THERE were always too many things to do and too little time to do them in.

And yet, as Geary walked restlessly through *Dauntless* on the day prior to transferring to *Inspire*, he found himself at the worship compartments. He paused, thinking of all the tasks yet to accomplish, then walked slowly to one of the small rooms that was currently vacant. He closed the door, shutting out the eyes of crew members, who were courteously pretending not to intrude on his privacy, then sat down on the small wooden bench. On a shelf before him sat a candle, which he lit.

The candle flickered in the slight draft caused by the compartment's ventilation, light and shadows dancing on the walls. Geary stared at the flame, trying to see any hint of images or guidance within it. *Everyone thinks I have some special knowledge, or special link to the living stars, but all I have is the hope that my ancestors will tell me things I need to know.*

All I have is what everyone else has, the hope that I'm doing the right thing.

Am I?

He tried to let his mind drift, open to anything that might enter. But despite his best efforts, he kept focusing on the upcoming mission. *It must be a trap. I have to assume it's a trap of some kind. Just as if I'm dealing with the Syndics, even though these aren't the Syndics.*

What exactly triggered the memory that came to mind? His father, looking angry, as he had in life often enough to have taught young Geary to face the disapproval stoically. *"Why didn't you ask me?"* his father had demanded.

Geary felt a remembered chill inside as his ten-year-old self had answered. *"I thought I knew what you wanted." And you would have gotten angry at being asked.*

"Don't assume! Don't assume you know what I want!"

He shook his head, coming back to the present, startled by the intensity of the memory. *Don't assume. Why did I remember that? I can't even recall exactly what that was about. I just remember that it was something I had been sure was right, and it wasn't.*

Was that a message?

Geary looked at the flame. *All right, Father. Maybe you've unbent enough in the light of the living stars to explain, something you rarely did when alive. I forgave you for that a long time ago.* It would be just like his father, though, to offer advice in the form of a lecture.

Am I not to assume this mission is a trap? I have to. That's the only safe option.

But that doesn't mean I should close my eyes to the possibility that there is something else going on.

Thank you, ancestors. Thank you, Father.

He snuffed out the candle and left the compartment, feeling oddly comforted by the ambiguous message he might have received.

INSPIRE felt subtly wrong. The same class and type of ship as *Dauntless*, *Inspire* had been thrown together as fast as possible, just like *Dauntless*, in the expectation that she would be destroyed in battle within a couple of years at the most, or so badly damaged that she would be broken up for parts and scrap. The layout of the ship was identical, and the design of the bridge and other critical spaces the same as on *Dauntless*.

But Geary had been aboard *Dauntless* long enough to be acquainted with every rough weld, every sharp edge, as well as every place where damage and repairs had resulted in minor changes from the original. *Inspire* had different rough welds in different places, different sharp edges in different places, and minor differences in equipment and its placement. It was like looking at an identical twin who wasn't . . . identical.

He sat in a fleet command seat that wasn't exactly like the one he was used to, next to the seat holding Captain Roberto Duellos instead of Captain Tanya Desjani, and tried not to let it all throw him off. *I am a fleet officer. It is ridiculous, and wrong, and unprofessional, to be tied to a single ship in the fleet. Besides,* Dauntless *is Tanya's ship, not mine, and—*

Dauntless *is Tanya's ship.*

Have I grown too dependent on her advice? Tanya is good. Very good. But I can't afford to need her support. As good a combat team as we are, I need to be able to handle things on my own.

Varandal's hypernet gate was close, Captain Duellos patiently wait-ing for Geary's approval to enter it.

But he paused a moment longer, gazing at his display. *Inspire* had not yet left Varandal, so he could still see *Dauntless* there, but already light-hours distant. He hadn't been so far from her since being awak-ened in this time, except for his brief honeymoon to Kosatka. Nor had he ever been so far from another "her," Tanya. *I shouldn't have made her fleet commander. I should have left her free to take some leave her-self, to go back to Kosatka and see her parents again.*

Who am I kidding? She wouldn't have gone. At least making her act-ing commander of the First Fleet ensures that she's tied down and can't come racing after me, with half the fleet at her back. "Captain Duellos, permission granted to enter the hypernet gate, destination Adriana Star System."

HE had expected to find a mess at Adriana Star System. He hadn't expected to find a hot mess.

As Geary's small task force left the hypernet, his display updated in a rush. It had already shown the seven planets orbiting the star, one of which at nine light-minutes from the star was slightly cold for human comfort but otherwise not bad at all. Another planet orbiting only two light-minutes away from the star was a scorching, bare rock. Farther out past the habitable world, a pair of mismatched planets whirled around each other as both circled the star, producing tidal forces so strong that humans avoided the two. The remaining three planets were gas giants sailing majestically through space, ignoring the human mining and industrial facilities orbiting them like parasitic insects.

That much matched Geary's few memories of Adriana. The human population had boomed thanks to the war and Adriana's position di-rectly behind the fought-over border star systems, resulting in many more towns, larger cities, and more installations in space. There hadn't been a hypernet when he had last been through this region of space, and Adriana wasn't a wealthy enough star system to have qualified for one of the extremely expensive hypernet gates on the basis of its economy. But the star's position near the border with the Syndicate Worlds had made a gate necessary, part of the defensive network built up during the war. For decades, that gate had been used to help quickly shift Alliance forces to wherever the Syndics had launched attacks, or to swiftly assemble Alliance forces for attacks on the Syndics.

There were numerous new defense installations. From this far out, even *Inspire*'s sensors couldn't immediately spot any signs of cutbacks here, but Geary suspected many of those installations were in worse shape than they looked. If his fleet had been ordered to send out inflated readiness reports, very likely the units here had received similar orders.

Basic bits of information about the star system were confirmed in a rush, then Geary focused on the activity here as new symbols popped into existence to reveal the current situation. What looked like a full squadron of aerospace forces short-range Fast Attack Craft was in orbit about the habitable world, trying to keep a motley collection of civilian freighters and passenger liners corralled. Many of those freighters and liners were aging Syndic models, as were another dozen scattered through the star system, fleeing attempts at being intercepted by more aerospace craft lunging out from the planets and moons on which they were based. Official comm channels were filled with transmissions of orders flying back and forth, as well as with demands, petitions, complaints, arguments, pleas, threats, debates, and explanations.

"There is a ground forces general in charge here," *Inspire*'s comm watch-stander reported tentatively. "But the aerospace forces colonel is issuing orders that contradict the ground forces orders. And the government of Adriana is giving orders to the general, while the general and the colonel are giving orders to the government. There are local police authorities also weighing in, as well as other varieties of local officials. And all of the refugee ships are demanding to be let go or to be granted asylum or pleading for help. That's just a basic rundown, sir. It's actually a lot more complicated than that."

Duellos ran through several possible expressions before deciding on simple acceptance. "Those aerospace craft don't have the legs to intercept all of the loose refugee ships. I recommend we send some destroyers after them, Admiral."

"Some destroyers? We're going to send all of them." He paused, wondering what he was expecting. *Oh. This is where Tanya would jump in and start helping assign specific destroyers to specific refugee ships. Duellos is deferring to me on the matter, waiting for orders, because we don't have that kind of established working relationship.* But there weren't that many destroyers or that many refugee ships, so it was a simple matter for Geary himself to tap units on his display, rapidly designating one or two destroyers to head for each fleeing refugee ship. "All destroyers in Task Force Adriana, execute attached orders. Intercept and round up your assigned targets, then escort them to join the other refugee ships being guarded in orbit. I don't want those refugee ships disabled or destroyed. Fire warning shots only. Request permission before firing on the ships if that proves necessary."

He sat back, watching the destroyers leap away from the formation, their paths forming a spray of graceful curves on the display.

"They would have preferred being sent to destroy those ships," Duellos commented.

"I know. But I don't have any stomach for massacring civilian refugees," Geary replied.

"I doubt they would, either, once they thought about it. You've gotten us all out of the habit." Duellos shook his head, making a face. "From the sound of the messages we're picking up, no one is in charge here."

"How is that possible? Why isn't the aerospace forces colonel paying attention to the orders from the ground forces general?"

Duellos shrugged. "Separate services. In a real crisis, they would hopefully cooperate well enough, but without an imminent Syndic threat to focus their attention, they're fighting for turf. Even though the aerospace commander here is a colonel, that rank is equal to the ground forces general's."

"It is?" Geary asked, eyeing one of the messages from General Sissons, the ground forces commander. The general's ideas of motivating subordinates and conveying orders appeared to depend heavily on yelling, profanity, and threats. Geary had been subjected to a few superiors like that in the course of his career. To their own superiors, they were unfailingly polite and proper, but the living stars help those unfortunate enough to work for them. "I can see why the aerospace forces aren't giving any ground when it comes to working with that guy, but why can they get away with it?"

Duellos raised his eyebrows at Geary. "You don't know?"

"No. And I want to know because I don't want this General Sissons trying to pull rank on me if I can help it."

"I'm sorry. Sometimes, I forget that your experience with the way things work these days is still limited, and I assume that things always worked that way. Yes, technically, General Sissons is very likely senior to you. Your promotion to admiral was less than a year ago. If you approach him as Admiral Geary to General Sissons, he can walk all over you. He can try, anyway," Duellos amended as Geary reacted to those words. "But as commander of fleet forces in this star system, you are his equal. See how the aerospace forces colonel is handling it? She always uses her status as aerospace forces commander when dealing with General Sissons, rather than her status as a colonel."

"That's . . . a little screwy. The Alliance has really allowed military command protocols to deteriorate to the point where no one is in charge of a star system?"

"You saw that at Varandal," Duellos pointed out. "The ground forces and aerospace forces there don't answer to Admiral Timbale.

But if there is a specific operation, in a combat zone, an overall commander will be appointed. If Admiral Bloch had brought a division or two of ground forces along when we made that ill-advised lunge for the Syndicate home star system at Prime, he would have been in charge of them as well as the fleet units because the assault force would have been organized that way."

The implications of that finally sank home. "If we're equals, I don't have to do what Sissons says, but I can't make Sissons provide whatever assistance I need to get those refugees back to Batara."

Duellos spread his hands. "You also can't make the aerospace forces colonel do whatever you want. You might be able to overawe them. You *are* Black Jack. But you'll have to convince them that whatever you are demanding is required to carry out the task specified in your orders and that your orders are consistent with their orders."

And General Sissons's orders surely also contained the old phrasing *all actions necessary and proper*, which offered substantial wiggle room, as well as substantial grounds to declare that anything he was asked to do was unnecessary or improper or both. In order to get this mission done, Geary might have to wheel and deal and convince and implore like some politician. He finally got a good sense of how fleet command processes had sunk to the level they had been at when he took control of the fleet at Prime. "How the hell did we avoid losing the war a long time ago?" Geary muttered.

"The Syndics are worse," Duellos said.

"Yeah. I guess they are. All right. I've already acted by sending my destroyers out after those loose refugee ships, which demonstrates my capabilities and my willingness to use them. I'll contact General Sissons and Colonel . . . Galland and see how they respond. It will take a day and a half for us to reach that habitable planet, which gives us all time to work something out."

In his earlier career, he would have been at a loss to formulate a message designed to convince other commanders to cooperate with him rather than either telling them what to do or submitting to their authority. But he had learned a few things since then. "To General Sissons, commander of Alliance ground forces in Adriana Star System, and Colonel Galland, commander of Alliance aerospace forces in Adriana Star System, this is Admiral Geary, commander of Alliance fleet forces in Adriana Star System." He marveled at the requirement to take a breath after that lengthy beginning to the message. "I look forward to working with both of you to resolve the refugee situation here. Your assistance and advice will be critical to a successful resolution of the issue. To the honor of our ancestors, Geary, out."

Duellos nodded approvingly. "Not bad. Spoken with authority, but not with enough force to get their backs up, and extending a hand for cooperation. You always say you're not good at politics, but that wasn't bad at all."

"I guess I've spent too much time around Victoria Rione. She's always made a point of explaining things like that to me."

"Ah. I see. That woman."

"Don't you start calling her that, too. It's bad enough that Tanya refuses to say her name."

Duellos grinned. "I just want you to feel at home."

"Thanks." Geary gestured toward his display. "Can your comm people do some analysis for me?"

"Certainly. What do have in mind?" Duellos asked, intrigued.

"According to what we're picking up so far, all of the ground and aerospace assets at Adriana are still at full strength and ready for action. But First Fleet's warships were ordered to send out deceptive status reports about their readiness."

"And the same might be happening here?" Duellos nodded. "But if it is, analyzing comm patterns will give us an idea of whether or not the external picture we're getting is a true one. Yes, Admiral, my crew can get you something on that. It will take a while to assemble a good picture, but within a day or so we should be able to tell you whether Adriana's defenses are still solid or just a hollow shell."

THE first reply came from Colonel Galland, about six and a half hours later. She looked tired, but her eyes were sharp. "Welcome to Adriana, Admiral. I see that your destroyers are already on the move. I appreciate your assistance in collecting the rest of the Syndic refugee ships. We've been overwhelmed by the number of ships and refugees, and my craft aren't designed for this kind of situation. The fleet always handled things like this, usually intercepting it at Yokai. But the last fleet assets were apparently pulled out of Yokai a couple of months ago. There were two fleet destroyers still here at Adriana, but they were withdrawn three weeks ago. Since then, we've been scrambling to handle the refugee problem with what we have on hand."

Galland smiled bitterly. "Half of my squadrons were supposed to be decommissioned by now, but I won a reprieve by getting the local government to raise hell with Adriana's senators at Unity. I'm still expecting the cutbacks to take effect at some point, though, so unless you're going to be stationed here for the long haul, we need to come up with a solution for what is going on at Batara. Once those squadrons are gone, my headquarters here will probably be downsized as well, and me with them. You might find this seat empty when you get back from Batara."

She smiled without visible humor again. "If you don't know General Sissons, fair warning. He's a neutron star. No light, no warmth, just toxic radiation that destroys bodies and souls in his vicinity. He'll want you to do everything, he'll find reasons not to do anything himself, and he'll take credit for everything that went right when it's done. But he sucks up to the right people, so he'll survive the reductions in force. He's only got a few months left here before he jaunts off to ground forces headquarters."

The sour smile shifted to grim resolve. "Admiral, I spent fifteen years fighting the Syndics and protecting Alliance star systems against them. My predecessor in this job died fending off an assault on this star system while your fleet was fighting its way back home from Prime. And now all that's left is coping with refugees, getting ready to turn off the lights when the last person leaves this building, and turning in my uniform when I get downsized, too. Which is why I'm being frank with you. I'd rather go out having accomplished something than playing along in hopes of prolonging my career another year or so. There's not much more I can do with my hands full just keeping the Syndic refugees from scattering into Alliance territory. Whatever else I can do, though, I will. To the honor of our ancestors, Galland, out."

The reply from General Sissons came in nearly six hours after that. By checking local planetary time, Geary could see that his message had reached the planet during the night. Sissons hadn't sent his reply until morning.

"This is General Sissons. Geary, I want full status updates on all of your ships and a briefing on your plan of action for returning the refugees to Batara using fleet assets only. My own forces have commitments that have stretched them to their limits. I see that you've already taken some limited actions to compensate for the lamentable lack of fleet support here in recent months. I don't approve of unilateral decisions regarding the movements of your forces, which should be coordinated beforehand with my headquarters. For your future information, all communications with local governments, local law enforcement, local aerospace command, or anyone outside this star system, including fleet headquarters, must go through my headquarters using established channels in accordance with existing protocols. If you still have questions about my expectations and your orders, contact my chief of staff. Sissons, out."

Geary's first reaction when the message ended was to say a heartfelt prayer of thanks to the living stars that he wasn't actually under the authority of General Sissons even though the general had done all he could to create the impression by his words that Geary would have to clear all of his actions and communications through him. Having finished the prayer, Geary mentally ran through a variety of entertaining responses he could send Sissons. *But I can't really tell him off like I want to. Anything I say to him has to appear reasonable and appropriate to others. I don't want Sissons to goad me into making myself look bad.*

He formulated a reply, imagining that first Tanya, then Victoria Rione were critiquing it. "General Sissons, this is the commander of Alliance fleet forces in Adriana Star System," Geary began, keeping his tone bland. "In reply to your suggestions, I must inform you that I will abide by standard Alliance fleet communications protocols and communicate directly with anyone I have to contact. I am always open to your suggestions for the most effective employment of the fleet forces under my command, but of course authority for such actions rests with me. Since you have been dealing with the Syndic refugee problem here for some months, and my orders specify that ground forces *will* provide security for refugee return operations, I am interested in seeing as soon as possible the contingency plans and options your headquarters must have already developed for resolving the problem using *your* forces. Geary, out."

He was still basking in the pleasure of having respectfully told Sissons where to stick his expectations when another message arrived, this one from the Adriana Star System government.

Most of the government seemed to have assembled to stand in the background as the elderly woman in the front spoke. Thanks to medical and genetic advances, age didn't visibly appear in people anymore until they were getting near the ends of their lives, so Geary realized this woman must have been born in the first decades of the war, making her the closest thing to a contemporary he now had.

"Welcome, Admiral Geary," she said with formal dignity. "The people of Adriana are honored beyond measure by your presence here and cannot express too strongly our gratitude for your assistance in dealing with our current troubles. We understand that you will be very busy with your labors, and will be contacting us regarding them, but if you have any time at all for social events we wanted you to know that the Adriana Academy for Children of the Armed Forces here contains a child who is descended from one of your crew on the *Merlon*. We know you would want to be aware of that. To the honor of our ancestors, President Astrida, out."

Once again, he found himself staring at the empty place where a message had been playing out. They wanted him to physically visit their world, their city. Everyone wanted Black Jack to do that. With rare exceptions, he had been able to avoid doing so, begging off on the grounds of duty. He had seen firsthand on Kosatka how the citizens of the Alliance reacted to Black Jack, and the hero worship there, worship for someone he knew he was not, had unnerved him and strengthened his resolve to avoid similar situations.

However, a descendant of someone who had been on his heavy cruiser during the battle at Grendel? Just what was an Academy for Children of the Armed Forces? Some sort of college or university?

Geary looked up the term and read it twice before the meaning sank in. *Orphanages established and funded by the Alliance government for those children who have lost both parents during military service in the war.*

Both parents. And according to the ship's database, there were enough children so afflicted that the Alliance had established dozens of those academies on worlds scattered throughout Alliance space. Captain Tulev . . . had he spent part of his childhood at such an academy after his home world was all but destroyed?

Geary himself had lost his entire living family to the war as well, though as an adult, when he literally slept through the rest of their lives while frozen in that escape pod. If he had been a child, it would have hurt so much more. He knew that. He didn't want to go. He didn't want to face those children. But . . .

Orphans. Why did it have to be orphans?

I'll go see them. I'll find the time. I owe them that.

"ADMIRAL, I have the information you asked for," Duellos said.

Geary looked over at Duellos. He was trying to stop the simmering anger caused by the latest reply from General Sissons, which had simply punted the problem back to Geary rather than offering either forces or solutions. The anger was aimed as much at himself as at Sissons. *I should have realized that Sissons could keep up this kind of thing indefinitely. I need a way to pressure him into supporting what it looks like will have to be my plan.*

The battle cruisers *Inspire, Formidable, Implacable,* and the light cruisers with them, were only twenty-four light-minutes, or about four hours' travel time at point one light speed, distant from the primary world at Adriana as they continued en route the planet. Geary, uncomfortable in the flag-officer quarters aboard *Inspire,* had come to the bridge to watch events and get a better feel for how *Inspire* ran. "Which information was that?"

"The true status of the military forces in this star system." Duellos gestured a tall, trim male lieutenant forward. "Lieutenant Barber, please give the Admiral a rundown."

"Yes, sir." Barber called up a virtual window and began explaining it to Geary. "These are aerospace unit and base designations. Over here are ground forces unit and base designations. These lines represent all of the comm traffic to and from those units and bases that we've been able to identify. More traffic, thicker lines, less traffic, thinner lines. Much of the traffic on Adriana's main planet would be by ground channels, such as buried cables, which we can't spot from out here, but by monitoring message sequence numbers, we're able to tell how many messages we're not seeing."

"That's clear enough," Geary said. "The aerospace units all seem to be pretty busy."

"Yes, sir. We assess that the status reports we're seeing from the aerospace forces are accurate and do represent the actual forces present in this star system." Barber paused, his lips thinning as he looked to the ground forces side of the image. "But for the ground forces, some units don't seem to be communicating with each other or with their headquarters except for those status reports saying all is well and they are at almost one hundred percent readiness."

Geary shook his head. "You're saying some ground forces units, but to me it looks like most of those units."

"Yes, sir. Which is especially odd since elements of those units are supposed to be on duty at facilities off planet. There would have to be a lot of messages we could see. There's nothing going to or from them, though, except daily status reports. One of my chiefs ran a pattern analysis on those status reports coming from units that had no other comm traffic. She found that when all reports are compared against each other, the number of minor problems reported each day, such as the number of personnel sick or percent of equipment temporarily degraded, closely matches the results produced by a simple random number generator."

"They're fake," Geary said.

"Yes, sir," Lieutenant Barber agreed. "My assessment is that those units do not actually exist."

Geary looked toward Duellos. "Some of those units have been assigned to Adriana for a long time."

"True enough," Duellos said. "But that doesn't mean they are still here."

"The units were disestablished, but they were left in the comm systems?"

"In the entire command and control system," Duellos corrected. "If you're going to maintain the illusion of an army, you have to ensure the command and control system reflects that illusion."

"My best estimate," Lieutenant Barber said, "is that each of the two ground forces divisions still assigned here actually only have a single brigade of soldiers still active. The rest of the ground forces organization is just an empty shell that, as Captain Duellos says, produces the illusion of a much larger force than really exists."

"Force reductions," Geary said as he studied the image showing Barber's analysis. "Done in such a way as to mask their impact. Ground forces divisions have three brigades these days? That means the ground forces in Adriana have been cut by two-thirds. The locals must know, though. You can't hide all of those empty garrisons and camps. You can't hide the lack of soldiers going out on liberty and spending money on the local economy."

"The locals may know the truth," Duellos said, "or they may be starting to guess the truth, but they may not wish to accept it. With what you told me about Yokai, it's clear that the Alliance is going to extensive efforts to conceal how the force reductions have impacted its defenses near the border with the Syndicate Worlds."

Lieutenant Barber pointed to some of the ground forces unit designations. "Sir, the locals may have been told that those missing soldiers were sent to Yokai. I saw a couple of reports that indicated the locals believe that the defenses at Yokai have been strengthened."

"Maybe those defenses were strengthened," Geary said, but he didn't really believe it.

"Admiral," Barber said with immense caution, "if, uh, if those missing units were at Yokai, there would not be any need to, uh, pretend they were still here."

"You're right," Geary said. "Lieutenant Barber, I don't mind people telling me when they have good reason to believe I may be wrong. In fact, I appreciate it. Thank you."

Barber smiled with obvious relief. "Yes, sir. It's just that . . . other admirals . . ."

"I know, Lieutenant. I've dealt with my own share of admirals who don't want to ever be told they might be wrong." Geary peered at the study again. "Both divisional headquarters are reporting that they are fully intact. Is that right?"

"As far as we can tell, yes, sir. Headquarters units appear to be fully operational. There are indications, requests for more workspace equipment and things of that nature, that they have grown a bit."

"They gutted the fighting units, and not only kept the headquarters at full strength but made the headquarters larger?"

"When money is short, you have to keep your priorities straight," Duellos observed sarcastically. "Thank you, Lieutenant. Excellent work. The Admiral and I will now discuss Great and Important Matters."

"Yes, sir."

Barber retreated to the comm watch station, and Duellos activated the privacy field around his and Geary's seats. "Colonel Galland told you that the locals raised a fuss to maintain her wing at full strength," Duellos said. "That probably didn't endear Colonel Galland to her superiors."

"No. I'm sure it didn't," Geary said. "And she said that General Sissons likes to suck up to his bosses though she didn't say it quite so bluntly."

Duellos smiled. "If General Sissons wanted above all to keep his superiors happy, he would have gone along without protest with any reductions in force passed on to him, and not told the locals so they wouldn't raise any fuss that might upset Sissons's bosses. We now know why Sissons hasn't offered you any ground forces," Duellos said. "He doesn't have any to spare. Those who are left are maintaining the image of two full divisions. Judging by how many refugee ships we're dealing with, we would need a substantial fraction of at least one brigade of ground forces to get this job done, and if that many more troops left Adriana, the whole imaginary house of cards would collapse as it became painfully obvious just how few Alliance soldiers were left here."

"If by a substantial fraction you mean two regiments, yes, that's what we need. Without those ground forces, I can't carry out my orders." Not a lethal trap, but a nasty one.

If that was the trap. Geary frowned at his display, which showed every portion of Adriana Star System and everything in it, though now he knew he couldn't trust some of that data. *If I fail to get this refugee situation resolved, it will be embarrassing for me. Not horrible or dangerous or unbearable. What sort of trap is that?*

What am I missing?

One of his hands moved, drawing out the focus on the display. Out . . . out . . . out. The details inside Adriana vanished as the scale shifted to interstellar distances, abruptly going from light-hour scale to light-year scale. Adriana, Yokai, and on out some more until Batara came into view as well.

The answer hit in a rush. What was happening in Adriana was important, but there were also Yokai and Batara. And maybe some other Syndic star systems were involved, as well as possibly the remnants of the Syndicate Worlds government or a local warlord CEO. The source of the problem, and any solution, lay in other star systems.

So would any traps.

NINE

SOMETIMES everything came together just right, like pieces of an intricate and finely machined puzzle in which every complex piece slid into place to form a perfect picture. Operations could be like that, where the mythical Murphy and his Law were nowhere to be seen, where friction appeared to be nonexistent, where even the enemy's moves contributed to exactly the desired outcome.

This wasn't one of those times.

"Rioting on some of the refugee ships in orbit! They're storming the supply shuttles!"

"The FAC squadron providing orbital security has suffered from a wing-wide control-system software failure! Individual FACs are operating their systems on manual and cannot conduct security ops!"

"The refugee freighter being escorted to the primary world by *Dagger* and *Parrot* is suffering life-support failure! The two destroyers don't have capacity to hold anywhere near all of the refugees!"

"Link has been lost to light cruiser *Forte*. Assess likely comm system failure."

"Two more refugee ships were just detected arriving at the jump point from Yokai! One is broadcasting a distress signal warning of equipment failures that could lead to power core collapse!"

"*Formidable* reports her main propulsion unit controls have failed during routine testing! She will be unable to maneuver until emergency repairs are completed!"

Geary, seated on the bridge of *Inspire*, waited as several seconds ticked by, knowing that everyone was watching him for instructions.

Captain Duellos, the palm of one hand pressed hard against his forehead, spoke in tight tones. "Is that all?"

His watch-standers looked at each other, then one lieutenant nodded. "Yes, sir. For the moment, sir."

Geary started issuing commands, letting them flow from somewhere inside without pausing to double-check or sanity-check them. That could come after he had put things into motion. He touched the comm controls. "*Implacable*, this is Admiral Geary. Proceed immediately at best speed to intercept the refugee freighter being escorted by *Dagger* and *Parrot*. Take aboard enough refugees to stabilize life support on the freighter and carry out whatever repairs you can. Geary, out.

"*Dagger, Parrot*, I have ordered *Implacable* to proceed to your assistance. Do what you can until the battle cruiser gets there. Geary, out.

"Captain Duellos, take all light cruisers and *Inspire* at best speed to assume security duties around the orbiting refugee ships. Take *Inspire* right into the middle of them and have the light cruisers form a perimeter. Pass orders to *Forte* via coded flashing light to accompany the rest of her squadron if she can do so. Alert the Marine platoon aboard *Inspire* to prepare for antiriot operations. Only nonlethal measures authorized."

His hand once again tapped the comm controls on the seat. "Colonel Galland, this is Admiral Geary. I am sending forces to assist your aerospace units in security ops. Keep me informed of your status. Geary, out."

Another tap. "General Sissons, this is Admiral Geary. There is rioting on the refugee ships orbiting the main planet. I have ships en route but require ground forces assistance to reestablish control. I expect military police in antiriot configuration to be shuttled up to assist my forces upon our arrival. If the military police do not arrive, I will immediately begin shuttling down every refugee on the orbiting ships and dropping them off at your headquarters landing field so your forces can deal with them there. That is a promise, General. Geary, out."

A third tap. "Unknown freighter coming from Yokai and broadcasting distress signal. None of my ships can reach you within the next twelve hours. You are ordered to divert immediately to the second gas giant in this star system, the one designated Adriana Sextus on navigational beacons. The orbiting facilities there will provide any necessary repair assistance, after which you will be required to proceed inward to the main inhabited world and place yourself under our control. Admiral Geary, out."

A fourth. "Commanders of Ninth, Fourteenth, and Twenty-first Destroyer Squadrons, be prepared to divert some of the destroyers escorting refugee ships in order to reinforce *Inspire* and the light cruisers. Have the maneuvers preplanned and ready to go if I call for help from you. Geary, out."

He sat back, taking a deep breath. "Did I miss anything?"

Inspire was already slewing about slightly, her main propulsion units kicking in to hurl the battle cruiser toward the refugee ships parked in near orbit about the planet the Alliance warships had been approaching at a more sedate velocity. Duellos waited until his ship had steadied out before replying. "I don't believe so. The locals at the second gas giant are obligated to provide emergency assistance, but you might tip off the local government just as a courtesy."

"I'll do that." Geary paused as another message flashed for his attention.

General Sissons's chief of staff was trying to look outraged but not succeeding very well. "For the commander of Alliance fleet forces in Adriana Star System, from General Sissons, commander of Alliance ground forces. We have no assets available to assist you. No landings at Alliance ground forces facilities on this planet are authorized. Ground forces, out."

"If he were a Syndic, we could just drop a rock on him," Duellos commented. "Ten minutes to joining up with the refugee formation, Admiral," he added.

"Thank you, Captain." Geary tapped the reply command. "For General Sissons, personal from Admiral Geary. Since you are unable to transport forces to assist in orbit, I will bring the refugees to you. Unless you are willing to fire upon my shuttles as they drop off refugees, you had better either find the necessary assets and get them into orbit immediately or stand by to receive those refugees on the ground, because they will be coming. Geary, out."

"*Implacable* reports she is one hour from intercepting the freighter with failing life support," *Inspire*'s operations watch-stander reported. "*Dagger* and *Parrot* are standing by the freighter, but one attempt to attach an evac tube to one of the freighter's air locks had to be abandoned when the freighter crew lost control of security at the air lock."

"Understood," Geary said. In his mind's eye it was all too easy to visualize what was happening on the freighter. The air increasingly unbreathable, the refugees panicking, the crew probably withdrawing onto the bridge and the engineering compartments and sealing the hatches for their own protection. He could see *Implacable*'s vector, see how the battle cruiser was accelerating all out for the intercept, but soon the warship would have to pivot and begin braking, using those same mighty propulsion units to slow her again so that she could match velocity with the lumbering freighter.

He, and *Implacable*, were doing all that could be done given the distances and the realities of acceleration and deceleration.

He prayed it would be enough.

Inspire was pivoting again, her own propulsion units flaring as the battle cruiser slid into position amidst the swarm of battered refugee ships, a lion suddenly present among a herd of sheep. On the outer edges of the gaggle of freighters, the Alliance light cruisers were also gliding into position, like cheetahs aiming to keep the herd from scattering away from the prime predator.

"Admiral, there are shuttles launching from ground forces bases on the planet."

"How many shuttles?" Duellos demanded.

"Eight . . . nine, sir. Here's three more coming around the curve of the planet."

"Twelve," Duellos said to Geary. "Enough?"

"Probably all Sissons has got," Geary muttered in reply. He gestured to *Inspire*'s communications watch. "I need a maximum override space shipping broadcast. All circuits."

"Yes, sir." It took only a couple of seconds before the chief nodded back to him. "You're ready, Admiral. Channel six."

"Thank you." Geary put on a stern expression, then hit the control. "All ships carrying refugees, this is Admiral Geary of the Alliance fleet. I am here to restore order, and I will do so. All activity is to cease on your ships. Armed and armored Alliance ground forces and Marines will be arriving on your ships. Any disobedience or unrest will be met with appropriate levels of response to reestablish calm and security. The commanding officers or executives of every ship carrying refugees are to contact the Alliance battle cruiser *Inspire* immediately and report the status of their ships. Any ships requiring assistance to restore order are to notify me on *Inspire* immediately."

What else would Syndics need to convince them to follow instructions? Geary recalled the phrasings he had heard at Midway among the former Syndics there. "Any failure to comply with my orders will be dealt with by whatever means are required. To the honor of our ancestors, Geary, out."

He had barely finished when another high-priority transmission came in. Not a message this time, but a direct call.

Colonel Galland spat out her words furiously. "An update! A damned, useless, bug-riddled software update that knocked my entire wing out of operation! My techs are restoring all systems to prior-day configurations, but my FACs will be out of commission for at least another hour while we do the resets, then bring everything online again."

"An update?" Geary questioned. "Someone planted worms in an update?"

She shook her head. "We haven't found any worms. That doesn't mean there aren't any. Right now, I don't know if the sabotage was malicious or just the routine sabotage-by-software-update that we usually encounter."

"What's the status of your supply shuttles that the refugees were storming?"

"There were three mated to freighters when the rioting started. One got clear. Two are stuck, with refugees packed into them and the air locks, and the flight crews locked down on the control deck. If those shuttles pull away, every refugee in them will die."

That settled one question. "I've got one platoon of Marines in riot gear. I'll send half to each ship where one of your shuttles is stranded so they can clear out the mess."

"Thanks, Admiral." Galland grinned ferociously. "I see ground forces on the way up, too. What did you do to General Sissons to get him to cooperate?"

"That's between me and the general," Geary said, even though he knew that in cases like this security only slightly slowed down universal knowledge of what had been in the messages he had exchanged with Sissons. Good gossip had a way of defeating any barrier and often seemed to exceed the light-speed limit in how fast it got around. "You've got a couple of FACs at the second gas giant, Sextus. There'll be a new freighter headed that way."

"The one claiming its power core is unstable? You're sending my guys a bomb? Gee, thanks, Admiral."

"You're welcome."

Duellos broke in. "Admiral, two of the freighters have lit off main propulsion and ignored warnings to stop."

"Have the light cruisers nearest them fire warning shots," Geary ordered. "And tell the freighter crews that if we have to fire on the freighters to stop them, we'll be aiming at the control decks of the ships."

He turned back to Galland to see her watching him appraisingly. "Admiral, as my FACs in orbit regain operational capability, I'll place them temporarily under your command. Once I get enough going to operate on their own, I'll have the squadron commander take over and coordinate with you. Are you all right with that?"

"That's fine," Geary said. "Does your squadron commander have experience working with ground forces?"

"Here? No. Sissons claimed he never had time or resources or money for joint ops. Do you have experience working with ground forces, Admiral?"

Geary smiled. "A little over a century ago. Two Alliance warships and a couple of platoons of ground forces. I was just a department head on one of the ships."

"Oh." Galland grinned back at him. "A little rusty, then?"

"Yeah. Let's get this done, Colonel. No, wait. What do you have on the refugees? None of the material I've seen since arriving here tells me anything about them."

"They're Syndics."

"Are they?" Geary asked. "Is Batara still under Syndic control?"

"I don't know, Admiral," Galland admitted. "I don't have any data on the refugees. I've had my hands full dealing with the freighter executives. The aerospace intel capability in this region was at Yokai, and as far as I know they all went home when everything else there closed down. Interrogations and collection at Adriana are the responsibility of ground forces intel."

As the call ended, Geary turned to Duellos. "Did you copy all of that?"

"Yes, Admiral." Duellos gestured behind him. "The two misbehaving freighters have seen the error of their ways thanks to very near misses from hell lances and have shut down their propulsion. My Marines are loading into my shuttles now. I need a rules-of-engagement question answered for them, though. They have CRV, riot-dispersal gas, and CRX, riot-suppression gas. The Marines want to use the CRX."

"What's wrong with the CRV?" Geary asked.

Duellos swung a hand across his controls and repeated Geary's question to the image of a Marine sergeant in battle armor that appeared.

"It's like this, Admiral," she said. "CRV is designed to disperse riots, to make people run by doing real unpleasant stuff to their eyes, ears, noses, skin, and so on. Nothing too bad, just real uncomfortable. But there's no place on a ship like that for anyone to run, and from the readings I'm seeing, the life support on those tubs is already shaky. We drop a bunch of CRV into that, and the rioting might get a whole lot worse as people try to run away from it but have nowhere to run."

"Could we end up with dead?" Duellos asked.

"Yes, sir," the sergeant replied. "Crushed and suffocated in the panic. And the overstressed life support will take forever to sweep out the CRV, so people will be suffering a long time. But the CRX will just knock them out. No warning, just boom, out go the lights. No time to panic and start stampeding. That's what I recommend if we run into problems, sir."

"Can the CRX cause casualties?" Geary said.

"Maybe," the Marine replied. "Very low odds, but if someone is already sick or something, it might push them over the edge. But it's as close to nonlethal as anything in the arsenal, Admiral."

Duellos nodded his recommendation to Geary, and Geary in turn nodded to the Marine. "Use the CRX if you have to employ gas, Sergeant."

"Yes, sir! Thank you, sir!"

After the Marine's image vanished, Duellos raised an eyebrow at Geary. "Marines don't usually get that excited about nonlethal options."

"From what General Carabali has told me, they really hate the idea of facing out-of-control civilians. There have apparently been some very ugly incidents on Syndic worlds where Marines had to fire to protect themselves from rioters who were just out of their heads with fear and panic."

"The glory of war," Duellos muttered. "We fleet sailors never had to see those who died when we dropped rocks on them from many thousands of kilometers away."

"That's over and done," Geary said, his voice sharp.

"Admiral," the operations watch reported, her voice carrying easily over the low conversation between Geary and Duellos, "*Implacable* reports fifteen minutes to intercept of the refugee ship with failing life support."

"Do we have any more reports from *Dagger* or *Parrot*?" Geary asked.

"*Dagger* reports . . ." The watch-stander hesitated, then continued speaking in grim tones. "Reports that the freighter crew says they are donning survival suits."

The combat systems watch-stander shook his head. "Captain, my cousin worked on a freighter. Breaking out those suits costs money. They don't do it unless they absolutely have to."

Duellos nodded slowly, his expression tightly controlled. "Would they wait until air quality was bad enough that it was necessary for survival? Or would they don the suits earlier to have a margin for safety?"

"Captain, from what my cousin said, they'd wait until the last minute."

"And we're twenty light-minutes distant from all of them," Duellos said.

Geary pressed his lips tightly together, then hit his comm control harder than necessary, knowing that anything he said would get there too late to make any difference. "*Dagger*, *Parrot*, this is—"

"Admiral, incoming from *Parrot*!"

Breaking off the transmission, Geary called up the new message.

Parrot's commanding officer seemed shockingly young, a product of the war when promotions could come very rapidly as more senior officers were wiped out wholesale in bloody engagements. Only her eyes betrayed the experiences which had aged her enough to qualify for command despite her youth. "Admiral, based on reports from the freighter crew about conditions aboard the ship, I decided to attempt attaching another evac tube. The attempt was successful, because conditions aboard the freighter are so bad that most of the passengers are either half-conscious or already comatose.

"We've linked an intake tube to our own life support to suck out what we can from the freighter and send back clean air, but we don't have nearly enough capacity. *Dagger* is mating a tube to another air lock and should join the effort within another few minutes. *Implacable* is only a few minutes away now, but . . . sir, we're going to lose some of them. Maybe a lot of them. We're doing all we can. Lieutenant Commander Miller, out."

A year ago, Miller would have been trying to kill those Syndics. Now she looked ready to howl with frustration at not being able to save them all. Despite the tragedy unfolding, Geary saw grounds for hope in that.

"Admiral, incoming from ground forces shuttles."

He shifted his attention to another screen, where a ground forces officer faced him, uniform and other aspects of his appearance reflecting a very hasty shuttle trip. "Major Farouk, One Thousand Seven Hundred Twelfth Military Police Regiment. I have six and a half platoons ready to assist you, sir."

Duellos indicated his display. "They should go to these ships, Admiral. I've been watching them while you handled the big picture, and they've got the most restive refugees. Our cruisers just had to fire more warning shots to keep a few more of those freighters from bolting."

"Thanks. Major, your assistance is welcome. I am tagging the nine freighters that we assess are most in need of riot control. My Marines are already boarding these other two. I have authorized the use of CRX riot-suppression gas."

Farouk stared blankly back at Geary for a moment before replying. "Sir, we have no CRX."

"You only have CRV?"

"No, sir. We don't have any gas."

"What *have* you got?"

"Screamers, flash-bangs, stunners—"

It was equipment more suited to dealing with serious law-enforcement scenarios than riot control. Geary held up his hands to halt the recitation. "Use minimum necessary force. We've got six warships out here to back you up. Are there any leaders among the refugees whom you can contact to help restore order?"

Major Farouk's expression reflected embarrassment this time. "I don't know, Admiral."

"Your intel people can't tell you?" Geary demanded, afraid that he already knew the answer.

"We have nothing on the refugees, Admiral. They are under the control of the aerospace forces. I asked, sir," Farouk added quickly. "As we were lifting. I was told the refugees are Syndics who came here for economic reasons, and if there was anything else, the aerospace forces should have learned it. That's all."

"Here are my orders to you," Geary said slowly and clearly. "As you board each ship, make sure you attempt to learn if there are local leaders who can assist in restoring and maintaining order. I want to know what you learn. Advise me immediately if you need any assistance or learn anything that I have to know. Any questions?"

"No, sir."

"Damned idiot bureaucratic foolishness," Geary grumbled after the call ended. "They're Syndics. Didn't anyone think it was important to know why so many were risking coming into Alliance territory?"

Duellos shrugged. "They're Syndics," he repeated. "Let me tell you how the people here probably have been thinking. First, since the refugees are Syndics, they'll lie if they're asked. Second, their motives don't matter because they're going back to Syndic territory. Third, they're Syndics, so who the hell cares? That's on top of what we already know about General Sissons's attitude toward cooperation and providing any support he doesn't absolutely have to provide." He checked something on his display. "My Marines are beginning boarding ops. Do you want to monitor them?"

He liked doing that, liked watching events through the viewpoints of the Marines, but . . . "Not this time. There's too much else going on for me to get that narrowly focused. Let me know if they run into problems."

"*Formidable* has propulsion controls back online!" the operations watch announced happily.

Geary felt himself smiling, too. Things were finally getting under control. "*Formidable*, this is Admiral Geary. Proceed to intercept with *Inspire*. I want these freighters to see another battle cruiser coming."

"Admiral, FAC 4657A is reporting in for instructions."

What should he do with a FAC? "Tell them to assist our cruisers in dealing with any freighters that start to leave orbit."

"Marines aboard one ship are employing CRX," Duellos said.

"What about the other one?" Geary asked.

"It looks like order was being restored before they boarded." Duellos looked to one side, said something, then turned back to Geary. "They've been contacted by two leaders who are asking them to refrain from compliance actions, whatever those are."

"When this calms down, I need to speak to those two leaders," Geary said. "On a secure, remote hookup. Have the Marines tell them now that as long as they can restore order, the Marines will have no need to act."

"*Implacable* has intercepted the stricken freighter and is assisting in rescue efforts," another watch-stander reported.

"FAC 1793B reporting for instructions."

"Ground forces boarding three freighters, shuttles still on approach for the other six."

"FAC 8853A reporting for instructions."

"Marines aboard freighter where CRX was employed need some fleet sailors to monitor freighter propulsion, power, and control systems until the crew revives."

Geary paused to rub his eyes. The bubble was slowly getting under control, or at least was no longer threatening to break into a million pieces flying off through space, but it would be a while yet before he could relax. He lowered his hand and looked to where on his display *Implacable*, *Dagger*, and *Parrot* could be seen clustered around the stricken refugee ship.

I've limited the damage, but I couldn't prevent some loss of life.

I'm going to get on top of this situation, find out how to get these refugees home, find out how to keep more from coming, and find out why they're coming here in the first place. And the one good thing about this recent mess is that it's put me in a place to start doing that.

IT had been a very long day, but despite his exhaustion Geary still felt keyed up. He needed answers, and these people might be able to give them to him.

The conference room aboard *Inspire* was nearly identical to that on *Dauntless*, but Geary still felt an irrational discomfort, including a sense that the standard-issue seat he occupied in this compartment was more uncomfortable than the standard-issue seat in the compartment aboard *Dauntless*.

Seemingly seated at the table across from him were the virtual presences of two individuals, the refugee leaders whom the Marines had found aboard one of the freighters. The Marines had set up the conferencing equipment, then backed off so that the two leaders would feel freer to talk to Geary. Both the leaders were in nondescript outfits that had clearly been worn too long under conditions that didn't permit baths or laundering.

The one who identified himself as Naxos was an older man of heavy build who reminded Geary of the more experienced senior enlisted sailors he had worked with. He did not seem comfortable with being someone in charge, and often looked down at his hands as if hoping they could do the talking for him. Naxos's words confirmed Geary's impression.

"I spent my life on a work line," he said. "At the lowest level. I started forty years ago. My last job was senior line supervisor. People think that means I know how to get things done. I hope they're right." Naxos glanced toward Geary, a flash of defiance showing, then quickly looked away again.

"I'm not a Syndic CEO," Geary said. "I like it when people look me in the eye."

The other refugee leader was younger, sharper, a blade not yet worn down by life in the Syndicate Worlds. She didn't have the same air of reflexive submission that Naxos did but lacked the confidence of someone who had occupied a high position. The woman, who gave her name as Araya, snorted skeptically at Geary's words. "Can we afford to take your word for that?"

"I don't see where you have any alternative," Geary said. "From what I know, I'm the first person in authority from the Alliance to talk to you, and I might be the last. If there's something we need to know, you need to tell me." As he spoke with these two, on top of his earlier conversations, he was slowly realizing how much Victoria Rione had schooled him on difficult talks. Without telling him she was doing so, Rione had almost constantly forced him to deal with oblique statements and unclear motivations. He had always assumed that was just the way she was, but now he wondered if Rione had done it deliberately with this end in sight. She had been very direct in their first conversations, after all. "What was your job under the Syndicate?" he asked Araya.

"Sub-executive Level Five," Araya replied as if daring him to comment on it.

"I can't remember exactly where that rank sits in the Syndic hierarchy," Geary said.

"It's not high. In fact, you can't get any lower without being a worker." Her eyes studied him. "I was blackballed by a CEO. No promotions. Ever."

"I see."

"Do you?"

"I've talked to the people in the Midway Star System, who revolted against the Syndicate Worlds. They told me a lot about the system they had been forced to live under, what CEOs could do to try to compel people." Geary pointed to Naxos, then Araya. "I've been ordered to take you back to your homes. But I want to help you."

Skepticism radiated from the two like a physical force. "Why?" Naxos asked, his eyes on his hands.

"Because I'm supposed to solve this mess. Just taking you home won't solve anything if you and the others just show up here again. You're refugees. Why? Why did you leave Batara, and why did you come to an Alliance star system rather than one elsewhere in Syndic space?"

"You're Alliance," Araya said, heat entering her voice. "You've bombed us and killed us and shot at us for a century. Why should we tell you anything?"

"Why the hell did you come here if you think everyone in the Alliance is evil?" Geary asked.

"It wasn't our—" Araya began hotly before cutting off her words. She glared at Geary, then shrugged. "All right. Batara threw out the Syndicate. We rebelled. But once we got rid of the snakes and the CEOs, we . . . we . . ."

He knew this story from other star systems. "You had been united against the Syndicate government, but after they were gone, the different factions at Batara started fighting among themselves. Is that what happened?"

"Yes," Naxos confirmed, his gaze flicking upward for a moment to look at Geary before lowering again. "We were given a choice. Leave, or stay in a Syndicate labor camp that was under new management, or die. The last two options were the same thing."

Geary nodded, leaning back in his seat as he thought. "Since you were rebels, you couldn't go to another Syndic star system."

"We didn't have any choice," Araya insisted. "That's the only reason we came here. Leave Batara or die. Fine. Where could we go? We've got three jump points at Batara. One leads to Alliance space."

"To Yokai," Geary agreed.

"You call it Yokai. We call that jump point the Mouth of Hell. For a hundred years, the people at Batara watched Syndicate forces jump from there and disappear, or come back in tatters. For a hundred years, we never knew when Alliance killers would appear at the jump point to attack us."

"There was a certain logic to it," Naxos offered, frowning at his hands. "The other rebels wanted to get rid of us, so they sent us through the Mouth of Hell."

"The other two jump points," Araya continued, "lead to Yael and Tiyannak. Yael remains under Syndicate control. They don't have enough forces to reconquer Batara, but they do have enough to send minor attacks at us. They pop out, bombard some installations and destroy some shipping, then run. If we resubmit to the Syndicate, they say they'll stop. But everyone in Batara knows that letting the CEOs back will be worse than anything the forces at Yael can do to us. And the ones who kicked us out of Batara didn't want us helping the CEOs, joining with them or just telling them lots of things about what was going on, so they wouldn't let us jump to Yael."

"What about Tiyannak?" Geary asked.

"Tiyannak!" Naxos said it like a curse. "There was a mobile forces refit facility at Tiyannak. Not much else. My brother worked there. They revolted, too, and took over the mobile forces that were at the facility. They've been raiding Batara for the last four months. No, six months, now. They want refined resources, specialized equipment, bulk food supplies, and other things. Batara can't hold them off with what it has got, which are mostly just lightly armed converted merchant ships."

"We had to go through the Mouth," Araya repeated. "We got to the star at the other end. Yokai. There wasn't anything there. Locked installations with automated security systems that warned us off. We had to keep going. So we came here. And they won't talk to us or let us go or anything. They provide just enough food to get by, and we have to stay in orbit here and wait."

"We can work," Naxos said with another glance at Geary. "We're skilled, and we're hard workers. We're willing to go where we could find jobs. There must be places other than the Syndicate and the Alliance. But if you just send us back, they'll kick us out again, and we'll be here again. Unless they kill us. Why won't you give us a chance?"

Geary looked at the two, seeing pride, defiance, and desperation. "You just described to me how you felt about the Alliance after a century of having war on your front doorstep. How do you think the people in Adriana feel about you after having experienced the same thing from the other side?"

"We didn't start it!" Adriana insisted.

"Actually, you did," Geary said in a matter-of-fact way. "The Syndicate Worlds, that is. It launched surprise attacks on the Alliance. I know, because I fought against one of those attacks."

"That's impossi—" Araya began. Then her eyes grew wide, and she moved back as far as her seat on the freighter would allow. "You're *him*. It's true."

"I am the man you know as Black Jack," Geary said. "I know that your leaders lied to you about who started the war, so even if you don't want to believe me, you might ask yourself why you still believe them."

"Our fault," Naxos said. He sounded drained and was looking fixedly down at his hands again. "Even after all this time, we must pay for the crimes of our ancestors. Is that it?"

"I don't see the point in it," Geary said. "Not if you no longer pose a threat to the Alliance. Do you?"

"Does what we say matter?"

"It does to me."

Araya met his eyes, bold again. "If you are him— We just want the Alliance to leave us alone. Let us go on and find some place. Or do you mean Batara? The people at Batara have their hands full dealing with attacks from Yael and Tiyannak. They don't want to keep the war with the Alliance going. But they won't take us back."

"They're going to have to," Geary said. "Batara can't be allowed to kick people into Alliance space, and if stopping that means forcing a change in government at Batara, then I am willing to do that." The basic lie-detector routines in the meeting software hadn't alerted him to any falsehoods by these two, and he was inclined to believe them anyway because no worthwhile government would be forcing so many of its own people into exile or taking over operation of Syndic labor camps instead of shutting them down.

"You want to conquer Batara now that the Syndicate is gone?" Araya asked. "You could do that, because there's nothing at Yael that could stand against your mobile forces, but you'd still have to deal with Tiyannak."

"I'm not interested in conquering anything. Just how many warships does Tiyannak have?"

"We're not sure," Naxos replied. "You mean mobile forces, right? At least two heavy cruisers, maybe a dozen light cruisers and Hunter-Killers. And a battleship."

"A *battleship*?"

"It was at Tiyannak," Araya explained. "Not in working condition. Damaged in some battle before the war ended. We think whenever Tiyannak gets the battleship working, they will use it to outright take over Batara. They've boasted to us about that. Tiyannak is going to be the strongest star system in this region. And not even the Alliance can stop them. That's what they claim."

And after Tiyannak took over Batara, a rogue star system with possession of a battleship would control another star system on the border of the Alliance, facing places like Yokai, where the defenses were gone, and Adriana, where Alliance defenses had been gutted by downsizing.

An annoying and difficult situation had just become ugly and dangerous.

TEN

DUELLOS had escorted Geary to *Inspire*'s shuttle dock, then paused at the end of the shuttle's entry ramp, giving Geary a pleading look. "You know what will happen to me if anything happens to you."

"Tanya wouldn't hurt you."

"How can you be married to her and not know what the woman is capable of?" Duellos asked. "Please, Admiral. Take a squad of Marines along. No one will blink at their accompanying you."

He shook his head stubbornly. "No. I'm not some Syndic CEO who needs bodyguards everywhere he goes."

"Captain Desjani said you might feel that way, her exact words were something along the lines of *he'll probably be a stubborn ass about it*, and requested that I remind the Admiral that various parties attempted to kill him while he was in Sol Star System."

"I haven't forgotten that," Geary said. "But, while there, Captain Desjani reminded me that Black Jack is an important symbol. What he does matters. How would it look, what message would it convey, if Black Jack thought he needed personal protection while walking around a planet of the Alliance among the people of the Alliance?"

"There is that. But you had agreed there was a trap waiting for you here," Duellos reminded him.

Geary laughed, surprising his companion. "There isn't a trap. Not like what we thought. Why do we have to worry so much about that battleship in the hands of Tiyannak? Because the defenses here and at Yokai have been gutted, right?"

"Right," Duellos agreed. "Not that a battleship could be discounted even if the defenses at Yokai were fully active."

"Who must have approved those drawdowns in forces and fixed defenses?"

"Fleet headquarters for our units, ground forces headquarters for—" Duellos ceased speaking, then smiled sardonically. "Admiral Tosic and General Javier. Who now find themselves in a lot of trouble because of those decisions. They have at least a hint of the threat from Tiyannak, don't they?"

"I'd bet on it," Geary said. "It's an awful mess as a result of their actions. They need someone to handle it, someone to bail them out."

"And who better than Black Jack?" Duellos frowned. "But if they knew about the battleship, why authorize only one division of battle cruisers to come with you to Adriana?"

"Because they can't admit that they know about the threat. They can't admit that they need a fire brigade in here to put out the blaze caused by their earlier decisions. If I put out the fire, they get to avoid awkward questions. If I fail, then, hey, they sent Black Jack with what should have been more than enough warships for the refugee return mission, didn't they? How can it be their fault that he failed?"

"Clever," Duellos admitted. "And the tendency of the press and the government and the citizens to focus on you would help ensure no one looked back to whatever actions various headquarters commanders had taken."

"Exactly. This isn't some great scheme to sabotage the Alliance or undermine the government. It's just good old-fashioned political maneuvering to protect the butts of the brass." Geary smiled again. "But it may serve a higher purpose than they plan."

Duellos looked around with exaggerated surprise. "I don't see that Rione woman anywhere, but I swear I could feel her presence."

"Working with her has given me some ideas," Geary admitted. "Tanya gave me more ideas. This will still be a tough operation if Tiyannak has the battleship operational. But it's the kind of tough I can handle."

COLONEL Galland was waiting at the landing pad where Geary's shuttle set down. She saluted him with an admiring smile. "I have seen people throw their weight around before, Admiral, but you take the cake."

"I'm not that bad," Geary said, returning the salute. "Not usually, anyway. Have the aerospace forces begun saluting again, too?"

"We're seriously considering it." Galland fell in alongside Geary as they walked toward a group of governmental dignitaries awaiting them. "When they take away your people and your aerospace craft and your training time and your lunch money, tradition is about the only substitute for those things that you can afford. Just so you know, nine months ago Adriana petitioned to have its contributions to the Alliance reduced. They have unilaterally reduced those payments by half while awaiting a response."

"And they'll probably be shocked to hear that Alliance spending on defending them has been cut." Geary looked around. "I don't see any ground forces officers. Nor any military police for security. General Sissons had better show up for this meeting."

"There's some regular police farther out occupying a security perimeter. Military police don't usually handle this sort of thing," Colonel Galland advised. "They're more focused on internal security."

Geary was so shocked that he came to a momentary halt. "Internal security."

"Yes." Galland eyed him. "I guess that's a change from your days. They look for threats from foreign powers in Alliance territory."

A military force conducting internal security operations? That explained why the MPs had been equipped with the sort of gear someone who broke into buildings would need. "Yes. That's a change from my days." Geary looked around, at the blue sky, at the utilitarian buildings clustered around the landing pad, at the citizens awaiting him. None of it looked strange, but suddenly it all felt alien. He had been stunned to learn the sort of tactics the fleet had adopted when fighting the Syndics, but it had never occurred to him that similar anger, fear, and desperation could have altered the behavior of forces inside the Alliance.

Colonel Galland watched him, puzzled, then with slowly dawning understanding. "It wasn't that way? At all?"

"No. What about ground forces intelligence?"

"Same thing. Monitoring internal threats and watching for external threats."

Ancestors preserve us. "In my time, the military, the intelligence services, were outward focused. They never would have been aimed at Alliance citizens. We had laws that prevented that."

"I guess the laws changed." Galland bit her lip as she gazed into the distance. "And I guess we got used to it. I just realized that while active military forces have been drawn down a lot recently, the forces aimed at internal threats haven't been. Maybe we need to start thinking about that."

"Maybe we do," Geary agreed as he began walking again.

The most senior leaders of Adriana's government were here, as well as a general whom Geary didn't recognize. "Yazmin Shwartz," she introduced herself. "Chief of Staff for Adriana Star System Self-Defense forces."

President Astrida led Geary to one of the ground vehicles that would transport them to the meeting place. During the short trip, Geary tried to study the interior of the vehicle without being obvious about it, noting fairly luxurious fittings and what seemed to be impressive active and passive defenses.

General Shwartz noticed his interest in the vehicle. "We haven't made any unauthorized modifications," she said, sounding defensive in the manner of someone expecting criticism.

"This is a standard government vehicle?" Geary asked.

"Yes. Standard specifications," she repeated. "Required for all governmental officials at star system senate level and higher."

There must have been a huge number of luxurious and heavily protected limos like this bought for officials, Geary realized. He had a suspicion that the spending cutbacks hadn't affected those purchases. "Are you related to Dr. Shwartz of the University of Vulcan's Nonhuman Intelligence Studies Department?"

"Not that I know of."

Neither General Shwartz nor most of the others in the limo appeared ready to relax, making it hard for Geary not to tense up as well. Apparently, they expected the worst from him.

Colonel Galland, though, leaned back in her seat and looked inquiringly at Geary. "Nonhuman intelligence? We've recently seen a lot of press reports about those you found, and what the ones with you did at Old Earth."

"That's all officially classified," General Shwartz cautioned.

"Everyone here is cleared, aren't they?" Geary asked. "You have as much need to know as anyone."

"Can you tell us more about them?" President Astrida asked eagerly.

It was a nice opening to break the ice before the meeting. He owed Colonel Galland for offering it.

Especially since they were going to be getting some pretty bad news at the meeting.

"GENERAL Sissons was unavoidably detained—" the colonel began.

"What?" Geary interrupted. He hadn't thought he had given the word any particular force, but the colonel paled and had trouble speaking again.

"The general will attend via conferencing software," the colonel got out this time, his words falling over themselves in haste.

Geary found the seat with the elaborate placard saying "Commander, Alliance Fleet Forces, Adriana Star System" and refrained from pointing out that it should have identified him as commander of the First Fleet. He stood, waiting, as the others took their seats, and the virtual presence of General Sissons appeared in his seat.

President Astrida looked around the table, clenched her jaw in a way that stood out clearly on her aged face, then gestured to Geary. "Admiral. You said this meeting was urgent."

He paused only to bring up the star display over the table around which everyone sat, momentarily startled when no less than four aides, military and civilian, rushed to do the job for him. Waving them off, Geary pointed to the region around Adriana. "We've got a serious problem."

"Your orders, as I understand it," an officious man in a suit worthy of a Syndic CEO noted, "are to return the refugees here to Syndic space. Why is that *our* problem?"

Enough other people around the table seemed to share in the sentiment that Geary decided to go straight to the heart of the matter. "Because if a battleship belonging to a hostile power arrives at Adriana, you're all going to get your butts blown off."

He gestured again in the sudden silence. "The battleship is owned by Tiyannak. That star system," he said, pointing to the display. "Tiyannak has indicated an intention to conquer Batara, where the refugees came from. That will make Tiyannak your next-door neighbors."

Someone finally found their voice. "The Syndics signed a peace treaty!"

"Tiyannak is in revolt. They're not a Syndic star system anymore."

"How did you learn all this?" President Astrida asked as she cast accusing looks at some of her own officials. "I have heard nothing of this."

"The refugees told me," Geary said.

"They've told us nothing!" one of those subject to the president's glower insisted. "I've been up to some of those freighters myself. All they would talk about is finding jobs."

"Is that what they said?"

"They said . . . they said they could work. They were looking for somewhere they could work. They wouldn't tell us anything else! I asked for military assistance in interrogations, but we couldn't get any because I was told the refugees were a civil problem! I threatened the Syndics, I told them what we would do, and they didn't say anything else." The woman focused on Geary. "What did you do? What interrogation tricks did you use? What finally scared them into co-operating?"

"I talked to them," Geary said. Those around the table stared back, uncomprehending. "That's all. I talked to them. It is possible to talk to Syndics. And these aren't even Syndics any longer. But we have to talk to them. Not interrogate them, not threaten them, just talk to them. Those people have spent their lives being threatened by their own leaders," Geary added, "and by an internal security service that had almost unchecked power. Our threats seem like child's play to them. They've learned how to avoid answering questions, how to avoid saying things, how to avoid any truth that might focus attention on them or get them into trouble. They would only talk to you about the work they could do because they thought that was the only safe topic—because they think that we are just like their own leaders."

"So, they're stupid," someone said scornfully.

Geary felt his face flush with anger. "No. They're survivors. They're operating according to the rules they know. They don't trust anyone. But when I put the discussion in terms of self-interest, both ours and theirs, then they understood. My fleet database had enough information about Tiyannak and the Syndic-controlled star system at Yael to confirm part of what the refugees told me. Tiyannak is a resource-poor star system that was positioned well for a big Syndic ship refit and repair base just behind Syndic front lines. Now they're not under Syndic control, and they're still resource-poor, but they've got the warships the Syndics had at that base. The refugees didn't understand the significance to us of the battleship that Tiyannak has. They just saw it as a threat to Batara. But if the battleship is at Batara, it's a threat to Adriana."

President Astrida glared at the star display. "The defenses at Yokai cannot stop it? Why not?"

"Because there are no defenses at Yokai. They've all been shut down. The star system has been totally abandoned by the Alliance."

General Sissons spoke loudly. "That information is classified. It should not—"

"Everyone here *should* be authorized to see it," Geary broke in. "I'm releasing it to them on my authority."

"But . . . for a hundred years we have been on the front lines . . . all right, near the front lines," a government official complained plaintively. "Right behind them. And the Alliance has been here to defend us."

"The Alliance government has been cutting expenditures right and left as the amount of revenue flowing in has dwindled," Geary said. "I shouldn't have to explain that. I know that some senators in other star systems who argued for the need for maintaining more revenue to the central government for Alliance-wide priorities were defeated in elections. I also know that everyone is tired of war, tired of the endless fighting and deaths and destruction. Ending the war has reduced the scale of the threat to us. But it didn't make it go away, and it has created some new threats."

He paused to look around the table, catching the eyes of each person in turn, except for General Sissons, who kept his gaze fixed firmly on the table before him. "You know my fleet was sent out far beyond the frontiers of the Alliance. You must have heard that we took losses. Ships. Sailors and Marines. Men and women."

President Astrida held up her hands in a gesture of half surrender. "You don't need to lecture us on the sacrifices demanded of the armed forces, Admiral. Too many of us have lost people close to us. Have you looked at the economies of the star systems in the Alliance? Very few are doing well right now. We are willing to pay . . . what is necessary to the common good, to the common defense. But it is very hard to know what is necessary when so much is kept secret from us. Colonel Galland told us when her wing was threatened with removal, and we moved to save them. We were not told of these other reductions. We were not given a voice in the decision."

"Why weren't we told?" someone else demanded.

Colonel Galland shook her head. "Your president already said why. Secrecy."

"Did you know?" the president demanded of General Shwartz.

"No, Madam President," Shwartz denied, her eyes on General Sissons revealing anger and betrayal.

"It had nothing to do with defenses in this star system!" Sissons snarled.

"What about the status of your forces in this star system?" Geary asked. "Has that been shared with those responsible for local defense?"

Sissons didn't answer, glaring down the table in such a way that he avoided eye contact with everyone.

"General Shwartz?" President Astrida asked.

"All I know is that a couple of joint training exercises have been canceled in the last few months," Shwartz said. "Lack of funding was given as the reason."

"There have been persistent rumors that ground forces units were leaving the star system," a short, thin man said. "We were told they were rotating into Yokai."

"They weren't," Geary said. "My best information is that Alliance ground forces in Adriana now measure about two brigades. Total."

President Astrida slammed her fist onto the table hard enough to make the stars themselves vibrate inside the display for a moment. "Why weren't we told? *Why weren't we told?* What excuse does the Alliance have for leaving us exposed this way?"

Geary spoke with slow clarity, driving home his point. "I understand that Adriana is one of the many star systems in the Alliance petitioning to have their payments to the Alliance reduced. Who did you think was going to pay for the defense of your own star system if you wouldn't?"

A long silence was broken by the president, who glared at Geary. "Adriana contributed a tremendous amount to the defense of the Alliance during the war."

"With all due respect, Madam President, I know what was at Adriana before the war, and I can see what's here now. Other star systems, a lot of them, must have contributed a lot of money that was used to defend this star system."

She smiled back at him, a thin-lipped expression without much humor to it. "I forgot who I was dealing with. You passed through Adriana in those days? Before the war?"

Everyone got that look as they stared at him, the one he hated.

Geary nodded, gazing steadily back at the president. "Star systems complained about their taxes to the Alliance back then, too. They paid a lot less, but they still complained."

"Why do we need to discuss money?" a woman demanded. "You are here, Admiral, with three battle cruisers. Surely you can defeat a single battleship with that force."

Geary made an uncertain gesture with one hand. "Probably. But even with three battle cruisers it won't be easy. And I am not authorized to stay here any longer than necessary to get those refugees back to Batara. Fleet accounts have been hit by serious funding reductions. I'm scrambling to keep as much of my fleet operational as possible."

"Surely there is still enough money for the most important purposes!"

"I can't swear that what money is left is being spent wisely," Geary said. "I can only say that any money being spent on my fleet is being used as carefully as possible, and there isn't enough. More to the point, I've got orders to take care of the refugee problem here, then leave. If we don't figure out how to not only neutralize the refugee problem but also that battleship, you are very likely to be facing it alone when it finally comes here."

He gestured to the nameplate at his seat, proclaiming him commander of fleet forces in this star system. "Adriana is used to having fleet forces committed to its defense. That has changed. I'm not happy to be the one who has to tell you that. I'm going to work to get some fleet units positioned near here again full-time, but I don't know when that will happen or how strong they will be."

"Colonel Galland," one of the government men spoke in pleading tones, "your craft can stop a Syndic battleship, right?"

Galland laughed briefly, as if she were genuinely amused. "Under ideal conditions, if the battleship came into low orbit, and if I have every single craft under my command available to me, there would be about a twenty-five percent chance that we could cripple or destroy a battleship. Our losses under those conditions would run between seventy and ninety percent."

"And, if conditions are not ideal?" the man pressed. "What are your chances of success under other situations?"

"How many ways can you say zero?" Galland replied. "My FACs are not designed to engage something like a battleship. That's not their function. We'll do it. Do not mistake me on that." She looked somberly around the table. "If a hostile battleship shows up here, my people will go out to engage it to the best of their ability. They'll do that knowing that the odds of success are tiny and the chances of death are very high. But their sacrifices will not guarantee victory. Far from it. They can buy time, they can harass, they can disrupt attempts by the battleship to bombard targets on this planet from low orbit. But they can't win. Not under almost every possible scenario."

"Ground forces can't make any difference at all against that kind of threat," General Sissons broke in. "That does not fall under my responsibilities. It is the duty of the *fleet* to stop major enemy warships from ever reaching this star system."

President Astrida sighed, shaking her head. "Admiral, you've given us a lot of bad news. But, if even a small part of your reputation is true, you must have some ideas, some plans for defending us."

Almost everyone cheered up at those words, looking to Geary with the sort of hope he remembered seeing too many times before. That faith in him, that hope centered on him, had often threatened to unnerve him, but this time he just met it. His growing sense of confidence, of purpose, was crystallizing. *This is just like commanding a ship, or the fleet. They need to see confidence, they need to see competence. And it's my job to give them those things. I've been lucky so far. I haven't let anyone down. Someday, I'm going to fail. It has to happen. But not this day.*

"The fleet will stop this threat," Geary said, seeing the immediate elation his words generated. "But I need the help of Adriana to do it. As far as the refugee problem, Adriana can help with that, too. Otherwise, I can take those people back to Batara, but they'll just show up here again."

"What can Adriana do?" the thin man asked.

"I need three things. I need some ground forces in enough numbers to board all of the refugee ships, maintain order aboard them, and ensure that they all come along when we go back to Batara. I also need ground forces to back up our demands to Batara's current government that they stop shoving people toward Adriana and provide security on the ground while we're dropping off the refugees. Those ground forces will need transport." They were already adding that up, some looking unhappy once more, but Geary plowed ahead. "And we need something at Yokai to stop threats coming this way before they get here."

"And you have no extra funding," President Astrida said.

"I have no extra funding. You can request reimbursement from the Alliance government, but I cannot promise that you will be repaid."

"What exactly do you need from us?" the old woman asked. "How many ground forces?"

"I need two regiments of ground forces, fully combat outfitted, and I need shipping sufficient to carry those ground forces."

"You said one regiment would be dispersed among the refugee ships to keep them under control while you take the Syndic refugees back to Batara," the very well dressed officer protested. "They won't need separate shipping."

"They will if you want me to bring that regiment home once we drop off the refugees and let those beat-up ships the refugees are on go about their business," Geary said.

"The request is impossible," General Sissons said. "I don't have the available assets to spare. My soldiers are committed to defense of this star system."

"General," the president said in something very close to a growl, "if the Alliance ground forces in Adriana are incapable of offering any support to an Alliance military operation in defense of this star system, I can promise you that information will be widely reported and discussed on the floor of the Alliance Senate at Unity. Are you prepared to answer the questions that will be asked by the Senate if that happens?"

Sissons got the look of a deer in the headlights as he saw his career being threatened. "That isn't needed. We're on the same team. What you were told isn't entirely accurate. That's all I was trying to say."

"What was inaccurate?" President Astrida pressed him.

"I still have personnel equivalent to two brigades. I don't have two combat brigades," Sissons explained hastily. "There are support personnel, my headquarters, intelligence, military police—"

"What *can* you provide?"

"A regiment. One regiment. I can provide that." Sissons smiled as if expecting praise.

Astrida turned to General Shwartz. "Do we have a regiment from the self-defense forces that can go on this mission?"

Shwartz pursed her lips and looked unhappy. "As you know, Madam President, our self-defense forces have also suffered from significant spending reductions in the last several months."

"I know we still have an entire division on the books, General Shwartz."

"Yes. But self-defense, and deployment on an offensive mission, are two different things," Shwartz explained. She took a deep breath, then nodded. "We can provide a regiment. I'll build it out of smaller units with the necessary training. But, Madam President, I must advise you that there may be political costs involved with deploying so many of our forces."

"I'll take those costs," the president said. "At least we know that the men and women we send on this mission will be under the command of Black Jack and not at the mercy of one of the clumsy, dim-witted butchers who never seemed to care how many died."

No one looked at General Sissons, and he once again avoided looking at anyone else.

But one of the female officials spoke up. "The Admiral is a fleet officer, not a ground forces commander. How do we know—?"

"We know," another official broke in. "A couple of the Marines who accompanied Admiral Geary's fleet have families in this star system. When I learned that Admiral Geary was here, I talked to those families. I asked them what they had heard, and they told me it sounded like every Marine in the Admiral's fleet would go through hell for him."

"It's not easy to impress Marines," Colonel Galland said. "I know I've never managed to do it."

The laughter helped to cover up Geary's embarrassment at the earlier statement. *That's one more I owe you, Colonel.* "And the transport for those ground forces?"

President Astrida spread her hands with an irritated expression. "Yes. We don't have much choice, do we?"

"You have a choice," Geary said. "I think there's only one good choice, but I can't compel you to take it."

"Actually," Colonel Galland said, "you could. Compel them, I mean. TECA."

"TECA? What's TECA?" He had surprised Galland, and the others, with the question.

Galland laughed again. "You *were* gone for a century! Temporary Emergency Command Authority. Part of the Temporary Emergency Defense Act."

"Which," the old president said, "is a temporary measure that has been in effect for longer than I've been alive. It gives you the authority to draft any self-defense forces or other resources from any star system in defense of the Alliance. Even though the war is over, we haven't been told that it has been repealed. I was grateful that you offered us a choice on whether to support your mission, but now I see that you didn't know that you did not have to ask."

Geary shook his head. "Yes, I did. I'm . . . old-fashioned when it comes to coercive measures aimed at the Alliance's own people."

Astrida smiled. "I'm sure our ancestors would approve of such an attitude. Thank you for asking instead of taking. There was one thing more. You mentioned stopping any more refugees or other problems from coming through Yokai."

"Yes. We've got what's needed here. The question is whether you're willing to commit to paying for deploying some of it, not knowing whether the Alliance will pick up the costs later. I think they will because it is necessary, but I can't guarantee it."

Colonel Galland shook her head. "Adriana's self-defense forces don't have anything that could effectively screen traffic through Yokai."

"No, they don't," Geary agreed. "But you do. If you could rotate one of your squadrons through Yokai—"

"Keep a squadron at Yokai? There's no money for that! Not in training, not in operating funds, and not in anything else available to me. And I have no authorization to expand my mission! I'd get relieved of command as soon as headquarters heard what I was doing, and I'd probably get put on the hook to personally pay back *unauthorized* expenditures."

"I think I know where this is going," President Astrida remarked. A couple of her associates appeared about to protest until her sharp gaze silenced them. "The Admiral wants Adriana to pay for that."

Galland eyed her skeptically. "It wouldn't be anything like war costs. I'd need a lift to get a squadron of FACs and personnel to Yokai and back. A heavy-equipment transport of some kind. But once I had a squadron out there, I could leave the equipment and only send in replacements when necessary. Then there'd have to be logistics support, getting food and other necessities out to the deployed forces, and to rotate people in and out. That would be a recurring cost."

"What about the operating costs?" the thin man asked. "And your orders?"

Galland frowned in thought. "I could justify a lot of it as training. Flying patrols and deploying equipment are all part of that. Even being at Yokai fits that because one of my secondary missions is to deploy there if required. That means we have to be familiar with operating in Yokai, right? We could reactivate one of the bases. A single squadron can live for a long time off everything that was probably mothballed at Yokai. As long as my spending doesn't exceed authorized funding, no one back at aerospace forces headquarters is likely to notice or care what's going on."

"We can move some money around in the budget," the thin man told the president. "I think this is doable."

"And then we'd have defenses at Yokai again," the president said with obvious satisfaction.

"Yes, but," Colonel Galland added as just about everyone began looking relieved, "while we can stop refugees in civilian shipping, and a squadron can stop Syndic Hunter-Killer ships, if Syndic light cruisers or heavy cruisers show up, all a single squadron of my craft can do is harass them. That kind of threat requires fleet support to handle, and I don't mind admitting it."

"You will be working to get us that support, long-term?" the president asked Geary.

"I'll do my best," Geary said.

"A promise from Black Jack is no small thing." She gazed at him, her thoughts unreadable. "We haven't heard everything about the losses suffered during the final campaigns of the war and during your subsequent missions, but they are rumored to have been substantial."

Geary nodded, letting his own eyes rest upon the star display to avoid looking directly at anyone else as the memories hit him. "The fleet took massive losses before I assumed command. We took more getting home, while the fleet units left to defend the Alliance were badly hurt fighting off Syndic attacks as I was getting the fleet home. Since then, we have had to fight the Syndics again and have fought the alien enigmas several times, as well as the alien Kicks."

"It's the sort of thing that has happened many times before in the last century," Colonel Galland sympathized. "To the fleet, to the ground forces, and to the aerospace forces. Massive losses and constant streams of rebuilds and reinforcement. The difference is that this time, replacements stopped coming."

"I understand the why of that," Geary said. "But we can't let our forces get too small, or we'll end up with more and more situations like this one."

"There should still be enough money available to fund a better defense than we've been left with," one official protested. "Where is it going? We have a rough idea of how much contributions to the Alliance have been held up from other star systems, and from this one, I admit that, and if the cutbacks here are any indication, the cuts have exceeded what I admit are large cuts in funding."

"I don't know where it's all going," Geary said. "Your senators may not know. I would recommend you task them with finding out. Waste and . . . ill-considered programs are not something we can afford. Not if we want to keep faith with our people, whether civilian or military."

"Be assured that we will look for those answers," President Astrida said. "Colonel Galland, members of my staff will contact your staff to work out the details of your, um, extended training maneuvers at Yokai. Admiral Geary, we will notify you of the shipping, which will be leased to convoy the ground forces to Batara. General Shwartz, I want you to take the lead for getting the two ground forces regiments ready to go as soon as possible. Let me know immediately if you run into problems." This with a dagger-sharp look at General Sissons. "Is there anything else?" she asked of the room.

"Just one thing," Geary said. "A small thing," he added quickly, as tension suddenly began ramping up again. "I had promised to visit a place on this world that's not far from here. Could I get some ground transport there?"

President Astrida nodded. "The Academy? Of course. I am sure you will be very welcome there, and I thank you personally for visiting those children."

Colonel Galland stopped Geary before he got into one of the limos. "You've made my life a lot more interesting, Admiral."

"Not as interesting as it would have been if that battleship had shown up here and surprised everyone," Geary reminded her.

"No argument there. I just wanted to point out that my FACs might be useful at Batara."

Geary let his puzzlement show. "How would I get them there?"

"You've got battle cruisers. Have they just got the regulation two shuttles each? One FAC can be crammed into a battle cruiser shuttle dock along with them. It's a real tight fit, but it can be done. If those shuttles need to make drops in a hostile environment, or if you just want a strong escort accompanying your shuttles to impress the locals, my boys and girls could really help out."

"Another training mission?" Geary asked.

"How did you guess?" Galland said with a grin.

"I'm probably going to take you up on that offer, Colonel. We're doing this on a shoestring, and every bit of capability we can add will give me a better chance of getting it done right. Thank you."

"No, sir. Thank you. It can be hard to keep the faith sometimes, you know? You work with guys like Sissons, and after a while, you wonder what the point is. But there is a point." She stepped back, saluted again with the care of someone who had recently learned the gesture, then waved farewell as Geary got into the vehicle.

BEING around civilians made him nervous.

It wasn't because he had spent so much time in the company of military personnel whose uniforms had not undergone radical changes in the century he had been frozen. No, it was because civilian clothing had undergone the usual shifts of taste and fashion, altering with the years and the decades. Granted, because of the long war, some of those fashions had borrowed much from uniforms. But other fashions clearly avoided any hint of the uniform or the functional in their designs. Among the military, he could pretend that not all that much time had passed since the battle at Grendel. Among civilians, he couldn't avoid seeing in the styles of clothing they wore how much time had passed.

"We're very grateful that you could come, Admiral," the man in charge of the Academy beamed. "My mother used to tell me about Grendel when I was a little boy, and I worried that the Syndics would come attack us in our homes. She would say that Black Jack would never let that happen, that he would come back to prevent it."

Geary cleared his throat, even more uncomfortable. "Well, I . . . um . . ."

"I admit I had stopped believing! We were all in despair. The fleet was gone. That's what everyone was saying even though the government claimed the fleet was all right. But everyone knows you can't believe official announcements. And, then . . ." The man actually put his hand to his heart, gazing into the distance with a wondering smile. "You brought the fleet back safe, and you had hurt the Syndics worse than anyone ever had, and then you won the war."

Everyone else was smiling, either at him or at the man enraptured by his memories. The media was here, of course, recording every moment for posterity and soaking up the raw sentiment on display.

Geary looked ahead to the doors of the orphanage, functional metal entrances adorned only by what looked like amateur paintings of the seals of the Alliance Armed Forces, paintings he felt certain had been done by the children who had lost their parents to those armed forces. He felt bitterness rising to mask his discomfort. "I wish I could have ended the war while these kids' parents were still alive."

The man's smile changed to a solemn nod. "Don't we all, Admiral. But that's not what the living stars decreed. We are grateful that there won't be any more orphans. That's a big thing."

"People are still dying," Geary said, thinking of the ships he had lost, of *Orion* being blown apart at Sobek Star System. He noticed the uncertainty and the concern appear in the man's eyes and tried to rally his own spirits. "I'm sorry. My fleet has been through some very serious fighting even though the war is over."

"Serious fighting?" a woman reporter called. "The government hasn't said much about that."

Geary saw police moving to silence her and held up a hand to halt them. "I'll be happy to answer questions later. My first responsibility here is to the children."

"Do you still support the Alliance?" the woman persisted.

He waited a moment to answer, feeling tension filling the air like something tangible. "Yes. I support the Alliance, I support the government, I support those things our ancestors believed in, and those principles so many men and women of the Alliance died for."

"How strong is that support?"

They would keep pushing that point, apparently. Geary turned to face the crowd. "I support the Alliance and the government. I have made my stand on those grounds. I will not retreat from where I stand, and I will not retreat from those words."

As he headed for the doors of the Academy amid the buzz of conversation following his statement, Geary found himself walking beside one of the teachers. Her face held the telltale smoothness that hinted at age held back by modern science, so that she could have been anywhere from fifty to eighty years old. However, a prominent burn mark marred one side of that downy face. It was the sort of disfigurement that could have been easily removed, but the woman had chosen to keep it. "I served in the fleet, Admiral," she said in a low voice that just carried to him. "I had six ships shot out from under me. I know it's hard to lose men and women, but don't forget how many you've saved by winning those battles as well as you have. No one else may tell you this, but this Academy and the others have been told to plan for consolidation and closing as the children in them grow up and leave. Do you understand? Don't dwell here on those who died. Dwell on the fact that this place and similar ones will no longer be needed. Thanks to you."

"Thank you," Geary said. "That does mean a lot. And thank you for helping to hold the line with your own service during the war."

Then he was inside the utilitarian building, functional enough and nice enough but without any frills or extravagance evident in the entry. It felt military. Not lavish-headquarters military, but field-offices military. He wondered how many of the furnishings here had come from the same contracts as fulfilled military requirements.

A short walk led to the entrance of a large multipurpose room filled with children standing in ranks, the smallest in front. They gazed back at him with a solemnity not in keeping with their ages. They were serious in the way of children who had experienced terrible blows at a young age, and as Geary looked at them, he wondered how he could possibly speak to them in any way that mattered.

A young girl spared him the need to search for words. "Did you talk to them?" she cried, as teachers tried to hush her. "The eldest ones? Did you?" Her eyes were too dark in a face too thin, but now hope had given her expression a measure of serenity.

Thank you, Tanya, for warning me to expect that question. Geary knelt, so his head was on a level with that of the child. "Do you mean on Old Earth?"

"Yes. The oldest ancestors of us all. What did they say?" Her eagerness almost caused her words to trip over themselves.

"I'm still trying to understand what I saw and heard on Old Earth," Geary said, having decided that a literal truth was the best answer for a question he would otherwise have to lie about. "It was . . . a remarkable place."

A boy, older, almost a teenager, spoke abruptly, anger clear in his voice. "Why didn't you come back sooner? Why did you wait?"

Geary stayed kneeling and looked up at the boy, knowing the unspoken part of the question. *Why didn't you come back before my parents died?* Once again, he answered with the only truth he knew. "I don't know. It wasn't up to me. I don't know why I was found when I was, and not before. I wish . . . If it had been sooner . . . My parents died while I was asleep. Everyone I knew died while I was in survival sleep. I woke up, and everyone was gone."

"You know how it feels, then," another girl said somberly.

"I think so. Not as bad as you. I got into the escape pod just before my ship was destroyed, and the survival sleep process immediately put me to sleep because the escape pod had been damaged and couldn't keep me alive any other way. I thought it wouldn't be long, but when I woke up . . ." He looked down as the old emotions flooded through him. "I'm sorry. I wish I could have saved everyone. I can't. I'm just an ordinary man. I'm doing my best, but I can't save everyone."

"You saved us."

He raised his head, meeting the gaze of another boy who had spoken.

"We won't have to die in the war. Not like our parents did." He pointed upward. "I want to explore. I can do that now."

"How many Syndics have you killed?" another boy demanded. "Did you kill a whole lot?"

Another adult moved to intercept the boy with a haste Geary recognized. The boy was asking the wrong questions. "Hold it," he said, then focused back on the boy. "I don't know how many I killed. But I do know that I did not kill one more than I absolutely had to, and I hope that I never have to kill another even though I know the odds are very much against that."

"They killed my family!"

"I can't bring your family back by killing Syndics," Geary said. "I can stop the Syndics from killing any more, but I can't undo the harm that was done."

"They all need to *die*!" the boy insisted, oblivious to the tears welling from his eyes and running down his face. "They need to know they can't treat us that way, that our honor will not allow us to be hurt like that, and we will kill anyone who hurts us or . . . or . . . insults our honor! We—"

"*Stop.*" Geary saw the reactions of the children and adults, heard the sudden silence fall, and wondered just how forcefully he had said that one word. He stood up, looking around at the boys and girls surrounding him. "Honor? You think honor is about killing people? That's not what your ancestors believed."

"But—" someone began.

"He *knows*," a girl cried. "He listens to the ancestors and he . . . he is one of them. He came back from the dead! Listen!"

Geary didn't want to claim such a role, but he knew it was the strongest argument backing his words. "Honor isn't about how others treat you. Honor is about how *you* treat others. The only way to gain true honor is to respect and honor other people. The only true way to defend your own honor is to defend the rights and persons of other people. Treat others as you would wish to be treated. Do they still teach that Truth? It's easy to say. It can be very hard to do. But, if you don't, if all you think about is your own self-interest, about killing to get what you want, then you're just like the worst of the Syndics. Their leaders didn't care how many might die in the war they started. All they cared about was what they personally might gain from it, and what they wanted, and what they could do. And we all paid for that."

"We paid too much," an older girl said, looking at him with the eyes of an adult. "We see the news, and it's all about people arguing and complaining, just as if we hadn't won the war. Everyone talks about the price we paid, and the debts, and how hard things are. Sometimes . . . sometimes I want to speak to my ancestors, and I can't feel that anyone is there. It is very hard to believe. I know that you are here. I don't know if you actually were somewhere else all this time, if you saw or heard things we can only imagine, but how can we fix everything that was broken? How can we bring back what was lost?"

She faltered, swallowing, then spoke in a very low voice. "How can we even know what our parents would have wanted? The answer used to be, don't give up. Keep fighting. But the war is over. What is the answer now? Do you know . . . Black Jack?"

"I . . ." He had no idea what to say, then suddenly he did. "Listen." It hadn't been necessary to say that. They were all hanging on his every word though he himself didn't understand where these words were coming from. "There is one thing I did learn on Old Earth that I can tell you right now. Something I was shown there. You have heard some of ancient history, haven't you? A little about the old days, before humanity reached the stars, when we were confined to one small planet in one star system? Did you learn about the wars? The disasters? I never really understood that when I studied it in school. It was too far away, lost in the far past."

Geary paused, looking around at the children. "But I saw it first-hand recently, saw what Old Earth and our oldest ancestors had endured, and I finally understood. Old Earth is covered with ruins and wreckage and remnants of the past. But not one of those ruins is the last word. Our ancestors on that one, small planet never gave up. They rose again from every war, every disaster, every loss, and they built again and they kept rising and they kept building until they reached the stars. That's why we're here. Because our ancestors never stopped trying, never gave up.

"There was a town we visited. An old, ruined town in a place called Kansas. It had been abandoned because of the wars and other things too awful for the people there to endure. But when I was there, the people with us from Old Earth said the town would live again. I asked before we left Sol Star System. Is it true? Will that town live again? And I was told that yes, it would, that people whose own ancestors had lived there, and had never forgotten it, had already begun preparations to rebuild. Just a small town. But even it would not be allowed to die, to be forgotten."

He had to pause again, overcome by emotions. "If the people of Old Earth, our ancestors and their descendants today who remain there, could keep building, could keep trying, how can we do less? We are their children, and while we brought to the stars with us all the faults and problems and flaws of the past, we also brought the good things,

the determination, and the willingness to help others, and the imagi-
nation to build things greater than every shortcoming humanity has
ever known. We, all of us, will save the Alliance, will rebuild and carry
on. Because it is not in us to quit. Our ancestors gave us that gift. And
you and I and everyone else will use that gift to honor them and to give
our children a better future than we once believed possible."

It was only then that he realized many of the children and adults
in the room had phones and other devices with which they were
recording his words. Very likely those words had already left this
building and were flying around the planet on wings of light, soon to
leave even this star, carried inside ships to go everywhere the Alliance
mattered.

And he wondered who or what had given him those words and if
those words would be good enough to help save what some thought
already unsaveable.

The older girl was crying. "My grandfather was on *Merlon*. Thank
you for saving him."

Somehow, she was hugging him, face buried in his chest, tears wet-
ting the fabric of his uniform, Geary feeling incredibly awkward and
fighting back tears himself as other children came close to touch him
and laugh or cry.

He had considered avoiding talking to the press again, considered
finding a back way out and fleeing to the privacy to be found in the
confines of a battle cruiser, but not now. He would face the press and
everyone else, and say what he could say to them because he couldn't
be any less brave than these kids.

THE conference room once again felt uncrowded, with just Geary there
along with Captain Duellos and the virtual presences of two ground
forces colonels. Colonel Voston, the commander of the regiment very
grudgingly provided by General Sissons, had that look Geary had seen

so much of since being reawakened. It was the look of a man who had witnessed too many horrible things for too long. When a massive war went on for a century, many, many people had that look.

Colonel Kim, commanding Adriana Star System's contribution to the ground forces, had a ready smile and a calm disposition. She had made no secret of her relative lack of combat experience and was paying close attention to everything said.

Searching for a means to open the conversation, Geary fell back on the old military standby of asking about prior service. "Have you been stationed at Adriana for long, Colonel?"

Voston paused to think. "About five years now. My unit was sent here to reconstitute after we got chopped up at Empyria." He stopped speaking as if no further explanation was needed.

Geary chose his words with extra care. "There's a lot of history I haven't been able to fully familiarize myself with."

"Oh." Colonel Voston had the slightly puzzled expression of someone trying to explain something he had never before had to explain. "Empyria was Objective One for the Auger Campaign. It was a lynchpin for Syndic defenses in that region of space. We were going to go in with overwhelming force, take it, hold it, and move on to another star system deeper in. Hit one star system after another, going deeper and deeper into Syndic space, until we . . ." Voston hesitated, then smiled slightly. "Actually, I don't know what we would have ultimately done. That was above my pay grade."

"There were other campaigns like that, weren't there?" Geary asked.

"Over the course of the war? Yes. Many. None of them had succeeded. But This Time Would Be Different," Voston said, pronouncing all of the capital letters with extra, mocking emphasis. He paused once more, a shadow crossing over his face. "The entire Third Army was sent in against Empyria. We took half a million casualties during the landings, then lost a million more dead and wounded over the next several weeks as we reduced all of the Syndic defenses."

"How many Syndics were defending that star system?" Geary asked, trying not to let show how appalled he was.

"They told us going in that estimates were about half a million defenders." Voston shrugged. "I'm guessing it was closer to a million. No telling what the real number was. Too many bodies got destroyed during the fighting, blown into fragments, and nobody had the time or interest to collect fragments of the enemy. We'd gone in with three million, the entire army, but our losses were so bad that after we took Empyria, instead of heading for the next objective, we were told to hold for resupply and reinforcement." Another shrug. "A month went by, the Syndics were popping into the star system and launching raids and counterattacks, logistics were a nightmare, another month passed, the next big offensive got delayed and delayed again; eventually, my division got sent to Adriana to rebuild, and here we've been since."

Colonel Kim nodded. "Logistics. My mother handled part of that for the Empyria assault. Supplying three million ground forces soldiers on the attack strained our systems in this region to the limit. We dropped in freshwater recyclers, but still had to constantly bring in huge amounts of food and ammo. Every Sillis we had in that part of space was committed to the job, and we were barely keeping up."

"Sillis?" Geary asked.

"SLLS. Super-Large Logistics Ship. There aren't many left, so you probably never saw one. The Syndics figured out that with how many supplies each Sillis carried, they could score a significant victory every time they destroyed one of them. The Syndics started launching raids targeted on every Sillis they could find, tearing past other targets to destroy the big prize."

Geary nodded as a memory came to him. "At Corvus, I saw a Syndic light cruiser that was designed to take out targets like that."

"Corvus?" Kim asked, puzzled.

"A Syndic star system. One jump away from Prime."

"Damn," Colonel Kim said admiringly. "You were right in the Syndics' guts, weren't you?"

"We never should have built something that was such an attractive target and couldn't defend itself," Colonel Voston grumbled.

"It made sense from a logistics standpoint," Kim said. "Just not from a war standpoint. You'd think after so many decades of fighting, the brass would have realized that."

"I don't spend much time assuming the brass will figure things out," Voston said sourly, then realized he had said that in Geary's presence. "Admiral, I apologize for—"

"Don't worry about it." Geary looked over at Duellos, who hadn't said anything since being introduced and apparently didn't plan on saying anything. "Let's get started. I understand that General Shwartz has recommended that your regiment, Colonel Kim, provide security on the refugee ships."

"Yes, sir."

"Get me a plan for dividing up your force. They won't be alone. We'll have all of my warships nearby, and if any emergency pops up, we'll have three platoons of Marines for immediate reinforcement on any ship that needs it, as well as Colonel Voston's regiment if more ground forces are needed."

Voston spoke slowly, as if trying to ensure his words were understood. "My regiment is full of soldiers who have lots of time in combat, Admiral."

"I've been told that," Geary replied.

"Yes, but . . . Admiral, there's a reason we haven't been sent back into offensive operations. I've got a lot of people who've been pushed to borderline status. I think they've been kept active only because the medical treatment costs for them once discharged would help overwhelm the treatment centers in their home star systems. They're good soldiers. Good fighters. Good people. But they've been through hell. More than once. They might shoot when they shouldn't. Do you understand?"

"Yes, Colonel, I understand. Can they still handle this kind of mission?" Had Sissons burdened him with useless troops, soldiers too burned out to function anymore?

"They're good soldiers!" Colonel Voston repeated, his voice rising. "Excuse me, Admiral. They can do the job. Put them in combat, and they'll know what to do. Tell them to set up a security perimeter, and they'll hold it. But if you put them into some more ambiguous situation, they might . . . overreact."

"I see." Geary nodded his understanding to the colonel. "How about you?"

Voston smiled crookedly. "I won't let you down. I won't let my soldiers down. But, yeah, I'm pretty burnt, too."

"All right." Geary activated the star display on the table. "There's going to have to be a lot of improvisation because of how little we know about the tactical situation. I intend coming into Batara ready to shove the refugees back down the throats of the government there. I want to do that in a manner that makes it clear they had better not toss any more refugees our way. Colonel Kim, your soldiers will make sure the refugees board shuttles to be dropped off at Batara without rioting or just passively refusing to go. Colonel Voston, your regiment will provide security at the place where we drop them off."

"The locals are going to object?" Voston asked.

"Very likely. From what I hear of the current local leaders, they're way too much like Syndics for my taste."

"We can handle anything they throw at us."

"You'll have fleet warships providing fire support," Geary added. "Once we have the refugees dropped off, I'm considering continuing onward to Tiyannak."

Colonel Kim gave him a doubtful look. "There's nothing about Tiyannak in my orders, Admiral."

"I shouldn't need you there. If the situation looks calm enough, I'll send you back from Batara with my light cruisers as escorts before proceeding to Tiyannak. There's a former Syndic battleship that needs to be eliminated as a threat. Ideally, we'll be able to hit it in the dock where it's being repaired."

"And if everything goes to hell?" Voston asked.

"Then we'll improvise and respond as necessary. My three objectives are to return the refugees, try to ensure that the refugees don't get sent here again, and take out that battleship. You two only have to worry about the first couple of those."

"No problem," Colonel Voston said.

"Yes, sir," Colonel Kim agreed.

"Let me know how soon we can get going. The sooner we hit Batara, the sooner we can hit Tiyannak, and if we hit them soon enough, Tiyannak may not have that battleship working yet."

After Kim said her farewells, her image vanished, but Voston lingered, eyeing Duellos.

"Captain," Geary said, "can I have a moment alone with the colonel?"

"Certainly," Duellos said. He stood up with careful deliberation, then saluted Voston with the same slow precision before leaving the compartment.

Voston watched him go, then looked at Geary. "Admiral, I think you know why General Sissons tapped me and my soldiers for this. He expects us to screw up. He expects us to fail. Which I guess might make you look bad, or at least cause you a lot of extra trouble. But I want you to know that we won't screw up. We're not angels in the barracks, but in combat we've never let anyone down. You can count on us."

"I never doubted it, Colonel," Geary said.

IT took close to two weeks for the two ground forces regiments to be organized and loaded, and for three of Colonel Galland's FACs to be eased onto the shuttle docks aboard *Inspire*, *Formidable*, and *Impla-*

cable. Geary watched the lethargic process with growing impatience, unable to do much as the wheels of the ground forces bureaucracy and the Adriana government bureaucracy ground slowly toward actually getting anything done. He had no doubt that General Sissons was tossing all of the sand possible into the gears driving the ground forces' wheels, and wished mightily that Victoria Rione were here to help bypass the countless layers of approval required for the Adriana government to lease the necessary transport for the ground forces.

More than once he found himself regretting ruling out employing TECA and envying the leaders of Midway. Having dictatorial control and the ability to throw laggards into prison just for taking their own sweet time to get things done seemed more attractive with every day that crawled by.

And with so many of Adriana's self-defense forces coming along to Batara, it seemed as if every soldier in that regiment, all of their families, and everyone else in Adriana Star System were talking about it. If Tiyannak didn't get advance warning of all this, it would be purely due to the vast distances between stars and the still-limited time for some ship to carry the word there.

Finally, the day came. The refugees maintained a sullen, watchful silence under the eyes of Colonel Kim's soldiers as the freighters carrying all of them began accelerating toward the jump point for Yokai.

Geary ordered his warships into motion, pacing the clumsy freighters and wishing for the thousandth time that auxiliaries and freighters could accelerate like warships.

Duellos sat next to him on the bridge of *Inspire*, watching his display. As the large convoy of refugee ships (which more closely resembled a swarm of gnats herded by the warships than an organized formation) settled onto a vector for the jump point, Duellos glanced at Geary. "We haven't seen any new refugee ships arrive from Batara since that one with the power core problems about three weeks ago."

"I noticed," Geary said. "Colonel Galland said they were formerly showing up at a rate of one or two a week."

"I have a feeling that's a bad thing," Duellos continued. "That it may indicate that conditions at Batara have already changed."

"I have the same feeling," Geary said. "The living stars know there's been enough time wasted for conditions to change. We'll be jumping to Yokai in combat formation."

ELEVEN

YOKAI did not prove to be as empty as hoped.

Geary had jumped there prepared for battle. The battle cruisers and half the destroyers arrived ten minutes before the light cruisers, the rest of the destroyers, and the clutter of refugee freighters. Nothing waited near the jump exit, though, except a few automated Alliance navigation buoys, which were continuing the same mechanically mandated roles they had fulfilled for decades. Amidst the quiet of the shut-down defenses elsewhere at Yokai, one object stood out as very much active.

"Syndic Hunter-Killer," the combat watch-stander said. "Right next to the jump point for Batara."

"A picket ship," Duellos observed. "But whose picket ship?"

The jump exit for Batara was on the other side of the star system, nearly seven light-hours distant. "Let's see what he does when he sees us," Geary said. "Are there any indications that someone is trying to set up shop here?"

"There aren't any signs that anyone has broken into any of the mothballed defense sites," Duellos replied.

"Monitoring and security systems at some of the sites do report a few attempts at entry, Captain," the operations watch reported.

"But no reports of actual entry?"

"No, sir. All of the sites are reporting their current status with no discrepancies, so nobody has gone in and shut down anything to try to hide their activities."

Lieutenant Nadia "Night Witch" Popova, the pilot of the FAC loaded onto *Inspire*, was also on the bridge and pointed out a large orbiting facility near the edge of the star system, only a couple of light-minutes from where the HuK was loitering. "That's where our squadron will be based. We'll reactivate enough of the station to handle our needs and leave the rest dark."

"You'll be able to intercept anything coming in," Geary said. "I wish your people were already there."

"Me, too, Admiral. I wouldn't mind having a HuK silhouette painted on the side of my warbird."

"What will your squadron do if it's something too big for them to handle?" Duellos asked.

Popova grinned. "Play dead and send off a courier drone to jump for Adriana with the bad news. The base had several of those drones for emergencies, and the colonel is pretty sure they were mothballed in place. While we're passing through, Catnap is supposed to ping the base's housekeeping systems to confirm the drones are still there."

"Catnap?" Geary asked.

"Lieutenant Alvarez, sir."

"She's on *Implacable*," Duellos said before turning a questioning eye on Night Witch. "Is there a reason why aerospace pilots use those nicknames so much, Lieutenant?"

Lieutenant Popova smiled wider. "Tradition, sir. And, it does drive the ground forces and fleet forces kind of crazy, sort of as a bonus."

"Who is on *Formidable*?" Geary asked.

"Nightstalker, Admiral."

I guess we're lucky we got Night Witch. "Were you ever at Yokai before they shut things down?"

The smile faded into seriousness. "Yes, sir. Just a rotation for familiarity. It was busy back then. Kinda spooky now."

"Let me know what, uh, Catnap finds out about the drones," Geary directed. "Make sure both of the others know to be ready to launch in combat configuration the moment we arrive at Batara."

Popova frowned toward Geary's display. "It's pretty quiet here, except that one HuK. That should be a good sign."

Duellos shook his head. "Ah, youth and its optimism. Lieutenant, the Admiral and I look at the lack of freighter traffic here and wonder why there are no refugee ships passing through en route Adriana. The flow of refugee shipping appears to have been choked off. We don't know why, so we are assuming it means something that will complicate our own mission. We also don't know who that HuK is here to warn, but it is certain now that we will not have the advantage of surprise when we arrive at Batara."

The pilot's frown turned into concern. "Yes, sir. When we get to Batara, we'll be ready for whatever is there, sir."

I sure hope so, Geary thought as he nodded encouragingly to the pilot.

COLONEL Kim appeared to be as cheerful as ever despite riding one of the refugee freighters. "There's a little bit of restiveness, Admiral, but most of the refugees were kicked out of Batara, or fled the star system to save themselves or their families instead of leaving because they wanted to. You were right about that. Sitting in overcrowded, stinking freighters for months has cooled any enthusiasm they might have had for being in the Alliance, even if they didn't think we were monsters to begin with. They seem to be happy to be going home now that we're actually on the way."

"They're not worried about what the government at Batara might do to them?" Geary asked.

Kim grinned wider. "They got kicked out in small groups. They're coming back in one big bunch, and from what I can tell, they don't intend getting kicked around anymore. If you ask me, it's the government at Batara that ought to be worried."

"That government deserves to be worried," Geary said, though he had been concerned enough about what might happen when they dropped off the refugees to have been running contingencies through his head for a while.

"Are we going to be doing any shooting?" Colonel Kim didn't seem to be worried or excited at the prospect, just curious.

"I'm going to try to avoid that," Geary replied. "How are your soldiers doing?"

"No problems there, Admiral, except the living conditions."

Geary smiled at the image of Kim seated opposite him in his stateroom. "Freighters don't offer luxury sleeping accommodations, I'm afraid."

"It's not that, Admiral. Ground forces don't expect opulent living conditions like the aerospace forces do," Kim explained with another grin. "It's the smell. Too many people on these freighters for too long. The people stink, the air stinks because life support can't clear it all out, and, of course, the field rations always smell awful. I expect the refugees will be as happy to get some good showers as my soldiers will be to get the refugees off-loaded."

"Are there any indications we'll have trouble doing the off-load at Batara?" Geary asked. "I want to be ready if any of the refugees decide they don't want to confront their government after all."

"No, sir. No indications." Kim looked around theatrically to ensure she wasn't being overheard. "I've been talking to those two leaders on this freighter. That Araya woman won't lighten up at all. She keeps acting like she expects me to cut her throat during the next sleep period. But Fred Naxos is all right."

"Fred?"

"Federico, but he prefers Fred," Kim explained. "You aren't going to believe this, Admiral, but the refugees are quiet in part because there's a big rumor spreading among them that Black Jack is on their side."

"What?" He had thought he was beyond being surprised by what people expected of Black Jack, but this one had blindsided him. "Syndics usually think of Black Jack as some sort of demon."

"But these guys revolted against what they call the Syndicate. And, before they left Batara, word had been getting to them about your blowing away the old Syndic leadership and defending some rebellious star system way off on the backside of nowhere from the Syndics and aliens."

"Actually," Geary said, "the old Syndic leadership was killed by their own forces. I suppose I did cause that to happen. The star system they've heard about must be Midway."

"Yes, sir! Midway. That's what they said." Kim grinned conspiratorially this time. "So there's this rumor going around among the refugees that Black Jack fights *Syndics*, but he's a champion of *the people*. And the refugees figure they're not Syndics, anymore, they're *the people*, and Black Jack is taking them back home, so maybe he's their hero, too."

Great. Another group of people expecting me to save the day. "So, they're coming around to not seeing the Alliance as enemies?"

"Oh, no, Admiral. They still think the Alliance is where ogres live. But any of us who are working for Black Jack are good ogres. Sort of." Kim looked thoughtful. "It's a start, though. The idea that the other guy isn't a monster anymore. It would be nice to be able to trade through Batara again, like in the old days."

"The old days?" Geary asked.

"Yes, sir. My family has been in trade for a while. We used to do a lot of business into and through Batara, before the Syndics took it over; and then the war came. But we remember before then." She paused, a variety of expressions flickering over her face. "I wonder if anybody in Batara remembers. We've still got our records from those days, the business contacts and all."

"I imagine that the Syndicate Worlds did a number on the businesses that were there before the takeover, and it's been more than a century since then. We'll find out what's survived." *And what survives once we're done.* "Ask Naxos and Araya about the HuK. I'd be interested in knowing what their impressions are as to who it belongs to."

THE mysterious HuK jumped from Yokai toward Batara ten hours after Geary's task force had arrived, long enough to have seen all of the warships and freighters and to have confirmed that they were heading for the same jump point.

"We were, that is the government at Batara was, trying to get a damaged HuK working," Araya had reluctantly admitted. "That might be it. It was all we had in the way of real mobile forces. But I don't know why they would have sent it here instead of positioning it near the jump point where raids from Yael come in."

Geary gazed at the stumpy vector line on his display that reflected the relatively low velocity of his ships and tried not to chafe inwardly too much over the time it would take to get to the jump point and head for the place that would have the answers. It was exasperating having to match the velocity of the warships to the freighters. The merchant ships could push themselves to higher velocities, of course. They just had to keep accelerating. But it would take much longer than with warships—and burn more fuel cells—and then it would take just as long and burn just as much fuel for the clumsy freighters to reduce their velocity again.

THE Alliance battle cruisers, surrounded by two squadrons of destroyers, popped out of jump space and into Batara Star System. Geary's display had shown the last-known status of the Syndic defenses at Batara, dating to just less than a year ago, but now he had to shake out of his head the mental grogginess caused by exiting jump and wait while the sensors on the Alliance warships tried to see what was still here and was still working.

The first thing he was aware of was that no alarms were sounding and no weapons were being fired by automated fire-control systems on the Alliance warships. Whatever might await them here, it wasn't waiting very close to the jump exit.

In fact, as his head cleared, he saw that there were no threats at all anywhere near them.

The jump point from Yokai was a bit above the plane in which the planets of Batara orbited, and nearly four light-hours from the star. Geary had a stronger-than-usual sense that the Alliance battle cruisers had a godlike vantage of the entire star system, looking down and across the vast distances between worlds as if occupying divine box seats.

Like other front-line star systems, Batara had been heavily battered during the decades of war. But the Syndics had followed the same perverse logic as the Alliance in rebuilding and reinforcing it time and again. Marginal star systems, those with barely any population like Yokai, could be turned into purely military enclaves. But any star system with a significant population, cities, and industries had to be maintained as much as possible no matter how many times the enemy hit it and no matter how much it cost to sustain the civilian population there. Anything less would mark yielding to the enemy, would be admitting defeat, and the century-long war had often been more about refusing to admit defeat than it had been about any hope of victory.

Geary could see the small cities on the main inhabited world at Batara, all of them characterized by roughly circular patches of similar buildings that marked reconstruction where orbital bombardments had hit, the patches often overlapping. In a few places, such battered cities occupied areas near the heavily cratered ruins of a former city too badly damaged to rebuild on its original site. Defenses sat in craters where generations of bombardments had knocked out generations of rebuilt weaponry and sensors in an apparently endless cycle. The "empty" spaces between worlds were filled with fields of debris, the remnants of warships from both sides, some of the debris widely dispersed over many years and other clusters fairly compact, marking the deaths of ships and their crews within the last few years. It was a depressing sight, but also an astounding sight. Humans could choose to abandon star systems, but if someone tried to force them to leave, then by all the grace of the living stars and all the blessings of their ancestors they would plant their feet and *stay*.

"Two light cruisers and four HuKs," the operations watch reported. "All standard Syndic construction and all orbiting near the primary inhabited planet. Most of the fixed defenses appear to be nonoperational."

Duellos cast a suspicious eye on Geary. "You told me that you expected those defenses to be out of commission. Was it a guess based on likely Syndic budget problems?"

"No," Geary replied. "If the defenses had remained active, the people at Batara wouldn't have had to worry about raids from Tiyannak or Yael. I knew something must have taken out most of the active defenses. But the deep shelters will still be there, meaning Batara's population can ride out a lot of raids even if they can't stop them."

"Those raiders," Duellos observed, with a gesture toward the light cruisers and HuKs, "don't appear to be raiding. They're close enough to that planet to be engaged by some of the defenses that still exist, but they're not shooting, and neither are the defenses. Are you looking for something?" he asked Geary.

"Yes. I'm looking for that HuK that was performing picket duty at Yokai and jumped here ahead of us. Where is he?"

"He must be one of the HuKs in that group near the primary world. He had plenty of time to join them before we arrived."

A reasonable assumption, Geary thought. *But, still, an assumption.* He parked a mental worry chit on the question of where that HuK was as more information about Batara came in.

"Captain," the operations watch-stander said, "we're spotting significant crowd activity in the cities that are visible to us. The population is in the streets, not sheltering against bombardment."

"Crowd activity?" Geary asked. "How full are the streets?"

"Packed, Admiral."

"Lieutenant Barber," Duellos ordered, "we need to know what's going on here."

"We're analyzing all the communications and other traffic we can pick up," Barber said. "There's a lot for a star system with a population this size. The official newscasts say nothing is happening."

"But we all know what official news amounts to, don't we, Lieutenant?" Duellos turned back to Geary. "What are you going to tell them?"

"Batara?" Geary said. "Nothing, yet. We'll wait here until the refugee ships show up, then all proceed in-system toward that inhabited world. I'll wait to send any messages to anyone until we have a better idea of what's happening."

A flurry of updates on the displays marked the arrival of the refugee ships and their escorts, scores of ships suddenly there in space near the battle cruisers. A thought struck Geary, and he tapped another control. "Colonel Kim, give the refugee leaders Naxos and Araya listening access to the comms on that freighter and see what they think the situation is based on what they hear and who is saying it." It was annoying not having Lieutenant Iger and his intel team available to handle all this, but he could improvise.

"Let's get going," Geary said. "Immediate execute, all units turn starboard one eight degrees, down zero seven degrees, maintain point zero five light speed."

Since the light cruisers and HuKs were near the primary inhabited world, and that world was swinging in orbit on the far side of the star relative to Geary's ships, it would be a bit over four hours before the light from here reached them and they learned that the Alliance warships had arrived. It gave him some time to figure out what the situation was in Batara.

It only took about half an hour before Colonel Kim called back. "The refugee leader Araya is certain from the transmissions we're picking up that what she calls the *damned cowardly greedy revolution-betraying traitors-to-the-people* who have been running Batara have sold out to Tiyannak."

"Sold out? They've allied with Tiyannak?"

Colonel Kim shrugged. "Even Araya isn't sure what their status is. Ally. Vassal. Slave. She and Naxos both say if they didn't know exactly whom to pay attention to in all the transmissions out there, they wouldn't know what was going on. There are a lot of broadcasts where even they can't figure out who's sending them and what side they're on."

"You're certain of that?" Geary demanded. "Araya and Naxos thought the transmissions we're picking up are unusual for Batara?"

"Pretty certain, yes, Admiral. While she was listening to them, Araya kept saying stuff like *what the hell?* and *what is this?* She kept asking Naxos who different people and different organizations were, and he spent a lot of time shaking his head."

"Thank you, Colonel." Geary turned to Duellos as Kim's image vanished. "How is Lieutenant Barber doing on his analysis of the situation?"

Duellos grimaced. "I checked with him while you were talking to Colonel Kim. Barber is doing his best, but he says it's very complex. He's a good, smart officer, Admiral. He'll figure it out."

"If he doesn't, it won't be because he isn't smart." Geary pointed to where the primary inhabited world showed on his display. "The refugee leaders say there are a lot of transmissions out there that they have trouble identifying, transmissions that confuse the situation and make it very hard to understand exactly what the status of Batara is."

"Confuse?" Duellos repeated, his jaw tightening. "The HuK that told them we were coming."

"And gave them plenty of time to fill space before we got here with misleading, confusing, and false transmissions in order to keep us uncertain about who is in charge at Batara and what they are doing."

Duellos gazed narrowly at his own display. "To what purpose? Those tricks will delay our understanding of the situation, but they won't stop us. They must mean to keep us guessing for a while. What advantage will that gain them?"

"Good question." Geary chewed his lip as he studied the situation. "They knew we had the refugee ships with us. Even a Syndic HuK has good enough sensors to ID those as old Syndic-make merchant ships at seven light-hours distance. Having the refugee ships with us meant we would head for that planet, but the only significant threat to us there are those light cruisers and HuKs, and we should be able to handle them easily."

"We've been keeping a close eye on them," Duellos said.

"I know you've—" Geary stopped, frowning. "We're watching them."

"Yes."

"*Focused* on them."

Duellos shook his head quickly. "We are watching for any other threats, Admiral. There's nothing else out there."

"There's nothing else we *see*," Geary replied. "If they want to delay our understanding of the situation, that means they have something that requires time to develop." He paused, eyeing his display, then tapped a command for it to project future movements at a greatly accelerated rate. Ships spun in orbit or raced along vectors, planets rocketed around the star—

Geary almost flinched as he saw something big coming toward the track his ships would be following, then recognized the object swinging toward that track as the largest of the gas giant worlds in Batara.

He froze his display, then tapped another command. "Ten light-minutes."

Duellos raised an eyebrow, leaning over to check what Geary was doing. "That gas giant? Yes," he confirmed, "its closest point of approach to our ships as they proceed, and it orbits, will be ten light-minutes distant." Duellos paused to think, tapping one finger against his lips as he considered this information. "Not awfully close in space terms, but not a long distance, either."

Geary nodded almost absentmindedly, his thoughts moving ahead as he gazed at the representation of the gas giant. It was fairly gorgeous as planets went, bands of colors rioting across the heavy clouds cloaking it and a single, bright ring marking the ancient fates of one or more moons which must have shattered into fragments long ago. In terms of size, as planets went, it was indeed a giant.

Ten light-minutes. Roughly one hundred eighty million kilometers. A very long distance in planetary terms.

But when he had to worry about a large number of merchant ships that could not run well or fight at all, ten light-minutes might be far too small a distance.

"We're in space. We're assuming we can see any threats. But what if," he asked Duellos, "something was hiding behind that gas giant, maneuvering to stay concealed until it could pop out when it was close enough that the freighters couldn't get away?"

Duellos nodded, his eyes also on the gas giant. "An ambush from that distance wouldn't work against warships, but against freighters is a much different matter. We'd also have trouble spotting small, stealthy satellites from this far away under normal circumstances, but that ring offers perfect secondary concealment. They could have a score of small satellites in orbit inside the ring, watching us and relaying their observations to each other by tight beams around the curve of the planet." He looked at Geary. "That's just a guess, though. We don't have any proof."

"We can get proof." He pondered his display a moment longer, then called the light cruiser *Spur*.

Lieutenant Commander Pajari, captain of *Spur* and commander of the light cruiser squadron, answered less than a minute later. "Yes, Admiral."

"Which one of the light cruisers has the most reliable propulsion and maneuvering?" Geary asked. He should have been able to get that data from the fleet's readiness reports, but since headquarters had ordered those to display exaggerated readiness, he could no longer trust the information in them.

Pajari didn't hesitate. "*Fleche*, sir. Her propulsion systems failed not long after we returned to Varandal last time, so she was moved up in priority for replacement of the equipment. Her other systems are as old as she is, for the most part, but propulsion and maneuvering are new and solid."

"*Fleche*?" Tanya had served on an earlier *Fleche*, which had been destroyed. There might have been a half dozen other *Fleche*s built and lost in the intervening years. This *Fleche* with the "old" equipment had been launched barely two years ago, her systems designed to last for the ship's life expectancy in combat, which had been less than a year. "Very well," Geary said. "You are to detach *Fleche* for a reconnaissance mission." Geary indicated the gas giant on his display. "We need to find out, as soon as we can, whether anything is hiding behind that planet. I want *Fleche* to go out there, pop over the top, swing wide to take a good look, and rejoin the formation."

"Yes, sir. *Fleche* is to go out, reconnoiter the far side of the gas giant by passing over its north pole, then rejoin the formation," Pajari repeated.

"*Fleche* is not to engage anything it spots," Geary emphasized. "If there is something there, it's probably a lot more than a light cruiser can handle. She is to take a look and get back here, utilizing whatever acceleration is necessary to ensure her safe return to formation."

"Yes, sir. I will ensure that *Fleche*'s commanding officer receives those orders word for word."

Only a couple of minutes later, Geary watched *Fleche* peel away from the formation and tear off toward an intercept with the gas giant as it lumbered along its own orbit. He could almost feel the eagerness with which the light cruiser embarked on the mission, a welcome diversion from plodding along with the refugee ships.

"If there is something there," Duellos said, "*Fleche* won't buy us much warning. It looks like she'll get her look at the back side of that planet when it's about fifteen light-minutes from our track."

"That's better than ten light-minutes."

"True." Duellos had turned somber as he watched the light cruiser arc away from the other Alliance warships. "This is one of those times when you should be grateful that I'm not Tanya."

"I'm often grateful that you're not Tanya and that she's not you," Geary said. "No offense. Why in particular this time?"

"She's very superstitious about light cruisers bearing the name *Fleche*." Duellos shook his head, avoiding looking at Geary. "Has she ever told you what she endured in the battle where her *Fleche* was destroyed?"

"No. She did finally say that I could read her citation for the Alliance Fleet Cross, but she still absolutely refuses to talk about it." Except once, and Tanya had mostly focused on what had happened afterwards.

Duellos relapsed into silence, but Geary guessed that he was also worried about using a ship named *Fleche* for this mission. Tanya wasn't the only superstitious sailor in the fleet. Something about being a sailor, about being out on the vastness of planetary seas or the infinite immensity of space, encouraged the sense of being surrounded by unseen forces that could help or hinder, save or destroy, depending on whether they were appeased or provoked. It was something older and vaster than any religion, and he had felt it often enough himself.

However, there wasn't a lot he could do in the way of appeasing or provoking the unseen while waiting for *Fleche* to reach the gas giant. Even with the light cruiser ramping her velocity up a little past point two light speed, it would still be close to three hours before the warship intercepted the gas giant in its orbit.

But he could move his ships around a bit, positioning the battle cruisers so that they were ahead of and to one side of the gaggle of refugee ships, best positioned if something dangerous did lurk behind that gas giant. And he could plan for when they reached the inhabited world, talking with both Colonel Voston and Colonel Kim about the security that would be needed, and with the three FAC pilots about how they would provide protection for the shuttles bringing down the refugees to the surface.

Night Witch, Catnap, and Nightstalker were all attentive as he talked to them, eager to reach the planet and fulfill their mission. Geary had looked up the statistics on FACs, learning that in an offensive combat situation their odds of survival were extremely small, but none of the pilots showed any signs of being fazed by that. They were, after all, pilots, just as the crews of Geary's ships were sailors.

When all of those preparations were done, and *Fleche* was still an hour from reaching the gas giant, Geary talked to the refugee leaders Araya and Naxos again. "What are you planning to do once we drop off you and the others?" he asked.

Araya gave him her scornful look. "Are you still pretending to care?"

"Actually, I do care," Geary replied. "You'll have a pretty large mass of people with you, most or all of whom think like you do. There are already a lot of people in the streets on that planet."

Naxos smiled, his eyes on the deck. "The people on Batara aren't happy. I, for one, will not be exiled again. I will walk into the Hall of the People and kick out the new CEOs who rule there."

"You'll have help," Araya said. "Lots of it. If we can get the ground forces and the security forces, some of them anyway, to back us, we can do it." Her face lit with dangerous enthusiasm. "And then those scum will find themselves in the labor camps!"

Geary looked at Naxos and Araya. "Do you both hate the Syndic CEOs who used to rule here?"

Both nodded immediately. "They just cared about themselves," Naxos grumbled, head still lowered.

"There was a revolt in the Midway Star System, too. After they kicked out the CEOs, they shut down the labor camps. Their leaders said there would never again be labor camps anywhere they controlled."

"How are we supposed to punish the enemies of the people?" Araya demanded.

"Is that the question you should be asking? How to keep doing things the way the CEOs did? Or should you be wondering why you want to act like the people you hate?"

Naxos raised his head and held it up this time, looking intently at Geary. "I said that. Many times. Why change leaders if we're going to be the same as the old leaders?"

"I can't make you do things differently," Geary said. "But I think you're right to be asking yourself that question."

"What guarantee would we have that doing things differently would be the same as doing things better?" Naxos asked.

"None. It's not enough to be different. And there will be lots of disagreement on what is better and what is worse or the same." Geary paused, remembering his own recent experiences. "But as long as you're talking, as long as people can change things they don't like, as long as you aren't refusing to listen to other people, then you'll have a chance of doing things better."

"Do you listen to other people?" Araya asked in acidic tones.

"All the time," Geary said. "Other people act as a mirror of sorts, second opinions on whether I'm doing the right thing, whether my preconceptions and assumptions are justified, and whether there are better answers than I've come up with so far. In combat, I often have to act quickly, but even then I listen when someone suggests alternatives. I don't have to agree with them, I don't have to do what they want, but I *listen*."

"I had a few good supervisors," Naxos said, looking at Araya this time. "They listened when I suggested things."

She flushed slightly, mouth tight, then nodded. "Yes. As a sub-executive, I tried to listen to the workers, including you. I prided myself on that. Did I stop listening?"

"You're listening now," Naxos pointed out.

"Ha! You're a very insubordinate worker, aren't you?" She addressed Geary again. "We can do more listening, and convincing and planning, if we are allowed to talk to those on the other ships."

"I'll tell Colonel Kim to give you access to comms."

"You're going to trust us?" Araya didn't bother hiding her skepticism.

"If you're going to create trouble, if you're going to organize a new dictatorship to replace the current one, I'd rather know now," Geary said. "And, as I'm sure you already expected, those comms will be monitored. Given the potential for riots on the ships, I have no alternative."

"Why tell us that?"

"Because, at this point, you're not my enemies, and I'd like to keep it that way. The Alliance already has enough problems and enough enemies."

Araya and Naxos stared at Geary for several seconds. "How could we ever be anything but enemies?" Araya finally asked.

"Batara used to be on friendly terms with the Alliance, before the Syndics took it over," Geary said. "If there are any records left in Batara that the Syndics didn't destroy or alter to fit their preferred version of history, you can look it up."

She shook her head. "That's a very big if. The Syndicate tried to destroy all hard copy, so they could easily alter all of the digital histories every time the official version changed."

Something suddenly became clear. "I was talking to someone else, a former citizen of the Syndicate Worlds like you, and they used the word 'history' as if it was interchangeable with 'lies.' I didn't understand that."

Araya shrugged. "We call what's real *hard copy*. History is lies, and hard copy can be lies, but you can't change hard copy once it has been printed. No undetectable updates, no invisible revisions, no additions you can't spot. Hard copy is what it is. My friend here"—she gestured toward Naxos—"thinks that you are hard copy, Admiral. I hope he is right."

By then enough time had elapsed for Geary to return to the bridge of *Inspire* and wait. The two light cruisers and four HuKs had not left their orbits near the inhabited world, and aside from a few small craft operating near orbital installations, nothing else human could be seen moving in the star system except the Alliance warships and the refugee ships they were escorting.

Duellos had not left the bridge and now shook his head. "I wondered if you were just being extra cautious, but the lack of activity is suspicious. They knew we were coming, and those ships orbiting near the main planet have seen us and had time to react yet haven't done anything."

"I ordered *Fleche* to be careful."

Shaking his head again, Duellos spoke in a low voice. "This fleet spent decades considering careful and cowardice to be two sides of the same coin. Aggressive action in any circumstance is almost engraved on their DNA. *Fleche* is less than two light-minutes from intercepting the planet, about seventeen minutes' travel time if she maintains her current velocity. I would strongly advise reminding her of your orders."

This seemed like another good time to not just listen but also accept the advice. Geary touched his comm controls. "*Fleche*, this is Admiral Geary. Maintain caution while conducting your mission. There is a possibility of a serious threat hiding behind that gas giant. Check out the back side, then return to the formation. Geary, out."

The message should arrive a couple of minutes before *Fleche* and the gas giant reached each other as the warship zoomed in from the outer star system and the planet swung along its orbit.

Fleche was fifteen light-minutes from *Inspire* when the light cruiser swooped over the northern pole of the gas giant and got its first look at the side hidden from view of the fleet. Geary watched intently as the images from *Fleche* appeared on his display. Everything he was seeing had happened fifteen minutes ago.

Fleche's combat systems sounded alerts as a HuK appeared around the curve of the planet. The HuK had been rising at a slow rate, heading toward the path that *Fleche* was taking, a dead giveaway that the HuK knew *Fleche* was coming.

The HuK spun about and accelerated downward, skimming the upper atmosphere of the gas giant as it fled.

Geary watched, appalled, as *Fleche* rolled, turned, and dove after the HuK in full pursuit. He felt a numbness inside and realized his hand was quivering above the comm controls, wanting to send the commands to the Alliance light cruiser to follow her orders, to finish searching the back side of the gas giant, and to return safely to the rest of the Alliance warships.

But this had all happened fifteen minutes ago. Any order he sent would take fifteen minutes to arrive, and he knew with a sick certainty that would be too late.

As Duellos had reminded him, he hadn't been in command of this fleet that long. He had been in charge a tiny fraction of the time since the war began, a war whose destructive and mindless path had favored ever-more-aggressive and mindless tactics as trained tacticians died en masse and new commanders sought to make up for lack of training and experience with a narrow focus on what they saw as courage and honor, and on a willingness to die rather than retreat.

Geary had done a lot to change those attitudes. But he could not in a short time eradicate the false lessons created by a century of stubborn bloodletting and pursuit of personal glory. The fact that such attitudes were partly justified by claims that they embodied the true spirit of Black Jack, of *him*, had only made it harder.

Now he watched *Fleche* in hot pursuit and waited for what he was certain would come.

Two Syndic-design heavy cruisers appeared around the lower curve of the gas giant, bracketing *Fleche* and on top of her too fast for the light cruiser to react. The heavy cruisers were too close, the moment of engagement too fleeting, for missiles to be employed, but the two enemy ships each hurled out a volley of hell-lance particle beams and the metal ball bearings known as grapeshot. The fire lashed *Fleche*'s shields, collapsing them, some of the impacts going on to tear holes in the lightly armored Alliance warship.

Geary could see the damage reports as they appeared on his display, showing that *Fleche* had suffered serious hits to her maneuvering systems as well as her weapons.

He saw the helm orders appear as *Fleche* tried to alter her vector.

Ten seconds after the heavy cruisers had flailed *Fleche*, the Alliance light cruiser caught sight of a massive shape like that of a squat shark rising around the curve of the gas giant. At the velocity the light cruiser was moving, there wasn't even time for the crew to react before they were within range of the battleship's weapons.

Two and a half minutes after diving in all-out pursuit of the HuK, *Fleche* disintegrated under the hammerblows of the battleship's weapons. None of the light cruiser's escape pods left the ship. None of the crew had time to reach them and launch them.

The data feed cut off as the light cruiser was blown apart.

Fleche, along with her entire crew, had died fifteen minutes ago.

Geary gradually became aware that the bridge of *Inspire* was totally silent.

The quiet was finally broken by a single word as a young officer spoke plaintively. "Why?"

"Why?" Geary repeated, wondering why his voice sounded so soft yet could be heard so clearly on the bridge. "Because the commanding officer of *Fleche* forgot that it was not about him. He forgot that it was not about glory. He forgot his orders, he forgot his responsibilities, he forgot his training and his duty. Because of that, he wasted the lives of his crew. Don't ever do any of those things."

Geary took a deep breath, straightened in his seat, then spoke in a firm voice. "We've got at least two heavy cruisers and a battleship that must have already popped out from behind that gas giant and will be seen by us at any moment! Do your duties, fight smart as well as bravely, and *Fleche* is the only ship we will lose today!"

It took them another fifteen minutes to see that the battleship, accompanied by two heavy cruisers and four HuKs, had risen over the top of the gas giant and begun accelerating toward an intercept with the mass of refugee ships.

"We threw off their timing," Geary said to Duellos. "*Fleche* accomplished that much. In another hour and a half, we should see those light cruisers and HuKs near the inhabited planet coming toward us, too."

Duellos's eyes were searching his display. "Didn't the refugees say that Tiyannak had four light cruisers?"

"At least four."

"The other two could be hiding behind this planet," Duellos said, pointing to a cold, barren world the size of one and a half Earths but lacking much in the way of atmosphere or water. It orbited thirty light-minutes from the star and would cross the path of the Alliance and refugee ships a few hours before they reached that part of space. "Everything else that someone could hide behind is too badly positioned in their orbits."

"I'll need to leave the light cruisers and destroyers to screen the refugee ships, while I take the battle cruisers against that battleship flotilla," Geary said.

"That's probably your best option," Duellos agreed. "Given enough time, my battle cruisers can probably wear down that battleship. But we don't have enough time. How are we going to stop the battleship before it reaches some of the refugee ships, causing them to scatter and become easy prey?"

"I'll think of something."

TWELVE

LOOKED at one way, the whole thing was pretty simple. He had to get his warships and all of the refugee ships to the primary inhabited world, off-load the refugees, and along the way deal with any threat posed by the warships, which must be from Tiyannak. A mission so simple it could be condensed into a single sentence.

But, as the ancient warrior sage had said, all of the simple things in war end up being really complicated.

Geary looked over at Duellos. "What do you know about Commander Pajari?"

"Not a lot," Duellos admitted. "I think she took command of *Spur* less than a year ago."

In that year, and since Geary had been reawakened, Pajari had apparently done nothing praiseworthy enough or stupid enough to draw Geary's special attention. That described many of the commanding officers in the fleet, though, since there were nearly two hundred fifty heavy cruisers, light cruisers, and destroyers. The captains of the battleships and the battle cruisers tended to speak up at conferences because of their seniority and influence. Usually, the commanders of smaller warships stayed silent except for general expressions of approval or disapproval. One of Geary's ongoing regrets was that he had never had the time to get to know all of those officers personally.

He checked Pajari's service record and found that she had been commissioned just four years ago, having served on three ships, two of which had been destroyed in battle, before gaining command of *Spur*. Like many officers in the fleet, she might be young for her rank and responsibilities, but she had immensely more combat experience than Geary had had at her age and rank.

"I'm going to trust her with command of the escorts for our convoy of refugee ships," Geary said. "Pajari will have to fend off threats to the freighters, using the light cruisers and all of the destroyers, while I take the battle cruisers to handle that battleship."

Duellos raised both eyebrows. "You won't take any destroyers with us?"

"Given the size of our group of freighters, and with potentially three enemy flotillas coming after them from at least three directions, Pajari is going to need all of our escorts." Geary zoomed in on the image of the battleship heading toward an intercept, accelerating ponderously but steadily, like a massive, armored animal building up unstoppable speed. Despite the intervening millions of kilometers, the image was crystal clear, the enemy warships appearing to be unmoving against the endless space around them despite their large and increasing velocity. The two heavy cruisers and two HuKs accompanying the battleship were not spread out, acting as escorts in a typical formation, but were instead tucked in extremely close to the battleship. "We won't be able to peel off the escorts with that battleship easily."

"No. An unconventional formation, and one that will be hard to counter," Duellos agreed. "Any firing runs aimed at the escorts will bring us within range of the battleship's weapons for certain. On the other hand, those four escorts with the battleship must have their maneuvering systems slaved to it. They're so close, that's the only way to avoid the tiny bobbles or variations in starts and stops of maneuvers that would otherwise cause a very nasty collision."

Geary nodded. "How can we use that?"

"I'm working on an answer to that question, Admiral."

To his own surprise, Geary smiled crookedly. "What about suggestions for dealing with the battleship?"

Duellos waved toward the back of the bridge. "My people are running sims to try to find solutions."

"What have they found so far?"

"So far?" Duellos shrugged helplessly. "They've found a number of plans that *won't* work."

"You and I both know what we have to do," Geary said. "We have to take the battleship out of the threat column. There are ways we could do that using the battle cruisers' superior acceleration and maneuverability to slowly whittle down the battleship, but that would take far more time than we have to work with. The only way to neutralize the battleship quickly enough to protect the refugee ships is to damage the battleship's main propulsion. If we can also take out his maneuvering capability, so much the better."

Duellos grimaced. "I've faced something like this situation before, Admiral. Three battle cruisers is the minimum possible force that could do what we need to do. Assuming the Syndic battleship's rear shields are at full strength, the only way to achieve a quick takedown of its propulsion is for all three battle cruisers to conduct close passes within a very short interval. Ideally, the first battle cruiser weakens the battleship's rear shields, the second scores enough hits to knock down the weakened shields or render them ready to collapse, and the third goes in with the shields down and actually gets a shot at hitting the main propulsion units. But the battleship isn't going to just sit still for that. He's going to be maneuvering, pivoting the ship, trying to ensure that all three firing runs do not hit the rear shields, and trying to hit our battle cruisers hard as each one comes in to attack."

Geary nodded, thinking through alternatives. "What if our battle cruisers go in close enough to employ the null-field projectors?"

"Against an undamaged battleship? We lose at least one battle cruiser. Maybe two. And with no guarantee those sacrifices will enable us to score disabling hits on the battleship."

"We won't do that, then." Geary shook his head. "Our advantages are our numbers, three battle cruisers to one battleship, and maneuverability."

"Whereas his only disadvantage is lack of maneuverability," Duellos said.

"No. He's also neutralized his own escorts by keeping them tucked in so close. We can't get at them, but they can't interfere with our attacks."

Geary closed his eyes, mentally running through what he would say next, then touched his comm controls once more. "Commander Pajari, I am placing you in charge of Formation Echo. You will have your light cruisers and all three destroyer squadrons. Your mission is to keep the refugee ships together and protect them from any attempts at attack."

Surprised, Pajari saluted. "I will not disappoint you, Admiral. Do you wish me to continue on a vector toward the primary inhabited world?"

"Yes. You can alter the vector as necessary to deal with threats, but you and I know that the freighters won't be able to do much. Colonel Kim's soldiers will keep the freighter crews from panicking and trying to run, but they can't do anything about the sluggish maneuverability of the freighters. Be advised that there's a chance further enemy warships are hiding behind this planet." Geary indicated the super-Earth farther in-system. "Maybe a couple of more light cruisers and HuKs. If the attacks on us are coordinated, within the next few hours we should see the enemy flotilla near the primary inhabited world coming out to intercept you, while anyone hiding near that other planet will pop out once they think we've committed our forces to dealing with the other two flotillas. If we can't stop all of the enemy ships in the battleship flotilla, you may have to help fend them off as well."

"Yes, sir," Pajari said, her eyes narrowed as she concentrated on Geary's words. "You call them enemy, sir. Are we free to engage any other warships in this star system as necessary?"

"You are. I am making the judgment that all other warships in this star system are part of the same forces as those that were at the gas giant. They have proven hostile intent by their destruction of *Fleche*." In that way, *Fleche*'s sacrifice had accomplished something very important. He would no longer have to wait for those other warships to fire the first shot. They already had. "Engage and destroy any threats to your ships or the refugee ships."

"Yes, sir!" Pajari's eyes had blazed at the mention of *Fleche*.

"Commander," Geary emphasized, "your mission is to protect those refugee ships. Don't forget that in pursuit of some of those enemy warships."

"I will not, Admiral." Pajari smiled slowly. "They think we will rush off in pursuit, that we'll forget our mission. We won't. But if they think we will, we can use that."

"You can use that," Geary agreed, smiling back. "Have you conducted convoy escort operations before?"

"Yes, Admiral. Not with an ill-disciplined mess like those refugee ships, but the principles are still the same. I know what tactics the Syndics use to try to pull escorts out of position and reach the convoy. I'll be ready for them."

"Good. I'll be dealing with the battleship. Geary, out." He ended the transmission, feeling much more confident about Pajari, then nodded to Duellos. "Captain, let's get your battle cruisers going. We've got a battleship to knock out."

Duellos grinned as the watch-standers on the bridge let out cries of approval.

Geary designated the three battle cruisers as Formation Alpha, then paused to look over the situation carefully before calling the maneuvers. The large, unwieldy formation of refugee ships and Alliance escorts was still a bit over three light-hours from the inhabited world, which orbited only seven and a half light-minutes from the star. If Batara had been Sol, the home star of Old Earth, that would have rendered the planet uncomfortably hot for humanity, but Batara's star burned a bit less fiercely, so the planet was only warm by human standards. Because the planet orbited so much closer to the star, the progress of the Alliance and refugee ships appeared to be aimed just slightly to the left of the star at this point.

What Geary now designated Flotilla One, the two light cruisers and four HuKs near that planet, was also directly ahead of the Alliance ships but light-hours distant.

Only fifteen light-minutes off the starboard bows of the Alliance ships were the battleship and its escorts, which Geary designated Flotilla Two. The battleship flotilla was coming in from the right as seen from *Inspire*, aiming to intercept the refugee ships as they headed inward. Because the enemy ships were on a direct intercept—even though the paths of the ships formed a huge arc across space—their bearing relative to the refugee ships would not change as the enemy drew closer and closer. To the freighters, the battleship would remain off their bows, but grow steadily and implacably larger as the distance between the ships shrank.

The super-Earth planet ahead of the Alliance formation had already crossed just beneath the Alliance ships' vector, orbiting oblivious to the tiny actions of humans. By the time the Alliance ships themselves reached the path of that orbit, the planet would be slightly off to their left and moving away at the relatively sedate pace of about twenty kilometers per second as it swung around the star. If there were also enemy warships hiding behind that planet, they would spring out at the right time and come at the refugee ships from the front and left.

Whoever set this up did some clever planning. If we had just barreled in and reacted to each attack as it developed we would have been in a real mess by the time that third attack force appeared. "*Inspire*, *Formidable*, and *Implacable*, this is Admiral Geary. You are now Formation Alpha. Our task is to take out that battleship. At time five zero, come port two seven degrees, down zero two degrees, accelerate to point one five light speed. Geary, out."

A few minutes later, Geary felt *Inspire* swing to the right. The command port meant to turn away from the star, whereas starboard or starward meant turning toward the star. Upon arrival in the star system, the Alliance warships had automatically designated one side of the plane in which the planets orbited as up and the other as down. It was all extremely arbitrary, a human system for establishing mutually understood directions of right and left, up and down, in space where such things didn't exist. If he had told *Formidable* to turn "right" the other battle cruiser might have swung in a direction one hundred and eighty degrees different from that of *Inspire*. But with the star just off to the left of the ships' bows, everyone knew which direction turning away meant.

Inspire's main propulsion kicked in at full power, the force of the acceleration causing the ship's inertial dampers to whine in protest. Geary felt himself being pressed back into his seat as some of that force leaked past the dampers. No other warship could accelerate like a battle cruiser, which carried more propulsion than a battleship but also sacrificed much of the armor, shield generators, and weaponry that loaded down the battleships. Battle cruisers were designed to get where they were needed fast with a lot of firepower. They weren't designed to tangle with battleships.

Geary watched the vector for the battle cruisers lengthen dramatically as they charged toward the battleship.

"One hour and ten minutes to contact with Flotilla Two," *Inspire*'s operations watch reported. "Remaining distance twenty nine point seven light-minutes. Closing rate point two seven light."

"They're coming on at point one two light," Duellos commented to Geary. "They won't slow down to fight us."

"No. I don't think they will," Geary agreed. "They want to get to those refugee ships and force us into desperate attacks to protect those ships. We'll brake before contact to bring the engagement speed below point two light." Above that velocity, distortion in the appearance of space caused by relativity got too bad for human-designed systems to compensate, rendering an already very difficult fire-control problem almost impossible.

"How are we going to do this?" Duellos asked after about a minute of silence.

"I'm still working on that."

"The captain of that battleship is Syndic," Duellos mused. "By-the-book thinking and behavior."

"Unless he or she is a rebel, in which case a more creative and unconventional junior officer might have suddenly been propelled into the position of captain," Geary said. "You remember what some of the former Syndic officers in the rebellious forces at Midway were like."

"That is something to worry about," Duellos conceded. "However, those former Syndics at Midway were experienced at ship handling. They hadn't been in the war zone facing the Alliance, dying in battle almost as fast as they arrived. Any Syndics here are the survivors of the last battles in the war, and any fighting since then. They probably have minimal training and not much experience."

"All right," Geary said. "I agree that's probable."

"And they've got four escorts tucked in very close, which would worry even a skilled, experienced ship driver."

"They'll use automated maneuvering as well as having the escorts' maneuvering systems slaved to their own?" Geary asked.

"I think it's pretty certain. We need to outthink that automated system, what it will do when it sees us coming toward the stern of that battleship."

There were circumstances in which an hour and ten minutes could feel like a very long time. But not when racing toward an encounter with an enemy battleship.

Geary tried tactic after tactic, approach after approach, as he ran sims, knowing that Captain Duellos and his crew were doing the same, trying out every option. Since the battle cruisers' superior ability to accelerate and maneuver compared to the battleship was their primary advantage, he kept pushing the velocity of encounters as high as possible. But each time the velocity of the battle cruisers went up, the complications got bigger as well. Higher velocity meant larger turn radii, which were already huge at the speeds warships traveled. It also made it harder to change vectors in short distances or times, and if they were going to counter the attempts of the battleship to pivot against their attacks, they would have to make significant last-moment changes in their approaches.

Geary sat back, glowering at his display in frustration. He was reaching to try another sim, one that pushed encounter velocity a little higher, when his hand paused in midmotion. *Why am I only thinking in terms of going faster? Why am I locked into focusing on that one advantage? Because while intercepting that battleship as quickly as possible is necessary, is making the actual encounter at higher speeds a good thing? The sims keep telling me it isn't. Instead of beating my head against a wall that just gets harder, why not try the opposite approach and see what happens?*

He cut the velocity of the encounter dramatically, enough so that the necessary braking maneuvers required far more time than he was comfortable with. But when the sim ran, he had partial success this time.

He cut the velocity more. He tried some options.

He smiled.

Duellos noticed. "I hope that means you've found something."

"We can't let the battle cruisers use their acceleration for the fastest possible attacks," Geary explained.

"We can't—?" Duellos peered at Geary. "What? That's why they're battle cruisers."

"That's how we usually employ them. Fast approaches and fast attacks. But what we need here is a slow approach." Geary pulled up his most successful try. "Look. We come in at a slow relative velocity, aiming for sequential firing runs on the battleship's stern. He starts pivoting to turn his stern away from us. He has to do that. Once he commits his maneuvering thrusters and momentum to that pivot, we use the battle cruisers' superior capabilities to alter the order in which they attack. That completely changes how the battleship wants to be oriented to counter each individual firing run."

Duellos nodded, smiling with satisfaction as well. "He'll see our vector changes, and start trying to change his pivot. But he's got so much mass and momentum driving it at that point, and has less ability to alter how he's moving, so we can readjust faster than he can." His smile faded. "But at those relative velocities, our ships will make much better targets for him if he can bring enough firepower to bear."

"If we can keep our approaches directly off his stern, that will limit his available weapons. How precise is our knowledge of Syndic battleship maneuvering capabilities?" Geary asked.

"On that model of ship? Very good. Alliance warships have watched them in action in many engagements and analyzed their movements afterwards. What we have in the sims is not perfect, but it is very accurate."

"So, we can predict when he'll start trying to change his pivot and how long it will take the battleship to react. This wouldn't work if the battleship had strong escorts to interfere with our movements and disrupt our attacks, or if there were two battleships that could cover each other's stern from receiving multiple attacks over a short period. But against one battleship, which has decided to protect its escorts instead of having the escorts protect it, this can work."

This time Duellos did not reply immediately as he studied every aspect of Geary's work. "Sir, I do feel obligated to point out that the extra braking time required to get the relative velocity to the battleship low enough for this is considerable. If this does not work, we won't have much time to come up with alternatives before the battleship gets within range of the freighters."

"You're right," Geary said. "Anything else?"

"Do you want me to set up the braking maneuvers for the three battle cruisers?"

"Yes." He knew he wasn't the most talented ship driver in the world, not nearly as good as Tanya Desjani and probably not as good as Roberto Duellos. This would be a good chance to see Duellos at work up close.

"Admiral," the operations watch said as alerts sounded, "Flotilla One is altering vector. They're turning outward and accelerating, coming onto an intercept with our Formation Echo."

"Preplanned maneuver," Duellos said.

Geary nodded. Flotilla One, light-hours distant near the inhabited world, had started its move hours ago. If the battleship flotilla had not been flushed early, it would have been sighted by Geary's ships only a brief time ago, followed closely by the sight of Flotilla One also heading for the refugee ships. "It'll be about an hour and a half yet before they realize their timing got thrown off. If they keep coming, Commander Pajari will handle them."

There was some superstition in that last statement, too, which was both an assertion of confidence in Pajari and an attempt to wish his hopes into reality with a bold assertion.

He focused back on the battleship, trying to feel the motion of all of the ships and the time delays between them caused by the vast distances that light had to cross, trying to anticipate and be ready for whatever the next moves should be.

He could hear the muffled sounds of the bridge watch-standers doing their jobs and speaking to each other in low voices, hear Duellos passing on the maneuvering orders and handling subsequent *what-the-hell-are-we-doing?* calls from the commanding officers of *Formidable* and *Implacable*.

Inspire pitched over, coming almost completely around. Her main propulsion lit off again. Nearby, *Formidable* and *Implacable* matched the maneuvers. The huge velocities built up earlier were now being fought against, the propulsion systems laboring to shed momentum along one vector and build it up again in the same direction the battleship was going.

The track of the battle cruisers through space bent, swinging downward toward the battleship and his escorts. The relative velocity kept slowing as the battle cruisers swept past the oncoming enemy, above and slightly to one side of the battleship, still out of range of all but long missile shots that the enemy chose not to attempt.

A moment came, aft of the enemy flotilla, when their vectors momentarily matched. For that instant, the Alliance battle cruisers and the enemy flotilla were suspended in space, unmoving relative to each other.

Then, their propulsion units straining at maximum, their hulls and inertial dampers protesting audibly at the forces being employed, the battle cruisers began accelerating straight for the battleship.

Duellos still sat in his command seat as if relaxed, but his eyes were on Geary, waiting for the orders that would, hopefully, make the attack runs as successful as they needed to be.

"All weapons ready," the combat systems watch reported. "Shields at maximum. Damage control at full readiness."

A blip appeared on Geary's display as two of the missile launchers on *Implacable* suddenly went out of commission. "Power junction failure!" *Implacable*'s captain reported, sounding as if she were ready to bite a hole in her own hull out of frustration. "I'll have them operational when we get in range if I have to jump-start the damn things by hand!"

She wouldn't have long to work on the problem. The battle cruisers kept accelerating, closing on the battleship. *Inspire* was lined up to hit the battleship first, followed by *Formidable*, then *Implacable*. There wasn't any fancy formation this time. *Formidable* was almost directly behind *Inspire*, but out slightly to one side, while *Implacable* was behind *Formidable*, slightly out on the opposite side. Geary had kept the formation as simple as possible, so as to present solutions as deceptively simple as possible for the automated maneuvering controls on the battleship and to lull the human officers into complacency.

"They're not cutting the escorts loose," Geary murmured, relieved. If the battleship commander had told the heavy cruisers to move off and attack the Alliance battle cruisers, it would have seriously complicated Geary's approach.

"There he goes," Duellos breathed in a very low voice.

The battleship had begun pivoting, his stern dropping and his bow coming up and over. Geary didn't have to check his maneuvering display to know that, if everyone kept on the same courses and speeds, the battleship would be pivoting at exactly the right rate to meet with its heaviest armament and armor in its bow each oncoming battle cruiser as it passed.

"Give him five more seconds to build up momentum," Geary said. *Three . . . two . . . one.* "All units in Formation Alpha. Immediate execute, main propulsion at zero."

The battle cruisers shut off their main propulsion. They were still closing on the battleship, but as they were no longer accelerating, their rate of closure was no longer increasing.

The automated systems controlling the battleship's maneuvers would spot that, would take the necessary action to counter it, firing thrusters at maximum as they tried to slow the turn of the massive battleship, still trying to ensure that when *Inspire* reached weapons range the battleship's bow would face the battle cruiser.

If the person in charge of the battleship was sharp enough, experienced enough, they had time to spot what Geary was doing, to guess what his plans were. They had barely time enough to override the automated controls and swing the battleship's bow back. The escorts could have done the same, and faster, but the overwhelmed command staff on the battleship had probably, for these few hectic, precious moments, forgotten that the heavy cruisers and HuKs couldn't maneuver on their own until released from control.

"*Implacable*, accelerate at maximum, adjust course as necessary to target main propulsion," Geary ordered.

Seconds later, "*Formidable*, accelerate at maximum, adjust course as necessary to target main propulsion."

And, as everyone on the bridge of *Inspire* waited anxiously, "*Inspire*, accelerate at maximum. Get his propulsion!"

The battle cruisers leaped forward again, but their order had suddenly shifted. Now *Implacable* would be the first in line, then *Formidable*, and finally *Inspire*. Along with the order of the attack, the exact times when they would be within range of the battleship had changed. The battleship's thrusters fired again in another attempt to compensate, trying to counter its own earlier moves. The enemy ship wavered under contending momentum and the push of its maneuvering controls, momentum trying to keep its huge mass turning in one direction while the maneuvering thrusters were working all out to reverse the direction of turn. A sudden shove from its main propulsion might have helped throw off the battle cruisers' attacks, but that would have been an unconventional move, not something that automated systems or officers trained to do as they were told would think of.

The battleship hung momentarily suspended between competing forces, its bow pointing straight "up."

The relatively few weapons on the battleship that could bear on a target coming in on its stern opened up for the very brief moment when *Implacable* was within range as the battle cruiser swept onward at a relative velocity of thousands of kilometers per second. Humans couldn't aim and fire under such circumstances. Only automated fire-control systems could judge the precise instant when a target flying past at such a velocity could be hit.

Geary saw *Implacable*'s two broken missile launchers report themselves ready to fire seconds before the battle cruiser tore past under the stern of the battleship, volleying out missiles, hell lances, and even grapeshot set for the smallest possible dispersion patterns at the farthest possible dispersal range. As the battle cruiser shot away from the battleship, *Implacable*'s hell lances fired repeatedly at missiles the battleship had launched despite the poor intercept angles, destroying most of the missiles before they could score hits.

Formidable came right behind, hammering the same stern area, her missiles, hell lances, and grapeshot flashing against shields already fading under the blows being absorbed. But the battleship was better prepared this time, more weapons coming to bear as it angled a bit off the vertical, slamming blows at *Formidable* as well as another volley of missiles that pursued the battle cruiser as it opened the range once more.

Geary had his eyes locked on his display, seeing the battleship begin to finally push over, more weapons coming to bear as *Inspire* made the last, most dangerous, and most important firing run.

Inspire raced past the battleship, hurling out shots toward the battleship's immense main propulsion in the moments after the rear shields collapsed and before they could rebuild.

Geary felt *Inspire* shudder, not just from the launching of her own weapons but from multiple hits. *Inspire* lurched heavily as something big struck aft, perhaps one or more missiles. Alarms went off, and portions of the display flickered as power was automatically rerouted. He could only hope the battle cruiser hadn't been hit too badly and remain focused on the battleship as the sensors on *Inspire* and the other battle cruisers looked back and tried to evaluate what damage had been inflicted.

"We'd better hope we took it down," Duellos said, his voice grim. "I've momentarily lost maneuvering control of *Inspire* and half of my own main propulsion."

Geary could hear the different watch-standers reporting damage from hits. "Hell-lance batteries 1A and 3B are out of commission. Missile launchers are off-line. Hull has been holed in several areas aft of amidships. Aft shields have collapsed and are rebuilding using emergency power, now at ten percent. Personnel casualty numbers unknown."

Damage reports were also showing up from *Implacable* and *Formidable*. Both had taken far less damage than *Inspire*, but neither was unscathed.

Debris from the weapons fired interfered with the evaluation of damage to the battleship, but Geary realized that the battleship's maneuvering thrusters were still pushing it over at maximum. "What's he doing?"

Duellos tore his attention away from his own ship's damage for a moment. "He's hurt."

The battleship kept spinning bow over stern, coming around faster. "His maneuvering controls have jammed," Geary said. "Wait. They're pushing his stern partway toward us."

The display updated triumphantly and Geary fell back into his seat with a gasp of elation. "Thank you, ancestors. We did get him."

Inspire's weapons had inflicted awful damage on the momentarily unshielded main propulsion units of the battleship. The massive, heavily armed and heavily armored ship was helpless to change her vector, spinning end over end through space. The impact of the hits had shoved the battleship slightly off of its earlier path, so that it would now pass slightly above the refugee ships instead of passing right through the middle of their very loose formation.

Taking out the battleship using conventional weapons would still take a long time. But . . . "He can't maneuver. Captain Duellos, do you have working planetary bombardment launchers?"

Normally, a ship could evade large projectiles thrown at it. The distances in space were too large, the ability to simply alter course very slightly to cause the projectile to pass harmlessly by too easy to employ. Even a miss by a single meter was all that was needed to avoid damage.

But the battleship couldn't even do that. He was locked onto his current path until his crew managed to repair the damage to the maneuvering systems, and Geary knew that Syndic warships did not carry nearly the same damage-control capabilities as Alliance ships. To the Syndic CEOs, that wasn't "cost-effective."

The ones who paid the price for that policy weren't the CEOs, naturally.

"I only have one that can bear on the battleship's path," Duellos said.

"Fire when you can," Geary ordered. "*Formidable, Implacable,* engage the enemy battleship with bombardment projectiles. Use everything you've got. Take it out before they can manage any repairs."

The battle cruisers began pumping out bombardment projectiles. The simple weapons, just solid metal shaped to pierce through atmosphere as they plunged toward targets on the surface of worlds, streamed toward the path of the battleship, forming an arc of deadly metal as they headed for the place it would be.

Despite the energy that would be unleashed when solid metal objects moving at thousands of kilometers per second slammed into an obstacle, the battleship could have shrugged off a few hits. If it could have jogged even slightly in its path, the battleship could have avoided the majority of the projectiles aimed at it.

The two heavy cruisers and two HuKs that had been following very close to the battleship suddenly broke away, either because they had been ordered to stop slaving their maneuvers to that of the battleship or because they had no wish to die helplessly and finally took matters into their own hands.

"*Implacable* and *Formidable*, get those heavy cruisers," Geary ordered.

"Get our maneuvering back online *now!*" Duellos roared at his crew, frustrated at being out of the fight.

Escape pods began leaping off the battleship as its crew sought safety, first a few, then a rush as the thousands of crew members scrambled to survive.

The first bombardment projectile hit, then a second, sparking massive flares as the battleship's shields parried the blows. Another hit, then two more, the last penetrating to slam into armor. A half dozen projectiles hit in a flurry, smashing through the armor, vaporizing sections of the hull, one bashing into the already useless main propulsion units as the battleship continued to twirl helplessly.

Three more hits, and in an instant the battleship vanished as its power core took too much damage and overloaded.

Geary sighed, feeling sudden weariness filling him as the cloud of gas and small debris that had once been a Syndic-built battleship began spreading out to join with the wreckage of countless other warships destroyed at Batara in the last century.

"Captain, we have partial maneuvering control back."

Duellos made a fist and rapped the arm of his command seat in barely repressed anger. "Those heavy cruisers and HuKs are going to get away," he said to Geary.

Sizing up the frantic flight of the escorts and the wide turns through space as *Implacable* and *Formidable* swung back in pursuit, Geary nodded. "You're right. Unless they turn to fight, we won't be able to get them. Cheer up, Roberto. *Inspire* got in the death blow on that battleship."

"True." Duellos looked down, breathing hard as if he had just run a race. "But we got hit hard. Casualty reports are still trickling in, but I lost people. That's really why I'm unhappy."

"I'm sorry."

"I know that. You're not one of those bastards who just shrug and say price of victory or something." Duellos looked at his display. "Now what?"

Geary looked as well. "If we try chasing those escorts, we could still be chasing them a week from now and be no closer to catching them."

"The HuKs will run out of fuel cells, eventually, as will the heavy cruisers, but so will we. I'll go ahead and recommend what I think you are already leaning toward. As pleasant as it would be to finish off the rest of these scum to avenge *Fleche*, chasing them is likely to be an exercise in frustration and may be exactly what they want. I believe we should return to the vicinity of the refugee ships to repair damage, protect the convoy, and keep an eye out for other surprises."

Geary checked the damage to *Inspire* again and resisted the urge to shake his head. Some of the repair work would be beyond anything that the crew could do. *Inspire* wouldn't be back in full fighting trim again until an auxiliary or a dock was able to work on her.

The refugee ships and Alliance escorts in Formation Echo had proceeded onward while the battle cruisers had dived off to the side and slightly down to intercept the oncoming battleship. Geary ordered the battle cruisers to head back, the commanders of *Formidable* and *Implacable* not hiding their disappointment at being told to break off the chase. But they did as ordered, something the example of *Fleche* had forcefully reminded him could not be taken for granted even now.

Inspire could still only limp along as the other two battle cruisers joined her, angling across the star system back toward the rest of the Alliance ships. A bit over a light-hour distant, the light cruisers and HuKs that made up Flotilla One were still heading toward the refugee ships, unaware that the battleship they were counting on was no more.

But Geary paid more attention for now to the heavy cruisers and HuKs that had been escorting that doomed battleship. Once it had become apparent that the Alliance battle cruisers were no longer in pursuit, the enemy ships had slowed and turned, holding their positions. "They're disciplined," he commented to Duellos.

"Who? That lot?" Duellos frowned at his display. "Well disciplined. What are we going to do about them? Even after destroying that battleship, what's left to Tiyannak is enough to control this star system once we leave here, and probably at least a few other star systems."

"Let's see how well disciplined they are and what else we can find out about them." Geary called Commander Pajari, still about fourteen light-minutes away. "I'm bringing *Inspire* back to you. I want you to detach the destroyers from the Ninth Squadron with orders to intercept some of the escape pods from the enemy battleship. I want to sweep up as many prisoners as possible. I will detach *Formidable* and *Implacable* to screen their operations and take aboard prisoners picked up by the destroyers. Geary, out."

Duellos looked even grumpier, but he nodded in understanding. "*Inspire* would just slow them down, the Ninth is the smallest destroyer squadron, and Pajari no longer has to worry about this flotilla threatening the convoy. You want to see if those heavy cruisers will race to the rescue of their friends when we start scooping up escape pods, right?"

"And, if they do," Geary said, "it will give our battle cruisers a chance to nail them. I know Captain Savik on *Formidable* is good, but I haven't had much chance to see how capable Captain Ekrhi on *Implacable* is."

"I think she's good, as good as Savik. Either one is capable of commanding the screening force. But James Savik is senior in date of rank."

Geary called Savik on *Formidable*. "I'll be detaching you and *Implacable* as Formation Beta. You'll be in command of the formation. Your job is to stay close enough to the destroyers to screen them against those two heavy cruisers and the HuKs if they try to stop us from taking survivors of the battleship prisoner. If you can lure in those heavy cruisers, so much the better, but I don't want to lose any destroyers, so don't get too far from them."

Savik nodded, grinning. "Understood, Admiral. How many prisoners do we want? A lot of escape pods got off that battleship before it blew."

"I want the prisoner-taking to last long enough for the heavy cruisers to see and long enough for them to react if they're going to. Use your best judgment. Don't keep it going past the numbers of prisoners you can easily carry."

"Yes, sir. What are we going to do with them? I mean, are they Syndics?"

"Technically? I don't think so. Interrogate them to find out what they can tell us about the situation here and at Tiyannak, and how many total warships Tiyannak has." Geary pointed toward the star. "When we get there, I'll drop them off on the primary world along with the refugees. I don't expect Batara to be thrilled about that, but I don't want to catch hell from fleet staff and the government for bringing home more prisoners of war for them to feed, confine, and otherwise worry about."

After detaching the two battle cruisers, Geary pondered his display a moment longer. It was probably a good time, having badly blunted the planned ambush of his forces, to finally give a call to whoever was running Batara. "I need a broadcast message aimed at the primary inhabited world."

The comms watch made a few taps on her display. "You're ready, Admiral."

"Thank you." He paused to think, then touched the control. "To the current rulers of Batara, this is Admiral Geary of the Alliance fleet. My ships have been attacked without warning by hostile warships operating freely in your star system. I require an immediate message from you, establishing your status as an independent star system or one subject to an external government and explaining the status of all non-Alliance warships in this star system. I will take any necessary actions to defend the ships under my control and under the protection of the Alliance. We are escorting back to your primary inhabited world refugee ships full of people from this star system. They will be landed on that planet, as will a regiment of Alliance ground forces to ensure nothing disrupts the return of your people to your world. Any attempts to interfere with our operation will be met with the full force at my disposal. Any attacks on Alliance military personnel or civilians under the protection of the Alliance will be met with the full force at my disposal. I await your reply and your explanations. To the honor of our ancestors, Geary, out."

"Tanya would approve," Duellos commented.

"Tanya would already be urging me to bombard the hell out of this star system as well as Tiyannak."

"And she would be complaining mightily about that thing crowded into my shuttle dock. Speak of the devil, here is Lieutenant Night."

"Night Witch," Lieutenant Popova corrected, but her smile was serious. "Admiral, I came to the bridge because there aren't any automated internal links to give you the status of my warbird. It didn't take any damage. Is there anything I can do?"

Duellos, who had been looking ill-tempered again as he went over the damage to his ship, gave Popova a wry smile in response to the sincere offer. "Not unless you want to take the FAC out and take *Inspire* in tow."

"You're already moving pretty fast, sir. My warbird could match you, but she'd burn her fuel out in no time, and then you'd be towing me."

"Save it for when we get to that planet," Geary told the aerospace officer. "Our shuttles and the ground forces are probably going to need all of the deterrence your warbirds can provide, and maybe the fire support as well."

"Admiral, the heavy cruisers have come about and are accelerating parallel to our course," the operations watch reported.

Geary checked his display. "They're not paralleling us. They're headed for the battleship's escape pods."

"Not if *Formidable* and *Implacable* can help it," Duellos said. The two battle cruisers were accelerating and adjusting their own courses to meet the heavy cruisers near the cloud of escape pods.

But the enemy ships veered off again when they saw the Alliance warships approaching. Geary hesitated, one hand poised over his comm controls, waiting to see what Captain Savik would do. But his fears proved unfounded as Savik brought the battle cruisers around to hang in orbit a good light-minute short of the escape pods. The heavy cruisers checked their own velocity, matching orbits, so that Alliance battle cruisers, escape pods, and enemy heavy cruisers all hung in space unmoving relative to each other, the escape pods occupying a perilous no-man's-land between the two groups of warships.

"The Ninth Destroyer Squadron is on its way to the escape pods," the operations watch said. "Admiral, they're at point one five light speed, so they should reach the pods in an hour and a half."

"Very well." Geary studied the movement of the destroyers, worrying about their fuel status. "If this high-speed maneuvering keeps up, we'll have to transfer fuel cells from the battle cruisers to the destroyers to keep them from running too low."

"What we have won't go far spread among that many destroyers," Duellos cautioned. "What's this?" he asked as another alert sounded.

Two light cruisers had appeared from behind the super-Earth planet, swinging around one side and heading for the refugee ships. "They jumped out early," Geary said. "They must have received orders to move up their attack."

"Anything sent from the battleship would have reached them at about the right time for us to see them moving now," Duellos agreed. "Let's see what they do when they see that the battleship isn't with them anymore."

After an hour spent watching for reactions, the answer was clear. "All enemy ships have seen the destruction of the battleship by now," the operations watch-stander said, "and none have altered their vectors. Both groups of light cruisers are still on an intercept with the refugee ships."

"And the heavy cruisers are still hanging around near the escape pods," Duellos added. "These may not technically still be Syndics, but they're still fighting like Syndics."

Geary nodded in reply. Despite what propaganda said, few in the Alliance military doubted the courage of the men and women fighting for the Syndics. Alliance fighters were baffled by the willingness of Syndic combatants to die for a system that was so obviously wrong, but they had learned through bitter experience that their enemy was tough and determined. But the Syndics were also subject to rigid discipline. They obeyed orders, to the letter, or else. "How are repairs coming on your main propulsion and maneuvering?"

"They're coming. *Inspire* is almost back to full maneuvering capability, but the two main propulsion units that are still off-line are very badly damaged. My engineers can't give me an estimated time to repair on them."

Inspire wouldn't be able to rejoin the escorts around the refugee ships before the enemy Flotilla One reached them. It would be up to Commander Pajari to keep those light cruisers and HuKs from reaching any of the helpless freighters.

Half an hour until that enemy flotilla closed on the refugee ships and their escorts, and half an hour until Destroyer Squadron Nine reached the escape pods and started hauling in prisoners. "It's time I talked to the people in this star system. Everyone. This time I want a broadcast blanketing all comm frequencies and directed to all points in the star system."

"Yes, Admiral," the comms watch acknowledged. "Wait one, sir. All right. You've got it, Admiral."

Geary straightened in his seat, made sure his uniform looked as good as it could, then touched the control. "To the people of Batara

Star System and all ships in Batara Star System, this is Admiral Geary
of the Alliance fleet. We are here for one purpose only, to return to this
star system the citizens of Batara who have been stranded in Alliance
space. Once we drop them off, we will not remain here. The Alliance
has no designs on this star system and no interest in dictating to the
people of Batara. However, we have been subjected to unprovoked
attacks by warships of unknown allegiance. We have responded to
those attacks and will continue to do so, taking all necessary steps to
eliminate any threats to us or to the people of Batara. To the honor of
our ancestors, Geary, out."

"I'm curious," Duellos said. "Why didn't you tell them outright that
we were on a humanitarian mission?"

"Because of something else I learned not long ago from talking to
former Syndics. To them, 'humanitarian' means 'scam.' It means
someone is lying about their motives and their objectives, and is simply
using the word to describe a scheme for personal profit. If I had said we
were on a humanitarian mission, it would have sounded to them like I
was admitting that I was actually out to cheat them."

Duellos gazed morosely toward his display. "Sometimes I almost
feel sorry for them. The Syndics. But then I get angry again, remembering how hard they fought for the same system that screwed them,
how many people of ours they killed in the name of that system."

"How many did *Inspire* lose in this fight?" Geary asked.

"The final casualty count is seventeen dead, thirty-five wounded.
All of the wounded are now out of danger though some will take a lot
more patching up. We were lucky it wasn't worse."

Implacable had only suffered a couple of wounded, while *Formidable* had lost one killed and had eight wounded. They had all inflicted
far more injury upon the enemy than they had suffered, but somehow
that wasn't very comforting.

Geary sat watching the movements of the warships and the refugee ships, seeming slow across the huge distances they had to cross,

waiting for any replies or reactions to his message. Commander Pajari had positioned most of her available escorts in two box-shaped formations, each facing one of the oncoming enemy flotillas. The destroyers of the Ninth Squadron continued their work hauling in escape pods and hauling out the men and women inside until they had all the prisoners they could carry, then heading over to meet up with either *Implacable* or *Formidable* and transfer the prisoners to the much larger battle cruisers.

He saw the movement before the combat watch reported it. "The heavy cruisers are accelerating toward our destroyers, sir!"

Moments later, the operations watch called out another warning. "Both light cruiser flotillas are accelerating onto attack runs against the refugee ships, Admiral."

THIRTEEN

"THEY'RE still using closely coordinated actions and still following the orders of some command authority who was not on the battleship." *Inspire*, and Geary, were five light-minutes from rejoining the refugee-ship formation, and nearly ten light-minutes from the region of space where the heavy cruisers were moving in to tangle with the Alliance battle cruisers and destroyers. "The heavy cruisers are a distraction."

Duellos nodded in agreement. "They won't press the attack. They just want you looking at them instead of whatever the light cruisers try against the refugee ships. They may think you're on *Formidable* or *Implacable*."

"I'm still far enough away from the escorts that I need to count on Commander Pajari to do the right thing." If he tried giving orders that would take five minutes to reach their intended recipients, based on information already five minutes older, he could seriously mess up the defense of the convoy.

The light cruisers were coming in from two directions, the original flotilla consisting of two light cruisers and four HuKs, and the second of just two light cruisers. They had pushed their velocity up to point one five light. With the convoy plodding along at point zero five light speed, that would still allow good fire-control solutions for the attackers while making it harder for the Alliance escorts to intercept the enemy. But while still short of the convoy, the light cruisers coming in from the right pulled up to race over the top of the convoy while the light cruisers and HuKs coming from the front dove down and over in a wide, reverse loop.

"Classic Syndic tricks," Duellos said. "They want Pajari to disregard the ones in front who appear to be fleeing and chase the two zipping past just out of range overhead."

Geary couldn't suppress a grunt of surprise as the four remaining Alliance light cruisers leaped away from their own formation, all apparently racing in pursuit of the enemy light cruisers passing above them. Had Pajari fallen for the bait despite her words of reassurance?

But only one of the Alliance light cruisers actually steadied out in pursuit of the two bait ships. The other three kept swinging about and turning, curving along a path aimed toward the front of the refugee convoy. Half of Pajari's destroyers had also jumped forward, moving out well ahead of the refugee ships.

The two enemy light cruisers and two HuKs there had, instead of fleeing, gone back into their loop, coming out finally, after having gone through a full circle, and heading for the refugee ships once more. But instead of finding a defense weakened by ships that had left their positions to chase the bait light cruisers, the small enemy flotilla found itself running headfirst into Pajari's countermove.

Three Alliance light cruisers and a dozen destroyers tore into the two enemy light cruisers and four HuKs. The slashing firing run wasn't one-sided. *Parrot* took two bad hits from the enemy HuKs, and *Spur* got battered as the enemy light cruisers concentrated their fire on her. But *Spur* and light cruiser *Flanconade* scored crippling hits on an enemy light cruiser, while the other enemy light cruiser reeled from fire coming from light cruiser *Nukiwaza* and a half dozen destroyers.

The Alliance destroyer *Flagellum* got in a lucky hit on one of the HuKs, knocking out its main propulsion and leaving it helpless as well.

The surviving three HuKs fled as Pajari brought her warships back around for another firing pass. One of the enemy light cruisers fired back as it tried to limp away, but the crew of the second fled in escape pods before the second Alliance attack reached them, as did the crew of the crippled HuK.

The second firing run tore apart the still-fighting light cruiser and the abandoned HuK. The abandoned enemy light cruiser blew up as its power core overloaded under a barrage of hits.

Above and now curving slightly back from the left of the refugee-ship formation, the two bait-ship light cruisers altered their vectors as they absorbed the destruction of Flotilla One.

"They're heading for the jump point for Tiyannak," the operations watch on *Inspire* reported. "So are the HuKs surviving from Flotilla One."

"More good news," Duellos exclaimed, pointing to his display.

Events that had taken place over ten minutes earlier were now visible to *Inspire*. The two enemy heavy cruisers had pushed their diversion moves a little too far, and Captain Savik had positioned his battle cruisers just right. A sudden burst of acceleration from *Formidable* and *Implacable* had brought one of the heavy cruisers within extreme missile range, and the resulting volley from the battle cruisers had scored enough hits to slow the heavy cruiser appreciably. As its companion fled along with the two HuKs accompanying it, the stricken enemy heavy cruiser fired back in futile defiance as *Implacable* and *Formidable* swung in and blew it apart in a single attack run.

By that time, one of the three HuKs running for the jump point for Tiyannak had veered off, making a dangerously tight turn to bring it back toward the inhabited world. That would be the one HuK that Araya had thought Batara had managed to get working, probably dragooned into service with the Tiyannak forces but now reasserting independence as the former conquerors fled.

"We have met the enemy, and Batara is ours," Duellos said with a grin.

"Not that we want it or intend keeping it," Geary said, trying suppress his own elation.

The job wasn't over yet.

EVERY one of Geary's ships and every spy sat dropped off by them was tied into a single surveillance net by automated systems. Anything one ship or satellite could see, anyone on any ship could see just as if they were looking directly at it. Now Geary sat on the bridge of *Inspire*, watching his display as shuttles dropped down into atmosphere with more refugees. Already, the off-load seemed to have been going on forever, and there were close to half the refugee ships still to go.

The entire contingent of Alliance warships and all of the refugee ships were in orbit about the main inhabited world. Batara's antiorbital defenses had chosen discretion over senseless valor, remaining silent as Geary's warships wove their way just above the atmosphere.

The image of a speaker for the government of Batara occupied a virtual window next to Geary's seat. "We must protest this continued violation of Batara's sovereignty," the speaker insisted for perhaps the sixth time since the off-load had begun with Colonel Voston's regiment being dropped into a large, central square of the main city.

The regiment had formed a wide perimeter, clearing a big open area in the square for the shuttles to land and refugees to stay once they were dropped off. The three FACs had all been launched, their sleek, manta shapes gliding through the atmosphere and alternately hovering over the drop-off areas or swooping around the perimeter in a distinctly menacing fashion. If Batara still possessed any FACs of its own, they had stayed hidden rather than tangle with the Alliance warbirds.

"We are returning your citizens," Geary told the speaker in a tone of voice that made it clear he wasn't going to yield. "We have already defended your precious sovereignty by destroying the warships from

Tiyannak that were operating at Batara. We will not tolerate any inter-ference with our mission. That's all."

He ended the call. "Captain Duellos, have your comm people screen any more calls from that source. Unless they have something new and important to say, I don't want to waste any more time with them."

As if on cue, another alert sounded. Geary found himself looking at another virtual window that popped into existence, this one showing the view from Colonel Voston's battle armor. "We got a situation developing, Admiral. My hack-and-crack platoon set up shop here when we landed and have been monitoring all comms and networks. The local government has been using code words to assemble a response to us."

Voston turned slowly, letting Geary view what Voston's armor was seeing. Rows of nondescript, brutally bland buildings were interrupted by openings for streets and alleys, all of them packed with people. "This is what's going on just outside our perimeter."

"I've been watching the crowds from overhead," Geary said. "The citizens have been protesting in the streets since before we arrived in this star system."

"It's what's been coming through the crowds that's the problem," Voston said. "They've been infiltrating and forming a screen between our soldiers and the crowds. Some ground forces, some of what look like police, and a lot of mob-militia types."

"That doesn't sound like something aimed at attacking you," Geary said.

"It's not. And they're not here to protect us from the outside crowds, either. There's a lot of comm talk going on, and a lot of it is ugly. The thugs are going to wait until we leave, then they're going to move in and do their best to massacre every single man, woman, and child we just dropped off here." Voston's distaste for those waiting to attack the refugees came through clearly despite his attempt to sound impassive. "Just thought you should know."

"What can we do?"

"You mean against the mob types? We don't have to wait for them to move. They're in a threatening posture. Give me the word, and we'll start wiping them out if that's what you want."

"You've only got a regiment on the ground," Geary said, appalled by both the situation and by Colonel Voston's casual suggestion for handling it. "If you start shooting, the crowds may start moving against you, and you'll be swamped."

"We'll go down shooting."

"Colonel, I didn't bring your regiment here so you could all commit suicide in a blaze of combat and glory! Between the refugees we're dropping off and the crowds gathering around the site, there are already close to fifty thousand civilians to worry about."

"Syndics," Voston said.

"Civilians," Geary repeated. "What are the numbers on the mob militias, police, and local ground forces?"

"Ummm . . . our armor sensors and my hack and cracks are estimating a few companies of ground forces, maybe five hundred cops, and a couple of thousand mob types. Odds are only the mob types will do the dirty work while the uniforms pretend to be maintaining security but actually hold back any crowds that might try to help the refugees."

"There are a lot more than a few companies of ground forces available to the local government in that city," Geary said.

"Yes, sir, but these are the loyalists, the ground forces that will do whatever the guys in charge say. The rest of the ground forces are probably not as high on assisting in the slaughter of their fellow citizens."

Geary sat watching the images of the crowds. *I only have a regiment of ground forces to deal with this, and another regiment tied up on the refugee ships and scattered around on all of those ships. Plus three FACs, which are doing a great job of intimidating the locals. But that's not enough. I can't leave Colonel Voston's regiment down there indefinitely, and I can't use my warships unless I want to start bombarding the city.*

Wait a minute. He focused on the crowds again, remembering what the two refugee leaders had told him in their last conversation. "Colonel Kim, where are Araya and Naxos right now?"

Kim answered up immediately. "They're on the way down. I watched them load into a shuttle half an hour ago, so they should be getting close to drop-off."

"Excellent. Colonel Voston, I want your hack-and-crack platoon to get together with two refugee leaders named Araya and Naxos, who should be landing soon. Give Araya and Naxos full access to your gear so they can break into every available network and comm system down there and start spreading the word about what's going on. Have both Araya and Naxos identify any other refugee leaders who can assist them in that."

"Tell them what's going on so they can tell the whole planet?" Voston asked. "I'm supposed to brief Syndics?"

"No, Colonel, you're supposed to brief people who will prevent the Syndics from controlling this planet again. The local government controls the planetary comm systems and networks, but we can break in and get out whatever information we want. No one here will believe anything *we* say, but they'll recognize the refugee leaders and listen to them. Once those crowds, and the not-so-loyal ground forces of this planet, find out what's happening, they may solve this refugee problem for good in a way that won't stain our honor."

"Yes, sir. It's your war."

The crowds around the landing site kept growing as Araya and Naxos were given access to the Alliance comm gear and began blanketing planetary communication systems with their pleas and calls for a new government, as well as images of the government toughs and military forces menacing the returned refugees. Geary had to admire the way the specialists in the ground forces unit managed to get images that didn't show any trace of the Alliance soldiers protecting the perimeter of the refugees' landing site. As far as the vids and pictures showed, the refugees were defenseless against the looming threat of government-controlled violence.

"More local military deploying," Colonel Voston reported, his voice and words terse. "Armor and heavy weapons as well as some leg ground forces."

Geary took a look at part of his display, where a partial globe centered on the refugees' landing site showed military bases over much of the planet. "They're moving everywhere, not just near you."

"Right. We can't tell where they're going, because all the orders we're picking up from the government are telling them to remain in garrison. Those forces aren't following those orders, though. My hack and cracks aren't picking up anything that might tell us their intentions from the units that are moving, so if they are communicating with each other, they're using means that no one can intercept."

"This was a Syndic star system," Geary said. "From what I've heard, figuring out how to communicate without being intercepted is a common thing in Syndic societies."

Voston frowned. "Admiral, we don't know why they're moving or where. We've got lots of Syndics crowding us from outside our perimeter, lots of Syndics crowding us from *inside* the perimeter, and the numbers keep going up as the crowds get bigger, and more refugees get dropped off. If more Syndic ground forces start showing up, things could hit the fan real fast."

"They're not Syndics, Colonel. We're watching them from up here, too. You've got three warbirds flying close support overhead and a lot of warships ready to provide bombardment support." He knew why Colonel Voston was worried. Another virtual window before Geary showed an overhead view of the landing site. There had been a wide, open band around the Alliance soldiers protecting the perimeter, but as more refugees had arrived, their numbers had pressed outward closer to the soldiers, and the growing crowds outside the perimeter had slowly edged their way inward. Colonel Voston's troops occupied a gradually narrowing space separating the much larger groups of what the Alliance soldiers still saw as Syndics. Even the calmest troops would be rattled under those circumstances.

"Captain Duellos," Geary said. "Have your comm officer try to get direct contact with some of those local ground forces units that are on the move. I also want a feed here so I can listen in to the soldiers of Colonel Voston's regiment."

Listening to the ground forces communications, Geary could feel the battle-scarred veterans growing more nervous and more dangerous as the crowds came closer and kept growing in size and intensity. Ironically, his idea to use Araya and Naxos to stir up popular unrest was succeeding so well that it threatened to cause a disaster. If Voston's battle-weary troops were pressed too hard and opened fire . . .

"Lieutenant Popova, this is Admiral Geary."

"Night Witch here, sir," Lieutenant Popova answered immediately.

"Take your warbirds as low over the refugee drop-off site as possible. I want them to look as intimidating as you can manage. We have to hold back those crowds."

"We're on it, sir."

He might lack enough of other assets, but at least he had a lot of shuttles since that had been necessary to off-load all the refugees. "Captain Duellos, have your ops people help arrange the shuttles so we can pull up Colonel Voston's regiment in only two lifts."

"That may be difficult, Admiral," Duellos cautioned.

"I know. That's why I want your people working on it. I know they can make it happen." It was half an expression of how he really felt, or hoped, and half a public statement of confidence in Duellos's crew that might inspire them to do more than they themselves believed possible. Automated systems could spit out the numbers and the load plan in seconds, but only humans could spot unconventional ways to get around obstacles that stubborn software saw as unconquerable.

"Admiral, this is getting worse fast!" Voston called.

"I am on top of this," Geary replied, trying to sound confident without seeming oblivious to the real problems facing Voston's soldiers. "The crowds—"

"It's the local military and those toughs working for the government! They're either pushing closer on their own or forcing civilians ahead of them closer to us! We—"

Voston broke off as a single Alliance FAC roared close over his head, pivoting and braking simultaneously to drift above the thin line of Alliance soldiers, its vertical lift drives thundering out a storm of exhaust that had no effect on the soldiers in their battle armor but physically drove back the nearest civilians.

Geary checked his overhead view, seeing the other two FACs similarly employed. "We're almost finished, Colonel. The last shuttles carrying refugees are on their way down."

"Understood, sir." Voston's grin was tense, a sheen of sweat on his face. "We'll hold the line."

"Admiral, we have comms with a local armored unit!"

Despite his worries about Voston and his soldiers, Geary had to switch his attention to a new virtual window that popped into existence, showing a grim-faced woman in a uniform only slightly modified from its Syndicate Worlds origin. She was clearly inside an armored vehicle, one that was moving rapidly. "I need to know your intentions," Geary said without preamble.

"Why?" the woman replied.

"Because I have troops on the ground on your planet, engaged in ensuring the safe return to your world of citizens of your world. We will leave as soon as that operation is completed. I don't want my troops harmed, and I don't want those citizens hurt, either."

"You're Alliance," the woman spat. "You don't—" Her eyes narrowed, regarding Geary. "My equipment gives me an ID on you. Are you Black Jack?"

"I am Admiral Geary, yes."

The eyes widened, then the woman nodded. "We aren't going to engage your forces unless they try to stay after returning all of our people. We are no threat to *our* people."

"You are heading toward the site where we are dropping off the refugees."

"There are others there who need to be dealt with. Internal matters."

An alert drew Geary's eyes to his display. "There are two drones closing on the site, as well."

"They're not ours," the woman said.

"Then I'm taking them down."

"Be my guest."

"Lieutenant Popova, take out those drones." He spoke to the armored forces commander again. "Hold off until I get my troops off the ground."

The armored forces commander eyed him for a long moment, then nodded. "We have no interest in engaging your forces," she repeated.

The window vanished, and Geary swung his head to focus on Colonel Voston once more. "The local military forces closing on your position intend engaging the other locals. They will not engage you."

"I'd rather not take the word of a Syndic for that, Admiral!"

"You don't have to. We're getting you out of there." Geary spared another few seconds to run his eyes down the lift plan that Captain Duellos's crew had put together. "Stand by to start the lift. Tell your hack and cracks to give those two refugee leaders, Araya and Naxos, a couple of minutes' warning before they shut down their gear to leave so the leaders can broadcast some final messages."

"Yes, sir. Does the Admiral understand how dangerous it will be between lifts? I'll only have half my regiment left down here against growing numbers of hostiles."

"I understand, Colonel. We'll get this done as quickly as possible. Lieutenant Popova," Geary added, knowing that Voston could also hear this transmission, "you are weapons free if you spot any threats to the ground forces or the shuttles."

"Yes, sir," Popova replied, sounding happy. "We've got your six, Colonel."

Minutes passed at a crawl despite all of the activity as the Alliance shuttles grounded, barely able to find room to land inside the now-crowded landing area, the local military forces that had left their garrisons came closer to the outer edges of the now-massive crowds surrounding that area, and the local forces and government toughs near the refugees pressed closer to the Alliance perimeter despite the aggressive movements of the FACs overhead.

"Even numbers, go!" Colonel Voston ordered. Every other soldier on the perimeter melted backwards, forming into clumps of soldiers racing toward the nearest shuttles. "Steady!" Voston called out to those still holding position.

Geary could see Voston's movement highlighted on the overhead view. The colonel wasn't leaving on the first lift, but was instead walking steadily along the perimeter. Geary could see majors, captains, and lieutenants from the regiment doing the same, and when he called up the data saw that every senior noncommissioned officer was still in place as well. Voston had sent up the first lift with just corporals in charge, keeping the rest of his command structure in place to help maintain stability in the half of his badly pressed regiment still forming a tenuous barrier between the refugees and local government forces.

"Back! Off! Now!" A sergeant and several Alliance soldiers had leveled weapons at local toughs, who were so close that the ends of the barrels of the Alliance weapons almost touched their bodies.

Several of the toughs paled, trying unsuccessfully to push back against the crowd behind them. They were used to beating up civilians, not facing armed and armored ground forces.

Geary was trying to figure out how to keep the situation from blowing up when he saw another sergeant leading a wedge of refugees toward the point of confrontation. "They're taking over security here!" the sergeant called. "Fall back!"

The toughs had only a few moments to relax and start to smile as the Alliance ground forces faded backwards, before the mass of refugees charged them and swamped their front ranks in a swirl of improvised weapons and swinging fists.

Everywhere along the perimeter, the refugees were surging outward as Voston's soldiers dropped back to where the second wave of shuttles would land. The government thugs found themselves trapped between the refugees and the antigovernment crowds pressing in behind, who had joined in the fight when violence finally erupted.

Geary hastily checked the status of the few local military units that had been backing the toughs and found them falling apart without fighting as other local forces allied with the crowds began arriving in vastly larger numbers. The local police, who had been protecting the thugs, had completely vanished, either overrun by the crowds or seeking shelter anywhere they could find it.

Voston's soldiers backed into the shuttles, the last ones raising their weapons in triumph and shouting encouragement to the refugees while the shuttle ramps closed.

As the last shuttles bounded upward, a single shoulder-fired missile bolted through the air after them.

Geary didn't have time to order any response, but he didn't have to. The FAC flown by Nightstalker whipped around, slicing between the rising shuttles and missile, popping out flares, chaff, and other decoys that caused the missile to weave back and forth before locking on a decoy and detonating far from the shuttles.

While Nightstalker handled the missile, Night Witch had taken care of the launcher. Geary saw a single shot slam into a small crowd of mob toughs on a flat rooftop, scattering the thugs and leaving a hole in the top of the building, along with three toughs who had never had time to regret their mistake.

The three FACs did victory rolls over the roiling mass of refugees and other civilians in the square, then sprinted skyward in the wake of the shuttles.

"Pilots!" Duellos muttered. "Do they always have to show off?"

"I think so," Geary said. "Pilots were like that a century ago, too. They can't just be good; they have to make sure everyone else knows how good they are."

"Black Jack!" Another comm window, this one showing the refugee leader Araya and, in the background, the local armored forces commander who had spoken to Geary earlier. "Thank you! Naxos was right, you are hard copy. But this is our fight now!"

"Good luck," Geary said.

By the time all of the shuttles were recovered and Geary led his task force away from the planet, he could watch intercepted broadcasts showing that the crowds were storming the hall of government, chanting demands for freedom, backed by substantial military forces which had joined the revolt.

"Freedom," Duellos repeated as he watched the reports from the planet. "Will they really get freedom?"

"That's up to them," Geary said.

He cut loose the former refugee ships, whose crews aggrievedly demanded pay for their long chore hauling and housing the refugees, but when offered the chance to plead their case to any of the governments in local star systems chose instead to head out in search of more profitable activities. The leased freighters carrying the two regiments of ground forces, Kim's now consolidated along with Voston's, were sent with a strong escort toward the jump point back to Yokai, then Adriana, while Geary took the rest of the warships to the jump point for Tiyannak.

"Is this covered by your orders?" Duellos said.

"Tanya wouldn't be asking me that. She'd be happy that I assumed it was a necessary part of solving the refugee problem. And it is."

It took an extra two weeks to jump to Tiyannak, ensure that the heavy cruiser, light cruisers, and HuKs that had escaped at Batara were still fleeing as fast as they could run, launch a mass of bombardment projectiles aimed at the former Syndic shipyards and refitting facilities there, where a few more warships still sat in various stages of repair and refit, then return to Batara with the knowledge that Tiyannak would no longer be able to support offensive operations against its neighbors.

The squadron to which Night Witch, Catnap, and Nightstalker belonged had begun setting up camp in the partially reactivated facility at Yokai. Geary dropped off the pilots and their FACs along with some sincere appreciation for their support, then headed back for Adriana.

As he prepared to leave the bridge of *Inspire*, the FAC base dwindling behind them, Geary paused to listen to Duellos as he spoke to a virtual window showing one of his senior noncommissioned officers.

"Give them whatever assistance we can," Duellos said, sounding unusually aggravated. "And let me know when our own is completely straightened out."

"Is something wrong?" Geary asked.

"Software updates," Duellos said in the same persecuted tone of voice that Colonel Galland had used a few weeks ago. He closed the virtual window and pointed astern. "The FAC base techs made a backdoor request for assistance from my code monkeys because they're having particularly bad problems running the accumulated updates on the gear that was mothballed here."

"Aerospace forces software techs asked fleet techs for assistance?" Geary asked. "Voluntarily?"

"Amazing, isn't it? Everybody's code monkeys tend to get along and help each other out regardless of institutional rivalries. I am told they actually call it the Code of the Monkeys though I may have been getting my leg pulled."

Geary cast a worried glance at the image of the FAC base, floating serenely in space. Additional lights could be seen on a portion of it, where the aerospace forces were reactivating enough compartments and equipment to support them. "What's their problem? The same sort of stuff that afflicted the FACs at Adrianna?"

"No. The warbirds appear to be all right. They were all updated before they deployed here. This time it's the software in the sensor and combat systems on the base." Duellos waved a grand gesture. "My senior chief code cracker says the *New! Improved! Intuitive!* updates on the FAC base appear to be causing fights between the base's subsystems."

Geary shook his head, wondering why news of troubles with software updates was ever surprising. "Are there similar problems on *Inspire*?"

"Nothing nearly that bad, but some of the updates aren't playing as well as they should with the others." Duellos gave Geary a lopsided grin. "The FAC base systems were even suffering bleed-throughs from training-sim software."

"Bleed-throughs?"

"Somehow, information from inactive training sims was showing up as active, real detections, before vanishing completely as their systems caught up with it, to be spotted by something else, then disappearing again almost as fast as the systems scrubbed the bad data."

"And they're sure these aren't real detections?" Geary pressed. "We've seen some unusual stealth capabilities with the Dancers."

Duellos smiled again. "The purported sightings were of a battle cruiser and two heavy cruisers. I think we'd be able to spot that bunch. My people cross-checked our own systems and confirmed that we'd seen nothing during the transient reports of those warships. If someone really could hide ships of that size, and those ships' stealth really had stumbled for a second or two, we would have seen them as well."

"You're right, and nothing the size of a battle cruiser could be hidden using even the best stealth gear. It wouldn't be the first set of updates that were buggy," Geary said. "Are we certain that's what this is? An update with bugs in it? Are there any signs of malware?"

"None, Admiral," Duellos answered. "That was the first thing my people checked. There's no sign of sabotage unless, like Colonel Galland, you believe that software updates are inherently acts of sabotage aimed at users."

"Based on my own experience, I have a lot of sympathy for Colonel Galland's opinion on that," Geary said. "Do we need to hang around that base in order to help the aerospace techs?"

"No, Admiral. I would have let you know if that was an issue. My people can provide any necessary assistance remotely."

"Good. I want to know when that's cleared up," Geary said. "That single FAC squadron has barely enough capability to maintain security here as it is. We can't afford to have them chasing after software ghosts when we have enough real problems to worry about."

Several hours later, Duellos reported that the software in the systems on the FAC facility was, if not totally pacified, at least no longer engaged in active friendly fire among its own subsystems.

Geary took advantage of the time spent getting the rest of the way through Yokai, and in jump to Adriana, to compile his report to fleet headquarters. He had a particularly hard time describing the loss of *Fleche* without using words and phrasing that cast guilt on the high-level fleet decisions that had ended up requiring his mission to Batara. As much as he might believe that, it had no place among the dry, official language of the report.

As they arrived at Adriana, Geary found that an official courier ship had shown up in their absence and was waiting near the hypernet gate.

"Probably dispatched by fleet headquarters," Duellos commented to Geary, "so they can find out as quickly as possible whether you've cleaned up their mess, or whether disaster has struck, and they need to start blaming you for the whole thing without any further delay."

"Let's not keep them waiting," Geary replied, transmitting his report. In a few hours they received the receipt for the report from the courier ship and watched as it accelerated into the hypernet gate. Clearly, it had been waiting just for his return.

Everyone at Adriana (except General Sissons) seemed happy with the outcome of the mission. Finally, with a sincerely fond farewell to Colonel Galland and a request that she look him up if she ever needed anything, Geary took his ships back to the hypernet gate, en route Varandal.

"MIND if I come in?" Geary asked as he stood in the hatch to Captain Duellos's stateroom. The enforced isolation of travel inside the hypernet had left him time to decide something.

Duellos stood and waved Geary inside. "Anytime, Admiral. Is this visit official or personal?"

"Both." Geary took a seat, once again unsettled a bit by the close resemblance of the captain's stateroom on *Inspire* to that on *Dauntless*. Aside from a few private mementos, this could have been Tanya's stateroom, a compartment he had rarely visited to avoid potential gossip. He waited until Duellos sat down again at his desk before saying more. "*Inspire* took some major damage to her main propulsion at Batara. Once we get back to Varandal, she'll be out of commission for a while as the repairs are carried out."

Duellos leaned back and twisted his mouth in a dissatisfied way. "I wish I could disagree with that assessment, but it is accurate. The only question is exactly how many weeks the repairs will take."

"Which leads me to the reason for my visit. Roberto, this is a personal counseling session. We're off the record. *Inspire* won't need you while she's laid up in dock. I would like you to take leave as soon as we return to Varandal so you have the opportunity to deal with some important matters at home."

It took a moment for Duellos to reply. "Tanya's been talking to you?"

"She let me know you're facing a difficult situation, and I could see during my time aboard *Inspire* with you that you've been more on edge lately. Don't mistake me. Your performance as a commanding officer has not suffered. But I can tell you're under stress."

"It's not an easy situation," Duellos said, sighing and seeming to sag in his seat as if he had partly deflated. "My wife isn't wrong. I have responsibilities at home. My heart remains at home. But . . ."

"You need to talk it out."

"I'm not sure that will help."

Geary looked down, biting his lip, before raising his gaze back to Duellos. "My executive officer on *Merlon* had the same difficulty. Lieutenant Commander Cara Decala. She loved being in the big dark, traveling to other star systems, doing everything the fleet did. Her spouse had close ties at home, no desire at all for extensive travel, and wanted Cara at home, too."

"I see. Somewhat like my own situation now. How did that work out for her?" Duellos asked.

"I . . . don't know. Cara was supposed to go on leave, go home, and talk it out, once the convoy we were escorting had reached its destination. But the Syndics attacked us at Grendel. I had to order her off the ship when the crew evacuated." Geary paused, his gaze distant as he remembered the chaos and alarm that had seemed to fill the universe as *Merlon* was destroyed around him. Events a century ago, which to him felt but a short time in the past. "I discovered after being reawakened that Cara had got off all right, and was picked up, but . . . she had died a few years later, commanding her own ship in another battle. I never learned whether she had ever had a chance to go home, to reconcile things, whether she had died still united in spirit even if separated by distance, or if she had been separated in all ways when the end came."

Almost a minute passed in silence before Duellos replied. "I see. You never know when the last chance to say the right things will come and pass by. But, Admiral, I don't want to leave while we don't know what might happen to the fleet. You do need all of us."

"I'll have Tanya again when we get back to Varandal."

"True. She's worth more to you than all the rest of us combined."

"And I suspect that your wife is more important to you than I, or this fleet, are," Geary added.

Duellos smiled. "That is true."

"Take leave as soon as we get back to Varandal. Go home. Talk.

Whatever happens, let it be something you decided on, not something you let happen."

"Yes. You're right. Thank you." As Geary got up to leave, Duellos fixed him with a demanding look. "What if I had said no? Would you have ordered me to go on leave?"

"Yes." Geary paused in the hatch, looking back at Duellos. "You've already given the fleet, and the Alliance, a lifetime's worth of sacrifice. I hope you'll be back. But if you decide otherwise, you've more than earned it."

"Thank you," Duellos said again.

Geary left, the hatch closing behind him, and walked slowly back to his stateroom, pausing to speak to some of the crew members whom he met on the way, asking about their homes and their lives, letting them know that he cared and that he knew those things mattered.

Because you never did know when it might be too late to say such things.

"I hope you're not expecting them to be grateful," Tanya Desjani grumbled as they left the shuttle dock on *Dauntless*, where the crew had just welcomed back Admiral Geary in nicely turned out formations and immaculate uniforms.

"The people of Batara?" Geary asked.

"Them, too. But I meant fleet staff. Just because you bailed them out of the mess they created doesn't mean they'll stop trying to undermine you."

Geary smiled. "Fleet staff will be busy for a while answering questions from the Senate about why they let the security situation around Adriana get so bad. I bailed them out, but I didn't take the fall for their decisions."

They reached his stateroom and Geary waved her inside, but Desjani hesitated. "I don't want anyone thinking we're having a warm reunion now that you're back."

"Oh." She had a point. It had been hard to avoid wrapping his arms around Tanya when he had seen her again. "Stand in the hatchway, then."

"Thank you for sounding disappointed." She leaned against one side of the hatch coaming, arms crossed. "I thought you wanted nothing more than to avoid the press."

"That's how I usually feel, yes," Geary admitted, sitting down and enjoying the sense of being back where he belonged, aboard *Dauntless*.

"Do you have any idea how much press coverage there has been of your question-and-answer session at Adriana? And the visit to the orphans?"

Geary blew out a long breath, leaning back resignedly. "What are they saying?"

"Most of them think it was all very Black Jack." She smiled at the expression on Geary's face. "In a good way. Some wondered whether you were positioning yourself to run for political office—"

"Ancestors save me, no!"

"—and others hinted at darker ambitions, but most just cheered on the protector of the Alliance."

"That could have been worse," Geary said. "I just want people to stop worrying about what others are going to do and start wondering what they can do. I wondered if going to the academy at Adriana was the right thing or if I'd be accused of using the children as political props."

"Yes, it was absolutely the right thing," Desjani said. "Those kids are sort of the conscience of the Alliance. Too many of us can too easily imagine being in their place, and worried about our own children ending up in one of the academies. You did the right thing, there," she repeated, then paused, just smiling at him.

"What?" Geary finally asked.

"I was watching you say those things, in all those press reports, about how we'd rebuild and make a better future because that was who we are, and I thought, I ought to marry that man because I'll never find anyone better. And then I remembered that I had."

He gave her an astonished look. "We're on duty."

"Well . . . damn. Yes, we are. Even I slip once in a while, Admiral." She winked at him, then adopted a studiously professional expression. "Have you talked to Captain Jane Geary since you got back, sir?"

"No. I wanted to talk in person, not over a comm line that would probably have eavesdroppers no matter what kind of encryption we used. It was a relief to see that she and her ships got back intact."

"Her mission wasn't a wild-goose chase, either. It may still have been intended to get her away from Varandal, but it was real enough. She's standing by to talk to you." Tanya saw his hesitation and smiled crookedly. "Relax. This is Admiral to Captain, not Great-Uncle to Grand-Niece."

Geary snorted. "My grand-niece is biologically older than I am, since she wasn't frozen for a century like I was."

"That's not what's bothering you. It still concerns you that she grew up hating the legend of Black Jack that has warped the life of every Geary for the last hundred years. You know she feels a lot differently now, having gotten to know you."

He shook his head. "I can't forget that her brother Michael probably died right after I assumed command. I don't see any way she can forget."

Desjani nodded, sadly. "She knows Michael Geary chose to sacrifice his ship and maybe himself as well. I honestly don't think she blames you for that. You know that Michael Geary himself didn't blame you. Stop blaming yourself. We don't know how many of his crew survived and whether he himself still lives. For now, Captain Geary is waiting to talk to you, Admiral."

"Thank you." He said it in a way that made it clear he was thanking her for a lot more than her last words. Tapping a control, he saw Jane Geary's image appear almost immediately in response. As usual, he couldn't help searching for resemblances in her to his long-dead brother, her grandfather. "Welcome back, Admiral," she said.

"Welcome back to you as well," he replied.

"I can provide a detailed report in person later," Jane Geary continued, "but to summarize, my ships brought back about ten thousand Alliance prisoners of war, most of them elderly, from the middle period of the war."

"You didn't run into any problems? The Syndics cooperated with the prisoner handover?"

"Yes, Admiral." Jane smiled thinly. "It was a matter of profit and loss for them. A few Syndic star system CEOs had gathered the Alliance POWs together to hand them back to us so they could close down the POW camps they controlled and save some money. I got the impression that the central Syndic government is offering many star systems a lot more autonomy because otherwise they might revolt."

Tanya nodded again. "In addition to Captain Geary's experience, Lieutenant Iger received a report, which is in your in-box, saying the Syndic internal security forces are going along because a more-loosely-controlled star system with all of the internal security apparatus intact and ready to mobilize is a lot better for them than a rebellious star system with the internal security forces all massacred by the locals."

"If they're thinking long-term for once," Geary said to both of them, "that would be a smart policy."

"Then let's hope they don't stick to it," Jane Geary said, her voice growing rougher with the old hate fostered by a century of war and reinforced by recent Syndic behavior. She made a face. "Captain Michael Geary wasn't among the POWs."

"I'm sorry." It was a grossly inadequate thing to say, but the only thing he could say.

Jane Geary nodded, a shadow of emotion crossing her face. "Judging by the way the Syndics have been messing with us in most matters, despite the peace agreement, if Michael was taken prisoner when *Repulse* was destroyed, they will be holding him as a hidden card to use against us. Have you . . . heard anything?"

The way the question was phrased told him that Jane wasn't asking about official reporting or anything like that. "Our ancestors haven't spoken to me about that. But I haven't sensed any message from Michael among them, either." The meaning of that was ambiguous at best, but messages from the ancestors were usually like that.

"I haven't, either." Jane frowned, realizing that they had veered onto personal topics better discussed in person. "That's all I have for now, Admiral."

"Let's get together tomorrow," Geary said. "It's always good to see you again."

As Jane Geary's image disappeared, Tanya, sensing his distress, abruptly changed the subject. "I hear that Roberto Duellos is going on leave for a while."

Geary nodded, feeling relieved to be back on more comfortable ground. "*Inspire* is going to be in dock to get her main propulsion units and some hull structure damage repaired. He didn't have any professional excuse to stay here, so I suggested he go home and talk to his wife. I told him they had to make some decisions together, or they'd each be making them alone before long."

Desjani regarded him closely. "You've been doing some thinking, too, haven't you?"

"Yes. Tanya, in some ways it was good to be away from you."

"What?"

"I mean, it's hard to think when you're there. You're distracting and you demand my attention and—"

She had stood straight, her arms coming out of their relaxed crossed stance. "I'm *demanding*?"

The temperature in his stateroom seemed to have abruptly dropped by several degrees. "You know what I mean."

"*No. No*, I don't."

Geary stood up, making a calming gesture. "Then let me explain. When you're there, I don't need to ask myself why I'm here. You provide all of the answers, just by being there. You're my reasons."

"Oh, please."

"I'm serious!" He gestured toward the star display with a wide sweep of one arm. "But out there, you weren't around. I had to think about that. I knew what I could do, but what should I do? I've had this growing sense that the answer was coming to me, and when I was in a meeting with the government of Adriana and the other Alliance commanders in that star system, I found the start of an answer. I thought more, and I talked to our ancestors, and I think I get it now."

Her hostility had vanished, replaced by curiosity. "And the answer is?"

Geary sat down, frowning at his hands in his lap as he tried to find the right words. "We think that the Dancers believe the universe is a pattern, that everything is a pattern, and we think they act to make the pattern right and strong. What if there's some truth to that which we humans can see? What kind of pattern do I want to exist, and how can I add to that pattern and make it stronger? Maybe the pattern of humanity is completely coming apart, shredded by our own actions, including the war, and the covert sabotage by the enigmas. Maybe I can still help fix it. Maybe I was given this ability to influence events so I can help make our pattern strong again."

She smiled, shaking her head. "How many times have I told you that exact same thing?"

"You never said anything to me about my place in a pattern."

"All right, maybe I didn't use the exact same words when telling you the exact same thing, but that doesn't matter. Maybe being away from me gave you time to finally listen to me instead of being, um, *distracted* by me."

Geary sighed. "I didn't mean distracted in a bad way."

"You know what, Admiral? I'm going to save you by not pursuing that line of conversation any further."

"Thank you." He moved his hands as if trying to shape something. "That's what I decided to do at Adriana and Batara, to do what I could to strengthen what I thought would be the best pattern. I got a lot of confidence from that because it finally focused me on something other than the mistakes I might make. I may get raked over the coals for talking to the press so freely and for exceeding the letter of my orders, but they said to deal with the refugee problem, so I did what I thought best to resolve that issue for the long term and to leave Alliance security in that region in much better shape. And I planted some seeds at Adriana and at Batara, while also knocking down the threat of Tiyannak, that might bear some good long-term outcomes for everyone in that part of space."

Tanya nodded, still smiling. "And you also blew up a lot of stuff. So I'm good with all that."

"Is there anything else I need to know that isn't in the official status reports and can't be said over any supposedly secure circuits?"

"Yes." Her smile disappeared. "You got a message from that woman. It came in two days ago."

Geary frowned at Desjani's tone, trying to parse the emotions behind it and failing. "I'll check it—"

"You don't have to. It was security-sealed eyes only for you, but it opened for me, too." Desjani didn't say what they both knew, that Rione must have set it that way. "The entire message was one word, and that was 'missing.'"

"The one word was missing?" Geary asked, confused.

"No," Desjani repeated patiently. "The entire message consisted of only one word, and that word said 'missing.'"

There was only a single likely meaning for that. "Her husband."

"Yeah."

"They were supposed to be lifting the mental block on him!" Geary yelled in sudden anger. "They were supposed to be repairing the mental and emotional damage the block caused!"

"Maybe they are, but wherever they're doing it, that woman can't find him."

"If Rione can't find him . . ." Geary muttered.

"Yeah," Desjani repeated. "I can't stand her, but I don't underesti-mate her. Her husband must be hidden very, very well."

Hidden along with the secrets her husband knew about an Alliance biological warfare program that would at the least embarrass some senior officials and might lead to some being charged with war crimes. "Unity Alternate," Geary said angrily.

"Unity Alternate? I can't remember the last time I heard that joke." Desjani grimaced. "But if a place like that existed, it would be a good place to hide him. And Admiral Bloch."

"Still no word on Bloch?"

"No. It's as if he vanished off the space of the galaxy, like someone dumped him out an air lock in jump space." She looked thoughtful. "I doubt we were lucky enough for that to have happened, though."

"I'm not sure I would wish that even on Bloch," Geary said, trying to suppress a shudder at the idea of body and soul being lost forever in the gray nothingness of jump space.

"I might," she replied. "He made a heavy-handed pass at me before that last campaign, you know."

"He . . . *what*?"

"Yeah. Came aboard, I escorted him to his stateroom, this state-room, and he went over by the bed, then looked at me and said some-thing like *You could make admiral yourself someday if you did the right things for the right people. You could start right now.*"

Geary's earlier emotions were lost in a surge of red rage. "You were already in his chain of command, you were a captain in the fleet, and he . . ."

"Yes, he did."

"On your own ship!" Geary's anger was replaced by a rush of puz-zlement. "You didn't kill him?"

"Killing superior officers is frowned upon in fleet regulations. Didn't we go over that at some point?"

"You could have brought charges!"

She shook her head. "I knew he was wearing the same personal security that the politicians do. Nothing he was saying could be recorded by any of the ship's systems. It would have been my word against his, fleet commander versus one of his subordinates who already had a reputation for her attitude. I've been known to fight hopeless battles, Admiral, but I took a pass on that one." Her smile held a very sharp edge. "But I also made it clear what would happen if he made another pass like that at me."

"If I see him again—"

"Admiral," Desjani interrupted. "I dealt with it. If it had gone beyond words, I would have brought charges. And I told him that I'd be keeping an eye on him, so I'd know if he tried anything with any of my crew."

Geary shook his head, still enraged. What surprised him was the realization that while he had been appalled by the idea of Bloch or anyone else breaking their oaths to the Alliance and staging a military coup, he was far more disgusted to know that Bloch had broken faith with his responsibilities as a commander, with his responsibilities to his subordinates, and with everyone else serving. *I was already determined to stop Bloch if he tried anything. But now, it's personal.*

THE next day, as he was working in his stateroom, still trying to catch up on the status of the First Fleet while fending off requests from the media for more interviews, an urgent call interrupted him. Geary felt a wave of guilty relief at the interruption because plowing through status reports for hundreds of ships and thousands of personnel had never been his idea of a fun time.

"*Diamond* is back," Desjani reported.

Diamond? It took a moment for him to recall what the special significance of that heavy cruiser was. "Are the Dancers with her?"

"Not y— Hold on. There they are. All six Dancer ships also arrived.

They all came in at a jump point two and a half light-hours from our current orbit."

General Charban had called in as soon as *Diamond* arrived at Varandal, his message arriving right after the light revealing the presence of the ships.

Charban looked fairly well rested for once, which Geary realized had to be because he had been able to relax in jump space, where communications with the Dancers were impossible. "You'll be pleased to hear that the Dancers had an understandable reason for going to Durnan Star System, Admiral. They wanted to check on the remains of a Dancer settlement that had once been there. I know what you're thinking. How did we miss the presence of ruins of a settlement belonging to an alien species on a heavily populated planet in a star system long occupied by humans?

"According to the local authorities, in the time I had to speak with them, the ancient ruins in question were so odd, so unlike those of any human structures, that they were labeled natural features that just happened to resemble the work of intelligent creatures. Apparently, the concept of alien remains a little unclear among our experts in the field. However, the Dancers also got across to me that their settlement should have been much larger than the small area of ruins that still exist. Somehow, most of the settlement was obliterated so thoroughly that no remains could be detected, nor signs of the destruction."

Desjani nodded sharply as she heard that part. "Enigmas. It must have been them. You remember how they wiped out any trace of human presence in places like Hina Star System."

"Something must have interrupted the enigmas in their work at Durnan," Geary speculated. "The arrival of the first human colony ships?"

"What the hell were Dancers and enigmas doing so deep in what became human space?" Desjani wondered.

Charban was still speaking. "I could not determine from the

Dancers why they had long ago attempted to place a colony at Durnan, which is a very long distance from the region of space they currently occupy. They did not express any desire to reoccupy the star system, they did not claim any ownership, they did not even try to claim the ruins. I got the impression that what mattered to them was that someone still lived in that star system. Someone intelligent, that is. After determining that no records or remains of their own kind were located at or near the ruins, the Dancers headed toward the jump point for Kami.

"All they did at Kami was transit through the system, heading straight for the jump for Taranis. At Taranis, they spent a long time traveling through the star system, but wouldn't explain what they were doing or why. Then they jumped for Dogoda.

"Long story short, we went on a tour of star systems, tending gradually back toward this part of space, until the Dancers finally jumped for Varandal again. Aside from the stop at Durnan, we're not sure what the purposes of any of the other visits were. Nor am I sure they will remain at Varandal."

Charban paused, looking worried. "I do have the distinct impression that the Dancers are agitated about something they refer to as unraveling. But who or what is unraveling, they don't say. I'll speak more with you as we get closer to your ship and a real conversation is possible. Charban, out."

"Maybe they were looking for signs of survivors from that settlement who might have tried to get back home," Desjani speculated. "Here's how their trip looks on a display."

The image popped up over the stateroom's table, a three-dimensional star map with the path of the Dancers through Alliance space marked by glowing lines. "If there's supposed to be some shape or pattern to that, I can't see it," Geary commented.

"It's sort of a warped sphere, isn't it? They came back here by a roundabout route so there would have to be something circular about their path. About that unraveling thing, Admiral. I've got a suspicion that the Dancers have some sort of faster-than-light communications capability just like the enigmas do."

"That's possible. We have no idea how long those two species have been in contact. But the enigma system isn't instantaneous and doesn't appear to be capable of sending much data or detail."

Desjani nodded. "Exactly. Maybe the Dancers themselves don't know what the problem is. Maybe they got a message that caused them to bolt for Durnan, then later some other stuff that got them worried but couldn't tell them exactly what's going on."

"That's possible," Geary repeated. "We can't know if it's true, though."

"If it is true, then I predict the next thing we hear from the Dancers will be an announcement that they want to go home."

It took barely six hours for Desjani's prediction to be proven accurate.

"The Dancers want to leave," Charban reported. "They want to leave soon. They want us to escort them back through Syndic space via the Syndic hypernet to Midway. I'm pretty certain that they intend saying farewell to us at Midway and going the rest of the way home on their own."

Oh, great. Geary gazed sourly at the representation of the Dancer ships on his display. *Here I am, reading the latest government communication directing me to convince the Dancers to visit the Alliance capital at Unity, and the Dancers instead want to leave without ever having gone there. And this morning I got a message saying a team of official alien liaison experts is coming to Varandal to take over all future interactions with the Dancers, but they're not scheduled to arrive for another two weeks at the earliest.*

Charban was wrapping up. "I'll try to get them to define what they mean by soon. Charban, out."

Back through Syndic territory. Through the Syndic hypernet, which could be manipulated by the Syndic government to block gates, and through star systems governed by people who had signed a peace agreement but were still waging a form of covert war on the Alliance. The Syndics had already demonstrated their intent to keep destroying Alliance warships when possible, and had not been thrilled to know that the Alliance was establishing friendly contact with the Dancers, a friendly contact that could be disrupted if the Dancer emissaries being escorted by the Alliance suffered from "accidents" while in Syndic space. "Tanya? We've got a problem."

She was in her own stateroom, the lights dimmed except the work light on her desk. "What is it this time?"

"We might have to take off, fast, to escort the Dancers back to Midway."

"I guess the living stars decided to shower more blessings upon us," Desjani commented. "Fast? We can't get the fleet ready to roll that far in a short time."

"I know. How much of the fleet should we try to bring?"

She spread her hands. "You said it. Fast. As many of the battle cruisers as we can get ready, and enough light cruisers and destroyers to match. We can cannibalize fuel cells from the ships that aren't coming to overstock the ones that are going. If we only have a few days to work with, that's the best option."

Geary thought about it, calling up ship status reports, then cursing under his breath as he remembered that they were all falsified. He would have to order individual ship captains to send him accurate reports. "I think you're right. We need to go fast through Syndic space. Get in and get out before the Syndic government on Prime can find out and block any of their gates to our use. Can we do that?"

"I'll have my officers run the numbers, but I think so. We'll use the Syndic hypernet gate at Indras again? Indras is a lot closer to Prime than Midway is, but that's all to the good since longer hypernet trips take less time than shorter ones. As long as we enter Midway's gate to get home before the Syndics can block it, we'll be home free."

"As home free as we can be in Syndic space," Geary corrected. "The Syndics shouldn't have time to set up any nasty ambushes."

Unless they already had some ambushes ready to go.

At least he had a little more time to get his ships ready for this operation.

"NOW," Charban said. *Diamond* had continued in-system and was only a couple of light-minutes distant from *Dauntless*, making a real conversation possible if also awkwardly drawn out waiting for a reply to come back. "The Dancers say they must leave now."

FOURTEEN

"BUT what does 'now' mean to them?" Geary asked, hoping for some ambiguity in the answer.

"It means *right now, this moment, this time, go*," Charban amplified when his answer came back a few minutes later. "That's exactly what the Dancers communicated to me when I asked that question. I also asked what would happen if we couldn't go now, and they said *we go*. It's pretty much an ultimatum. We escort them home, or they start off on their own."

"They must be bluffing! Jumping back all that way would take forever."

"They could be bluffing," Charban admitted. "I'd never gamble with a Dancer because I can't read their emotions at the best of times. But we can't rule out the possibility that the Dancers have tricks we don't know about when it comes to jump drives," Charban said. "As well as the possibility that they may be able to endure much longer periods in jump space than humans can. They somehow got to Durnan a long time ago."

And if the Dancers headed home on their own, leaving the entire Alliance with no idea of whether or not they had made it through Syndic space in one piece, there would be hell to pay. "I need twelve more hours to get a task force together," Geary insisted. "That's the absolute minimum time. I need a strong enough force to protect them, and a strong enough force to defend itself against any threats we might encounter. Tell them that. Twelve hours. Have they said anything about our offers to send a ship all the way back with them, with representatives?"

When the reply came, Charban was rubbing his head with both hands as if trying to drive away a headache. "Their answer is *not yet*. They're not saying *no*, they're not saying *yes*. The Dancers are saying *not yet*."

What did "not yet" mean to a Dancer? With humans, it could mean a delay of minutes, hours, days, or years. And yet the Dancers hadn't had any trouble conveying exactly what they meant by "now." "The government won't like hearing that, but I don't know what we're supposed to do to change the Dancers' minds. That ship carrying the official alien liaison team won't be here for close to two more weeks at best anyway. What about individual representatives?"

"I have suggested myself, I have suggested Dr. Shwartz, I have asked if there is anyone they would be willing to accept." Charban smiled. "*Not yet*."

"What about the unraveling thing? Is that related to their sudden desire to leave now?"

"They won't say."

Geary felt a headache of his own coming on. "General, I have to admit if it was me dealing with the Dancers I would be having a very hard time not getting really, really upset with them. I know they think differently than us, but I believe that you are right that they are also deliberately not telling us some things."

Charban nodded and sighed. "Yet I am certain that they mean us well. Maybe they are treating us in the same way they would treat others of their own species. I don't know. I can't get angry about anything with them because that might shut off my ability to learn more. I have learned that the only way to maintain my sanity when dealing with the Dancers is to take a very contemplative approach, meditating at appropriate times and frequently telling myself not to keep carrying the old woman."

Geary eyed Charban's image. "The old woman?"

"Haven't you ever heard that story? It's a very old one." Charban paused to think. "There are two men walking through a town where the streets are muddy. They come to a place where an old woman who has been shopping is trying to leave her vehicle and reach the sidewalk. But all of her helpers have their hands full of her packages, and if they put the packages down to help her avoid the mud, they will get the packages muddy. All they can do is stand there while the old woman screams at them. One of the two travelers walks up to the old woman and gives her assistance to reach the sidewalk. She doesn't thank him but just stomps off, followed by her helpers, as the two travelers go on their way. The other traveler spends the rest of the afternoon wondering why his friend helped that mean person, and finally, as they stop for the night, he asks, *Why did you help that unpleasant person?* His companion looks at him in surprise, and says, *I put that woman down this morning. Why are you still carrying her?*

"I have to be like that with the Dancers. I have to not carry anything that frustrates or angers me but approach every communication without that kind of baggage."

Geary laughed despite his worries. "You're a better man than I am, General. Put together a detailed report of your conversations with the Dancers since you returned to Varandal. I need to have that left here and sent on to the government and fleet headquarters after we depart, so no one accuses me of kidnapping the Dancers. Tell them twelve hours. Get more time if you can. But I need twelve hours."

"Understood, Admiral."

Geary rapped his head with one fist out of frustration, then checked the status of frantic efforts to prepare ships for the unexpected mission. He called Captain Smythe on the auxiliary *Tanuki*. "What are the chances of *Inspire* being ready to go in twelve hours?"

"Can't be done," Smythe said. "We couldn't even close up all our work in that time frame, let alone finish the repairs."

"That leaves me with only thirteen battle cruisers."

"Twelve," Smythe corrected. "I've gone over the status of *Intemperate* with Admiral Timbale, and we can't get her ready, either. Half her systems are torn out and being replaced. Since we gave priority to getting the other battle cruisers in shape, and you didn't bang up *Implacable* and *Formidable* too badly on your last jaunt, the other twelve should hold up. But watch *Adroit*. Her systems were all 'smart-evolved,' which is the latest bureaucratic speak for cutting corners to save money. They're almost new, but I don't trust them."

"How's the money situation look?"

"Oh, that's fine. This is an emergency. You get to spend and let higher authority figure out how to pay for it later. One other thing, Admiral. I know you're just planning on taking light cruisers and destroyers and escorts, but from a purely logistical point of view, it would be good to have some heavy cruisers along. They've got the acceleration to keep up with the battle cruisers, much better endurance than the lighter ships, and they can stuff in enough extra fuel cells to help resupply the destroyers when they start to run low."

"Thanks. That's good advice. Let me know if any other problems develop. Have we ever given Lieutenant Jamenson a look at the Dancer communications?"

"Why would we do that?" Smythe asked, looking unusually surprised.

"Because General Charban suspects the Dancers are avoiding telling us things and sort of, well, dancing around the questions we ask."

"They're trying to confuse us?" Smythe's expression shifted to intrigued. "That is right up Jamenson's alley."

Geary could almost see the wheels turning in Smythe's head. Jamenson's ability to produce accurate and complete reports that were also nearly impossible to understand was invaluable to Smythe, as was her ability to spot the truth in documents that others had tried to write in a confusing manner. But having an in on communicating with the Dancers or other aliens would boost Lieutenant Jamenson's value immensely. Even if she didn't continue working for Smythe, she would surely be open to requests for favors that could be extremely important and perhaps extremely profitable as well.

"Would you like to borrow Lieutenant Jamenson for this mission?" Smythe asked in a completely guileless manner. "Since it is so very important."

Geary pretended reluctance. "But her work with you is also very important."

"A few weeks won't make a big difference, and this is important to all humanity!"

"I didn't know you were such a humanitarian," Geary said, thinking once more of the Syndic definition of the term.

"I've been known to surprise people," Smythe said with a disconcerting smile.

"But not me, Captain," Geary said. "No surprises for me."

"Of course not, Admiral!"

JANE Geary didn't argue with his rationale for leaving the battleships behind, with her once more in temporary command of the fleet. "But be careful. Syndic space is a snake pit."

"You don't have to remind me of that," Geary replied.

"I know you're unlikely to encounter any more POW camps since you're going through only a few Syndic star systems, but keep an eye out for Michael. Good luck, Great-uncle."

Geary ended the call, gazing morosely at his display. Twelve battle cruisers. Two divisions of heavy cruisers. Three squadrons of light cruisers. Four squadrons of destroyers. "It doesn't feel like enough."

Desjani snorted. "It isn't. But taking more wouldn't help. At least this time we've got *Steadfast* with us."

"*Steadfast*?" Geary knew he looked puzzled. "Is there some particular significance to *Steadfast*?"

"Of course there is! *Steadfast* represents the spirit of the fleet. There always has to be a *Steadfast*. That's why we got a replacement for the last *Steadfast* so quickly when she was lost at Heradao."

Geary remembered that, the new *Steadfast* showing up as quickly as the new *Invincible*, but he had been wrapped up in so many other issues, he hadn't taken special note of it. "When did that start? The idea that *Steadfast* represents the spirit of the fleet?"

"Hasn't it always been that way?" Desjani asked, startled.

"No." There must have been a battle, sometime in the last century, in which an earlier *Steadfast* had performed so well, fought so hard, perhaps sacrificed herself, that the name had taken on a special significance. There had been a *Steadfast* a century ago, Geary recalled. It might have been that very ship, helping to hold off the first Syndic attacks and gaining a singular status for her name in the process. "Why weren't you particularly upset at the loss of the prior *Steadfast*?"

"Because *Steadfast* always comes back," Desjani explained. "Not in a bad way, like *Invincible* always shows up again, but in a good way."

"I've still got a lot to learn about things today," Geary said. "Let's get going." He tapped the comm controls. "All units in Task Force Dancer, this is Admiral Geary. Immediate execute, proceed to stations in Formation Delta, form on guide ship *Dauntless*."

Geary nodded to Desjani. "Head for the jump point for Atalia, Captain."

"Yes, Admiral." Under Desjani's helm orders, *Dauntless* swung about and began accelerating slowly, giving the other warships plenty of time to take station around her. They came gliding in from all angles, forming into three boxes, which were arranged in a staggered V shape. Leading them was the box centered on *Dauntless* and also holding the rest of her division, *Daring*, *Victorious*, and *Adroit* which was taking the place of *Intemperate*. Joining them were one squadron of light cruisers and two squadrons of destroyers.

Off to port, behind and slightly above, Captain Tulev's *Leviathan* took up station in her box, surrounded by *Dragon*, *Steadfast*, and *Valiant*. Around them, a division of heavy cruisers and one squadron each of light cruisers and destroyers formed up.

To starboard, also behind but slightly below, Captain Badaya's *Illustrious* moved into position, along with *Incredible* as well as *Formidable* and *Implacable*, which had been temporarily assigned to Badaya's division. They also got a division of heavy cruisers, a squadron of light cruisers, and one of destroyers.

"Looking good," Geary approved.

"Duellos is going to give you hell when he gets back and finds out he missed this," Desjani cautioned.

"If I'd hauled him along to the limits of human space again, his wife might have told him to stay out there instead of coming back." Geary waited until the last ship was on station, the three boxes aimed like an arrowhead for the jump exit, then gave new orders. "All units in Task Force Dancer, immediate execute, accelerate to point one light speed."

General Charban had transferred back over from *Diamond*, along with his communications gear. He was not on the bridge of *Dauntless*, instead occupying the compartment set up for communicating with the Dancers, and he now called Geary. "The Dancers have indicated they understand that we are leaving and that they should close on you so you can all jump together."

"How are you and Lieutenant Jamenson getting along?" Geary asked, hoping that the Dancers would indeed do as they were asked.

"She's the finest green-haired officer I ever served with," Charban said, then grinned. "And I've actually served with two others. It's not hard to spot people from Eire Star System. Once we enter jump, she's indicated a desire to spend some time with the intelligence cell aboard the ship, if that's all right with you."

"As long as she's getting enough exposure to Dancer communications," Geary said.

The conversation reminded him of another call he needed to make. "Lieutenant Iger, if we get any updates on the situation in Atalia or Syndic space before we jump, I need to know as soon as possible."

The intelligence officer nodded quickly. "Yes, sir. As of now, my latest from Atalia is that report from the last courier-ship rotation. Atalia is pretty much unchanged."

"Let's hope it stays that way," Geary said. "Lieutenant Jamenson may visit the intel compartment while we're in jump. I assume you'll have no problems with that."

"Lieutenant Jamenson, sir? No, sir! No problem!"

When he ended that call, Desjani was grinning. "Let's hope Lieutenant Iger doesn't get too distracted by Lieutenant Jamenson."

Geary took a discreet glance to the back of the bridge. "Speaking of lieutenants and personal relationships, how are our quarantine cases doing?" he asked in a low voice.

Desjani gave him a sidelong look. "Lieutenant Castries and Lieutenant Yuon are professionals. They are carrying out their duties without regard to any personal emotions created by past developments."

"Really?"

"Really. Of course, I also told them each separately that if there was any drama on the bridge, I would crack heads so hard they'd both end up back in sick bay. But I think they're doing all right now that it's over. Say, mind if I borrow that green-haired lieutenant while we're in jump? I'd like her to take a look at the books in Master Chief Gioninni's division."

"I want her to be able to get some sleep," Geary said.

"Sleep? This is the fleet. Sleep is for wimps, right?" Desjani loudly asked of the bridge.

"Yes, Captain!" the watch-standers chorused back at her.

"Sometimes," Geary said, "I can't tell whether or not you're joking."

She lowered her voice to a whisper as she leaned toward him. "Sometimes," Desjani said with a grin, "neither can they."

JUMP space was never a particularly restful place. You could get physical rest, but mental relaxation grew harder with every day in a place so strange that humans had no right to be there. As the old saying went, the longer a ship stayed in jump space, the jumpier the crew got. For Geary, the worst part was usually the itchiness, a day-by-day growing sense that his skin no longer fit properly.

But this time it felt worse in some small and indefinable ways. One thing he could identify was odder-than-usual dreams because the same one repeated during the days en route Atalia.

He dreamed he was indeed out in jump space, alone, surrounded by the gray nothingness that filled whatever jump space really was. Panic began to set in, but before it could overwhelm him, the lights emerged.

No one knew what the lights that appeared randomly in jump space were. Scientific theories abounded, all lacking in evidence or any form of proof. Metaphysical theories were fewer, simpler, and equally impossible to prove or disprove. The vast majority of sailors believed that the lights were linked to their ancestors and to the living stars. Beyond that, exactly what the lights meant or signified was just as mysterious to believers as it was to nonbelievers.

When Geary had been awakened from his century in survival sleep, he had been told that many believed he had been among the lights all of those decades, communing with the ancestors. He would have liked to categorically deny that, but couldn't since he had no memories from his time frozen in space.

Now, in these dreams, as he drifted alone in jump space and fought against panic, he saw the lights appear. But they didn't come alone. They appeared in clusters, they flashed off and on, they seemed to be almost forming a picture. A pattern. And then . . . he awoke, to stare at the darkened overhead in his stateroom with the feeling that something very important had been almost within his reach but had vanished in an instant, leaving nothing behind but memories of a dream he couldn't understand at all.

GEARY greeted their arrival at Atalia with more relief at leaving jump space than usual. As Lieutenant Iger had said, very little had changed here. Atalia, like Batara, had been a front-line star system fought over during the war. It had been among the first star systems to rebel against the Syndics and had quickly requested Alliance protection.

However, an Alliance reluctant to fund protection for even its own territory in the wake of the war had no interest in taking on responsibility for a battered star system that had recently been enemy territory. The Alliance's sole commitment to the protection of Atalia was a single courier ship hanging near the jump point for Varandal. If Atalia was attacked, the Alliance would know it.

But the Alliance hadn't actually promised to do anything with that knowledge.

"We're just passing through," Geary told the crew of the courier ship. "We'll be back soon."

He sent a similar message to the government of Atalia, which technically had to approve the Alliance task force's transit of its star system. In practice, Atalia wouldn't do anything to offend the Alliance and actually welcomed any presence by Alliance warships as a deterrent to attempts by the Syndic government to regain control of the star system.

From Atalia they had to jump through Kalixa, which had once had

its own hypernet gate. But the enigmas had caused that gate to collapse, wiping out the human presence at Kalixa and rendering the
once-habitable main world a lifeless wreck, hoping that the Syndics
would blame the Alliance for the atrocity and begin making the gates
in Alliance star systems collapse. The plan had almost worked.

Geary took the task force through Kalixa as quickly as possible.
The Dancer ships stayed close to the Alliance ships, not following
their usual practice of zooming off to whirl around each other in the
graceful movements that among humans had earned the aliens
the nickname Dancers. Geary wondered if the ruined star system
of Kalixa marked some sort of mar in the patterns the Dancers val-
ued, something that unsettled them, but Charban's attempts to ask
the Dancers about that produced no replies understandable to the
humans.

From Kalixa, they finally jumped into a star system still controlled
(when last heard) by the Syndics. Indras was fairly well-off, fairly
wealthy as star systems went, far enough from Alliance space to have
taken relatively little damage during the war, and possessed the working Syndic hypernet gate that Geary needed.

The few, minor Syndic warships present avoided getting anywhere
near Geary's ships as they thundered through the star system on the
fastest route to the hypernet gate. The two Syndic light cruisers and
five HuKs, some still bearing scars of combat not so long ago, showed
no interest in confronting the Alliance Task Force in any way. But the
senior CEO in the star system was not so circumspect.

"We must protest this violation of Syndicate Worlds space by an
armed expedition of the Alliance," CEO Yamada declared. Yamada,
with his impeccably tailored suit, perfectly coifed hair, and well-
practiced expressions designed to conceal any real emotions, looked
like almost every other CEO that Geary had encountered. Judging by
his girth and other signs of rich living, Yamada had also not personally
suffered much during the war. "You are to cease aggressive actions

against the Syndicate Worlds and vacate Syndicate space immediately. Forthepeople, Yamada, out."

"Yeah, he's for the people," Desjani commented sarcastically. "Are you going to bother answering?"

"Just with the standard legalities. But not yet. And apparently there are some intelligence reports I need to know about."

"About Indras? Why didn't they brief you before we got here?"

"Ask the people who make up the rules the intelligence community has to follow. They're probably the only ones who understand whatever logic is involved."

A few hours later, Lieutenant Iger briefed Geary in his stateroom. "Thank you for taking the time for this, Admiral." He brought up some images of individuals, star systems, and businesses, all connected by various colored strands. "This is the best picture we have at this time of Syndic covert operations in this region against the Alliance and their own rebellious star systems."

The point of Iger's presentation wasn't hard to grasp. "It looks like Indras is at the center of a lot of that."

"Yes, sir. We can't tie CEO Yamada specifically to what is going on. He may not personally even know about some of the things being done by the central government, but it's likely he knows about some of it. A lot of covert activity is being coordinated through Indras."

Geary hunched forward a bit, resting his elbows on the table and gazing at the interrelationships and activities being shown. "Is there anything I can do about this? Is there anything I'm supposed to be doing about it?"

"No, sir," Iger said with a regretful shake of his head. "This briefing is for informational purposes only. We are at peace with the Syndics. Alliance military forces can't just launch open attacks on the basis of evidence like this which can't even be shown to the average person. As for other alternatives, we don't have the sort of proof that could be presented in any court, and there aren't any courts that would handle this sort of thing between the Syndics and the Alliance anyway."

"Is anybody else doing anything?"

Iger hesitated, then spoke slowly. "Admiral, I can't say."

"As in you don't know, or you do, and I'm somehow not cleared for it?" Geary tried to keep from sounding angry and accusing. It wouldn't be Iger's fault if the matter was out of his hands, so Iger shouldn't be personally held to account.

"I don't honestly know anything, sir," Lieutenant Iger protested. "I've heard rumors that counteroperations are under way, but nothing specific and nothing official."

"Counteroperations? Aimed at what's going on here?"

"Vague rumors, sir. That's all I have."

"I hope that's all they are," Geary said. "Because it would look very suspicious to everyone if something blew up in this star system while we were here or soon after we left." He wanted to add that surely no one would plot covert actions that, by their timing and placement, would imply Geary's ships were involved, at the very least not without warning him, but recent experience with the government's mania for secrecy left him with no confidence on that count. "Let me know if anything else comes in that relates to this."

Geary waited almost another day, until the Alliance warships and the Dancer ships were almost to the hypernet gate, before he called up the Syndic CEO's message again and tapped the reply command. "CEO Yamada, this is Admiral Geary. We are permitted by the terms of the peace agreement with the Syndicate Worlds to transit Syndicate space to and from the Midway Star System, and to make use of the Syndicate Worlds' hypernet system when we do so. We will continue to operate in accordance with our rights under the peace agreement. To the honor of our ancestors, Geary, out."

"They probably already knew we were going to Midway," Desjani said.

"The longer we could keep them guessing, the better. Let's get out of Indras before the Dancers decide to go sightseeing." *Or something blows up,* he added to himself.

To his relief, the stolen hypernet key dialed up Midway without any problems, and a moment later they were safe inside the nowhere of the hypernet.

THE hypernet allowed Geary's ships to cover the distance to Midway in a few weeks, a voyage that would have required several months if conducted by jumping from star to star. Oddly enough, even though the other discomforts of jump space weren't present, Geary had the same dream a couple of more times, ending in the same frustrating fashion. Whether it was his subconscious or something else trying to send him a message, the meaning of it wasn't coming through.

As the Alliance ships left the hypernet, the stars reappeared around them, and displays began updating with the newest information. "It sounds like they've been busy around here," Lieutenant Iger reported. "Lots of comm traffic, official and unofficial."

"Anything bad?" Geary asked. "There's a battle cruiser here. Whose is it?"

"We're trying to ID it, Admiral. Wait. We're picking up references to *Pele.*"

"That's the next star system toward the enigmas," Geary said with more patience than he felt.

"No, sir. I mean, yes, sir," the intelligence officer corrected hastily. "This *Pele* is a ship. It looks like it correlates to that battle cruiser."

"The Syndics don't name their ships," Desjani said.

"No, but the Midway people do," Geary said. "To emphasize that they're not Syndics anymore. Where did they get a battle cruiser?"

"No idea, Admiral," Iger said. "It sounds like there are civil disturbances on the primary inhabited world. Rioting. The government is trying to deal with it."

"How are they dealing with it?" Geary asked, his voice flat. There were Syndic ways of handling riots and rioters, and the rulers here had been Syndics not long ago.

"I can't determine that yet, sir."

"Hey!" Desjani's startled exclamation drew Geary's attention. "The Dancers just took off!"

Took off was putting it mildly. The alien ships had dashed away from the Alliance formation at the strongest acceleration they could manage, a rate of increase in velocity that even the Alliance battle cruisers couldn't match. "They're heading for the jump point for Pele. General Charban!"

"Here, Admiral," Charban replied from the compartment where he and Lieutenant Jamenson were once again seated at their comm gear. "I just received a message from the Dancers. *Watch the many stars.*"

"The many stars? What does that—? Sorry." For once, Geary avoided asking a question that he already knew Charban had no answer to. He stopped to think as he watched the Dancers tear away. "I guess they're going home as fast as possible."

"I concur," Charban said. "I'll try to get more out of them before they leave."

"Thanks. If—"

"We just got another message from the Dancers," Charban interrupted, looking startled. "It says *until next time, see you later, good-bye for now.*"

Tanya raised both eyebrows. "They're not taking any chances that we won't understand that."

"No, they're not," Charban agreed. "They want us to know that they will be back."

"Do they expect us to wait here?" Geary demanded, exasperated.

"I don't—" Charban began, then paused again. "Another message. *You go your home. See you there.* Admiral, I don't know why the Dancers have suddenly shifted from vague ambiguities to clear meaning, but I have no doubt that they mean exactly what these messages say. They are not mistakenly saying something we might misinterpret. They want us to go home, and they want us to know they will come back and meet us there."

"How are they planning on getting back through Syndic space?" Desjani wondered.

"How did they get to Durnan in the first place to plant that colony long ago?" Charban asked.

Geary made a helpless gesture. "We'll have to take the Dancers at their word. There's nothing in this star system that can catch them or hurt them before they reach that jump point."

"Something might come out of the jump point," Desjani suggested.

"Yeah. That's true. We'll hang around the hypernet gate until the Dancers jump and we know they're out of human space, then we'll head home." The Dancers themselves obviously didn't feel that the Alliance had any further obligations to escort and protect them, but Geary still felt a sense of responsibility toward them. He wouldn't feel comfortable leaving Midway until the Dancers had.

As the hours went by, the Dancers racing toward the jump point for Pele while the Alliance warships orbited near the hypernet gate, Lieutenant Iger's people were able to build up a picture of events at Midway that was only slightly reassuring. "They haven't started shooting at the protesters yet, and I haven't detected any orders for the local warships to move into position for precision bombardments. A lot of the ground forces seem to be missing, and there are references to General Drakon's being gone from the star system."

"Do you have any idea where he is?" Geary asked, remembering the stolid general who had seemed glad to shed the trappings of a Syndic CEO.

"There are a couple of mentions of Ulindi, a nearby star system."

It was odd how someone having a dozen battle cruisers at his beck and call could feel powerless, Geary thought as he watched the Dancers dart away too fast to be caught up with and viewed images of events in Midway Star System that were hours old by the time he saw them. "At the rate the Dancers are going," Desjani said, "their total transit time to the jump point for Pele will be less than twenty hours. They're moving faster than sailors heading for the liberty shuttle."

"Is their return that urgent?" Geary asked. "Or are they hurrying because they know we can't leave until we know they have?"

"Or are they just sick and tired of us ugly humans?" Desjani added.

"I'm going to get some sleep," Geary said as he realized that he had been on the bridge for more then seven hours straight. "There's nothing anywhere near us and nothing I can do. When something does happen, I want my mind to be a little rested. If I'm not back in six hours, give me a call."

He made a futile effort to sleep, staring up at the overhead from his bed, before eventually calling up some paperwork. But this time not even routine paperwork on the most soul-deadening of topics could make him drowsy.

Geary returned to *Dauntless*'s bridge, noting that it had been thirteen hours since arrival in this star system. "Anything new?"

"How did you know?" Desjani asked. "We just got a message from that woman who calls herself president. I was reaching to call you when you showed up."

For someone who had cities full of rioters, alien spaceships on the edges of her star system, and a large force of warships present belonging to an Alliance that had until recently been her bitter enemy, President Iceni appeared remarkably calm and confident. Geary was certain that it was an act, which made it all the more impressive to him.

"Admiral Geary, my friend, I am hoping it is you who have returned to this star system," President Iceni began. "We are currently undergoing some minor domestic disturbances, which I regret to say are occupying my full attention. General Drakon is at Ulindi, assisting the people there in throwing off the chains of the Syndicate. You will be pleased to hear that your Captain Bradamont has proven to be an exceptionally valuable resource in our attempts to both defend this star system and create a more stable system of governance for it. I regret that she is currently aboard our battleship *Midway*, which is also at Ulindi and cannot speak to you directly. I assure you that she is both safe and highly respected by the officers and specialists of our military forces.

"From what I can see, it appears that the aliens called the Dancers are returning home. I would appreciate confirmation of this. They sent us a message directly. *Watch the different stars.* We have no idea what that means.

"I am certain that our current domestic disturbances are the work of foreign agents. I will be focusing my efforts on calming the situation here without resort to Syndicate methods.

"Please advise me of your plans. I remain your friend and ally, President Iceni. For the people. Out."

Geary sat thinking for several seconds after the message ended. "The Dancers told the locals at Midway to watch the *different* stars," he finally said.

"They got a different message than we did," Desjani said. "Interesting. Too bad we don't know what either message means."

"Iceni claimed she was trying to put down the riots without resorting to Syndic methods. I'm sure I know what you think of that."

"No, you don't," she replied. "I believe her."

He stared at her. "You believe a former Syndic CEO?"

"That's right." Desjani indicated the image of President Iceni that still hung suspended next to their seats. "You see, I know that kind of woman. She doesn't like being pushed around."

"Yeah, I know that kind of woman, too."

"Please let me finish, Admiral," she continued with a sharp look at him. "You heard what she said. This Iceni knows that somebody triggered those riots, that somebody is trying to make her put down the riots using the standard Syndic methods involving lots of dead and wounded demonstrators. And she's mad enough that she might do that. Except that she knows that's what the people behind this want. They're probably working for the Syndic government on Prime. And they're trying to make her do something."

Geary pondered that. "Iceni won't do it because she knows they're trying to force her into taking that option."

"Not unless she absolutely has to," Desjani agreed. "Which she might. This isn't entirely about her being a Syndic. It's about her being that kind of person."

"I hope you're right. And I hope that Iceni can stop the riots without resorting to mass deaths, or any deaths at all. But we can't wait around to find out."

"So, what are you going to tell your friend and ally?" Desjani asked.

"Just the truth. And she really is already an ally of sorts. I hope Iceni turns out to be someone we can call a friend as well someday." Geary took a slow, deep breath, then touched his comm controls. "President Iceni, this is Admiral Geary. We came here only to escort the Dancers back to Midway. They are proceeding home from here on their own. We cannot remain in this star system one minute longer than absolutely necessary because of the danger that the hypernet gate may be blocked before we can leave. I don't know when any Alliance ships will be able to come through here again. Perhaps not until we figure out how to override that ability to block access to the gates. I regret that we cannot offer any assistance at this time and also that we cannot offer any suggestions as to the meaning of the message the Dancers sent you. Good luck, and may the living stars aid you. To the honor of our ancestors, Geary, out."

Desjani rolled her eyes. "You didn't have to ask the blessing of the living stars for her."

"I thought you liked her!" he protested.

"I *understand* her. That doesn't mean I *like* her. Aren't you ever going to figure out things like that?"

"It doesn't look like it."

He sat silently after that and actually dozed a few times in his seat, waking to realize with a guilty conscience that the watch-standers on the bridge had been working as silently as possible so as not to disturb him.

"Admiral," Lieutenant Castries reported, "the Dancers should have jumped one minute ago based on our projections."

"Thank you." Geary stared at his display, trying to decide what to do. It would be another six hours before the light reached this part of the star system showing whether the Dancers had actually jumped. He could wait for that confirmation. Maybe he should wait for it. But every hour, every minute, brought them closer to the possibility the Syndics might block this gate and leave his task force stranded at Midway, or once more forced to go home through a deadly gauntlet set up by the Syndics.

"The Dancers have proven they can take care of themselves," Geary said out loud. "My responsibilities to the Alliance and to the crews of these warships require me to return now rather than risk them by waiting for unnecessary confirmation of the Dancer ships' departure."

"I concur," Desjani said.

He brought the task force around to approach the nearby hypernet gate, wondering if he would ever see Midway again.

"Hypernet key set for Indras," Desjani said. "Field size set to encompass all ships of the task force."

"Do it," Geary said.

And once more the nearly infinite multitude of stars vanished.

Watch the many stars. Watch the different stars. What the hell did those things mean?

THEY came out at Indras to find a star system under attack.

"Who is it?" Geary demanded as his display rapidly updated, revealing that numerous Syndic installations had been turned into new craters by bombardments. Dispersing wreckage marked the remnants of several merchant ships and one of the Syndic light cruisers that had been here before.

"They must have just left, Admiral," Lieutenant Yuon said, his eyes darting over the sensor findings. "There aren't any—"

"A HuK just blew up!" Lieutenant Castries announced. "Something just ripped it apart! Whoever did this is still here."

"Enigmas," Geary said.

"We can spot enigmas, Admiral," Desjani reminded him. "I'll have my security teams sweep our systems for quantum worms again just in case they got some past our last routine scans." Desjani spun in her seat to face her watch-standers. "If we can't spot whoever is hitting Indras, we can spot what they're doing. Track weapons firing, track bombardment projectile launches, track anything that shows where and what these attackers are."

Geary hit the command to talk to his intelligence cell. "Lieutenant Iger, I need answers. Who has just hit Indras so hard? There must be something in the comms in this star system that tells us."

Iger looked rattled but pulled himself together. "Sir, there's a lot of chatter about dark ships."

"Dark ships?"

"Yes, sir. Dark warships. There's— Here's something else. It sounds like the dark warships showed up and opened fire without any communication or warning. Most of the targets that we can see have been hit were Syndic government or military, but some are civilian. Indras has taken a lot of damage."

"Captain," Lieutenant Yuon called, "our systems are not registering any signs of weapons fire. There are zero indications of any attacking ships in this star system."

Geary fixed a hard look on Iger. "Did you hear that? Do you concur that we can't see any sign they're still here?"

"Yes, Admiral. I have to agree."

"When did the dark ships leave? Can you tell?"

"Admiral . . ." Iger shook his head helplessly. "Even though we can't spot any trace of them, from what we're picking up from the Syndics, they are still here."

FIFTEEN

"LIEUTENANT Iger," Geary said with slow force, "do you know anything about this? Anything that could explain this? Even in rumors?"

"No, sir. I have no idea what's going on here." Iger sounded uncharacteristically angry. "There's something . . . odd. We're intercepting video that's supposed to be showing the dark ships, and there's nothing on it. I would think everyone at Indras has gone crazy, but there's no doubt that destruction has taken place and is ongoing."

Geary fixed a glare on his display, which continued to report attacks under way but offered no trace of any attackers. "Communications. Set up a conference call for me, Captain Desjani, Captain Badaya on *Illustrious*, and Captain Tulev on *Leviathan*."

A little more than a minute later, Geary appeared to face Captains Badaya and Tulev in their command seats on their own ships, Desjani also linked in next to him. "Does anyone have any idea what's happening here?"

"They're definitely under attack," Badaya said. "I recommend we maintain all of our ships at full combat readiness until we figure out who is attacking them and whether they are also hostile to us."

"It is like the enigmas," Tulev said. "But we have rescreened the systems on *Leviathan* and can find no trace of software of any kind that might be corrupting our systems to hide these attackers from us."

"What would the enigmas be doing at Indras, anyway?" Badaya demanded. "This is probably some Syndic secret weapon that has turned on them. Or something one of their rebel star systems is using to hit back."

"The locals are reporting that they can see what they call the dark ships," Geary said. "Why would the attackers of a Syndic star system blind our sensors and not those of the Syndics? The Syndic government itself has no reason to attack one of their own star systems, and from the amount of damage we can see, the attacking force has to be much larger than anything we believe the Syndics or any rebellious star systems have in this part of space."

"If it's a Syndic worm," Badaya began again.

"We would have found it already!" Desjani insisted. "My code monkeys are good. As good as they come."

"Could the Dancers have planted something in our systems?" Tulev asked. "Something as different from what we know as the enigma quantum-coded worms were?"

"That's not impossible," Geary said. "But why? What possible reason could they have for doing that, and why would the Dancers somehow assist whoever is attacking Indras?"

"I just double-checked," Desjani said. "We've maintained full isolation of the comm gear that talks to the Dancers. The only way they could have infected our systems is if they have worms that can leave the gear, invisibly crawl across the deck to other compartments, and wriggle into the equipment there. And if they can do that, then we're dealing with tech so much higher and different than ours that the odds of even spotting it seem impossible."

"Then what about the Kicks?" Badaya asked, instantly shifting focus. "We had that ship of theirs with us for a long time. Something aboard that, which leapfrogged through the Marine and Fleet systems, slowly infecting every ship."

"A contagion off of *Invincible*?" Geary considered that, his eyes shifting briefly to his display as another Syndic installation at Indras blew up under the impact of bombardment projectiles that were invisible to the Alliance warships.

"These can't be Kick ships attacking Indras," Desjani protested. "How would they have gotten here? And the attackers are using bombardment projectiles, which as far as we know the Kicks don't even carry. Besides, according to my people, the stuff we found on *Invincible* was totally different from our own. How could Kick software have migrated to our systems when their systems and software don't match ours at all?"

A momentary silence fell. "We seem to have run out of possible sources for whatever is blinding our systems," Tulev finally said. "What other enemies does this fleet face?"

"Do you mean besides our own headquarters and government?" Badaya asked sarcastically.

Geary stared at him without speaking for a few seconds. "Tanya, you say your code monkeys are absolutely certain that there's nothing in our systems that isn't supposed to be there?"

"Yes, sir," she replied forcefully. "Not unless it's something totally new and unusual, using principles totally different from anything we've used or considered or encountered or imagined up to now."

"Captain Tulev? Captain Badaya? Do the system security people on your ships concur in that?"

Both of them nodded. "I wish we still had Captain Cresida here to address the problem," Tulev added. "But I do not think even she would have any answers."

"There goes another HuK," Desjani said. "He was obviously running from something that caught him. I've never been in a fight where I can only see one side. Admiral, what are you driving at?"

"I used to read old detective stories," Geary said. "Really old stuff. In one of them, the detective said that once you eliminate all other possibilities, whatever is left must be the answer. I never forgot that. And now, it seems we've eliminated the possibility of unauthorized software messing up our systems and even wiping out images of these attackers from Syndic videos that we're intercepting. What's left?"

"Authorized software?" Tulev asked, a rare amount of surprise inflecting his words.

"Yes. Something that's supposed to be there that's causing this and isn't tripping any security screens because it's not a worm or a virus or anything else. It's part of the official system software."

"Why would fleet headquarters do such a thing?" Tulev said.

Badaya began to answer, but Geary spoke quickly to cut him off. "Maybe they didn't. Maybe the government didn't. Maybe certain offices or secret programs did it, and a lot of high-ranking people don't even know it was done. Maybe part of the government did it, maybe segments of fleet headquarters. If my guess is true, that is. Get your people looking."

"For what?" Badaya asked, plaintive now.

Tulev answered with dispassionate logic. "We do not know under what name or subsystem the software can be found, but we do know what it must be doing. If we know what it must do, then we can search for software that carries out such functions, no matter where it is located."

"Exactly," Geary said. "While we search, I'm going to take the task force toward the jump point for Kalixa, but only at point zero five light speed."

If he had felt powerless while observing events at Midway, here at Indras Geary felt a sense of bizarre incomprehension watching a literally one-sided battle as the Alliance task force swung along the outer edges of the star system.

"Admiral, we have a call from the Syndics. An emergency comm routing. They must be using some alternate command systems."

That would hardly be surprising given the amount of damage they could see to the regular command systems at Indras. "Bounce it to me."

The CEO Geary saw was not Yamada. Neither was she immaculately dressed and displaying a false, calculated expression. She looked, in fact, like someone who had just had her normal routine bombed out from under her. "This is an act of war! The Alliance has blatantly and openly attacked us without any warning, causing immense property damage and loss of life! I demand that you cease all attacks and withdraw from this star system immediately!"

Desjani exhaled in exasperation. "She thinks we're attacking them? Can't she tell we're not firing, and that this attack was well under way before we even got here?"

"I wish I knew who or what was attacking them," Geary said. He tapped reply. "To the leaders of Indras, this is Admiral Geary of the Alliance fleet. We are not attacking you. None of my ships have fired on you, nor will they unless attacked themselves. We are currently trying to determine the identity of the ships that are attacking Indras, but I swear on my honor that they are not under my command and not subject to my orders. To the honor of our ancestors, Geary, out."

Over the next hour, there were signs that the attack was tapering off as fewer targets were destroyed. "Captain," Lieutenant Castries said, "from the pattern of the attacks, it looks like the attacking ships may be withdrawing toward the jump point for Kalixa."

"Could they be a threat to Atalia?" Geary wondered. "And will they stop at Atalia or go on to Alliance space?"

Desjani kept her voice very low. "If we can't see them because of something that official sources in the Alliance did, that implies—"

"I know what it implies. I also know that even if that is true, I can't assume those ships aren't a threat to the Alliance as long as I don't know who they are."

Hours later, the same female Syndic CEO replied to Geary, her suit slightly neater and her expression much angrier. Whatever emergency bunker she occupied was overcrowded, filled with both people and a sense of shock that Geary could feel even through the medium of the message. "You must think us fools. The attackers are withdrawing toward Alliance space. I have no idea how many people have died today! Your government had better be prepared to answer for this!"

Geary looked down, his jaw tight enough to hurt. "If this was the work of someone in the Alliance, they just bought us a lot more trouble then we had before."

Desjani sounded more subdued than usual as she replied. "My guys think they've found something. They're seeing what they can do with it."

Geary's display rippled. As it did so, two new contacts suddenly appeared for a moment near the jump point for Kalixa. "What was that? Are they gone?"

"They probably jumped," Desjani confirmed. "We're lucky we caught a glimpse of them. My code monkeys think that they've found the answer. There's at least one subroutine hidden in part of the sensor-system software that seems to be selectively blocking some detection data. It's— What the hell happened to the images of those ships we spotted before they jumped?"

"Captain, they're . . . gone," Lieutenant Castries said, sounding horrified and mystified. "They vanished from the displays, and I can't find any traces of them in system records."

"Looks like there's more wonky software to find," Geary said.

"It does, doesn't it?" Desjani looked as angry as he could recall ever seeing her. "What my guys found is definitely human work and definitely part of one of the regular system software updates. That's how they found it so fast, by focusing on the updates instead of going through the bajillion lines of code on these ships line by line. They are pretty sure it ties in with integrated subroutines in other system software throughout the ship, which this disappearing imagery just confirmed. They are trying to run those down now."

Geary stared at his display. "Someone officially inserted subroutines into our ship's software that prevent us from seeing those dark ships." He didn't feel triumphant at his guess having been proven right.

"Yes, sir. We have to assume the software on every Alliance warship has the same subroutines." Desjani bit her lip, thinking. "What the enigmas did must have given someone in the Alliance an idea. They took that idea from the enigmas and ran with it."

"Not just the fleet," Geary said. "Did I tell you that at Yokai there were momentary ghost sightings by an aerospace orbital facility being reactivated? We thought it was a software problem, with training-sim data leaking through into active systems before it was scrubbed out. We were right, it was caused by the software, but not because it was creating false targets. The new software updates were actually having trouble making the systems not see real targets."

"Aerospace forces, too? Maybe all civilian space tracking as well. Those dark ships might be invisible to everyone in Alliance space." Desjani turned her head to meet his eyes with hers. "Which means they're ours. Which means the Alliance *did* just trash Indras, only this task force is going to get blamed for it because we happened to stumble through the star system as it was going on."

"What did you see of those ships before the image vanished?"

Desjani made an angry gesture with one hand chopping the air. "Not much. It looked like a battle cruiser and a heavy cruiser. Could have been our designs, could have been Syndic."

"Why did the Syndics call them dark ships?" Geary asked, trying to remember the brief look he had gained at the unknown craft. "They did look a bit odd that way."

"Yes. Like something, some hull coating maybe, was blurring visual details."

"Let Tulev and Badaya know what your security people have learned." Geary considered his options, then tapped his controls. "All units in Task Force Dancer, immediate execute, accelerate to point one light speed."

"Are you going to try to catch those ships?" Desjani asked.

"Maybe."

"What will you do if you do catch them?"

"I don't know, yet. Whoever ordered the attack here did so either oblivious to the possibility that this task force would be blamed for involvement with it or intentionally seeking to tie me and the rest of the fleet to the action. I will not accept such behavior, no matter who was behind it."

LIEUTENANT Iger, summoned to Geary's stateroom, shook his head in stubborn denial. "Admiral, I don't know anything about this. If official software is sabotaging our detection, it's also affecting my intelligence work by blocking images of those ships."

Geary was standing before him, far enough away not to seem threatening but close enough to make it clear that he was expecting answers. "Did you get a look at them before we lost that one image?"

"Yes, sir, briefly. I was zooming in on it when the image dropped out of my systems like it had never existed."

"Did you make out any details?"

"Not many, sir." Lieutenant Iger spoke with the careful stiffness of someone who knew what he was saying would not be well received. "Admiral, all I can tell you is that from what little time I had to see them, the designs of the two ships we saw were definitely human and share an ancestry with Alliance warship designs. But Syndic warships share much of the same design ancestry."

"Lieutenant, on our way through Indras last time, you told me that this star system was being used as a hub for covert actions against the Alliance."

"Yes, sir."

"And now we come through here and find Syndic facilities at Indras being destroyed."

Iger had been looking straight ahead as protocol required, but now looked directly at Geary. "Admiral, I'm not saying no one in the Alliance might have decided to . . . to . . . to send a message to the Syndics. But I know nothing of it."

"A lot of civilian targets got hit, too," Geary said. "A lot of freight-ers, and some places on planets or in orbital locations."

"Yes, sir."

"This wasn't a surgical strike, Lieutenant. Someone might have thought it would be, but those ships targeted places and things that should not have been targeted unless we're returning to a policy of indiscriminate bombardment. And in the process, they may have set in motion a resumption of the war with the Syndics. You and I both know how unpopular that outcome would be with the population of the Alliance."

Iger looked away, obviously uncomfortable now. "Admiral, there are segments that might welcome that. You know that, as do I. Not even near a majority. But this . . . sir, this was clumsy. Unprovoked attacks by the Syndics would be one justification for renewed war that the majority of the Alliance might accept. But not something like this."

"If those ships go to Atalia," Geary said, "and on to Alliance space, I will not remain silent about them and what they did at Indras."

"I understand, sir. I can offer no reason you should do so since nei-ther of us has been read into any program that covers such activity."

"Let me know if, once we get back, someone tells you to officially read me into such a program. Will you tell me if you're given such information and told not to share it with me?"

Iger didn't hesitate. "Yes, sir, I will tell you."

THE short jump to Kalixa offered more time for the security teams aboard *Dauntless* to identify the special subroutines woven through many portions of the ship's software. "Somebody really put a lot of effort into this," Tanya told Geary.

"Have we got it all now?"

"We think so. We'll find out at Kalixa. We should be able to spot some of those ships before they jump." She glowered at the nearest bulkhead as if it were guilty of a heinous crime. "The subroutines didn't just block the information from being seen by us. They deleted it so thoroughly that my best code monkeys can't find any trace of it. Is this how the government is keeping secret that new fleet that they're building?"

"We don't know that they're Alliance ships. Not yet."

"The hell we don't." Desjani made a fist and hit the offending bulkhead. "But if Admiral Bloch is in charge of that fleet, I'd like to know who is commanding the individual ships. How are they keeping secret the reassignments of personnel to crew those ships? Are they even crewed by military personnel?"

"If we can catch up with them, I intend demanding answers," Geary said. "Can your people put together a software patch that we can send to every other ship in the task force that will neutralize those stealth subroutines?"

"They're already working on it, Admiral."

KALIXA wasn't empty.

"There they are," Desjani said, baring her teeth in a grin. "Do you think that's all of them?"

"Six battle cruisers," Geary marveled. "Four heavy cruisers. A dozen destroyers. What can we tell about them?"

"They're not standard Alliance designs, Admiral," Lieutenant Yuon said. "They're also not broadcasting any IDs. They have some sort of surface coating that is blurring visual details, but we can see enough to spot a lot more weapon launchers and projectors than on ships like this one. Each of those battle cruisers is about the same size as *Dauntless*, but our systems estimate each carries up to twice the armament we do. The heavy cruisers and destroyers look like they follow similar designs."

"How did they fit all that armament on those ships?" Desjani wondered. "Admiral, are we going to send a message to those guys?"

Geary shook his head. "They'll jump for Atalia before anything I send would reach them. But that means they won't know we're following them. We'll be able to stay on their tails until they show us exactly which star system they came from. Is that software patch ready to distribute?"

"It will be before we leave Kalixa."

HE had expected to find a similar scene at Atalia, the dark ships traveling toward a jump point and almost there, heading back to wherever their base was located.

"Ancestors," Desjani breathed, stunned at what their displays were revealing.

Atalia hadn't boasted much in the way of defenses or other facilities, just what had survived the war and wave after wave of Alliance attacks. Its cities resembled those of Batara; small, often pummeled, and often repaired. Since the war ended and Atalia had broken away from the Syndicate Worlds, claiming a tenuous independence that survived more as a result of Syndic weakness than Atalia's ability to defend itself, the star system had been painfully trying to rebuild infrastructure from the rubble of war.

Those efforts had been reduced to rubble once again.

The dark ships weren't concentrated together, but were ranging through the star system, almost all of them in the inner star system, where they were methodically smashing target after target.

"They're attacking Atalia?" Geary said, disbelieving. "Why would they attack Atalia? They're destroying every ship, every small craft. There goes a freighter that was flagged to an Alliance star system!"

"Admiral," Desjani said, her voice hardening, "look up there. Toward the jump point for Varandal."

He looked, seeing the Alliance courier ship hanging near the jump point, light-hours distant from where *Dauntless* was. The crew of that courier ship must be as baffled at seeing the destruction under way in Atalia as Geary's ships had been while watching the attack on Indras. They were probably debating whether to continue observing in hopes of learning something about the attacks or to head for Varandal and report what little they knew.

Then he spotted the two dark ship destroyers swooping upward toward the courier ship. "Those look like firing runs, not approaches to the jump point."

"Yes," Desjani said in tones devoid of all feeling. "And the courier ship can't see those two coming."

It was one of the awful moments that had to be endured by those who operated in space. He wanted to send a warning, he wanted to do something, to somehow prevent what he could see about to happen. But there was nothing that could be done because what he was seeing had happened hours ago. It was history, and he was unable to do anything but watch it and futilely wish he could change the past that was about to occur before his eyes.

Geary watched the dark destroyers close on the courier ship, tearing past in a perfect by-the-book firing run that tore apart the unsuspecting courier ship with multiple hits by hell lances and a barrage of grapeshot delivered at point-blank range against the lightly armored and unarmed craft. Geary knew none of the courier's crew could have survived that attack. "Ancestors preserve us. They just annihilated an Alliance fleet courier ship." He looked back to where the Alliance-flagged freighter had been destroyed, just in time to see another dark ship riddle the freighter's single escape pod as it fled for safety, leaving a lifeless ruin in its wake. "Are they insane?"

"Maybe they are. What do we do?" Desjani asked, looking at him. For the first time he could recall, Tanya seemed totally lost for answers or suggestions.

"Lieutenant Iger!" Geary put a lot more force into that call than he usually did.

Whether because of that or because of what he was witnessing happening at Atalia, the intelligence officer had trouble speaking. "Yes, sir," he finally got out.

"Lieutenant, I want to know if there is any possible justification or rationale for what we're seeing here. I know what Indras was involved in. I have heard nothing similar about Atalia."

"Th-there is nothing like that about Atalia, Admiral," Iger managed to get out. "There are agents here. Their agents, our agents. It's a . . . a transit point. The reports I have seen say Atalia has been trying to keep us happy, so we'll protect them. This . . . I have no idea, sir. The . . . the courier ship. Sir . . . if I knew *anything* . . ."

"Thank you, Lieutenant. I just wanted to be sure."

Desjani spoke again, still not betraying her feelings. "From the way they're hitting space traffic, the dark ships are doubling down on what they did at Indras. That means they're going to go after more civilian targets next."

"And they've already destroyed Alliance civilian and military shipping." Geary felt a grim resolve filling him despite the enormity of the decision he had to make. "There's no possible justification for this. There's not even any possible reason for it. I don't care who those ships answer to. They're not broadcasting their identities, they are of unknown design, and they are attacking the Alliance as well as Atalia. That makes them pirates. We will stop them."

He reached for his controls and spoke with perfect clarity. "Unknown warships operating in Atalia star system, this is Admiral Geary of the Alliance fleet. You have attacked Alliance shipping and killed Alliance military personnel, as well as conducting wanton attacks on the people of the neutral star system of Atalia. You are to immediately cease any use of weaponry of any kind, you are to power down and deactivate all weapons, you are to lower shields, and you are to adopt fixed orbits pending the arrival of my ships in your vicinity. Failure to comply with these commands will result in my using the full force available to me to eliminate you as a threat to anyone in Atalia

Star System or elsewhere. This demand will not be repeated. To the honor of our ancestors, Geary, out."

He touched another comm switch. "All units in Task Force Dancer, immediate execute, come starboard five three degrees, up zero four degrees, accelerate to point two light speed. All unidentified warships is this star system are to be treated as hostile. You are authorized to engage any that pose any threat to you."

Tanya waited until *Dauntless* had swung onto the new vector before she activated the privacy field around their seats and leaned toward him. "Are you sure?"

"Yeah, I'm sure."

"If these are Alliance warships—"

"Then they've got a very short time in which to start acting like Alliance warships."

"Yes, sir." She sat back, smiling crookedly. "We're either going to come out of this as heroes, or they're going to hang us."

Captain Tulev called in with essentially the same question as Desjani's and seemed equally satisfied with Geary's reply.

Badaya didn't question what was happening at all. He probably, Geary thought, was enjoying having his long suspicions of parts of the Alliance government proven true. If that was what was happening.

"At point two light, we're thirteen hours from intercept with the nearest of the dark ships," Lieutenant Castries said, "assuming it remains on its current vector."

"Thank you, Lieutenant." Geary eyed his display, thinking that it would be another two and a half hours before the dark ships saw Geary's task force and received his orders to surrender. "All units in Task Force Dancer, stand down from maximum combat readiness. Rest your crews and maximize your equipment readiness over the next twelve hours."

SURPRISINGLY, the first dark ships to see Geary's ships and hear his message didn't react at all, continuing whatever they were doing while

Geary watched the destruction with growing anger and frustration. It was almost six hours after the task force's arrival at Atalia before the dark ships responded to the appearance of the Alliance warships.

And when they did react, it brought more bad news.

He watched the individual dark ships veer about, altering vectors at an impressive rate as they began gathering together. "Tanya, is it just me, or—"

"It's not just you. They're extremely maneuverable," she said, her expression reflecting cold concentration on her tasks. "Significantly more maneuverable than our ships."

"They may look like human ships, but the maneuvers remind me of enigmas."

Lieutenant Castries had already been running an analysis, and now reported the results. "Admiral, they're not a match for the enigmas, but their maneuvering capabilities are closer to enigmas than our ships are. There's a roughly thirty percent improvement over what we can do based on the limited observations we have so far."

"The enigmas don't have battle cruisers," Lieutenant Yuon protested. "They don't have anything that big."

"Maybe the enigmas copied our ships," Desjani said. "They've seen them. They could have copied the external appearance. Maybe this is all really another attempt to get us and the Syndics at all-out war again."

"If the enigmas were trying to fool us, why wouldn't they have made exact copies instead of ones that differed from our ships in external appearance and the number of weapons they carry?" Geary began to say more, paused to think, then looked at Yuon. "We're seeing their weapons fire now. What can you tell me about the signatures on their weapons?"

"It matches Alliance weaponry, Admiral. The signatures on the hell lances are exactly like ours, and one of the dark ships fired a missile that is either a specter or a perfect copy of a specter."

Several seconds passed in silence while everyone thought.

"Who or what the hell are they?" Desjani finally demanded. "They maneuver more like enigmas, and our software was covertly modified not to see them, which also matches enigma tactics. They attacked a Syndic-controlled star system, but also a neutral star system and Alliance assets here. And now it looks like they're getting ready to attack us, all of which would imply either enigmas or some other alien race. Like the Kicks, they won't respond to attempts to communicate. But they have Alliance designs, and Alliance weapons, and the software modifications that left us blind to them came through official channels rather than being some kind of cyberattack. What are they?"

Geary looked at his display, where the tracks of the dark warships were converging with each other. "I don't think the answer matters any longer. With that sort of advantage in maneuvering capability, and us having come this far from any jump points, I don't think we can avoid them if they come after us. We'll have to defeat them, then find answers in the wreckage."

"They're gathering into three formations," Lieutenant Yuon said.

Geary watched his display, frowning. It looked like the dark ships were going to arrange themselves in a smaller, but mirror-image, set of box formations in a V like the task force was still using.

"No answers to your message, no communications of any kind, and they're adopting combat formations," Desjani said. "They're definitely going to fight. This doesn't make any sense at all. What those ships did at Indras could be explained partly, but what they're doing here is just pure destruction. And now fighting us instead of outrunning us, which they could do? It's like they're berserkers."

"Berserkers?"

"You know, those mythical warriors who just go nuts in battle and fight like maniacs until they're cut to pieces."

"Maybe that is what we're dealing with," Geary said. "Here they come."

"They're accelerating to an intercept with us," Lieutenant Castries confirmed.

If these had been typical warships, the situation wouldn't have been too serious since Geary's forces outnumbered the dark ships by better than two to one in escorts and two to one in battle cruisers. But if the estimates produced by the sensor systems were correct, each of the dark ships had the same punch as two of Geary's ships, and they had a significant advantage in their ability to maneuver as well. "We'll have to hit each of his subformations hard in turn."

He decided to make one last check, to see if any other paths might exist. "Lieutenant Iger? Have you heard anything from the dark ships? Anything in any form?"

Iger had recovered his equilibrium and now looked as bleak as Geary felt. "We've seen no comms from the dark ships, Admiral. Atalia has sent them messages, attempting to surrender, but they haven't responded at all."

There simply wasn't any alternative to fighting. Geary started planning out the moves in his head. The dark ships were also accelerating to point two light speed as they charged toward the Alliance task force. If the two groups met at a combined velocity of point four light speed the odds of anyone getting a hit were very near zero. They would be tearing past each other at one hundred twenty thousand kilometers a second, which didn't offer much of a window for hitting a target even if views of the universe weren't pretty significantly distorted at that velocity.

With the dark ships coming toward an intercept so quickly, the curve of their vector sweeping toward a meeting with the long arc formed by the path of the Alliance task force, the time to meeting had shrunk dramatically. "Two hours to contact on current vectors," Lieutenant Castries reported.

Geary blinked his eyes, ran one hand through his hair, and straightened in his seat before touching his comm controls. "All units in Task Force Dancer, this is Admiral Geary. We have encountered ships of unknown type and allegiance, which have attacked and destroyed Alliance military and civilian shipping. They are now targeting us. We will destroy them, then determine their origin and motives. All ships are to come to full combat readiness in one hour. To the honor of our ancestors, Geary, out."

There weren't any cheers this time. The crew's emotions matched Geary's, a somber recognition of the need to deal with this mysterious and murderous threat.

The only good part about the next hour was that the concentration of the dark ships on Geary's force had halted the attacks against other targets in Atalia Star System. A stern resolve had settled among the crew of *Dauntless* and the other Alliance warships as word spread about what the dark ships had done and about the weapons and maneuvering capabilities they could bring to bear.

He waited until time to contact was forty-five minutes out, only nine light-minutes from the enemy, before ordering the braking maneuver, bringing the warships around to reduce their velocity to point one light speed.

"The enemy is also braking velocity," Lieutenant Castries announced.

Desjani had a puzzled look. "They started braking seven minutes ago, at almost the same time as you did, before they could have seen you had started doing so."

"Coincidence," Geary said. He was eyeing the enemy formations. Tanya had warned him that he tended to favor attacks up and to the right. Instead, he would aim for the dark ship subformation that was on the right and behind the leading dark ship formation. It contained two dark ship battle cruisers along with one of their heavy cruisers and four destroyers. *If I can hit them with most of my firepower while avoiding the rest of the dark ship subformations, I can knock out a third of their combat capability.*

They were one and a half light-minutes from the enemy, both sides having reduced their velocity to point one light so that the time to contact was still fifteen minutes away, when Geary made some minor adjustments to his formations, readying them for the sudden twist to the right and down that would avoid two-thirds of the dark ships and hit the remaining third as hard as possible.

Tanya was usually completely calm during moments like this, absorbed in the battle. But this time she was frowning at her display as if she were seeing something that bothered her.

"What's the matter?" Geary asked.

"I don't know. Something."

"Let me know the instant you figure out what it is." He focused back on the enemy force. The dark ships were coming onward without any alterations in vector, aiming straight for the center of the Alliance subformation at the tip of the task force's V. Aiming for the subformation centered on *Dauntless*.

It was almost time to make his move. Almost time to make that small, last-moment adjustment in vectors. Geary's hand hovered over his comm controls, ready to send the command.

"Admiral." Desjani spoke abruptly but with utter certainty. "Break off the attack. Now. Take every ship wide of a firing run. Any direction."

He had literally only a second or two in which to decide whether to do as she said and lose what seemed to be a perfectly set up firing run, or to ignore Tanya's advice and stick with his plan.

Only a second or two.

Damn!

SIXTEEN

GEARY'S hand came down on his comm control. "All units in Task Force Dancer, immediate execute, up one five degrees!"

Dauntless jolted upward, along all of the other Alliance warships. Geary fought down a wave of disappointment over the lost opportunity, matched with anger at Tanya for spoiling the attack run. He was only partially aware of the moment in which the dark ship formations rocketed past beneath them, some of the dark ships tossing out shots that scored a few hits on the lowermost ships in Geary's formations.

Wait a minute. "How could any of them have been in range when we made that big a vector change? Even with their advantage in maneuverability, they shouldn't have been able to do that."

"Because they did last-minute maneuvers to bracket one of our formations with all of theirs," Desjani said, pointing viciously at her display. "If you'd executed your firing run as planned Badaya's subformation would have been torn apart. Replay the last maneuvers on the display if you don't believe me."

Geary began to turn his ships farther up, planning on bending them all the way around to reengage the enemy. "How did you know that they'd do that?"

"Because it's what you would have done. Have you ever run sims based on your previous engagements?"

"You mean replayed the battles we've fought? No." Once of each had been more than enough.

"I have," Desjani declared. "Because I wanted to learn more about your way of fighting. I've played the enemy against you in those sims, and as those dark ships came at us, I suddenly realized that it felt exactly like one of those sims replaying *your* moves. That's what was bothering me."

"They're copying me?"

"This isn't just copying! This is *you*. They're using automated maneuvering tactics based on what you've done, based on how you fight. They've got a simulated Black Jack calling their shots."

Things had just gotten a lot worse. "How do I outsmart myself? Why didn't we understand this hours ago, so I could review those battles and see what lessons that sim would be using?"

She gave him an annoyed look. "Well, pardon me for not figuring it out sooner!"

"That's not what I—" He saw his formations reaching just past the vertical as they turned to reengage the dark ships, and he hit his comm controls. "All units in Task Force Dancer, immediate execute, turn up one two zero degrees." That would curve his task force away from an intercept, throwing off the dark ships, whose own courses would be based on the assumption that he would reengage as quickly as possible. Because that was what Black Jack did.

But the dark ships were reacting fast, twisting into tighter turns than Geary's ships could achieve and accelerating at faster rates than his ships could match. "All units, immediate execute, come starboard eight zero degrees."

All three Alliance subformations swung over at almost a right angle from their previous vector, heading almost straight for the distant star once again.

"I need time to think. Maybe if I split off the other two formations, have them operate independently—" Which was just what something programmed to think like Black Jack would want, he realized, because while Tulev was a good commander, and Badaya wasn't bad, either one could more easily be caught and overwhelmed if Geary was trying to deal with three formations moving on totally different vectors against an opponent as good as he was.

How could he break contact with a force that was more maneuverable and could accelerate faster?

"We've got to try another firing run," Geary said. "I need to disrupt them enough to gain time to think about this, and only a firing run offers the chance to do that."

Desjani hesitated, then nodded, a slight sign of worry creasing her brow.

He brought his ships all the way down and around, swinging the course change as tight as he could to try to catch the back end of the three dark ship formations as their V passed overhead.

But the dark ships reacted too quickly, tightening their own turns even more and changing vectors for another head-on encounter.

Geary tried to decide which part of the enemy formation to aim for, which subformation was most vulnerable. The geometry of the situation left him unable to turn tightly enough to go high, and he didn't want to aim right and low again, so he aimed for the left side.

Did he actually see, in the last moments when it could make a difference, the beginnings of a countermove by the dark ships? A countermove that would catch Badaya's subformation in a deadly vise? Or did he just sense it?

"All units, immediate execute, down two zero degrees!"

The Alliance warships lurched through the sudden change, sliding dangerously close to the dark ships, which were indeed diving straight toward where Badaya's ships would have been.

They missed each other by far too close a margin, out of range of most weapons but close enough for the dark ships to volley out missiles.

"All units pivot and engage missiles," Geary ordered.

Every battle cruiser, heavy and light cruiser, and destroyer swung completely around, their heaviest armament aimed toward the oncoming wave of missiles while the ships themselves continued moving backwards at the same rate they had been going. Hell lances lashed out, destroying most of the missiles short of their targets, but some ships had to fire point-defense bursts of grapeshot to hit missiles on final approach.

And the dark ships were coming around again.

He could feel what was happening. He was reacting. The dark ships had the initiative and weren't letting go. This was a path leading to disaster.

Geary looked toward Desjani, who was gazing fixedly at her display, not saying anything, not offering advice as she usually did. *Because she knows this isn't the usual situation. She doesn't know what advice to give when I'm fighting myself. And I miss having her suggestions because sometimes they have saved my butt and—*

Of course. "Tanya, they may have a sim of how I fight battles, but they don't have you."

"That's very flattering," she said in a tight voice. "But I don't see the relevance in terms of winning this fight. I wasn't single-handedly winning the war before you showed up, remember?"

"My point is, we work as a team," Geary explained with a patience he didn't really feel. "You see things I don't, I see things you don't. Whatever Black-Jack sim the dark ships are using won't have that. And I feel certain they loaded that sim with century-old tactical procedures that people had increasingly ignored during the war, but I have used because they're what I knew. I noticed the attack on the courier ship was carried out exactly how those procedures mandated that specific type of operation. That means the sim is programmed to counter *my* tactics."

Her eyes lit up with a fierce enthusiasm. "The more I influence your tactics, the more I suggest the ways we did things that don't match your tactical training, the less that sim will be able to predict them."

"Exactly. You said you were studying those sims of my past battles to help you learn how to fight more like me. Now we need you to help me fight less like me. But still good enough to kick the butts of the dark ships."

She grinned. "Then I can tell you exactly what to do on the next firing pass."

"What?" he demanded, watching the dark ships steady out below and behind the Alliance task force, a couple of light-minutes distant on a stern chase.

"Do the exact same thing that you planned to do last time. Hitting the left and back subformation, right? Do exactly that again."

"What?" Geary repeated, baffled.

"You never repeat a maneuver right after you've used it, Admiral. *Never.* Those ships will expect you to aim for another attack point. They will act assuming that you are aiming for another attack point because their sim will tell them you never hit the same spot twice in a row in the same way."

He stared at her. "I love you."

"Excuse me, Admiral?" Desjani asked, though she also smiled.

"Sorry." If the rest of the bridge crew had heard his words, they were doing a very good job of pretending not to have.

He brought his task force on down, all three formations completing a vertical loop that found them facing back toward the dark ships. If there had really been an up or down, his ships would probably be upside down compared to their previous alignment, but that didn't matter in space. What mattered was that the dark ships had adjusted their formation as well, coming down a bit to head for another direct intercept.

"That's exactly how I would have lined them up if I were commanding those dark ships," Geary said. "You're right. You are absolutely right."

"Have we reached the point where you can just start assuming that?" she asked.

"We already have. I pulled us out of the first attack run, didn't I?"

The two V formations weren't aligned in the same plane. Geary's three subformations were tilted up on one side relative to the subformations of the dark ships. Which was all to the good this time around. "Formation Delta One, come port zero two degrees, down zero one degrees at time four one. Formation Delta Two, come port zero six degrees, down zero three degrees at time four zero point five. Formation Delta Three, come port zero one degrees at time four two. Engage targets in the farthest port enemy subformation."

This is all wrong. Every bit of training and experience he had told him not to do this, not to aim to hit that left side of the dark ship formation again in an approach as nearly identical as possible to the last one. *But if I feel that way, then it's actually right this time.*

In the last moments before contact, beginning with Badaya's formation on the upper left of the task force, the three subformations altered vectors, swinging slightly to concentrate on where Geary expected the farthest-left dark ship formation to be as the dark ships also moved to intercept where they thought Geary would go.

The instant of firing came and went, automated fire-control systems hurling out weapons during the vanishingly small moment of time when the opposing ships were within range of each other.

Geary felt *Dauntless* shuddering from hits and felt a tightness in his gut, wondering if she had been badly damaged.

Then the displays updated as the sensors on the Alliance warships peered backwards to evaluate the results of the encounter.

It hadn't been perfect. Not quite. But the dark ships had swung up and to the right, expecting him to target there. The swift, precisely executed maneuver had resulted in most of the dark ships being out of position, but with the Alliance warships nearly surrounding the left-hand dark ship subformation, subjecting it to the concentrated fire of all twelve battle cruisers, eight heavy cruisers, thirteen light cruisers, and twenty-five destroyers.

One of the dark ship battle cruisers was completely gone, a cloud of debris marking where it had been. The other had broken into several pieces, which were slowly flying apart, shedding smaller fragments as they went. The dark ship heavy cruiser had been crippled, spinning off down and to one side with no maneuver controls and almost all weapons out of commission, while of the four dark ship destroyers in that subformation, three had been blown apart, and the fourth was nearly broken into two large pieces which were barely holding together.

Geary took that in, then looked for the damage to his own ships. The enemy, in the seconds before contact in which he could spot what had happened and prioritize targets, had clearly concentrated his fire on the central subformation of Geary's task force. Despite being badly outnumbered, the extra weapons on the dark ships had allowed them to score some blows. *Daring* had taken several hits and lost a hell-lance battery as well as two missile launchers. *Victorious* had also been hit and lost half her missile launchers, but both battle cruisers had not suffered any maneuvering or propulsion damage. *Adroit*, though, was sliding off to port without any maneuvering control at all.

He could hear the damage reports coming in to Tanya Desjani. Hits amidships. Two hell-lance batteries out of commission. Minor damage to maneuvering systems. Through luck or her position in the subformation, *Dauntless* had come off relatively lightly.

The heavy cruisers *Bartizan* and *Haidate* had taken hits on their bows but not serious damage. Light cruisers *Absetzen* and *Toledo* were hurt but still able to keep up, but their sister ship *Lancer* had been totally knocked out and was tumbling away.

Oddly, only two Alliance destroyers had been hit, *Kururi* and *Sabar*. The dark ships had managed a better than usual concentration of fire against major combatants.

Geary was already bringing all three formations around again, curving toward the star and slightly upward to meet the dark ships as they came around also toward the star. He was tempted to break two of the Alliance subformations loose, to maneuver each of the three separately to confuse an enemy already reeling from unexpected losses, but realized that was what Black Jack would do. "What do you think?" he asked Tanya.

"Third time's a charm."

"Do it again? But there isn't any more left-hand subformation."

"There's still a subformation to the left of the other one!" she insisted.

Doing a third attack in the exact same manner was, his instincts told him, a recipe for disaster. "It's really hard to do this," he muttered. "I feel like I'm going to destroy half my ships."

The V of the Alliance task-force formations was now almost tilted on edge relative to the plane of the solar system, coming back toward the dark ships, which had closed down smoothly into a single, rectangular box formation with one long side facing forward. If neither opponent adjusted vectors, the three Alliance subformations in their V would slice through the dark ship rectangle at a right angle, like an arrowhead tearing through a bar of butter.

But the dark ship formation was more like a bar of steel. The arrowhead might slice right through the center, carried by velocity and momentum, but it would take tremendous damage in the process.

"The left," Geary muttered.

"Yes, the left," Desjani affirmed.

But where would the dark ships go? Would they wait for him to hit the center? No. Black Jack wouldn't do that.

Geary pivoted his point of view, imagining he was commanding the ships in the rectangle and trying to take down the arrowhead. *I'd assume they were going to hit one side of my formation, and I'd go up slightly and swing one wing around to concentrate fire on the top of the arrowhead. And they won't expect me to go left again. They'll assume I'll*

hit their right. Which means their last-minute maneuvers will be like . . .
"Got it."

His focus wavered as the dark ship formation passed close enough to the drifting *Adroit* to fire another volley of missiles, all of them aimed at the helpless battle cruiser. There was no way that *Adroit* could survive that attack. "*Adroit*, abandon ship. I say again, *Adroit*, abandon ship immediately. Get your crew off as fast as possible."

Adroit's crew apparently hadn't needed any encouragement. He couldn't blame them for that, though, as escape pods launched from the sole surviving example of what the fleet had jokingly nicknamed "economy-class" battle cruisers. In a few minutes, when the dark missiles arrived, the last surviving one of those ships would be gone.

Reassured that *Adroit*'s crew was as safe as he could manage at this point, Geary called Captain Tulev. "Delta One took the brunt of the enemy fire on the last pass, so I'm going to adjust final approaches so Delta Two comes in ahead this time."

Tulev, as unshaken and impassive as ever, nodded. "They are concentrating fire on the battle cruisers, I see."

"Yes. But the heavy cruisers and light cruisers in Delta One took some hits, too. I'll have Delta One and Delta Three coming in very close behind you to split the attention of the dark ships a bit."

The huge curves through space were steadying out as the two formations came around to face each other and raced toward another encounter. "Get those shields at one hundred percent," Desjani snapped.

"Captain, one of the shield generators was clipped during the last firing pass and we're still—"

"We're ten minutes from contact. Get it done."

Geary, having given his orders, sat next to Desjani, watching the two groups of ships rushing toward contact. "It's funny," he said.

"I could use a laugh," she replied.

"Not that kind of funny. I told you earlier that I thought I needed to work on building and strengthening the right patterns. Well, here we are facing the pattern of my own tactics, and we have to break that pattern."

"Maybe it's an antipattern," Desjani said. "You have to break it because it's the anti version of your real pattern."

"Works for me."

In the last minutes before contact, the dark ship rectangle didn't just pivot one wing forward and up to concentrate fire on Geary's expected countermove while the rest of the rectangle swung upward as well. Instead, taking advantage of their superior maneuverability, the entire formation compressed and climbed. If Geary had done as their tactical model had predicted, his formation would have been badly raked.

But his ships weren't there.

Instead, the Alliance task force had swung down and left again, buzz-sawing through the far left wing of the dark ships' formation.

Dauntless jerked only twice in the wake of the firing run, Geary watching his display tensely for the results. Damage reports were flowing in, most of them from Tulev's ships, where the battle cruisers had once again been the target of most of the enemy fire. *Leviathan* and *Dragon* had taken the most hits, but were still moving. Behind them, in Badaya's subformation, *Steadfast* had also accumulated a series of blows.

But as Geary replayed in slow motion the hyperfast combat encounter, he saw that *Steadfast* had taken those hits because she had swung close enough to one of the dark battle cruisers to employ her null-field projector. The null field had eaten a huge hole out of the dark ship, leaving it rolling out of formation, most systems dead.

Another dark battle cruiser had been destroyed, along with a dark heavy cruiser. Two more dark heavy cruisers had been hit hard and three destroyers either crippled or completely blown apart.

"Come on, you guys," Desjani said to the representations of the dark ships on her display. "One more time."

But as Geary began bringing his ships around again, he saw that the remaining two dark battle cruisers, one heavy cruiser, and five destroyers weren't continuing their own turns in order to reengage. Instead, they had pivoted and were accelerating all out for the jump point for Varandal.

"Looks like our berserkers have had enough." He tried to keep triumph from his voice as he sent the next command. "All units in Task Force Dancer, immediate execute, come port four five degrees, up zero seven degrees, accelerate to point two light speed."

"We'll never catch them," Desjani said.

"No, but we need to be on their tails if they jump for Varandal." But her words broke his intense focus on the dark ships. Geary leaned back, looking at everything his display showed. A few crippled dark ships were drifting through the star system, as well as a few badly hurt Alliance warships, including the large number of escape pods from *Adroit*. *Steadfast*, whose close firing pass had taken out one of the dark battle cruisers, had partially paid for that with some hits on her main propulsion and was already lagging behind the rest of Captain Tulev's formation. In Atalia as a whole, mercilessly battered by the dark ship attack, there were enough needs for rescue and support to keep a fleet busy.

It all added up to a requirement to leave some ships here, and even if *Steadfast* hadn't been unable to keep up, Tulev would have been Geary's choice for the independent assignment.

"Captain Tulev, I am detaching Formation Delta Two under your command. Your ships are to remain at Atalia and rescue everyone you can, recovering escape pods, assisting repairs to the damaged Alliance ships, and helping anyone you can in any of the damaged orbital facilities or other locations belonging to Atalia. Make sure none of those badly damaged dark ships get going again. I want them permanently neutralized. Get every prisoner you can off those dark ships. I need to know everything that you can learn from the prisoners as well as everything you can learn from examining the wrecks. We'll bring the prisoners back to stand trial for war crimes. When you feel you have done all you can, return to Varandal."

Tulev saluted, his expression betraying no reaction to the orders. "I assume that if more dark ships appear, I am to treat them as hostile."

"Yes. I'm really hoping the surviving crews on those dark ships can explain—" Geary stopped speaking as he realized something. "We haven't seen any escape pods leaving the dark ships we crippled."

"No. We shall approach the damaged dark ships with care, remembering the example of the enigmas."

The enigmas, who had destroyed their damaged ships in order to keep humans from capturing any or learning anything about their crews. But how could the crews of these ships be enigmas?

"We're going to pursue the surviving dark ships," Geary told Tulev. "If they try to attack Varandal, the Alliance defenses there will need our system patches in order to see who the attackers are. If the dark ships keep going, we'll follow them. We need to know where they came from."

Tulev's face still revealed nothing of his feelings. "As far as we can tell, the problems in our software came from official sources. What if the answer to where these ships came from is not one we wish to know?"

"I have to know. *We* have to know. This is the Alliance, not the Syndicate Worlds."

"I agree. You reminded us of that before. Perhaps there are others who have forgotten."

The tension, the constant worry of a short time before, had been replaced by a long stern chase with no possibility of catching their prey. The dark ships could always reverse course and charge back to the attack, but Geary did not expect that to happen. No tactical system based on his decisions would come up with that course of action unless the situation was incredibly desperate and left no alternative.

"How's *Dauntless*?" Geary asked.

"Ready and willing," Desjani replied, her expression serious. "I'm going to be honest with you. Those dark ships creep me out. I'm glad that Tulev's boys and girls are the ones going in to investigate them."

"He'll be careful."

As if mocking Geary's words, an urgent alarm suddenly pulsed. "Admiral!" Lieutenant Yuon cried. "One of— Two of the— All of the crippled dark ships have self-destructed!"

"No escape pods," Desjani commented.

Geary slumped back in his seat, wavering in his assessment of who and what these dark ships were. "At least none of Tulev's ships were close enough to any of them yet. What the hell did they use to self-destruct? Even the broken segments that should have been nowhere near a power core have been blown into dust."

"Power-core-equivalent explosions in all segments," Lieutenant Castries confirmed. "Those ships were rigged to be able to leave nothing for anyone to exploit."

"Would human crews sign on to that?" Desjani asked Geary.

"I . . . Dammit, Tanya, I don't know. How could they be enigmas this deep in human space? How could they have Alliance weapons? Why would the survivors be fleeing toward Varandal?"

She laughed briefly and derisively. "Fair enough. I asked you a question you couldn't answer. I deserved some back at me."

"We'll stay on those survivors," Geary said. "Until they either turn and fight, or they lead us to their base. Then we'll get some answers."

"How about another question first?" Desjani was looking at her display, her expression somber. "Why did we spot those guys attacking Indras?"

"How could we miss it?" Geary asked. "We couldn't see them, but we couldn't avoid seeing the destruction."

"Because we were transiting through Indras," she emphasized. "Why were we transiting through Indras?"

"That's two questions. Because— Because the Dancers insisted on going home immediately."

"And they knew from previous discussions that our preferred route was through Indras."

Geary eyed her, troubled. "You think the Dancers might have intended us to go through Indras during a period when we could spot the attack?"

"They told us they needed to go home right away, and then they told us to go home right away," Desjani emphasized.

"How could the Dancers have known what the black ships were going to do?"

"I don't know. Maybe that long, spherical route they took from Varandal and back was designed to collect information. I don't know," she repeated. "But doesn't it feel as if we were led there?"

"Maybe." It could have been a coincidence. But he had a vision of the Dancers weaving a vast web, one spanning a good part of a galaxy, the web leading Geary and his ships to one particular place and one particular time. "If they did, at least they still left the decision on what to do up to us."

"True," Tanya agreed. "You can lead a human to something, but figuring out what they'll do once they get there is a lot harder."

One more complication. Perhaps a very big complication. Geary felt too tired to think it through. He checked his display. Even accelerating for all they were worth, and that was a lot, the dark ships would take about eight hours to reach the jump point for Varandal. Geary's ships would take a few hours more.

He should rest. He should relax. But he stayed on the bridge, watching his display where the ships all crawled with what seemed snail-like slowness across the vast, empty reaches of a star system.

"Admiral?"

Geary jerked back to alertness, wondering whether he had been dozing or just zoned out. A virtual window had opened next to his seat, revealing not just Lieutenant Iger but also Lieutenant Jamenson. "Yes?"

"Sir, we have some important information," Iger said.

Shaking the last traces of fuzz out of his mind, Geary sat up and eyed Jamenson curiously. "We?"

"Yes, sir. You did authorize Lieutenant Jamenson access to the intelligence compartment and to our information and, well, sir, my specialists and I thought it couldn't hurt to bring in a fresh viewpoint because we hadn't been able to reach any conclusions."

"And what has Lieutenant Jamenson concluded?" Geary asked.

Lieutenant Jamenson's usual ready smile wasn't in evidence. Even her green hair seemed more a shade of somber Lincoln green than the usual bright Kelly green. Lieutenant Iger appeared equally solemn. "What is it?" Geary asked.

"We don't know any more about who built and controlled those dark ships," Iger said, "but we, I mean, Lieutenant Jamenson, has managed to unravel how they were constructed."

Jamenson brought up a display next to her. "Admiral, I was looking for things that didn't fit because that's what I'm good at, and I thought, what's missing from the wreckage? Or the dust from the wreckage, rather. Something should be there, and it's not. A lot of somethings. There should be the usual amount of water molecules and organic matter from the supplies on the ships. And from . . . from the remains of the crew. There should be . . . pieces . . . of the crews, unless the ship was totally vaporized. There should be escape pods, and pieces of escape pods."

"There wasn't any of that?" Geary asked, appalled by the implications.

"No, sir. They weren't there. But from the percentages of different kinds of molecules, there were an unusually large number of hull structural members, and there were all those extra weapons on those ships, and there was the way they maneuvered, as if they didn't have to worry about the impacts on their crews."

"They didn't have crews," Geary said, making it a statement, not a question.

"No, sir. They didn't. They are all, at least all of the ones we destroyed, completely robotic, controlled by artificial-intelligence routines."

Iger nodded, his eyes downcast. "That may explain what happened here at Atalia, sir. The AIs may have suffered a malfunction, a problem with threat identification, a misinterpretation of their attack orders, any number of things that afflict automated systems at random, unpredictable times, and that human crews intervene to stop when they occur on a normal ship."

"That may explain a great deal," Geary agreed, feeling numb inside. "Thank you. That's a critically important thing to know. Well done."

He ended the call and looked at Desjani, who was staring back at him with a horrified expression.

"You heard?"

"I heard," she said. "Fully robotic ships controlled by AIs? Sent out to operate totally independently with no human oversight? No one could be stupid enough to do that."

"They thought they were being smart." The answers had come clearly to him, as plain as if they were spelled out in large letters in the air before his face. "That's why they built the secret fleet and gave command to Bloch. Someone convinced them that this time the AI software was infallible, this time the software wouldn't ever fail or have glitches or perform oddly or in unexpected ways."

"They all use computers," Desjani said, anger replacing her earlier shock. "They must know that's impossible. Things go wrong. They're not magic. They're electronics and other pieces of equipment and software, and they break or malfunction or screw up because they're not magic. And the more complicated they are, the more things can go wrong. I'm just a damned battle cruiser captain, and I know that! How could they not know it?"

"Because it seemed like a perfect solution," Geary said. "Bloch in command, because he was the one fleet officer of sufficient seniority who seemed capable enough to lead the robot fleet and could be certain to follow orders against me. And, with a tactical AI built on a simulation of me, Bloch would be able to beat me if anyone could. But the AI would have safeguards built in to keep Bloch from using the robotic fleet against the Alliance government. The most powerful fleet out there, as close to zero personnel costs as possible, guaranteed loyal, and able to counter the ambitions of me, Bloch, or anyone else, as well as ultimately take over defense of the Alliance. That's why enough of the Grand Council voted for the program. It seemed to have every answer they needed. It seemed foolproof."

Desjani's hand clenched as if seeking a weapon. "Only fools would think that was foolproof. AIs that will never malfunction? Did they also get promised visits by the Tooth Fairy?

"Don't those idiots know what they've done?" she demanded. "In the name of protecting the Alliance, they've created the means to destroy it! What happens if those dark ships slip their leashes again and shoot up some Alliance star systems the way they did Atalia? The Alliance will collapse like a house of cards on the surface of a neutron star, and no one will ever be able to rebuild it. They've—" Desjani struggled for words. "How could they think creating the means for the Alliance to commit suicide would preserve the Alliance?"

"I don't know, Tanya. All I know is that their plan is blowing up in their faces and our faces and in the faces of a lot of innocent people." He remembered the words of the woman on Old Earth, as she looked toward the crumbling remains of the ancient, autonomous, robotic ground war machines. "They chose to entrust our safety to something incapable of loyalty, morality, or wisdom. The same folly as the ancients pursued. How has humanity survived when we fail to learn from even our greatest mistakes?"

"We've survived because people like you and me pick up the pieces. When we can." She lowered her voice, speaking with almost violent intensity. "We're going to try to follow those dark ships home? Find out where they are based?"

"Yes."

"Didn't you tell me the construction program for this secret fleet called for twenty battleships, twenty battle cruisers, and an appropriate number of escorts for that many capital ships?"

"Yes."

"Based on our experience here, all of them more heavily armed than our comparable warships, and all of them able to maneuver and accelerate better than our ships can?"

"Yes," Geary said again.

"With a tactical AI that is designed to match you. It can't, but it's tough as all hell. If it has a good learning curve, it's going to get tougher. You know I'm not afraid to go into battle," Desjani said. "You know I will follow you into the mouth of hell if you tell me to. So will the rest of this fleet. But how in the name of all ancestors can we beat that secret fleet?"

"I don't know, yet. But we have to find its base, and we may have to beat it if the government can't shut down the monster it created. If we don't destroy it, the Alliance won't survive."